Hell's Diva Saga

Hell's Diva Saga

Anna J.

www.urbanbooks.net

Urban Books, LLC
97 N18th Street
Wyandanch, NY 11798

ISBN 13: 978-1-62286-942-8
ISBN 10: 1-62286-942-7

First Trade Paperback Printing October 2015
Printed in the United States of America

10 9 8 7 6 5 4 3 2 1

This is a work of fiction. Any references or similarities to actual events, real people, living or dead, or to real locales are intended to give the novel a sense of reality. Any similarity in other names, characters, places, and incidents is entirely coincidental.

Distributed by Kensington Publishing Corp.
Submit Orders to:
Customer Service
400 Hahn Road
Westminster, MD 21157-4627
Phone: 1-800-733-3000
Fax: 1-800-659-2436

For Nyser and Tynayjah

Anything is possible when you put your
mind to it. Believe in your dreams!

Also By Anna J.

Hell's Diva: Mecca's Mission
Hell's Diva 2: Mecca's Return
Snow White: A Survival Story
My Little Secret
Get Money Chicks
My Woman His Wife
The Aftermath
My Woman His Wife 3: Palying for Keeps
Exposed: Good Wives Go Bad

Prologue

"You got in way over your head, Mecca," Tah shouted as he paced back and forth in front of the bed. He had the look of pure evil on his face, and a harsh scowl that made his handsome face look ghoulish, hardly resembling the guy who women fell head over heels for.

"Tah, what are you talking about?" Mecca cried. She couldn't believe the state she was in either. Never ever get caught off guard, that was the motto, but tonight she got caught slipping in a major way.

"You're not your aunt, Mecca. She's gone!"

"Put the gun away, Tah, and untie me, nigga. You high on them pills?" Mecca lay naked on the king-sized bed in her Hamptons villa apartment, struggling to get loose from the ropes that were tied to her wrists and ankles. Tah, her boyfriend of five years, stood at the foot of the bed pointing a chrome .50-caliber, Desert Eagle at her.

"Bitch, I ain't your flunky! You hear me?"

"Tah, who the fuck said you was a flunky? You my peoples, nigga, not no flunky! You listening to them lame-ass niggas you be with, and they put this shit in your head. Be your own man, motherfucker!"

"Fuck you, Mecca!"

Boom! Boom! Boom! Mecca felt the first slug slam into her forehead, then everything went black, and a few seconds later she saw a bright light. In the bright light she noticed a silhouette walking toward her. When the person got closer, Mecca stared into the eyes of a tall, bronze-colored man with a perfectly round Afro, and a long, neatly shaped beard. The whites of his eyes looked as if there were flames burning behind his pitch-black pupils. His long, white robe looked as if he never moved in it. There were no signs that he traveled in it. When he spoke, his voice sounded as if he were in Mecca's ears. It was like she had headphones on, and the volume was turned up to its maximum.

"I've been expecting you, Mecca. I'm glad you could make it," the man chuckled.

Mecca looked down at his feet. The color of his feet matched his face, and his toes looked as if he had the best pedicure Mecca had ever seen. His nails were evenly trimmed and glowing. Mecca didn't have a foot fetish, but if ever she'd seen feet like that on a nigga she dealt with, she would have sucked his toes without hesitation. Bringing her eyes back to his face, she gave the strange man a puzzled look. One he seemed to find amusing.

"Am I dead?" Mecca asked nervously.

"Are you dead? Are you dead? Physically, a few minutes ago, you died." The man paused, shaking his head. "Mentally, you have been dead almost all your life."

"What is that supposed to mean, and who are you anyway? What, you Jesus or God or somebody? Get it over with and take me where I'm going," Mecca responded, her fear quickly turning to anger at what the man had said.

She knew Tah had killed her and wished she could be brought back to life if for only a second so she could send him straight to hell. She hated Tah, and the feeling grew stronger as the years had gone by. She knew eventually one of them would have to die; she was just pissed he got to her first.

"So many questions," the man said sarcastically. "I love your feistiness, Mecca. We'll make the best of friends, just please don't mistake me for that Jesus guy. And no, I'm not God. You're not on his good side, Mecca."

"So you're the devil, and I'm going to hell?" Mecca asked after sucking her teeth.

"We don't use the word 'devil' around here. That's a word man made up to separate himself from the evil that exists inside of all men. We don't play word semantics, either. It is what it is. I'm just someone who knew that the evil inside of men would prevail over the good inside of them," the man laughed. "You see the semantics man used to hide what's inside of them? They put a 'd' in front of 'evil' and added an 'o' to 'God'; hence the words 'good' and 'devil'."

"What's all that got to do with me?" Mecca asked.

"Mecca, you let evil prevail, proving me right. And you know what? You had so many opportunities to go the other way, but you didn't see the signs."

"What signs? I ain't see any signs!"

"Of course you didn't. So many people around you let evil prevail, but even the people who let the evil prevail were signs for you to go the other way. You didn't take notice."

"I don't know what you're talking about," Mecca said, frustrated.

"I know you don't. That's why I'm here. I'm going to show you the signs, and when I'm done, hopefully you'll be able to accept your future. Judgment day is near," the man said while rubbing his hands together.

Mecca just stood there staring at the man, wondering what was truly going on. Was she dead or what? At any rate, she knew he was running the show, so she just stood and waited to see what would come next.

Chapter One

So are the ways of everyone that is greedy of gain which taketh away the life of the owners thereof.
                                                    —Proverbs 1:19

Brownsville, 1982

Eight-year-old Mecca Sykes lay on her stomach under her bed, frightened, crying silently, as she watched two masked men bind and gag her mother and father with duct tape around their mouths, ankles, and wrists, placing them on the living room couch. The one-bedroom project apartment smelled of dirty cat litter and cigarettes, although there wasn't an actual cat present. Mecca's wood framed bed sat in the corner of the living room opposite the couch with a dingy, sky blue, fitted sheet covering it.

Mecca was still as roaches crawled over her hands and face. She could have sworn the roaches were drinking her tears and eating the crumbs on the corners of her mouth from the bowl of Cap'n Crunch cereal she'd just finished eating. She felt them crawl into the legs and arms of her yellow pajamas, but she still didn't move. Mecca watched one of the masked men take a plastic sandwich bag filled with a grayish-colored powder out of the freezer and place it into a brown paper bag. The other masked man with the big, black revolver pointed at Mecca's parents turned to look at his partner.

"You got the shit, Darnell?" the guy holding the revolver asked. The masked man with the brown paper bag, along with Mecca's father's, eyes widened at the mention of his name.

"What the fuck is wrong with you, dude?" Darnell yelled at his partner. "Nigga, have you lost your fuckin' mind or something?"

Mecca heard her father mumbling words under the duct tape, but his words weren't audible enough for them to comprehend. The man with the brown paper bag placed it back in the refrigerator, removed his mask, and walked over to the bound couple.

"Yeah, Blast, it's me, mu'fucka. You won't be bagging this shit up for Stone no more," he shouted, spit and small pieces of food flying from his mouth and landing on Blast's face. Darnell looked in Mecca's father's eyes, and with the gun in his hand he patted his chest. "It's my turn now, nigga," he continued while Mecca's father was mumbling, shaking his head, staring at the masked men.

"God, please, let us come out of this alive. If not, look over my daughter. Let her have a life where she doesn't have to face situations like this. Please, God, I beg you. Take my daughter out of Brownsville."

Mecca's mother had tears in her eyes. She silently prayed that they would come out of this alive. She prayed for her daughter's life even if the men decided to kill her and her husband.

Mecca, by staring at her mother's face, tried to block out the fear and the roaches that crawled on her. Her mother was so pretty. She reminded Mecca of Thelma from the television show *Good Times*. Her mother looked just like Thelma and wore her black, shiny hair in a ponytail like the actress did. The only difference between Thelma and Mecca's mother was the complexion. Mecca's mother was a shade lighter than Thelma. She had a cream-colored skin tone with three black moles on her right cheekbone.

Mecca inherited her mother's complexion and features, and people often commented on her looks, playfully referring to her and her mom as twins. Mecca looked at her father and smiled. Mecca was proud to have a father who all the women in the neighborhood gawked over. He was known as Blast in Brownsville, but some called him Pretty Blast from Langston Hughes projects. With the same complexion as Mecca and her mother, Blast was a tall, muscular man with curly black hair. Everybody in Brownsville said he looked like a lighter complexioned Billy D. Williams.

Blast supported his wife and daughter by bagging up dope and stashing the dope for the neighborhood kingpin known as Stone. Blast, whose real name was Bobby Sykes, got his nickname from Stone, when in 1979, Stone stood on the corner of Mother Gaston Boulevard dressed in his usual full-length mink with diamond studded rings and necklace. When a man walked up to Stone and pointed a gun at him and told Stone to give up his stuff, Blast was coming out of the gas station on Mother Gaston and Sutter Avenue, across the street from where Stone stood.

Blast had a bottle of Crazy Horse in his hand that he couldn't wait to get home to drink. He looked at Stone from across the two, way street. Stone and his robber stood under a street light, which made the gun in the robber's hand appear to glow. It was dark outside, so the stick up man didn't notice Blast walking toward them with his black .38 Saturday Night Special. Blast nodded his head to Stone. Stone understood that Blast wanted him to run, which he did. Before the stick up man could get a shot off, Blast emptied his .38 into the man's body, leaving him dead on the corner with blood leaking from his head into the sewer. Stone ran a block up to Rockaway Avenue, where he met up with Blast.

"Damn, you blasted the shit outta that nigga. Good looking, baby!" Stone said, relieved that Blast was there to have his back. From that day, he was known as Blast. Stone put him under his wing and put him on the payroll. Knowing that about him didn't deter the two men who were there from doing what they came to do. Tired of hearing Blast mumble, Darnell took the duct tape off his mouth.

"Yo, Darnell. You ain't got to do this, homeboy. I'll tell Stone to put you on baby bro," Blast said, hoping that his life would be spared.

"Nigga, you think I was born yesterday? You think I don't know that nigga is going to try to kill me? Who the fuck you think you talking to, Blast?" Darnell laughed, and then his face turned serious quickly.

"Darnell, my word is bond! I'll make sure . . . ."

"Your word is what? Oh, you think this is a game?'" Darnell said with rage on his face, pointing the gun at Blast's forehead.

Pap! Pap! Pap! Darnell put three bullets in Blast's face, sending blood and flesh flying against the beige painted wall and on Blast's wife's face and blue cotton robe. No one heard Mecca flinch and whisper her father's name. Her mother tried to break free of her restraints, but to no avail. She screamed under the duct tape, which muffled the sound.

"Oh, shit, Darnell! What the fuck?" Darnell's partner barked.

"Nigga, shut the fuck up. You the reason I had to do that, and this!"

Darnell put a bullet in Mecca's mother's head. Her body slumped over onto Blast's already slumped body. Darnell grabbed the bag of heroin out the refrigerator, and looked down at the slumped bodies on the floor.

"C'mon, stupid," Darnell said, putting his gun back in his waistband.

Mecca watched both men rush out of the apartment. When the door was closed Mecca waited for a few seconds before she came out from under the bed, making sure that the men wouldn't be back forgetting something, or remembering that Blast had a daughter who looked just like him.

Meanwhile, the white-robed man looked at Mecca after showing her the vision of when she was eight years old watching the murder of her parents.

"You didn't see then why you should have chosen a different lifestyle?" the strange man asked in an almost caring voice. Mecca could detect an undertone of sarcasm and that only pissed her off more.

"No, all I saw was my reason to make them pay! Why are you doing this? Who are you anyway?" Mecca responded angrily.

"Who I am is not important, and I'm doing this because this is my job. The question is why did you do the things you did?"

"It's all I knew," Mecca said, putting her head down, defeated. "If you're not God or whoever and you mad or if God is mad because of my life, then why did He put me in that situation? Why did He let them kill my parents? What type of God lets an eight-year-old watch her moms and pops get murdered like that? Answer that." Mecca said gravely.

"You can't blame God for the evil that men do. Those men and people like them decided on their own to do what they do. No one made you do what you did in life," the man countered.

Mecca folded her arms and rolled her eyes, looking away from the man. "Well, I was too young to comprehend or see the signs you're talking about. Whatever your name is," Mecca said sarcastically.

"Call me Lou, and I haven't finished showing you the signs you missed. I like showing you this. Your life is very interesting. You could have made a lot of money writing a book about it." Lou smiled.

Chapter Two

Thou shall not kill.
—Ten Commandments

"Mommy, Daddy, get up! Please, Mommy!" Mecca crawled out from under the bed and ran to her parents. Mecca cried, shaking her parents. Both of their eyes were open with the blank stare of death in them. A look Mecca would never forget. Mecca ran to the phone that was hung up on the kitchen wall near the refrigerator. She stood on her toes to reach the phone, and dialed a seven-digit number.

"Hello."

"Aunt Ruby? My mommy and daddy gone," Mecca cried to her mother's younger sister.

"Baby, where they at?" Ruby asked tersely.

"They lying on the couch," Mecca said, sniffing and sobbing loudly. "And they won't get up, they bleeding."

Ruby instructed Mecca to open the door when the neighbor knocked. Ruby had called a friend of the family who lived on the ninth floor along with Mecca and her parents, and asked her to go check on the apartment and Mecca until she got there. It would only take her about a half an hour.

The neighbor, a girlfriend of Mecca's mother and Ruby, knocked on the door. When Mecca let her in, the woman, used to seeing murders growing up in the rough Brownsville section of Brooklyn, still reacted as if this were her first time seeing dead bodies. She covered her mouth, ran into the bathroom, and the food she ate for breakfast and lunch found its way into the roach-infested toilet. Afterward, she called the police. They arrived just as Ruby did. Ruby saw her niece sitting at the kitchen table with a plainclothes white female officer kneeled down in front of her. Mecca ran to her aunt as soon as she saw her. Mecca cried as they made contact. Ruby picked her up, and while hugging Mecca she looked at the bloodstained sheet that covered her sister's and brother-in-law's bullet-scarred bodies, not believing what took place.

"Everything is going to be okay, baby. Auntie's here," Ruby whispered in Mecca's ear as she tried to offer her some comfort. Her parents were killed right in front of her, so Ruby knew there was only so much she could say or do at the moment.

"Don't tell these cops anything, okay, baby? Don't ever speak to the cops. They are bad people! They're just like the people who did this bad thing to your mommy and daddy. Auntie gone take care of this, all right?" Ruby gave the white female cop a menacing look, whispering to Mecca as she rubbed her back.

"Uh-huh," Mecca mumbled, agreeing to her aunt's wishes. Mecca whispered in her aunt's ear, "Auntie, I know who did it!"

"Tell Auntie later, okay?" Ruby whispered in Mecca's ear before putting her down on the floor.

"Is it okay if we talk to your niece?" the officer asked indistinctly, approaching them with a notepad in her hand, poised to write whatever Mecca was willing to share.

"No, it's not okay," she said. "She didn't see what happened. Her mother and father are dead, she's eight years old, and she's been through enough."

Ruby grabbed Mecca by the hand and they left the apartment. Mecca's mother's prayer was answered. Mecca left Brownsville, but her life in Brownsville was traded for another notorious Brooklyn neighborhood, Coney Island. On the drive to Coney Island in Ruby's 1982 black and yellow Camaro, Mecca informed her aunt about what she saw and heard when her parents were killed.

"Daddy talked to this guy. His name is Darnell. He's Tamika from my school brother," Mecca said in her childish tone.

"Auntie knows who you're talking about," Ruby said in a hoarse, scratchy voice. She held up two fingers to Mecca while she switched lanes on the Belt Parkway. "It was two of them?" Ruby asked.

"Yup, two of them. The other one didn't take his mask off."

Ruby nodded her head. She tried to hold back the tears because she wanted to be strong for her niece. Mecca needed her aunt, and if she saw Ruby crying, Ruby figured Mecca would be deeply affected by first the loss of her parents, and the sadness of her aunt. Ruby wiped her eyes and tried to swallow the lump in her throat. She glanced over at Mecca, who was staring out the passenger window at cars and the grimy Brooklyn neighborhoods that lay along the side of the Belt Parkway with tears running down her face. Ruby watched a roach crawl out of the collar of Mecca's pajama top. She grabbed it and smashed it in her hand.

Mecca turned and stared at her aunt as Ruby smashed the roach. They looked into each other's eyes, both understanding the silent language that Ruby would smash the people who killed her sister and brother-in-law, just like she did that roach. Without any words, Mecca continued watching the scenery through tear-blurred eyes, knowing her life from then on would never be the same.

Chapter Three

Twenty-five-year-old Ruby Davidson was the total opposite of her now deceased older sister, who Mecca was named after and was known around the way as Big M. Ruby was a dark brown, five feet eleven inches, big-boned woman. She kept her shoulder-length hair constantly wrapped with a blue bandanna, and she refused to wear women's apparel.

Ruby was a beautiful woman under the masculine mask she kept herself under. Ruby and Big M shared the same birth mother but had different fathers who neither knew. Ruby and Big M's mother was a young teenager at the ages of fifteen and sixteen when she gave birth to her two daughters. Big M's father was found dead behind a Bedford Stuyvesant bar with multiple stab wounds to his chest. His killer was never found. Ruby's father was killed in the Attica riots serving a twenty-five-to-life sentence after killing a cop walking the beat in his Brownsville neighborhood.

Ruby and Big M never met their fathers' families so there were no grandmothers or aunts or uncles they could spend weekends or holidays with. Their mother's family was spread out down south from Georgia to Louisiana, and their deep religious roots prevented them from dealing with their northern kin, who were into drugs and other sinful activities. Ruby and Mecca's mother raised her two daughters on her own until she fell victim to heroin.

One day a neighbor found Ruby's mother in the staircase with a needle in her arm almost dead. The neighbor contacted the Board of Children's Welfare, also known as BCW, and informed them of what was happening in apartment 5B. The city placed Ruby and her sister in a foster home on the premise that they would be returned to their mother when she cleaned up. She never did.

Ruby, the youngest, and her year-older sister, ran away from their foster home when they were twelve and thirteen. Even though she was a year younger, Ruby was more mature than her older sister. She had more leadership qualities. It was her idea to take off from their foster home in Queens and make their way back to Brownsville. Ruby felt like she would rather deal with the street life in which she grew up and was comfortable with, than deal with foster parents who didn't like her and her sister and only wanted them there because they were getting a check.

Ruby's body developed faster than her older sister so she looked older than her twelve years. Boys as old as eighteen approached young Ruby looking for a chance to get in her pants. Ruby had her first sexual experience on a project roof with this boy named Ron who was sixteen years old. She told her older sister afterward, revealing to her how painful it was. Ruby thought Ron was her boyfriend because he let her and her sister live in his two-bedroom apartment he shared with his ailing grandmother in the Langston Hughes projects.

He gave Ruby money and brought her clothes. The money he gave her she bought her older sister clothes with. When Ruby and her sister left the foster home, they dropped out of school. Ruby's boyfriend sold drugs in Brownsville, and eventually Ruby began to hold his drugs while he stood on the corner. He would send the customers to Ruby after the customers gave him the money.

He paid Ruby one hundred dollars a day. She saved money so one day she could get her and her sister an apartment. Mecca got a job at a local McDonalds when she turned fifteen after Ruby talked her boyfriend into taking Mecca down to get her working papers. Ron put Ruby on the lease of the apartment and when his grandmother died three years later the apartment was in her name. Ruby in turn put her sister on the lease because she had a job. Because Big M's job was a minimum-wage job, the rent would be lowered to accommodate her income.

Ron was arrested for a murder he committed against a rival clan in the Langston Hughes projects. Eventually, he pleaded to a five to fifteen-year bid and was shipped upstate to the same prison Ruby's father was killed in, Attica. Ruby was devastated.

She loved him. He was her first. She visited him faithfully. She sold the drugs he left behind and made sure his commissary account stayed in the three-digit range. She snuck in balloons of heroin for him to sell on the inside and accepted his collect calls. Ruby was always there for his calls. She wrote him love letters every night, crying herself to sleep. She never looked at another man, ignoring the advances guys made around the projects. Even some of his friends tried to get a piece of her.

"Damn, that nigga got you sucked up, girl! Let me hit it while he gone," they would say when she was seen around the projects. She ignored them all.

At the same time, her older sister was seeing a guy from the neighborhood named Bobby Sykes. The prettiest nigga Ruby ever saw. Her sister was happy and that's what made Ruby like Bobby. Ruby sometimes became jealous of her sister's relationship because her man was in jail while her sister enjoyed the company of Bobby. Bobby bought her sister anything she wanted. Her sister stayed with the latest trend of clothing and he decorated her with diamond-studded trinkets, rings, bracelets, and necklaces.

Ruby had a rough time selling dope in the projects because she was a female. At first the hustlers accepted it because they knew she was doing it to take care of her man, who they respected, but that didn't last. Ruby knew she had to get her own respect if she was going to continue to hustle. She bought a gun from an old timer who ran the neighborhood number spot. Even though it was a .25, Ruby had to make do until she was able to buy and handle a bigger one.

The day came when she had to put her weapon to use. The cousin of the guy her boyfriend had killed heard that Ruby was making money for his cousin's killer. He had to put a stop to that. He was a known troublemaker around Brownsville. Anywhere he went, something was bound to happen. He was also known to carry around a blue steel .44 Magnum and wasn't scared to use it. For that, he was given the moniker "Blue."

The rain poured down heavily on that Brownsville night, sending the dopefiends into the staircases to shoot up and the hustlers into project lobbies to hustle. Ruby stood in the hallway of her building wearing a black sheepskin with the hat to match, a black pair of Vidal Sassoon jeans, a black sweatshirt with "Ruby" written on it in white letters, and black Pumas. She had a plastic bag in her coat pocket with two bundles of dope in it, and her .25 in her other pocket.

Blue walked into the lobby with a black rain suit on with a black hooded sweatshirt underneath it. He took his hood off and glanced at Ruby while she leaned up against the silver mailboxes on the wall. He pressed the button on the elevator, acting as if he were waiting for it to come.

Ruby knew who he was. Everyone in Brownsville knew who he was. Seeing him around the way almost every day, Ruby didn't think anything of him coming into the building. She definitely didn't expect him to try to rob her as he pulled his blue steel .44 and pointed it at her chest.

Ruby had never had a gun pointed at her before and the shock of it made everything seem as if it were in slow motion. The graffiti on the walls looked as if it were moving. The pissy smell in the lobby seemed as if it were new to Ruby. She already had her hands in her pockets so she pulled out the plastic bag containing the two bundles and she put her other hand on the trigger.

"Where's the money? I know you got money. If I search you and find some I'ma blast you, bitch!" Blue said between clenched teeth.

"That's . . . that's all I got," Ruby stuttered in a fearful voice.

"Don't play with me, I know you sending that bitch-ass nigga of yours money. He lucky I wasn't around when he got my cousin or I would have murdered that punk-ass nigga!"

Hearing Blue say vulgar things about her man made all the fear in Ruby vanish. Her fear was replaced by a burning rage in her chest. With the gun still in her pocket, she pointed it at him and squeezed five times. All five shots hit Blue in his stomach, his groin, and his thighs, sending him falling face forward. His finger pulled the trigger on his gun as he fell, sending a bullet into the building's front door.

"Who's the bitch-ass nigga now, you faggot!" Ruby bent down and took his gun as he lay on the floor, moaning, then spit on him.

She ran out of the building and disappeared into the Brownsville night. A bullet had traveled to Blue's spine and he was paralyzed from the waist down. Ruby moved to Coney Island after she shot and paralyzed Blue. Blue didn't tell the cops who shot him, though. He was embarrassed by being shot by a female, let alone the girlfriend of his cousin's killer, so he told his friends that some cat he never saw before ran him down. When Ruby visited Brownsville, Blue, now being pushed around in a wheelchair by his little brother, only glanced at her, not wanting to stir up any trouble.

Ruby's world came crumbling in on her when she took one of her weekend trips to Attica to visit her boyfriend. The prison allowed inmates five visitors at one time. The prison only informed visitors that an inmate had visitors if the limit was reached; otherwise, they would allow a visitor to visit an inmate who was already on a visit. When Ruby was let in she immediately noticed her boyfriend hugging and kissing on a girl she recognized from Langston Hughes. She walked over to the couple just as they finished kissing.

"Who the fuck is this bitch, nigga?" Ruby yelled, standing between her boyfriend and the girl. Looking at the both of them, tears began to form in her eyes.

"She's a friend, Ruby. Chill out, girl," her boyfriend explained, trying to grab Ruby's hand. He could tell by the look in her eyes that she was about to go off. The other visitors and inmates all watched the drama unfold. Even the correction officer positioned at a desk at the front of the visiting room watched.

"After all I been through for you, this is how you pay me back? This is what I get, you bastard?"

"Yo, you buggin', Ruby. She's my friend!"

"Friend? Fuck you mean friend, nigga? You just asked me to marry you, and I'm your friend? You better tell this bit—" the girl responded. She was shorter and smaller than Ruby, but she wasn't the least bit afraid of Ruby's stature.

She didn't get the chance to finish her sentence before Ruby was all over her. The correction officer had to intervene before total chaos broke out. He had to call for backup to get

Ruby off of the girl because she was already bleeding from the nose and mouth. The visit was terminated, and Ruby left the prison distraught and heartbroken. She never visited him again. She didn't respond to his letters or accept his calls. She told her sister about the incident and the next day his name was taken off the lease. Ruby threw all of his clothes, pictures, and anything else that was his or reminded her of him in the incinerator. Ruby developed a deep hatred for men after her ordeal, and she swore to her sister that she would never let another nigga have her heart again.

As Ruby and Mecca drove the streets toward home, Ruby tried her best to get these thoughts out of her head. She couldn't help but notice how much Mecca looked like her now-deceased sister, and vowed to herself that she would do everything in her power to help Mecca get through these trying times that were clearly too much for a child to handle. Ruby also knew she couldn't dwell on the past, and had to keep the flow going in her own life.

Ruby brought her niece to her Coney Island apartment a few blocks away from the amusement park the neighborhood was famous for. Her duplex apartment on Twenty-fourth Street between Surf and Mermaid Avenues was decorated with mirrored walls and bright-colored furniture. It had a seventies look to it. Ruby was living in the apartment with a female companion, but she was currently serving a ten-year sentence for possession of a half kilo of heroin found in a backpack she attempted to bring on a Greyhound bus headed to Virginia. When they entered the apartment, Ruby turned on the television for Mecca to watch.

"You hungry, baby?" she asked while walking into the kitchen. Ruby didn't know why she asked that question, knowing her niece's appetite probably was gone by what she had seen. She didn't have an appetite herself. She just wanted to take Mecca's mind off of what had happened as much as she could.

"Yes, Auntie, do you have Cap'n Crunch?" Mecca replied to her surprise. Ruby knew at that moment that Mecca was tougher than the average girl her age. If she could get through the death of her parents with no problem, anything else that would come her way would be a breeze.

Chapter Four

*He that killeth with the sword must
be killed with the sword.*

—Revelations 13:10

After two weeks of taking Mecca shopping for new clothes and furniture for the room once used by Ruby's roommate, Mecca returned to school. Ruby allowed Mecca to continue to attend school in Brownsville with all of her friends. She, along with some of Mecca's teachers, noticed a change in Mecca's attitude immediately. Her temper, to be exact.

Her first explosion was directed toward a girl her age named Tamika, the sister of her parents' killer. Tamika didn't know it was her brother who had killed Mecca's parents. Tamika hardly saw her brother, and when he did come home it would be after a week of him missing and he would come home while Tamika was asleep. When she got home from school, he would be gone. It all popped off when Tamika asked Mecca for some candy during lunch period, something she was better off leaving alone.

"Can I get one of your Now and Laters?"

"No! Get your own," Mecca replied to Tamika while rolling her eyes.

"Forget you then," Tamika came back, sucking her teeth and rolling her eyes at Mecca. When she turned to walk away she didn't see Mecca charging at her like a speeding train. By the time she turned around, hearing the footsteps coming toward her, Mecca was swinging wildly, punching and scratching Tamika's face. She pulled Tamika's hair, forcing her to the floor and causing Tamika to squeal in pain.

"Mecca, get off me! You're hurting me!"

Mecca had rage in her eyes and she didn't hear Tamika's cry. She didn't hear the other students laughing and screaming for Mecca to "beat her up!" and "stop, Mecca, you're hurting her!"

Teachers heard the commotion and went to break it up. When Mecca was pulled off of Tamika, she had patches of her hair missing. Her face was scratched and bruised. Mecca was breathing hard and just stared at Tamika while the teachers walked her to the principal's office, where Mecca was told she was on a three-day suspension. Mecca thought she would come home to an angry Ruby. Instead, Ruby waited for Mecca to return home to a diamond bracelet and brand new Sergio Valente jeans and Reebok sneakers. Ruby was usually high off of the weed she constantly smoked, and smiled at Mecca.

"You beat that li'l bitch ass, Mecca?"

"Yeah, Auntie, I beat her ass." Mecca smiled back at her aunt.

Ruby hugged her niece and said, "If anybody says something you don't like or tries to hurt your feelings, you beat they ass. If they beat you, you grab a bottle, a knife, anything you can find and you make sure they feel pain, you hear me?" Ruby asked. With a serious look on her face, she held Mecca's shoulders and continued, "If I ever hear you let somebody hit you and you ain't do nothing, I'll beat your ass myself."

Ruby smiled again and handed Mecca her gifts. When teachers complained to Ruby, she told them she would deal with Mecca. Eventually Mecca got expelled at numerous schools in Brooklyn. By the time she reached junior high, Mecca had been to six elementary schools, and ended up in a school for problem kids known as "six hundred schools."

Ruby sold dope out of the apartment and didn't have to worry about standing on corners subjected to harassing beat cops, and detectives or the stick up kids. Coney Island was full of stick up kids. Ruby had regular clientele. People she knew. She didn't run a spot where just anyone could come cop; her customers were also friends she invited in to drink and gossip with, most of them women.

Ruby had some of the same customers she had before leaving Brownsville, and it was from her Brownsville customers that she received info she needed about the goings-on in

Brownsville. The who's who and what's what of the neighborhood. This is how Ruby received the information she needed
to make her move against the man responsible for killing
her sister and her brother-in-law, and making her niece an
orphan.

The kids in Mecca's new Coney Island neighborhood
learned the hard way that Mecca wasn't the social type. Ruby
kept Mecca's hair tightly corn-rowed, which made Mecca's
eyes seem catlike. The look in Mecca's light brown eyes scared
a lot of the kids. A lot of the kids envied Mecca, due to Ruby
making sure that Mecca's clothes were of the latest fashion.
Mecca wore clothes that kids in Coney Island wouldn't see
until months later and wouldn't be able to have because their
parents couldn't afford them.

What Mecca didn't know was that her clothes were from
boosters that Ruby paid for with dope or were given to her
by her friends. The only things Ruby bought for Mecca were
jewelry, sneakers, and shoes. Mecca wore two-karat diamond
earrings, diamond-flooded wrist and ankle bracelets, and
she had every cartridge for the Atari 2600 and the 3200 ever
made.

When the summer of 1983 rolled in, Mecca met a girl her
age named Dawn who lived down the hall from her tenth floor
apartment. Dawn's mother was one of Ruby's customers and
asked Ruby if Dawn could stay at her apartment while she
went out on "dates," which everybody in Coney Island knew
were Johns. She sold her body to support her habit. At first,
Mecca hated the dark-skinned, thick, bushy-haired girl. Dawn
wore dirty clothes, smelled like piss, and she was always ashy.
Mecca didn't like her out of jealousy. Ruby started giving
Dawn new clothes; she bathed Dawn, and did her hair the
same way she did Mecca's.

Mecca found her excuse to try to physically hurt Dawn when
Dawn tried to steal one of Mecca's Atari cartridges. They were
playing each other in a game of Frogger when Mecca noticed
out of the corner of her eye the print of a cartridge in Dawn's
dungaree pockets. Mecca dropped her joystick and went to
grab Dawns pocket.

"What are you doing?" Dawn jumped back and yelled.

Mecca gave her the look that usually scared other kids away from her, but to her surprise Dawn returned the look. Mecca was caught off guard. She was not used to anyone not being scared when she gave them that menacing stare.

"Gimme my cartridge, you thief!" Mecca barked.

"This ain't yours!" Dawn grabbed her pocket when she saw Mecca stare at it.

"Yes, it is!" Mecca yelled, charging at Dawn, who was no pushover.

This was no easy fight for Mecca. Dawn was just as strong and ferocious as she was. Ruby, in her bedroom, was bagging up heroin into small, white packets, wearing a hospital mask over her face as not to inhale the fumes, when she heard the argument going on between the girls, and ran out to see what the commotion was. When she entered the living room she saw Mecca and Dawn both with ripped T-shirts, hair out wild, and both had scratches and blood coming out of their noses. They were both out of breath holding each other's hair, and swinging their arms at each other. Ruby watched them fight for a few more minutes, grinning, then when she realized they had both had enough, she stepped between them, holding them apart from each other.

"All right, you two! Y'all know damn well y'all had enough. I don't know what y'all was fighting for. . . ."

"She tried to—" Mecca replied, pointing to Dawn, out of breath.

Ruby cut her off. "I don't want to know. The way y'all fought each other y'all better off being friends and holding each other down against them people that's going to hate you for who you are. Whatever it was, don't let it come between y'all again. Don't let nothing come between y'all, I want y'all to be like sisters, you hear me?"

Both girls stared at each other, neither not wanting to fight each other again. Mecca had to admit to herself Dawn was tough and Dawn thought the same of Mecca. Dawn also thought Mecca was a spoiled brat who was spoon-fed and didn't have to fight for anything, but she had a change of heart after the fight Mecca had put up.

"I said did y'all hear me?" Ruby grumbled. Both girls nodded their heads.

Dawn never tried to take anything from Mecca again. In fact, she stole cartridges from other kids that Mecca didn't have, and gave them to her. Afterward, Mecca started to like Dawn, and when Mecca realized Dawn's mother was a fiend she felt sorry for Dawn and their bond got tighter. Ruby enrolled Dawn in the same school as Mecca and the two became inseparable. When you fought one, you fought the other. Eventually no one messed with the two girls. Kids in their Brownsville school started calling them The Devil's Daughters.

The man in the white robe laughed loudly while Mecca just stared. "The Devil's Daughters!" the white-robed man called Lou yelled, chuckling.

"I didn't tell anybody to call us that. So what's so funny?" Mecca asked with anger in her voice.

Lou stopped laughing and said, "I know you didn't tell no one to call y'all that. It's what they saw in you and her. People see you better than you see yourself, Mecca. That's why now I'm giving you the opportunity to see yourself from day one and the people around you, I'm giving you the opportunity to see how your life affected others and how people saw you."

"I don't care how people saw me," Mecca said sternly.

"After this, you're going to wish you had cared, Ms. Mecca."

Chapter Five

The Summer of 1987

The summer of 1987 was one of the best summers Ruby ever
had. Crack was on the scene and Ruby became acquainted with
the rock form of cocaine, and established a relationship with it
that fattened her pockets. The Langston Hughes projects were
full of crackfiends looking for the dealer who had the best stuff.
A lot of good people fell victim to the lure of the three-minute
high that crack gave.

A lot of people Ruby knew from her younger days were now
strung out, people who were once a part of the in crowd. The
people who everyone in the hood wanted to be like, dress like,
and talk like got bit by the crack epidemic, even Stone.

When Stone, the once kingpin of the projects became a
full-fledged crackhead, he eventually lost the respect of his
soldiers and confidants. He started smoking his own product
until he went broke. Darnell, the man who killed Ruby's sister
and brother-in-law, made his move. He had the product and
the product was good. With that came the soldiers. Stone's
ex-soldiers. In no time Darnell was the biggest cat in the projects. Ruby set up shop in Coney Island, and she had her friend
Monique sell her stuff in Langston Hughes. Ruby wasn't
making as much as Darnell was, but it was enough. Most of
her money was being made on her Coney Island block.

"Girl, guess who home?" Monique asked as if she was about
to deliver bad news.

"Who?" Ruby asked while she chopped up a rock the size of a tennis ball on a white china dish with a razor blade. She placed the pebbles inside small vials with yellow tops.

"Your ex-nigga a Five Percenter now. They call him Wise, like the dumb nigga wise or something," Monique giggled.

Monique was the only person Ruby talked to about the ordeal with Wise. Monique and Ruby had been friends since they were kids growing up in Brownsville. Ruby talked to Monique about men because Monique was an expert when it came to dealing with the opposite sex. She had men wrapped around her finger. Her voluptuous body and striking good looks were the keys to making men bow at her feet. She had a caramel complexion and hazel eyes with firm C-cup breasts. Monique had an exotic look having been born to a Panamanian mother and Cuban father. Oddly, Monique didn't know a lick of Spanish.

The thought of seeing her ex made Ruby nervous. She wondered how she would react or feel when she saw him. She wondered how he looked. Was he buff from lifting weights in jail? Did he still look the same with his fine self? His curly hair that looked wet, his chinky eyes, and those dimples . . . damn.

"Girl, what you thinking about?" Monique asked, snapping Ruby out of her daydream.

"I was thinking how much product I left in Coney Island," Ruby lied. Monique knew she was lying, also. She knew her girl and knew when she was hurt, happy, and lying.

"Please, Ruby, you thinking about that clown Wise or whatever he call himself." Monique laughed at Ruby's expense, causing Ruby to laugh too.

"You know me too good. I got to change my ways."

"What's there to think about? That nigga old news," Monique said, hoping Ruby wasn't thinking about reconciling her and Wise's relationship. She knew how hurt Ruby was when she had gone on that visit and saw him hugging and kissing another woman. She didn't want her best friend to go through that again. People just didn't know how much Ruby changed after that episode.

"You right, girl. Fuck that clown," Ruby said, continuing to chop on the crack rock she had on the plate. "It's about money and you know what m-o-n-e-y means to us!"

In unison, Ruby and Monique yelled, "Money Over Niggas Every Year!" They both howled in laughter.

Mecca was now thirteen years old and still a virgin. Her body developed quickly. The boys in her junior high school noticed the feisty thirteen-year-old, and her friend, Dawn, who had also developed quickly.

Dawn had already lost her virginity in the school bathroom to a Puerto Rican boy in her social studies class. They started off passing notes to each other, then Dawn answered the last letter with a check in the "yes" box when he asked if she wanted to go out with him. He motioned for her to meet him when the bell rang to change classes. They snuck to the basement and had sex in the bathroom.

"Did you like it?" Mecca asked curiously.

"At first I didn't, because it hurt. Then it started feeling good," Dawn replied shyly.

"You so nasty." Mecca smiled and playfully hit Dawn on the shoulder.

Dawn sucked her teeth. "Please, you better get you some before your stuff dry up and die."

Both girls laughed. Mecca and Dawn had to gain their respect back when they entered junior high. It was a new school and there were new foes at the time, and some of the kids from their elementary schools were there and spread the word that Dawn and Mecca were not to be fucked with. But with some people, examples had to me made.

The opportunity presented itself when the girlfriend of a guy who had a crush on Mecca found out that he liked her. Instead of confronting her boyfriend, she chose to approach Mecca, who didn't even know the boy. The girl made a bad choice. A choice that she had to carry for the rest of her life.

Dawn and Mecca both dressed in tight-fitting Lee Jeans. Mecca with burgundy pinstriped ones with burgundy on white shell-top Adidas, and a white sweat shirt with "Mecca" written in script on the upper left corner, and giant door knocker earrings. Dawn wore black ones with black on white shell-top Adidas, and a white sweatshirt with matching earrings. They both walked down the crowded hallway heading toward the exit, when a light-skinned girl with a short Jherri curl that left stains on her no-name brand, button-down blue shirt approached Mecca with an angry look on her face.

"You better stay away from my man!"

Mecca and Dawn looked at each other, then back at the girl, confused. "Who you talking to?" Mecca asked.

"I'm talking to you! Stay away from Tah or I'm gonna . . ." the girl replied, stepping closer to Mecca's face.

Mecca didn't give her the opportunity to finish her threat. She was punching the girl in the face and pulled her Jherri curl, pulling the girl down to the floor. Dawn started kicking the girl in the stomach and the face. The girl screamed as the crowd in the hallway gathered around, watching the two fly girls beat up the girl who had approached them with hostility. While the girl was down, she managed to look up and spit in Mecca's face. Mecca turned as red as an apple. Mecca reached in her back pocket and pulled out a Gem Star razor that she had found on the kitchen table. Ruby used them to chop up her drugs.

Grabbing the girl by the back of her head, holding her hair, she sliced the girl's face from her ear to the corner of her lip. The blood squirted from the girl's face. She tried to hold her face closed so the blood wouldn't leak out.

"She cut me! Get this bitch off of me!"

When the crowd saw all the blood, they started walking away. Mecca and Dawn both ran to the exit and rushed to the bus stop to catch the bus heading home. Later that day, two cops knocked on Monique's door in Langston Hughes looking for Dawn and Mecca. The girls used Monique's address so they could go to school in Brownsville. They had to live in the zone in order to attend the school. If the school found out they lived in Coney Island, they wouldn't be allowed to attend. The cops told Monique that they had a warrant for the arrest of Dawn and Mecca. Monique informed both of them that Dawn and Mecca didn't return home that day. When they did she would bring them to the station. She lied.

"Who the hell is Tah, Dawn?" Mecca asked Dawn while they rode the bus home.

"You know him by face. He's in my math class," Dawn replied, looking out the window while the bus rode through the Pitkin Avenue shopping area.

"How he look? He better be cute after all this bullshit we going through," Mecca said.

"He all right. He ain't no LL Cool J. He gets fresh and all that. He pump jums in Brownsville houses."

"You know we can't go back to school, right?" Mecca said more than asked.

Dawn sighed. "Yeah, I know. Fuck it, I'm tired of school anyway. I'm ready to start making some dough."

"What are you talking about, Dawn?" Mecca asked with a look on her face that said, "I know you ain't talking about what I think you're talking about."

"I'm talking about the way your aunt gets money. Like everybody else. I'm tired of taking handouts from Ruby, Mecca. I'm ready to get down with the program."

Mecca shook her head at her friend. *Dawn is going crazy,* she thought. It's probably losing her virginity that messed her brain up. Mecca hoped Dawn was just talking and not dead serious about it.

"Dawn, you crazy, girl," was all she could say before riding the rest of the way to Coney Island in silence.

The white-robed man named Lou folded his arms and stared at Mecca for a few seconds.

"What?" Mecca asked tersely.

"Did that girl deserve to have her face sliced up like that?"

Mecca sucked her teeth and looked away from Lou. "Shoot, she spit on me. I ain't letting nobody spit on me, for real."

"Don't you see how reckless you were, Mecca? I could under-stand you being young and in emotional pain from the tragic loss of your parents, but to live your life blaming everybody for it? It's not fair, Mecca. Two people are responsible for what happened to your parents. Not the eight million people that live in New York City."

"What do you care? It wasn't your family!" Mecca barked. "You don't know what it feels like. How you going to tell me how I should have felt?"

"I didn't tell you how you should feel. I'm just saying you should have learned how to deal with your feelings better than the way you did," Lou shot back.

"What's the point then?" Mecca asked, lifting her hands in a protesting manner while shrugging her shoulders

"I haven't gotten to that yet. When I do you'll be the first to know."

Chapter Six

His mischief shall return upon his own head, and his violent dealing shall come down upon his own plate.
—Psalms 7:18

"Damn, Stone. How you let yourself go like that, man? This ain't you, man!" Wise said as he and Stone stood on the corner of Rockaway Avenue and Dumont in Tilden Projects.

It was a hot, sunny day.

Stone, dressed in a dirty, blue suede–front jacket with holes in it and ripped-up jeans and dirty, red suede Pumas, looked down while his mouth twitched, looking for an answer to Wise's question.

"I'll be back on my feet in no time, kid! Watch, ain't nothing change, baby." Stone smiled, showing yellow-stained teeth with some missing. His skin was ashy and dull, and though he was in his late thirties he looked to be in his fifties.

Wise looked at Stone, disgusted. This was a man Wise had looked up to when he was younger. This was his idol. Stone had it all. The women. The big caddies. Diamond-studded jewels and name belts. He wore the flyest clothes money could buy. Minks, silk suits, gators, crocs, and other reptiles on his feet. He was a legend. He was a stone cold killer everyone looked up to. Now, look at him.

"So what's going on around here, Stone? Who's doing what?"

Wise wore a bright red BVD nylon T-shirt, showing his muscular build from years of working out in prison. His black Calvin Klein jeans matched his black Reebok Classics. His once curly hair was now cut low with 360 waves.

"You know Darnell from the projects got things sowed up over there. Boy blew up something decent," Stone said in admiration.

"Word?" Wise asked, nodding his head.

"The only person besides Darnell getting some money is your girl Ruby. She doing okay for herself." Stone continued rocking back and forth on one leg at a time.

The mention of Ruby's name brought back memories for Wise. He also still felt the same guilt he felt for years after being caught on the visiting floor with a girl who was actually a mule bringing up weed and dope for him to sell. The kiss was the girl passing him dope. He led the girl on to thinking they were in a relationship because she wouldn't do what she was asked if he didn't give her the attention she wanted.

He didn't need her to do it because Ruby was doing it for him. His greed got the best of him, though. He never stopped loving Ruby; he dreamed of her every night for the four years he did time. He secretly cried in his cell when he didn't hear from her. When she wrote her last letter, it tore Wise up inside. The letter was stamped in his mind forever.

Dear backstabbing motherfucker,

I guess you wanted your cake and you wanted to eat it, too. I hope that bitch is worth losing someone who would have walked through hell with you. All the risk I took to make your bid comfortable and this is what I get? You a selfish bastard and you know what? I don't hate you for this. I'm bigger than that. It's a learning experience for me. I learned you ain't shit and you never gonna be shit. I hope you have a happy marriage. From someone who used to worship the ground you walked on.

Bye Forever!

Wise vowed to prove to Ruby that he was a better person than she thought he was. He vowed that he would make it up to her and try to win her heart back. When he began studying under the teaching of the Five Percent Nation, he had a different outlook on women. They were queens of civilization, goddesses of the universe. Wise needed a queen and he wanted that queen to be Ruby. What Wise didn't understand was a woman. He didn't understand a woman scorned. When she's done with you, she's done.

"That girl ain't nothing to fuck with, baby bro. She got her thing mapped out. She takes care of business, you hear me?" Stone said, while Wise was in deep thought on how he would win Ruby's heart back.

"I hear you, man," Wise replied.

"Speaking of the devil," Stone said excitedly, pointing toward Ruby walking toward them. "There she goes now!"

Both Ruby's and Wise's hearts beat fast as they caught eye contact with each other. It was like Ruby was walking in slow motion when he looked at her. Dressed in a tight, blue Calvin Klein jeans set that showed her thick thighs and bulging hips, which left no doubt about the size of her ass, her bootie socks had a black stripe on the rim matching her black and white Diadoras. Her rope chain was the size of a small child's arm. As usual, she wore her hair in a black bandanna scarf, this time with thick "baby hair" showing out of the front of it.

Ruby had to make a stop in the building Stone and Wise stood in front of. It was just a coincidence that she would run into him in another project only a few blocks from Langston Hughes. Ruby had customers in Tilden projects so her face was a regular around there.

Noticing him, Ruby became nervous, with perspiration beginning to cover her palms. It was just the way she imagined. He would come home buffed and beautiful and ready to fuck some woman's brains out with all those years backed up in him. He had the glow guys have when they come home from the penitentiary. His hair was sharply shaped up and his waves did a perfect circle around his head. His arms bulged and his chest muscles showed through his shirt. Ruby's mouth turned dry and she felt her body shaking as she came face to face with him. Wise smiled, showing pearly white teeth.

"Ruby, what's up, girl?" he asked while reaching out to hug her.

Ruby didn't hug him, but she let him embrace her. She felt the hardness of his body and her pussy began to throb. When she didn't return the hug, Wise backed up and looked at her with a questionable look.

"It's like that?"

"How you doing, Ron?" Ruby asked, using his birth name purposely.

"My name is Wise now. Please don't use my government name."

Ruby already knew he was calling himself Wise. She purposely called him that to irritate him. She held her grudge, something he would find out the hard way.

"What's up, Stone?" she asked, smiling at Stone, then returning to the serious look when she looked back at Wise. "It was nice seeing you, Ron, I mean, Wise. Welcome home," Ruby said, walking toward the entrance of the high-rise building.

Wise grabbed her hand and tried to pull her toward him. "Ruby, can I talk to you for a minute?"

Ruby, rolled her eyes. "I got something important to take care of. Time is money and my time is valuable, something you didn't realize a few years ago."

"Ruby, how many times do I have to apologize for what I did? I told you she was a mule. I had to act like I liked her so she would keep bringing my shit up north," he pleaded.

"I wasn't mule enough for you?" Ruby asked. "Listen, Wise, that's old shit. Like our relationship is. Good to see you home, have a good life. I'm too old to be carrying on about this. So what is it that you want to say to me?"

Stone was right, Wise thought. She definitely changed. *She's colder than she was before.* Ruby always had a good heart and she was loyal to those she loved. Her heart was no longer warm, and she had a look in her eyes that said, "Don't fuck with me."

"I heard you getting money pushing rock," Wise said. Ruby cut her eyes at Stone who was still rocking his body, acting as if he wasn't paying attention to the conversation. "I wanna help you expand, lock all this shit down around here."

"And how do you plan on doing that?" she asked skeptically. Ruby faced him with her arms folded.

Wise looked at Stone from the corner of his eye then back at Ruby. "I can't discuss that here. Can I take you to get something to eat later on?" he asked.

I can't let him do this to me. He's trying to sneak back into my life. Once a dog, always a dog. He'll only hurt me and I won't let another man do this to me, Ruby thought.

Ruby's dealing with men had drastically changed since the day she found Wise kissing another woman on the prison visiting floor. It took her a year to even entertain her desire to have sex with a man, and when she did, it was hit and run. Mecca found out how drastic the change was on one of her numerous suspensions from school; she walked in on Monique's face deep between Ruby's legs. Monique was doing such a good job that Ruby didn't even notice Mecca walk in the house. Ruby lay on the couch with her eyes closed, holding Monique's head. Both women were stark naked.

"Meet me in Langston Hughes at seven thirty," Ruby said to Wise.

She walked away thinking, *I won't let him back in my heart, but he could be of good use for the plan I got. When I'm done with what I got to do, then I'll be rid of his no-good ass. Let another woman go through the heartache that these niggas come with.*

Wise turned to Stone, who looked at him with a look that spelled pitiful.

"Never let a once a month–bleeding bitch think that you need her. She'll do nothing but play on it," Stone said.

Wise shook his head. "See, that's why you're in the position you're in. You can't see ahead. You can't see the big picture. Sometimes, you gotta fake it to make it, baby." Wise grinned.

Wise knocked on Monique's door at seven thirty on the dot. Ruby answered the door and thought, *Damn, this nigga really look good.*

Inside the apartment, Rakim's "I Ain't No Joke" blasted out of the speakers. Ruby wore a pair of acid wash jeans by Calvin Klein with the matching jean jacket. She had gotten rid of the low cut years ago and wore her hair in a ponytail with bangs in the front. On her feet she had a pair of white and green Gucci sneakers. Wise took Ruby to Juniors restaurant in downtown Brooklyn before this meeting. He told her his plan to take over Brownsville.

"What you going to do about Darnell? He got things locked," Ruby asked as they sat at a table in the crowded restaurant.

"Once I get Tilden locked, I'ma move on Van Dyke projects. By then I'll be ready for Darnell," Wise replied. "For now I need to get product. I need a connect, and I heard your shit is good shit."

Ruby knew Wise had something up his sleeve. He wanted her connect. He didn't even have any soldiers to set up in Tilden and Van Dyke. Those niggas over there wouldn't be trying to hear that shit. Wise just came home thinking this was 1982. *These niggas is playing with guns now.* Ruby listened to Wise ramble on and on. Ruby leaned over the table to get close to Wise's face. He leaned in, thinking she wanted to kiss him.

"Nigga, you got toast?" she asked, trying to call his bluff. Wise leaned back, surprised that Ruby was on top of her game like that.

"Not yet. You know anybody who got some?"

Ruby sighed, then answered, "I got a better plan. You can get rid of Darnell quicker than your plan. Come see me tomorrow."

Wise walked Ruby to Monique's door. Ruby knew he hadn't asked her out to try to start over. He wanted to use her to get to her connect. *That nigga ain't change. He's even worse than he was before he went in, a selfish nigga with plans to get rich by stepping on toes. What niggas in jail don't realize is that times change and people do too. They think things are supposed to be the way they were before they went in. This is why a lot of cats come home and get killed.*

Wise set up a meeting with Darnell on the pretense that Wise knew of a heist where the score would be twenty or more kilos of cocaine. Even though Darnell was doing good pushing dope and crack, grossing ten kilos of cocaine and three of heroin, he would still participate in a heist. It was in him. That's how he got in the position he was in now. Selling drugs made him hood rich, but robbery was his first love. It's the Brownsville way.

Wise had Darnell meet him at Monique's apartment. He showed up in style just to show Wise that he was the man in Brownsville. Darnell loved to show off. He always wanted to be like Stone. Darnell wore a four-finger ring with his name in diamonds. He wore diamond-flooded name buckles with a large diamond in one ear. He entered Monique's apartment wearing a leather blazer with a black turtleneck, and a big rope chain with a medallion the size of a small china plate. His name was on the medallion flooded with diamonds, and he had on black Levi jeans and black-on-white Nike Cortezas.

"Peace, God," Wise said to Darnell. Darnell was also a Five Percenter, which made him willing to meet with Wise without being skeptical about it. Wise told him of the heist in the lingo of the Five Percenters.

"Yo, God. One of the gods I was in Comstock with built with me about this eighty-fiver who's making a lot of Divine Cipher Equality. He said this cat is sex. He lives in Mecca in Grant projects. We can get era," Wise said to Darnell, telling him that a non-believer he met in prison was getting mad dough but he was soft. He wanted Darnell to know that getting his money would be a piece of cake. Darnell agreed to meet with Wise to plan it.

"You want something to drink, God?" Wise asked. "I just got some Old E."

"Yeah. It's cold?" Darnell asked, sitting at the kitchen table, taking his blazer off and placing it on the back of the chair.

Wise got up from the table. "Why equal self?" he said, meaning "yes" in the coded language of Five Percenters. He went to the refrigerator and poured beer in milk glasses. After giving Darnell his drink, Wise sat down at the table across from Darnell.

"How much this cat got in the crib?" Darnell asked.

"The bitch said wisdom cipher or more," Wise answered, meaning twenty or more.

"She supposed to call you in an hour, right?" Darnell asked, drinking the beer.

"Yeah, she said as soon as this cat call and tell her he on the way. That's how he do, so the broad could tell him if it's clear for him to come through. Real cautious nigga."

"What you plan on doing with the coke?" Darnell asked Wise curiously.

"I was hoping I could team up with you and we could take over the whole villa. Tilden, Brownsville Houses, Sethlow, and Van Dyke. We'll be billionaires, God!" Wise said, but what he was really thinking was that Darnell was a dumb-ass nigga.

Ain't no coke. The coke that he'll get is going to be Ruby's, and once I get close to her connect, I plan to get her out the way, too. This nigga think he going to be alive after this heist, he got another think coming. I'ma blow this nigga head off. Who the fuck he think he is? He do a little bid and think he's going to come home and get rich in my hood?

Darnell smiled.

"It sounds good. Yeah, God, we'll be dumb rich."

After a half hour, Darnell began to get real tired. His speech started to slur and his eyes got heavy. He shook his head, trying to wake himself up.

"Damn, a nigga feel real crazy fucking with that beer."

Wise watched as his eyes began to shut. The sleeping pills Ruby gave him were powerful. He put more in the beer than what Ruby had told him. *"Put three in. He'll be knocked out for hours. If you put too much, nigga fuck around and die."* Wise put in six.

Darnell fell out of the chair and passed out on the kitchen floor. Ruby, dressed in a green velour Nike suit from Dapper Dan, and Monique, dressed in the same suit but in white with green trimming around the word Nike on her chest, came out of the bathroom after sitting in it for an hour. What Wise didn't know was that both women were armed with black 9 mm Berettas equipped with silencers.

"I got Darnell, take care of Dumb," Ruby whispered, calling Wise the name she and Monique jokingly called him.

"Search his pockets" Wise said to both women, walking to the bathroom. "I gotta take a piss."

When Wise closed the bathroom door, Ruby whispered to Monique, "Mo, open the window right there." Ruby pointed to the kitchen window.

While Monique opened the window, Ruby dragged Darnell's limp body to it. Monique looked at Ruby, confused.

"What you doing, Ruby?" she whispered with confusion written over her face.

"Grab his legs. I'm throwing him out of the window."

Monique shook her head while grabbing Darnell by his feet. Monique thought that Ruby was really insane. She'd be damned if she ever crossed her.

Both women shoved Darnell's body out of the window, letting it drop nine stories to his death. People sitting around and walking around the projects heard a loud thump, then turned to see Darnell's body slam head first into the cement and watched his brain pop out of his head. Women screamed and guys around the projects gaped at seeing their boss, friend, and some enemies to Darnell, splattered on the concrete.

When Wise came out of the bathroom, Ruby stood in front of the bathroom door as he came out. Ruby put her finger to her mouth, gesturing for Wise to say nothing. "We gotta get out of here," she whispered.

"Where's Darnell?" Wise asked, trying to look around Ruby's shoulder.

"We threw him out of the window," Ruby replied.

"Y'all did what?" he yelled, pushing Ruby out of the way. "Y'all bitches is crazy! We were supposed to tie him up! Then when he woke up make him take us to his stash!" Wise said. Wise walked to the door, pissed that the plan had somehow changed. "I'm outta here! Y'all bitches is stupid!"

Ruby and Monique followed him out the door. In the piss-smelling hallway you could hear Slick Rick and Doug E. Fresh's "The Show" blasting from someone's apartment.

Wise mumbled all the way to the elevator. He changed his mind, walking to the staircase with Ruby and Monique in tow. When they entered the graffiti-covered stairs, Monique and Ruby pulled out their silencer-equipped 9 mm, and as Wise descended, they both pumped bullets into his back and the back of his head.

As his body rolled down the stairs, Ruby stood on top of him and emptied the clip in him. Ruby didn't hear the footsteps coming up the stairs, and she couldn't see behind the walled staircase.

When Mecca came around the landing, she almost stepped on Wise's body. Mecca jumped back in shock, and then looked up at Ruby and Monique, both with guns in their hands.

"Mecca, where are you coming from?" Ruby whispered.

Mecca looked at Wise, then back at Ruby, barely able to speak. "The . . . the elevator is broke."

***

"You didn't see where that life was headed then Mecca?" Lou stared at Mecca, shrugging his shoulders with his hands up.

"That had nothing to do with me." Mecca snorted.

"I didn't say it did, but you saw the evil that's attributed to the lifestyle. After that, why didn't you see it wasn't worth it?"

"What other choices did I have? My aunt was everything to me. She was what I wanted to be. It was all I knew!" Mecca cried.

"I doubt that, Mecca. There were people in your life who didn't live like that. There were people who wanted better for you. You turned your back on those people," Lou said.

"Who? What people? I don't remember anybody trying to change me. Most people I knew either was in the game and the ones that weren't had they hands out for money for things they didn't have," Mecca countered.

Lou shook his head. "That's why I'm here. You have a bad memory, Mecca. So I'll remind you."

Chapter Seven

Many waters cannot quench love;
neither can the floods drown it.

— Songs of Solomon 8:7

By the time 1990 came around, Mecca and Dawn were knee-deep in the drug game. They gave Ruby's workers the packages of crack and collected the money. Dawn managed the spots in Coney Island while Mecca managed the spots in Brownsville.

Ruby had spots in each project in Brownsville. Each spot was making over $20,000 a day, and she paid the workers $2,000 a week. She put Stone in a rehab program with a promise to put him back on his feet if he completed it. When he completed the program, Stone made sure each spot ran smoothly. He was security, and Ruby paid him the same she paid Mecca and Dawn.

The spot in the Brownsville Houses was having problems with a local stick up crew headed by a guy named Tah. When Mecca was told about it from the workers, she remembered the name from somewhere but couldn't put a face to it. When she informed Ruby, Ruby barked, "What the fuck do I pay Stone for? And what's up with those punk-ass workers? None of them got crons?"

Mecca told Stone about the stick up crew and all he said was "I'll handle it." He never did. Word on the street was that Stone got soft and the young cats lost respect for him. Tah and the stick up crew took advantage of the word about Stone going soft and stuck him up at a block party in Brownsville houses.

"If I gotta go to them projects myself and handle these clowns, I'll fuck around and kill them niggas, then I'll kill Stone's punk ass!" Ruby growled.

Ruby stayed away from Brownsville as much as possible. The gritty section of Brooklyn was too unpredictable for her. Stick up kids and killers were born and raised on the Brownsville streets every day, and she didn't want to be some young hot head's first of many bodies. When she did show up in Brownsville in her ocean green Sterling with BBS rims, it was usually in the early morning hours to see Stone and to remind the residents of Brownsville that she was still around, and she wasn't hiding in the villa she bought in the Hamptons where she and Monique now stayed.

Ruby and Monique had become full-fledged lesbian lovers. Monique treated Mecca like a daughter. She loved Mecca as if she were her daughter, and she became concerned with Mecca being on the street. After a lovemaking session with Ruby, Monique expressed her concern as they lay naked on their king-sized, heart shaped waterbed with red satin sheets and pillows.

"Ruby, them streets are dangerous. You shouldn't have Mecca out there. She needs to get herself a job or something or finish school. Niggas don't care if she a girl or not, they'll treat her just like a nigga when it comes to that money. She still damn near a baby."

Ruby folded her arms under her head and sighed. "She's young, but she got a old soul. Mecca knows how to handle herself." Ruby looked over at Monique and continued. "Monique, you know that girl ain't gonna listen. Her and Dawn are hardheaded."

"Don't let them work for you no more. They won't have a choice but to get a job. Them girls are materialistic like hell. They ain't trying to be broke," Monique said with concern filling her voice. She knew firsthand how the streets would eat you alive and spit you out. She barely made it out of the very same streets Mecca and Dawn were now on, and she wanted better for them.

"All they'll do is go to work for someone else, and they won't treat them like I do. Or they'll become strippers or hookers or something, and I'm not trying to hear that, Mo," Ruby said in a matter-of-fact tone. Monique knew when to back off. The last thing a person wanted to do was piss Ruby off. She was liable to do anything with no remorse.

Ruby rented Mecca and Dawn an apartment in Sutter Gardens, an apartment complex in the East New York section of Brooklyn. The neighborhood was just as dangerous as Mecca's Brownsville environment, but she would have it no other way. Her reason for staying in the slums was simple.

"If niggas think you hiding, they'll come looking. If you in their face, they know you ready for whatever."

Ruby also bought Mecca and Dawn Volkswagen Jettas. Mecca's was china blue, Dawns was silver.

Mecca and Dawn pulled up in their Jettas at a basketball tournament in Miller Park in East New York. Even though there were hustlers out there with Benzes and BMWs, Sterlings, and Alfa Romeo Milanos, the two young chicks made everyone look in their direction.

They wore black body suits that hugged the curves on their well-developed frames. Mecca wore a pair of red snakeskin boots and Dawn had black lizard-skin boots. They both wore large bracelets that resembled Wonder Woman's and giant doorknocker earrings. They both kept their hair laced with Anita Baker hairdos.

As Mecca and Dawn exited their vehicles, two cars pulled up behind them. One of the luxury cars blasted Big Daddy Kane's "Ain't No Halfed Steppin'" and the other blasted KRS One's "My Philosophy." They were a vintage, candy-apple red 1950 Jaguar XK and a sky blue Porsche.

The young cats that emerged from the vehicles were all decked out in the latest gear and jewelry. The driver of the Porsche stood out the most with his Gucci short set and sneakers. His diamond-flooded Figueroa chain with Mary holding baby Jesus was the size of Slick Rick's chain. He had a high rise pinky ring flooded with ice as well. He and Mecca caught each other's eyes and he smiled at her. Mecca looked away. At sixteen years of age, Mecca was still a virgin, unlike many of her peer group. Mecca was more into making money and fashion than boys. Also Mecca was afraid to fall for a boy after seeing how it had affected her aunt when Wise broke her heart.

Besides all that, Mecca had to stay focused. It took a lot for her to prove to Ruby that she could handle the responsibility that was given to her. When it came to business, Ruby didn't take any shorts, and since she was able to convince Ruby that helping her out was a better choice than going back to school, she had no choice but to stay on top of her game.

"It's not good to fall in love with no nigga because all they do is use you for sex. That's all they want, they care nothing about your feelings. So to avoid being hurt, don't fall in love. Use them for what you need the same way they do us," Ruby had always reminded Mecca.

During the game, the guy in the Gucci short set stared at Mecca. She glanced at him as she walked around the park with Dawn. Other girls in the park glared at her and Dawn with envy. All the boys in the park were either staring at the duo or trying to get with them. Dawn flirted with some, then she stopped and talked to one of the members of the guy who wore the Gucci short set's crew. She found out that crew was from Brownsville Houses and Dawn thought one of the guys looked familiar, but she couldn't place his face right away. She figured if they didn't know Mecca or Mecca didn't know them, then most likely it was the stick up crew that was sticking up Ruby's spot in the projects. Her suspicions were confirmed when the guy with the Gucci suit walked up to the guy she spoke to.

"Son, tell shorty to tell her friend I'm trying to get with her. Shorty look right," the guy in Gucci said.

"Yo, Dawn, tell ya girl my man Tah wanna talk to her!"

Dawn took another good look at him and remembered his face from when they were in junior high. Her mind flashed back to the girl Tamika, who she and Mecca jumped. Tah had dropped out of school, Mecca never got the chance to see what he looked like. Dawn thought better than to ask him about Tamika or explain why she asked. One of the guys in his crew could be related to Tamika and might want to get some payback for the lifetime scar Tamika wore on her face.

"Son, they from the ville," Tah's friend said to him about Mecca and Dawn.

"Word?" Tah asked, pointing at Dawn. "I knew you looked familiar. Where you live at in the ville?" he asked. Dawn just flashed him a flirtatious smile and sauntered over to where Mecca was sitting.

Mecca sat on the bleachers, drinking a wine cooler, watching the two teams, run a full court.

"Girl, you won't guess who the nigga in the Gucci short set is!" Dawn said, sitting next to Mecca.

Mecca swallowed the drink and, still watching the game, responded, "Who is he?"

"Remember that chick Tamika? We beat her ass in school and you cut her?" Dawn asked as Mecca looked at her attentively. "That's the boy she thought you were messing with," Dawn answered.

Mecca looked over at Tah, and she found him to be attractive. He was a caramel-complexioned, brown-eyed brother who stood about six feet tall. He had a medium build, not too big and not too small. He wore a fade-style haircut. The top of his hair was wavy with the sides faded. Mecca laughed at the thought of Tamika approaching her about a boy Mecca never met.

"They from Brownsville Houses. You never seen them?" Dawn asked.

Mecca shook her head, looking at the crew to see if she recognized any of them. Mecca didn't. "Nah, I don't know them."

"Well, the boy in the Gucci short set wanna meet you. He said you a cutie," Dawn said.

She didn't want to tell Mecca the guy's name because she thought maybe it wasn't the stick up crew. If it was, if Mecca got with him he would stop, and Mecca wouldn't have to worry about the crew anymore because she would be dating the leader. Plus, she needed to get her cherry popped. Tah came and sat next to Mecca on the bleachers while his friend grabbed Dawn's hand and led her off the bleachers to talk privately.

"What's your name, shorty?" Tah, asked showing his bottom teeth that were covered with gold.

"Mecca," she said tersely.

Tah nodded his head. "That's a pretty name. It fits."

Mecca smiled and thought, *He can't come up with something more original?* How many times had she heard that? She turned to look at him.

"You nervous or something?" she asked.

"Me?" Tah asked, pointing to his chest with a confused look on his face. "Hell no, why should I be nervous?" Tah asked, shaking his head.

"'Cause I know you can come up with something more original instead of my name is pretty, it fits!"

"You buggin'. I really meant it!" Tah said, sounding sincere. "I don't need to borrow lines from no one, shorty. I call it like I see it." Mecca ignored him and continued to watch the game.

"So what's your name? What do they call you?" she asked.

"Tah."

"Oh, yeah, Tah. You're Tamika's boyfriend!" Mecca said.

Tah snapped his head back, surprised to hear his ex's name spoken from a total stranger. He gave her a look like he was trying to remember her from somewhere else or place her face from someone he may have met in the past.

"That's old news, shorty. How you know though?"

Mecca giggled. "I used to go to school with her and she thought I was messing with you, because I guess you looked at me one day when you picked her up from school."

"I knew you looked familiar!" Tah said. "Oh, shit! You ain't the one who blast 'Mika on her face?" Tah asked, making a mock slashing with his hand. He remembered seeing Mecca in passing at school, but never saw her after the fight she had with his then girlfriend.

"She shouldn't have come up on me like that," Mecca replied with candor.

"Okay, shorty. You a wild one on the hush," Tah said.

"I told you my name. Stop calling me shorty!" Mecca barked.

When she thought of his name again, it hit her. One of Ruby's workers in Brownsville Houses said a crew led by a nigga named Tah was sticking them up. Mecca didn't want to bring it up yet. If it was him, she didn't want to wake him up to who she was. She had to investigate first. If it was him, she would have to formulate a plot on how to stop him. *Then*, Mecca thought, *getting to know him could be part of my investigation of Tah and his crew.*

"I'm sorry, Mecca. Calling you shorty is just a figure of speech. I'm not trying to be disrespectful at all," Tah replied before asking, "Do you have a man?"

"No, I don't," Mecca replied.

"I hear you from Langston Hughes. That's up the block from Brownsville. Maybe I can give you a call or come take you out one night. You know, a movie and a bite to eat," Tah said.

The way her attitude was, Tah thought she would deny giving him the number and say she would see him around, letting him down easy. To his surprise, Mecca said she would give him her number for him to call later. Tah smiled, then reached in his back pocket and pulled out a pen. He reached in his front pocket, and pulled out a hundred-dollar bill to write the number on. Mecca thought he was fronting. She grabbed the money and wrote her number on it. She stood up, ready to leave the bleachers to find Dawn, and she gave Tah a seductive look.

"Hopefully, I'll hear from you soon."

Tah put the money in his pocket. "Oh, you will," he replied, looking back at her and letting his eyes undress her.

When Mecca met Dawn, she grabbed Dawn's hand, pulling her away from Tah's friend. "Call me!" Dawn yelled to the boy as Mecca pulled.

"Dawn, I think these are the niggas robbing my aunt's spot in Brownsville Houses!"

"Word?" Dawn responded as if she was shocked at the thought that she already had.

"Yeah, remember I told you the worker said some nigga name Tah and his peoples were robbing them?"

"Yeah."

"I'm not sure, but I'm almost sure it's them. I'm going to find out. I'ma hang out with that nigga, Tah," Mecca said before the girls entered their own cars.

Dawn shook her head and thought, *Mecca is as crazy as her aunt, and if it is Tah and his crew robbing Ruby's spots, and if Tah doesn't catch on to what Mecca is up to, he'll be dead within a few weeks.*

Two days had passed since Mecca had given Tah her phone number. On the third day he called, and he and Mecca spoke for hours. They talked about the people they both knew in Brownsville. Mecca joked about Tah and Tamika's relationship.

"What you did to her? She must have been really in love with you."

They both laughed when Tah responded. "I don't know. There's something about me I can't figure out. Maybe it's my chain?"

Mecca found talking to Tah easy to do. He was smart and funny. He made her laugh the entire conversation. Mecca found herself unintentionally opening up to him. She began telling him things that she planned on not telling him. Mecca told him that she lived in Sutter Gardens on Blake and Hendrix Street, and she told him she was a virgin, which excited Tah and made him want her even more.

On their first date, Tah took Mecca to a Tony Roma's restaurant in Queens. Riding in Tah's Porsche made Mecca want one. She reminded herself to save up money to get one. Mecca was surprised at how much of a gentleman he was. He opened doors for her and he picked her up with roses in his hands. Tah took her to Coney Island where they walked on the beach. They took pictures together holding each other. He never let Mecca pay for anything, even when she begged him to let her pay for at least a movie.

"It would make me feel less than a man if I let a woman pay for anything," Tah would tell her.

Mecca realized Tah was a man of pride. Mecca got so caught up with Tah that she forgot why she started seeing him in the first place. Just like Dawn predicted, when Tah and Mecca got together, the workers in Brownsville Houses didn't have any problems with Tah and his crew. What Mecca and Dawn didn't know was that Tah was extorting Stone. Stone paid a thousand dollars a week for them not to rob the spot. Stone paid him out of his own pay.

When Tah wasn't around, Mecca found herself missing him. All she talked about to Dawn was Tah. Dawn was happy for her. She noticed Mecca's attitude change since she had started seeing Tah. Her explosive temper simmered down. Mecca usually was not someone who smiled, but she had a smile on her face almost all the time. Ruby noticed the change in her niece and she expressed it to Monique to see if Monique could shed some light on why Mecca's attitude changed.

"What's up with Mecca? She's been acting different lately," Ruby said.

"You acted the same way when you were in love," Monique replied.

"Love!" Ruby yelled, not believing the words that came out of Monique's mouth. "She's in love with who?" she asked, sounding angered by the news.

"Some guy in the ville."

"Why she ain't tell me?" Ruby asked, this time sounding hurt. She thought she and Mecca had the kind of relationship where they could talk about these kinds of things.

"Because she knew you would act the way you acting now. You got to let her be, Ruby. You said it before: she knows how to handle herself."

"I just thought she would share something like that with me. At least let me see the cat, you know." Ruby sighed. When Mecca finally got around to telling Ruby, she didn't react the way Mecca expected, and it shocked Mecca.

"Don't rush to give up the pussy, Mecca. Make him wait until he proves he deserves it."

Mecca said she would take Ruby's advice. She told Ruby things that Tah did for her, and she showed her the diamond tennis bracelet he bought for her. It was Monique that Mecca confided in most about her relationship with Tah, and it made Ruby jealous. Monique was happy for Mecca but warned her about how guys could be.

"It's risky dealing with niggas who are in the streets. You got to be prepared for him going to jail or getting killed. It's gonna hurt real bad, Mecca, so be careful with your heart."

"I hear you, but I love this nigga, Mo," Mecca revealed, feeling like she was already in too deep.

Chapter Eight

*Y'all some "well wishers," friendly
acting, envy hiding snakes . . .*

—Nas

"This is crumbs compared to what you could get from her," Stone complained to Tah while he handed him the $1,000 he gave him a week not to rob Ruby's houses. Both men stood in the pissy-smelling dark hallway of a building in Brownsville.

"You talking about that bitch with the green Sterling? You work for a bitch?" Tah asked, grinning and shaking his head. "Damn, Stone, you really fell off. How the fuck you let it get to that point?"

"It ain't as sweet as you think it is, Tah. She ain't your average bitch, kid. That bitch is a stone cold murderer. Remember Darnell from Langston Hughes? It was her that threw that nigga out the window. I don't think you knew Wise, but she bodied that nigga, too. She's the real deal, Tah," Stone warned, holding his head down, ashamed. Tah, with menace and anger in his tone, put his finger in Stone's face and gave him a warning as well.

"Nigga, I'm the real deal. Ain't no bitch or nobody else going to put fear in my heart. You's a bitch-ass, washed-up nigga. I ain't like you, mu'fucka. You just get that bitch to bring something heavy to you. Tell her somebody you know want three of them pies, and I'll take it from there."

Stone nodded grimly, agreeing to the setup. The pressure that Tah put on Stone, coupled with the fear of Ruby possibly finding out that Stone agreed to help set her up, caused Stone to relapse, and he started smoking crack again. When he got paid, the monkey on his back caused him to even cop crack from the workers he collected money from for Ruby. To his demise, word got back to Ruby that he was smoking again. When she confronted him about it he denied it, and she was full of anger.

"This nigga tryin'a insult my intelligence, Mo," Ruby said to Monique back at her Hamptons villa.

"Bitch, you must really be pissed. I'm down here with all your pussy in my face, and you rambling on about Stone," Monique complained to Ruby from her place in between Ruby's thighs while Ruby sat in a beach chair out on the patio.

Monique wiped Ruby's wetness from her face with a pink beach towel, opened up the sliding glass door and marched into the house, angry and naked. Ruby took a puff on her blunt, and blew circles into the air before she yelled for Monique to come back.

"Mo, come here. I'm sorry."

Ten minutes later, Monique appeared on the patio fully dressed in a sexy, tight-fitting pair of Gap jeans, a white button-down shirt from the Gap as well, with a cute pair of Gucci stiletto sandals to match the Gucci hobo bag dangling from her wrist.

"You need me to bring something back? I'm driving to the city," Monique asked Ruby, not bothering to make eye contact.

"I'm sorry, Mo. I'm just stressed a little, you know?" Ruby replied, pleading for forgiveness with her eyes.

"Yeah, I know. Do you need anything?" Monique asked again, not willing to forgive Ruby that easily.

"When you coming back?" Ruby asked her, now seeing her through a weed-filled daze. Monique just shook her head.

"I'll be back by midnight."

"Bring me back some cheesecake from Juniors."

Monique drove Ruby's Sterling into the city. She knew in order to get Ruby's attention back on their love life she'd have to get rid of whatever it was that got in the way. What got in the way was Stone. Monique felt for the nickel-plated .45 in her Gucci bag as she drove the two-hour drive into Brooklyn. While driving, she half listened to the New Edition tape that was playing. She loved the sound of Johnny Gill's voice when he sang "Can You Stand The Rain."

When Monique reached the dark, grimy streets of Brownsville, she drove to Rockaway and Dumont where Stone usually hung out. There were groups of hustlers and stick up kids standing on the corners. Some waved to Monique and some just stared at the Sterling as it drove by. Everyone knew Ruby drove the Sterling, but the mirror-tinted windows blocked anyone from seeing Monique driving it. She looked in front of a brightly lit liquor store and in front of a few bodegas and couldn't find Stone.

Monique then drove to the block she hated going to: Mother Gaston Boulevard and Sutter Avenue. Stone usually hung out up there, either at the gas station or on the opposite corner. He wasn't there, either. Driving around her birthplace, her native Brownsville, Monique looked at the neighborhood like an outsider. She could not believe the decaying, dilapidated houses were occupied by human beings. Living in the Hamptons made her beloved Brownsville leave a bad taste in her mouth.

She could not believe she felt this way. What was wrong with her? This is where she was from. This place made her who she was, and she loved who she was. She inhaled deeply in thought. *I love the ville. If it ain't rough it ain't right.*

Monique drove to what was said to be the most dangerous projects in the ville, Brownsville Houses. She drove around the projects looking for Stone, but still didn't see him. She noticed groups of young men sitting on benches with boom boxes blasting the latest hip-hop joints. Groups of extension-wearing young girls with big, gold earrings and bangles walked around the projects, flirting with much older men.

Monique smiled at what used to be her way of living. She felt a sense of pride now. Places like Brownsville make a person appreciate the little things in life. People in Brownsville are survivors. That's what Monique was, a survivor.

Monique stopped at a light on Rockaway Avenue in Brownsville Houses waiting for it to turn green. She looked at a group of men in front of one of the tan and brown buildings to see if she spotted Stone among them. With her focus on the men in front of the building, she never got the chance to see the teenager dressed all in black walk up to the passenger-side window with his .44

Magnum pointed at the tinted glass. The loud shots from the gun could be heard within a five-block radius.

Monique heard the first shot clearly. The rest were muffled and her vision became blurry. Everything began to turn dark, and her hearing faded out. She didn't hear the teenager yell, "That's for Darnell, bitch!" People in the projects saw the teen run from the car while the horn blared from the weight of Monique's slumped body pressing against the wheel. Stone heard the gunshots while he loaded his stem with crack while sitting on the staircase on the roof of a Brownsville Houses building. One of Ruby's workers ran up the stairs while Stone inhaled the lit crack inside.

"Yo, Stone! Somebody just bodied that chick Ruby. She's slumped in her Sterling on Rockaway right now!"

Stone almost choked on the smoke he inhaled when he heard what the worker said. He had to see it with his own eyes. He couldn't believe Ruby slipped up and got herself killed. He started thinking Ruby was invincible, that she couldn't be touched. He knew how cautious she was. She trusted no one except Mecca. Stone didn't even think she trusted her lover Monique.

Stone ran down the stairs thinking it couldn't be Ruby. *Nah, not Ruby!* He ran toward Rockaway Avenue still not believing what he just heard. When he saw the Sterling he still couldn't believe it. He saw a crackhead he knew reaching inside of the car with the driver-side door open.

"Yo, Smoke, get the fuck away from her!" Stone yelled as he approached the car. The smoker backed up out of the car, holding a gold chain in his hand.

"She won't be needing this, Stone. She deader than a mu'fucka, man."

"Smoke, put that shit down before I peel your skull back, nigga," Stone said, pointing a .38 revolver at him. The crackhead dropped the gold chain and ran off, not wanting to test Stone's patience. Stone approached the car, putting his gun back on his waist. He exhaled loudly when he realized it wasn't Ruby.

"Damn, Monique. What the fuck you doing over here, girl?"

Stone heard police and ambulance sirens headed toward the scene and he didn't want to get caught up out there. He

walked over to the pay phone a few blocks down and paged
Ruby.

*The backdrop of Mecca's vision of a white-robed man
named Lou changed from bright light to total darkness.
Lou's robe turned blood red. Mecca looked at herself for the
first time, noticing she was naked. Seeing Monique killed
made her cry. She wasn't there when it happened, but seeing
exactly how it went down hurt her to her soul.*

*"I don't want to do this anymore. Why are you doing this?"
she sobbed.*

*"Monique loved you, Mecca. She didn't want you in the
streets. Not only did she express that to your aunt, but she
also told you plenty of times to get it together. You didn't
listen. Or was it that you didn't take her seriously because
she continued to play the game?" Lou asked.*

*Mecca still shook her head, sobbing. "I don't know! I don't
know!" Mecca sobbed as she heard Monique's voice in her
ears warning her about the streets.*

"Mecca, don't be like me and your aunt. You see what
happened to your moms and pops. Your mom wasn't even in
the game like that, but she still died for what your pop was
into. You got your whole life ahead of you. You don't want
to die young, or end up in jail forever. These streets don't
discriminate. Just because you're a pretty girl don't mean shit.
You can't change the direction of a bullet with a fat ass and
good looks."

*"And you know what, Mecca?" Lou continued, "She wasn't
the only one who wanted what was best for you. You were
blinded by greed and lust."*

*Lou posed with his hands on his waist like a female posing
for a photo shoot and said, "You were a diva in the streets.
You were invincible, right, Mecca? Nobody could touch the
Queen of New York." Lou laughed out loud, then, just as
quickly, his expression turned serious.*

*"You were wrong though, but it's my job to show you what
you failed to see. Let's carry on," he said, clapping his palms
together to continue Mecca's journey.*

Chapter Nine

For she hath cast down many wounded; yea, many strong men have been slain by her.

—Psalms 7:26

Hundreds of people convened in the Brownsville funeral home to pay their respects to Monique. Monique's oak wood casket was surrounded by expensive wreaths and flowers paid for by Ruby and Mecca. Ruby paid for the funeral, the casket, and the mausoleum that Monique's body would be laid in to rest.

Ruby had Monique's body dressed in a white pants suit with gold buttons down the front of the jacket. She made sure Monique was made up beautifully. She almost looked more elaborately dressed and made up as a corpse than she did alive. When people tried to hug Ruby, offering her their condolences, people she didn't know or had ever seen Monique associate with, she verbally assaulted them.

"Who are you? Did you even know Monique?" To some of Monique's family members, she growled as they walked by.

"Stop being phony, when was the last time y'all saw her? What you do, chew an onion to get them fake-ass tears in your eyes?" she asked as they came up to view the body, causing everyone to avoid her.

She paid her workers to keep their eyes open. If they find out who killed Monique, she wanted to know. She offered a $50,000 hit for the person who found the person. She had a plan for Stone's ass too, who showed up at the wake high off crack, and smelling like he hadn't bathed in months. He went up to view Monique's body, and Ruby gave him a look that he missed. He was definitely going to pay.

"Ruby, I'm gonna find out who did this. I swear to God, someone is gonna pay!" Stone whispered in her ear before he walked away. Little did he know he would have to pay for this too.

Damn near every killer in Brownsville tried to cash in on the hit. There were thousands of rumors about who did it. When the rumor of Tah's involvement spread around the streets, Mecca quickly put an end to that, letting everyone know that Tah was with her that night.

It was the most memorable night in Mecca's life. After she and Tah dined at Red Lobster, Tah rented a room at the Ramada Inn near LaGuardia Airport. Mecca sat in the passenger seat of Tah's Porsche feeling the wind blow against her face as Tah sped down the Van Wyck Expressway. She tried to mentally prepare herself for the physical act of sex. She had never been this nervous, except when she first felt the flow of blood leak from her vagina. Instead of running to talk to Ruby about her period, she confided in Monique.

"Monique, come here," Mecca whispered from the bathroom, standing behind the door and sticking her head out.

"What's up, girl?" Monique asked, concerned.

Mecca opened the door all the way and pulled Monique into the bathroom by her hand. She showed her the drops of blood on the panties she held in her hand, and Monique started laughing. Mecca was confused.

"Why you laughing, Mo? I'm bleeding!"

"Girl, ain't no reason for you to be scared. It's your period. It's all a part of being a woman. It's going to happen every month, so get used to it," Monique said, opening the door. "Stay right here, I'll be right back." When Monique returned, she handed Mecca a Maxi pad.

"Put this on your pussy, and change it throughout the day until you stop bleeding. It usually takes three to seven days. Here is a bag of pads. I'll get you a douche to clean yourself afterward. You don't want your pussy smelling like trash truck juice."

Mecca sat at the funeral home staring at Monique's body, thinking of her. She felt a lump in her throat as she tried not to cry. Monique wouldn't be here to talk to her about sex, and she didn't think sex was a topic Ruby wanted to speak to her about. Mecca's mind wandered back to that night with Tah, and it saddened her how she wouldn't have anyone to talk to now. That was one of the most memorable nights of her life, and she zoned out as she thought back.

"You all right?" Tah asked, seeing Mecca's facial expression in deep thought. "If you're not with it we can wait, Mecca."

"No, I'm all right. I don't want to wait any longer. I love you, Tah." Mecca sucked her teeth before responding to him.

Tah was caught off guard with the four-letter word that he swore he would never say or feel toward a woman except his mother or grandmother.

A lot of cats got killed over women, and Tah swore to himself that it would never be him. He really liked Mecca a lot, though. He even dared to say he cared about her. She wasn't like the girls he usually dealt with. She wasn't the neighborhood freak like the girls he and his crew got a piece of. She was a virgin, and she wanted him to be her first. That sent Tah on an ego trip so far he had to pack a year's worth of luggage. But love? That's a whole other level that Tah didn't think he was ready for. Not wanting to ruin the night, Tah told Mecca he loved her too, and was almost convinced that he believed it.

Tah and Mecca entered the plush hotel room with cream wall-to-wall carpeting, mirrored walls, and a Jacuzzi shaped like a martini glass. Tah surprised her with a pair of hoop earrings with diamonds on them. Mecca hugged Tah, then their mouths met and their tongues began to wrestle with each other. Tah tried to be as gentle as he could. He wanted this night to be special for her. He wanted her to be strung out on him and never want to share her love with anyone else. He felt he was experienced enough to pull it off.

Tah began to suck on Mecca's earlobe, then slowly moved down to her neck. Mecca felt chills through her whole body as Tah began to unbutton her shirt. Her black satin bra came into view, and Tah had to make himself slow down. He picked her up and walked her over to the king-sized bed to lay her down, afterward softly kissing her belly button while caressing her breast. Then suddenly he stopped.

"Hold on, Mecca. Let me use the bathroom."

Tah went into the bathroom and looked at himself in the large mirror over the beige porcelain sink. His manhood bulged against the crotch of his red Fila velour sweat suit. As was routine with every girl he bedded, Tah took out his dick and began to masturbate so that when he had sex with Mecca he wouldn't cum quick. Mecca unhooked her bra while she waited for Tah to take off her tight-fitting jeans. Her panties matched her bra. Remembering what Monique had said about keeping her pussy smelling fresh, Mecca rubbed her hand against her pussy and smelled it. She was satisfied with the smell the vinegar-and-water douche left behind.

Three minutes later, Tah came out of the bathroom ready to give Mecca the best first sexual experience ever.

Tah took off his pants and crawled on the bed in his Calvin Klein boxers. He looked at Mecca's body and he felt his dick begin to stiffen. Her firm breasts and plump rear end didn't fit a sixteen-year-old's body. Her body fit a woman in her twenties. Mecca could tell that Tah worked out. He wasn't bulky or too small; his body was well defined from the eighteen-month sentence he served in D.F.Y.

Tah let his tongue explore Mecca's body, taking her on a high she had never experienced before. She gasped when she felt his warm tongue on her nipples. He licked down her belly button while removing her jeans and panties. He continued to taste and caress Mecca until he was sure she liked what he was doing.

"Tah, that feels so good," she moaned.

Mecca tried to get away from Tah, but it felt too good. She felt waves of pleasure run through her body. She didn't know why she kept feeling her entire body when Tah put his tongue inside of her. He brought her to multiple orgasms in no time.

He wanted to loosen her up some; the tightness of her pussy made Tah grind his teeth. Not that Mecca was his first virgin, but she felt a lot tighter than previous ones he had encountered. Slowly he opened her legs in the missionary position, and glided his rock-hard dick inside of her.

"Wait . . . wait, Tah. It hurts!" Mecca screamed out loud, holding on to Tah tightly. Tah kissed Mecca's lips and whispered in her ear to calm her down.

"I'm sorry, Mecca. I didn't mean to hurt you."

"I know, Tah. Please try again, I want you in me."

After Tah's first orgasm, he took Mecca into the Jacuzzi and they enjoyed a bottle of Moët while they relaxed. Tah stared at Mecca and it reminded him of something his partner Boogie had told him awhile back, and it had him feeling confused.

"Yo, Tah. Your chick Mecca is the bitch with the Sterling niece."

"Get the fuck outta here, Boog!" Tah responded in disbelief.

"Word is born, son. Your chick work for her aunt, too. She manages her spots in the projects."

"How you know all this, son?" Tah asked, not wanting to believe what he was hearing.

"You heard of Blast right?" Boog asked, and Tah nodded his head, indicating that he remembered. "That's her pops. Darnell bodied her mom and pop and her aunt took her in. That bitch from Langston Hughes."

"Mecca, let me ask you something," Tah said as he took a sip from his glass of Moët.

"Go ahead, ask me whatever," she answered, hoping he wasn't going to back out on her.

"Where you be getting money from? How you get all that fly gear?" Tah asked, registering the look on her face. The smile left Mecca's face. His question surprised her. She wondered why he asked that after all this time they been together. Mecca put her head down, looking at the bubbling water.

"My parents are dead, and I get SSI checks."

It was true, Mecca did receive SSI, but it was a mere $500 a month. She put that in a bank account and spent the money she made working for her aunt on the things she had. Tah was glad that she didn't lie, figuring since he had heard her parents were dead, that just maybe she was getting SSI. He chalked up the idea that she may be working for her aunt as just a rumor.

"Damn, sorry to hear that. Do you mind me asking how they died?" Tah replied consolingly, hoping she would open up more to him.

"Yes, I do mind, so don't ask," Mecca said, cutting him off.

Tah watched Mecca's facial expression change into one that he had never seen on her before: the look of pure rage. It was more than rage; it was more like pure evil. Tah knew it was time to change the topic before the mood got messed up. Besides, he wanted some more pussy because his dick was hard again.

"I didn't mean to make you angry, Mecca. I'm sorry." Tah smiled, then reached over to kiss her.

He kissed her cheek, and his mouth traveled down her neck. He placed his hand between her thighs and his fingers found their way to her clit. The evil look on Mecca's face disappeared, and she expressed pure pleasure. Deciding to not even leave the Jacuzzi, Tah sexed Mecca in every position imaginable until the wee hours of the morning.

A week after Monique's death, Stone had just finished making his rounds at each of Ruby's spots. He stopped in Langston Hughes to chat with some of the workers who were mostly young teenagers whose parents were customers. Stone saw one of the workers running through the projects, and stopped to see what was happening. By the time he and the other workers realized what the young guy was running from, they were all surrounded by unmarked cars, undercover detectives, and federal agents.

People in their apartments, and hoes standing outside in the area, heard cars screeching and the sound of police yelling for them to get on the ground and put their hands in the air before they blew their brains out. At the same time there were raids conducted in Langston Hughes, Ruby's spots in Brownsville and Coney Island were being raided as well. Ruby was watching an episode of *As The World Turns* when she heard a knock on the door. Dressed in only a long blue and yellow Polo robe with thong to match, she hated to have to get up from in front of the television, but she had no choice. She got off the couch and walked to the large, white double doors, grabbing hold of the gold-plated doorknobs.

"Who is it?" Ruby yelled on her way to the door.

"It's the police and we have a warrant. Open up!" an officer yelled through the door.

"Hold on, let me get dressed," Ruby yelled back, not knowing what move to make next.

"Open up, now!" the officer yelled before busting through the door and rushing Ruby to the floor before she had a chance to get one of her guns from the closet. Ruby didn't plan on getting arrested. She planned to go out in a gunfight, but it was too late.

"You have the right to remain silent. Anything you say can and will be used against you in a court of law. You have the right to an attorney . . ."

Chapter Ten

*A faithful witness will not lie, but a
false witness will utter lies.*

—Proverbs 14:4

The government had received information from a confidential informant about Ruby and her organization. The informant couldn't provide how much money Ruby was pulling in from her distribution of crack cocaine, but the government estimated that her gross amount was in the hundreds of thousands. So when the judge in the federal courthouse in Brooklyn placed Ruby's bail at $2 million, Ruby got out within a week.

The F.B.I. knew they stumbled onto an organization that was beyond your average drug gang. The informant either didn't know the part Mecca played in the organization or just didn't want her in jail. Stone's bail was set at $100,000, and Ruby made sure he was bailed out.

"What makes you think it's Stone?" Mecca asked innocently, not wanting to jump the gun.

"Who else could it be? Who else knows all about me besides you and him? Monique is gone!" Ruby yelled at Mecca as they sat in Mecca's Sutter Gardens apartment's living room.

Mecca's apartment was simply decorated. Her living room had a black, big pillowed couch, a forty-two-inch television that sat on a crystal television stand, and a six-disc Sony surround sound system that was surrounded by black art on the walls with cream frames to match the curtains she had hung at the window. Over the television she had a large picture of her parents that was hand drawn by a street artist, and a wooden wall unit with family pictures on it as well.

"He's a crackhead, Mecca. They'll do anything to get a hit. Those crackers probably gave him a hit just to snitch," Ruby said while trying to calm down.

"Why didn't he say anything to me or Dawn?" Mecca wondered out loud.

"Where is that bitch anyway?" Ruby asked skeptically.

"With her boyfriend," Mecca responded, but she had a skeptical look on her face. She didn't think Dawn would do anything like that. What would she gain from it?

All Dawn thinks about is that no-good boyfriend of hers. One of Tah's flunkies. Dawn hasn't been around lately since she met him, and that nigga has her strung out. Then Mecca remembered something that Dawn said, and it made her wonder.

"Mecca, I think we better leave this game alone. I feel like something bad is gonna happen if we keep going on like this. We gonna end up either in jail or dead."

"Don't go getting paranoid now, bitch. I can't just bounce up out the game like that," Mecca said to Dawn, not believing her ears. If it weren't for the game, they wouldn't have all the shit they had.

She brushed off the thought, concluding that Dawn was just paranoid at the time. Shit, she was the one who said they should get in the game in the first place.

"Since y'all bitches got them boyfriends y'all been on some real slackin' shit. Y'all let them niggas get the best of y'all. Mecca, you know better," Ruby scolded her, trying to talk some sense into Mecca to keep from punching her in her damn mouth.

"So what we gonna do?" Mecca asked, wanting to get off the boyfriend subject.

Ruby rubbed her temples and sighed. "I took a big loss. That bail really fucked me up. I got to get consignment off these Dominican mu'fuckas and start from scratch. What's up with these Sutter Garden niggas? They gettin' money?"

"Please. Those sorry-ass niggas hustle for outfits. You see the ones in front of the building? They stand there all day every day like they doing security and none of them niggas even got a Honda scooter. They some bus' ass niggas," Mecca replied, sucking her teeth.

"Those the types of mu'fuckas we want. Niggas who don't want much. That's how we get rich. If all they want is outfits then they will go hard for them. If we offer them more than

what they got now, they'll gladly work for us. C'mon, Mecca,
wake up, girl!" Ruby said, smiling.

Ruby kept quiet while she and Stone drove, then she parked
on a small block on Twenty-third Street and Surface. The
beach was at the end of the block. The block was deserted on
the chilly night. Stone was always nervous in the presence
of Ruby: he knew she was unpredictable and would kill in a
heartbeat.

"Somebody snitching on us, Rube. We got to find out who
did this. If you want, I'll handle this kid who got Mo—"

Ruby drew the .45 with a silencer so quick, Stone didn't
have time to finish the sentence. His head exploded against
the passenger side window as Ruby sent one bullet into his
temple. Ruby got out of the driver's side and walked over to
the passenger side. She opened the door and let Stone's body
fall onto the sidewalk. She smiled when she heard the waves
crashing into the beach. No one would hear her.

She went to the trunk of the car and removed a bottle of bleach
and a dirty rag. She poured the bleach on the rag, stepped over
Stone's body and wiped the blood off the window and door.

She looked at Stone's body and ripped open his black silk
shirt to see if he was wired. He wasn't. She removed the
gold Gucci link chain from his neck, and searched his black
corduroy pants pocket, and removed $500 from his pocket.
She left them turned inside out to make it look like he had
been shot right there in the street. Ruby pumped more bullets
in his head and body, and then she got back in the car and
slowly drove off.

The next morning, Ruby drove into Manhattan with her
hair in a ponytail, wearing a beige cotton skirt that reached
her knees, a white blouse under a beige blazer, black sheer
pantyhose to match, and black, five-inch heel shoes. The office
of Gilmore, Stein and Bloomberg was located on Thirty-ninth
Street and Park Avenue. Ruby walked in the office of Stanley
Gilmore, Esq., the senior partner of the law firm. She had
had him on retainer since 1987. He had a perfect record of all
wins, no losses. She had met him through Stone.

Stone killed a Jamaican cat in front of the entire Langston
Hughes projects during an annual Langston Hughes day, the
day the project celebrated when it was built. Every project in

New York has a day like that, as if the residents are celebrating the fact that they live in poverty-stricken, low-income projects with conditions a fence away from being a prison.

No one from the projects gave information to the police. There was no need to. Stone killed the man in the view of a housing cop walking the beat. Gilmore had the cop on the stand for almost two hours and when he was done with him, the jury was ready to convict the cop for the murder.

Ruby placed a brown paper bag on Gilmore's desk while he sat in his large, black leather recliner with an expensive, three-piece black, pinstriped suit resembling a 1920's Mafioso. He tried to conceal his receding hairline by combing the little hair he had left on the top of his bald spot.

"That's fifteen. I'll have the rest for you next week," Ruby said, sitting in one of the smaller leather chairs in front of Gilmore's large wooden desk. Gilmore grabbed the paper bag, looked in, and then placed the brown paper bag in one of the drawers in the desk.

"So how are things looking?" Ruby asked, folding her leg over the other, watching Gilmore stare at her finely toned thighs. Gilmore stood up and paced behind his desk with his hand in his pockets.

"I'm still waiting on the government to turn over the discovery. From what I do know," Gilmore said, pausing to face Ruby, "there's an informant that gave up a lot of info. They're making it a RICO case. You getting out on that two million raised some flags in the IRS, too. How are you going to account for that?" he asked.

"My life savings and donations from friends to get me out," Ruby replied with a straight face.

Gilmore shook his head.

"I don't think that the government's going to buy that. What about the cars, the house in the Hamptons? They're gonna want to know how you went from a Brownsville housing project to the Hamptons with no job."

"You're my lawyer; tell me what should I do," Ruby barked.

Gilmore sighed. "As an officer of the court, I can't give you incriminating advice." Gilmore then smiled. "But as a friend, I can show you how to clean your cash."

"You can't find out who this snitch is now? I mean, pull some strings?" Ruby asked.

Gilmore walked to the front of his desk and sat on it in front of her. Ruby already figured she knew that Stone was the rat, but she wanted to make sure. "I know what you want, you freaky mu'fucka!" Grinning, she unzipped his pants and pulled out his small, shriveled-up, pinkish penis and gave him a hand job. While she jerked his dick, she smacked him on his face hard. He smiled.

"You like that, huh, you cracka!" Ruby growled, stroking him faster, thinking, *Men are so simple. The things they will do for a nut.* They are all the same. "If you cum in my hand, I'll beat the shit out of your old ass," Ruby threatened.

"I won't, just don't stop," Gilmore moaned, holding the corner of the desk tightly. He reached on his desk for a piece of tissue in a Kleenex box.

"Oh God! I'm cummin'. . . ."

Mecca felt someone placing a robe on her naked body. She couldn't see who it was. When she turned her head, it was dark. She looked down at her body, and a white linen robe was covering her. Lou stood with his arms folded, still in a red robe.

"How much death and mayhem does it take for a person to realize that what they are into is wrong?" Lou asked. He then counted on his fingers and said, "Your parents, Darnell, Wise, Monique, Stone. Then your aunt goes to jail and everybody involved in the organization except you and Dawn are caught up. You didn't see the blessing in that, huh?"

"Blessing! What blessing? Where's the blessing in death and jail?" Mecca yelled.

Lou became angry and it could be heard in his raised voice. "The fact that it didn't happen to you. That's the blessing!" He paused, then shook his head and continued in a low tone. "But, once again, Mecca, you had a veil over your eyes. It's all a game, right, Mecca?"

"Why you gotta yell like that? I can hear you," Mecca snapped, causing Lou to laugh.

"We all know you can hear. You just have a problem seeing. We all know you can hear, but you don't listen. Soon you're going to see and listen to what you didn't listen to before, whether you like it or not."

Chapter Eleven

Every wise woman buildeth her houses but foolish plucketh it down with her hands.

—Proverbs 14

"I don't care who's first or who's last, I just know y'all better rock this at the drop of a dime, baby!" Marley Marl screamed on the intro of "The Symphony," a collaboration of Master Ace, Craig G, Kool G Rap, and Big Daddy Kane as Mecca and Dawn walked through the crowd on the dance floor of the Union Square club in Manhattan. This was a crowd Mecca and Dawn didn't stand out in, regardless that Mecca wore a Louis Vuitton three-quarter jacket with the matching boots, and bucket hat with the brim flipped up, while Dawn wore the same getup, but the brand name was Gucci.

There were people in the club from all five boroughs and surrounding areas like Mount Vernon, Yonkers, and Jersey who came to the Union Square in their best. There were girls and guys in full-length minks, shoes and boots from various reptiles, diamond-studded jewelry from neck to wrist, and mouths full of gold. Moët was the main beverage. The high rollers had cases of Dom Pérignon at their disposal.

It wasn't unusual to run into hip-hop celebrities in the crowd. Nice & Smooth, Doug E. Fresh, and Special Ed were in attendance. The crowd was usually split into groups according to the group's geographical location in the city. The Harlem cats stood in one corner, the Bronx cats in another, and the Queens cats had theirs. The Brooklyn cats usually were spread out, scheming on people to remove their jewelry or clothing from. Along with their fake IDs, Mecca and Dawn came with razor blades hidden under their collars, taped with Scotch tape. Before Mecca taped a razor to Dawn's collar, Dawn asked why they needed them.

"Just in case some jealous-ass bitch gets out of line, or some drunk nigga tries to touch you. You know how niggas is."

When Big Daddy Kane's "Ain't No Half Steppin'" roared through the club, the crowd reacted enthusiastically. Some wallflowers hit the dance floor, screaming, "That's my shit!" while other groups of cats who didn't dance leaned against the walls giving other cats evil stares.

If the crowd of guys made up of Harlemites didn't look in a certain direction, Mecca and Dawn would have never noticed Tah and his crew walk in the club, most of them wearing camouflage jackets with Champion hooded sweat shirts under the jacket, black jeans, and black Timberlands. Mecca noticed Tah didn't have any of his jewelry on, and he and his crew looked at the crowd as if they were looking at everyone individually for someone. Dawn was about to walk over to them, seeing her boyfriend with Tah, when Mecca grabbed her by her shoulder.

"Chill out, Dawn. Don't go over there. Them niggas look like they up to something, and it's something you don't wanna get caught in the middle of."

Dawn looked around the club and noticed girls and guys who were showcasing their jewelry moments ago stuff their chains inside their shirts. Some girls put their earrings in their pockets and some headed to the exit. To add to the fear and tension lingering in the air, the D.J., who was from Brooklyn, put on a Slick Rick song called "The Moment I Feared" where Slick Rick spits, "Boogie Down was performin' hey they ain't no joke/ And a bunch of Brooklyn kids was lookin' all down my throat/ Was it my big chains with the big plates on 'em?/ Then they rolled on me and told me to run 'em/ This was the moment I feared."

Tah and his crew split up and walked around the club. Tah made his way to the bar and bought a bottle of Dom P. He grinned at some women at the bar, who probably thought that because of the way he looked he wouldn't be able to afford Dom Pérignon. They could tell he was from Brooklyn, and Brooklyn cats had a reputation of not being high rollers, but cats who lived off of robbery. Mecca stepped in front of him, rolling her eyes at the women at the bar.

"What's up, nigga? What you doing here?"

"The question is, what you doing here?" Tah shot back.

"I told you I was coming here tonight. Me and Dawn." Mecca smiled and grabbed Tah's hand. "Dance with me."

Tah pulled his hand away and smirked. "Dance! I look like the type of nigga to dance? You buggin', Mecca."

Mecca figured Tah wasn't the dancing type but she wanted to avoid him getting into trouble, and possibly getting hurt or going to jail. A lot of niggas in New York were hip to what went down in the clubs. Everybody came to chill and show off the latest gear. Guys came to meet girls and vice versa, but Brooklyn guys came to see what they could take and start trouble. Niggas from other boroughs knew the deal, and some came prepared for it. Some didn't.

"Dancing is for herbs," Tah continued.

Dawn was walking behind her boyfriend, who was walking toward Tah. Dawn looked frustrated to Mecca when he leaned and whispered in Tah's ear. Tah nodded. Dawn looked at Mecca with her arms folded and rolled her eyes. Tah and his partner started to walk off. Stopping briefly, Tah turned to Mecca.

"I'll see you in the ville."

With an anxious look on her face, Mecca yelled, "Where you going?"

Tah walked off. Walking over to Mecca, Dawn leaned to her ear and said, "They stupid, Mecca. They always starting something."

Mecca watched Tah and his crew walk to the exit and out of the club. The crowd seemed relieved. Five minutes later, Mecca and Dawn noticed some guys in the crowd talking to each other and hyperactively walking toward the exit. Then a bunch of girls and guys all headed toward the exit.

Mecca heard a girl tell another girl, "Something happened outside. It's probably them grimy-ass Brooklyn niggas!"

Mecca had a feeling whatever happened outside had Tah and his crew written all over it. Mecca grabbed Dawn and headed toward the exit. When they got in the front, a crowd gathered around someone lying on the ground. Mecca and Dawn broke through the crowd to see who the person was and what had happened to him.

"That's what niggas get when they try to rob somebody. Good for his ass!" Mecca and Dawn heard someone in the crowd yell out.

Dawn's legs gave out from under her when she saw her boyfriend laid out on the concrete with blood flowing out of his neck. He was making a gurgling sound. Dawn crawled to him as Mecca tried to hold her. Mecca looked up and down the block to see if she saw Tah or anybody in his crew, and they were nowhere to be found.

Ruby started second-guessing her decision to turn everything over to Mecca. Mecca was strong and could handle herself on the streets, but she had a weakness. A man. Ruby constantly told Mecca that a man would be her downfall. She introduced her to her Dominican connect in Harlem. She told her connect that she was hot, and she told him about her arrest and the arrest of her workers.

"Don't worry, Ruby, my friend. Everything good for you. You beat the case," he responded in his thick Spanish accent. Ruby nodded grimly.

"Yeah, hopefully. Until then, I'm laying low. I'm going to let her run things until this shit is over. She knows what's what. This is my niece."

Ruby asked the Dominican for three kilos of cocaine on consignment so she could get things back in order. He told her to pick things up in two days. Back in Mecca's East New York apartment, Ruby gave Mecca instructions on how to run the show.

"Dawn is gonna have to manage all the spots for you. You're the boss now. You got to lay low. I'm going to give you the three pies, one for Coney Island, one for the ville, and the other for around here. Li'l Shamel got these cats around here in check. He's going to make sure these niggas do what they have to do. What's up with Dawn? You think she can handle this?" Ruby asked.

"Yeah, she knows what to do," Mecca replied.

Ruby's face turned sad. "I might have to do some time. Hopefully, this lawyer could get me a good plea or beat this shit. I'ma need you to hold shit down though, Mecca. You got to be strong. Don't let nothing slide. Don't show no weakness. The minute these niggas think that you going soft, they will be all over you like vultures. Somebody fuck up something small, treat it like it's big. These niggas y'all dealing with, don't let them in your business. Let them continue doing their own things. In fact, don't let them know nothing. The minute a nigga know you're doing better than him, his eyes will get in the way and cause serious problems."

Mecca nodded and soaked in everything Ruby said. She felt tears about to well up in her eyes at the thought of Ruby going to jail for a long time. Things wouldn't be the same without Ruby. She didn't know how she would be able to hold things down without her being around. She knew she had to do it, though, for Ruby and to prove to herself that she was a survivor. That night, Mecca decided to celebrate her new position, and she and Dawn headed to Union Square. Dawn would never be the same afterward.

The night Dawn's boyfriend was shot and killed at Union Square, Mecca was angry at Tah because it was their trouble-making that got Dawn's boyfriend, his partner, killed. Mecca decided she wouldn't talk to him for a few days. On the other hand, Dawn went to Brownsville Houses to confront Tah face to face.

"Why did y'all leave him?" Dawn yelled at Tah in an apartment rented by a crackhead Tah used as a hangout. Tah hugged Dawn, placing her head against his chest.

"Yo, we ain't know dude had a K-tone on him, Dawn. Son grabbed the nigga chain and yapped it before I could walk up. Then dude let off."

Dawn sobbed harder. "Why y'all gotta do that? Y'all got money! What y'all need a chain for?"

Tah couldn't answer that. He never thought of it like that. It's just the way he and his friends he grew up with were. *Dawn doesn't understand, it's the Brownsville way.*

Tah was caught off guard when Dawn grabbed his face and began kissing his lips. Tah kissed her back on her lips, at first gently, then their kissing became almost savage-like. They licked each other's faces then Tah pulled off his hooded sweatshirt.

Before either could make the conscious decision to stop and think about Mecca, Tah already had Dawn naked and there was no stopping them. In all honesty it felt so good they didn't want to stop, but after the act was over they both knew they had fucked up. Mecca was like Dawn's sister and she was Tah's girl. Trying to avoid eye contact as they got dressed, they both knew they would have to take their betrayal to the grave. If Mecca ever found out what they had done, they would be in the grave a lot sooner than they would have liked to be. Without saying a word, Dawn left the house vowing to never get caught up with Tah like that again. Tah, on the other hand, knew he was wrong, but figured Dawn was weak and he could probably hit it again. As long as Mecca didn't know, they would be cool.

Mecca tried to block the vision of Dawn sucking Tah's dick out of her head, but she couldn't. She couldn't close her eyes to the vision because it was in her head.

"Why are you doing this to me?" Mecca yelled to Lou.

"You did this to yourself, Mecca. You chose this life. You made your bed. You ever heard the phrase 'life is what you make it'? Well, so is hell," Lou replied, laughing. "Ain't it hell watching your whole life recur?"

"Whatever point you tried to prove, you did it, okay?" Mecca yelled.

"Don't you wish you knew that your best friend was messing with your man, when you were alive?" Lou teased. "You would have killed her, right, Mecca?"

Mecca stood silent. She imagined herself finding out about Dawn and Tah. She envisioned herself walking in on them, pulling out a gun from her Coach bag, and shooting Tah first while Dawn watched in horror, then turning the gun on Dawn. She played the scene out in her head while Lou watched in amusement.

She snapped out of her vision when Lou said, "Betrayal hurts like hell, don't it? Trust me, I know how it feels. The creation of you human beings was a betrayal," Lou said, looking off in deep thought. "But that's another issue. Right now, Mecca, don't you wish you could start all over? Do you think you would do things different?"

Mecca held her head down with her eyes closed, shaking her head. "What's the reason for all of this?" she asked.

Lou smiled while rubbing his palms together as if he were warming them. "I wouldn't use the word 'reason'," he said, putting his index finger up on his temple with his arms folded. "I would say . . ." Lou paused, going into deep thought, then, pointing his finger at Mecca, he concluded. "Purpose. The purpose for all of this."

"Well, what is the purpose?"

"I can show you better than I can tell you."

Chapter Twelve

*Time waits for no man, can't turn back
the hands, once it's too late, gotta learn
to live with regrets.*

—Jay-Z

"I'm going uptown real quick, wait for me at your crib. I'ma bring those through. We are going to bag up in them tall caps. Go get them thirty ones illusion black tops," Ruby commanded Mecca over a pay phone on the corner of Bedford Avenue and Fulton Street.

The corner was crowded with men and women dressed in the clothing of Arabs. The men and women weren't Arabs though. They were black men and women attending the mosque on the corner where Ruby used the pay phone. The smell of incense and oils permeated the sunny Bedford-Stuyvesant morning air.

While Ruby talked on the phone, she scanned the area up and down the street for any tails; police, or somebody trying to rob or kill her for something she did to her numerous victims. Fulton Street was a crowded street full of vendors selling T-shirts, children's and cultural books, and bootleg clothing and music, grocery stores, and guys hanging out hustling or looking for girls who paraded down one of the boroughs' main strips.

Ruby eyed almost everyone, thinking any of these people could be her killer. It was that way of thinking and paranoia that kept her alive as long as she had. Still it was impossible for her to see everybody, especially when that person was sitting in a burgundy Honda Accord with dark tinted windows watching her every move and following her.

"I'll be there in two hours. Don't go anywhere," Ruby concluded before hanging up. She got into her black Saab and drove. Ruby constantly checked her rearview mirror for any tail. The burgundy Honda Accord stayed three cars behind knowing where Ruby was headed.

She looked at her Bulova watch with gold numbers and hands against a black face. It was 9:30 a.m. *Them Dominican niggas be taking forever with the shit. I'll be in East New York by twelve o'clock.*

Ruby drove up the FDR Drive and got off at the 155th Street exit. She pulled over, seeing her connect waiting on the corner. He smiled at Ruby as he got in. He was a skinny, dark-skinned Dominican cat. He wore a silk shirt opened at the chest, showing his multiple gold chains against his hairy chest. He reeked of cheap cologne, and his hair was slicked back. A midnight shadow adorned his face.

"Wassup, my friend?" he asked Ruby.

"What's up, Papi? Where we going?" Ruby asked driving slow.

Papi turned in his seat, looking out the back window. "Drive to the Bronx. It's hot around here. T.N.T. everywhere."

"The Bronx!" Ruby barked, frustrated. "Why all the way up there?"

"It's not far. It's right over the bridge," Papi countered.

Ruby sighed. No sense in arguing with him. Better safe than sorry. Ruby drove over the small bridge connecting the Bronx to Harlem. They drove a block away from Yankee Stadium, still being tailed by the burgundy Honda Accord, and pulled in front of a run-down tenement.

"Wait right here a few seconds. You got the money?" Papi asked.

If it were somebody else, Ruby would have killed him for asking for the money without showing the product. But she'd been dealing with him for years and they had a good repoire with each other. Ruby reached in the backseat and handed Papi a black Jansport book bag with $60,000 cash in it.

"You wait here. I come right back," Papi said, opening the door and jogging into the tenement. The area was also crowded with Spanish men on corners. Some were at small tables, playing dominoes and listening to salsa music. Women were hanging out of tenement windows looking at the men or watching their children play stickball in the streets.

The man in the Honda Accord fit right in with the neighborhood. He was a short Spanish man with a low haircut and a red Sergio Tacchini jogging suit. He slowly got out of the Accord while concealing behind his back a black .380 with a silencer on it. Ruby kept her eye on the tenement that Papi had gone into. Fortunately for her, a police cruiser stopped across the street from where she was parked. The driver of the Accord walked back to his car. Ruby, using her street smarts, drove off and didn't return. She drove back into Manhattan and the Spanish guy in the Accord followed. Ruby thought about the $60,000 she gave Papi, and decided she'd go back uptown tonight and meet him.

When Papi came out of the tenement, he saw the police car across the street and he walked to the corner store. He came out of the tenement without Ruby's Jansport. Ruby stopped at a pay phone on 125th and Eighth Avenue. Mecca picked up on the first ring.

"I'm going to be running late. It's hot. I had to get ghost for a minute. Just make sure you in the crib around eight o'clock tonight." Ruby hung up, paused, then dialed another number. After three rings a voice came over the line.

"Gilmore, Stein and Bloomberg, how may I assist you?" the secretary said in a squeaky voice, sounding as if she were holding her nose.

"I need to speak to Gilmore. Tell him it's Ruby Davidson."

"Hold on, Ms. Davidson." Ruby held on for what seemed like hours.

"Ruby! What's up?" Gilmore said excitedly.

"Damn, you had me on hold long enough."

"Sorry about that. I was in a meeting with the partners. By the way, I got the discovery this morning. I need to go over some things with you. If you need a copy, I'll have my secretary do them now," Gilmore said wearily.

"I'll drop by and pick up the copies. I have to make some runs so we can discuss it tomorrow," Ruby said.

"All right, that'll be fine. I'll tell my secretary to have them ready. When can you stop by?" he asked.

"I'll be there in a half." Ruby hung up.

The Spanish guy driving the Accord watched Ruby from across the street while he ordered a hot dog from a vendor. With the crowds of people walking up and down and hanging around the world-renowned Harlem street with the famous Apollo Theater a few feet away, Ruby couldn't notice if anyone was following her. The Spanish guy kept a good distance between himself and Ruby.

A half hour later, Ruby picked up the copy of the government's evidence against her from Gilmore's secretary. The file was thick. There were hundreds of surveillance photos of Ruby and Stone getting into her Sterling in Brownsville. Stone's rap sheet was twenty pages long. There were mug shots of Ruby's workers in Brownsville and Coney Island.

Ruby was shocked to see a picture of her and her Dominican connect sitting in a Spanish restaurant on Amsterdam Avenue. There was a picture of Mecca in Langston Hughes and underneath the picture it said, "Davidson niece." There was a report on Mecca behind the picture. Ruby read the report.

Daughter of Bobby "Blast" Sykes and wife Mecca Sykes, who was killed in 1982 by masked men who invaded the home to rob Bobby Sykes of money and drugs. Present during the home invasion and murder of her parents, but couldn't identify the killers. Ruby Davidson took legal custody of her niece subsequently. G.I. Number 1 informs us that Mecca Sykes is not involved in her aunt's organization. This has to be investigated.

Ruby sighed as she parked on a side street in Midtown Manhattan reading the file. Before continuing to read, she took a sip of a Sprite she bought from a corner bodega. She turned to another page that had a picture of Dawn. Ruby spilled the Sprite on the car floor from the shock of what was written over Dawn's name. In bold, black print it said, **G.I. NUMBER 1.**

Blinded to what was going on in the street outside of the car, Ruby put the file on the passenger seat and reached down to get the soda can. The Spanish guy who drove the Accord exited his vehicle and sped toward her car. Ruby opened up the door and got out to wipe the car floor with a rag she took out of the glove compartment. The busy Manhattan day was buzzing with the sounds of loud talking, car horns, and trucks.

The Spanish guy approached from behind, but before he could raise his gun, Ruby spun around and pulled the trigger of her nickel-plated .45 that sent three bullets into the Spanish guy's face. The loud boom of the gun sent people on the streets running for cover. There were screams.

A police officer walking the beat saw Ruby standing over the Spanish guy, pumping three more bullets into his chest. Ducking down, she ripped the Spanish guy's pocket in his jogging suit and took a wad of bills. She picked up his gun and put it in her dark blue Fila velour pants and started walking back to her car.

"Lady, don't move! Drop the weapon and put your hands up!"

Ruby hesitated. She thought about Mecca. Her mind flashed back to when she was first born, when her sister had to get a C-section at Kings County Hospital. *What would Mecca do without me?* she thought. She had to tell Mecca about Dawn. She had to live. Ruby did as the cop ordered and dropped her weapon. Tears rolled down her face. She couldn't remember the last time she cried.

"Drop to your knees!" the cop yelled.

A crowd gathered around, looking at the dead Spanish guy with his blood flowing into the gutter. Cars stopped, blocking traffic, to see the bloody scene. The world seemed as if it were spinning to her. The cop's voice echoed in her ears.

"Put your hands above your head!"

Ruby put her hands behind her head and put her head down. She knew this was the end of her life of crime . . . at least on the streets.

"The feds gave your aunt four life sentences and almost three hundred years and you still didn't get the message!" Lou barked at Mecca.

Mecca unfolded her arms and tried to turn her back on him, but everywhere she turned, Lou's image was in front of her.

"You didn't have to remind me," Mecca replied gravely. For the first time in her life Mecca felt like maybe she should have gotten out of the game earlier. Dawn had suggested it years ago, but now Mecca felt like she was a snake, too, and anyone she loved couldn't be trusted. Mecca was confused, and was trying to make sense of her life . . . the only life she knew how to live.

"Wow! Then your so-called best friend informed on her. Y'all call it snitching these days, ratting, whatever term y'all use. But your best friend? How much betrayal and loss of lives you've witnessed and experienced and you're not convinced that the life you were in wasn't worth all you went through?" Lou grinned as he spoke. Suddenly, he looked off to nowhere and spoke as if someone else was there with him and Mecca.

"I told you they would prove me right, Your Majesty," Lou yelled. Mecca looked around to see if she could see whom Lou was talking to, but saw nothing. "Why did I have to belittle myself for these beings who caused so much bloodshed and havoc among themselves? I deserve better," he screamed. Mecca had to hold her ears. In a split second Lou became calm again and turned back to her.

"Why did you have to kill Dawn? She didn't inform on you. She did what she did to save your life. To save you from the destructive life that your aunt, your own flesh and blood, led you to?"

"She did it to save her own ass."

"I beg to differ," Lou replied, snapping his fingers.

The snap made Mecca close her eyes and rub her temples as if she were suffering a migraine headache. An image appeared in her head. It was after Mecca received Dawn's photo with "G.I. Number 1" on it in the mail from Ruby.

Mecca, dressed in a blue Polo sweat suit and blue Reeboks, with her head wrapped in a blue bandanna scarf, held the papers in her hand as she and Dawn sat on a bench in Brooklyn's Prospect Park on a late night.

Mecca waited almost a month after Ruby's letter, which simply said, "If you don't get rid of her, she will be your downfall. Remember, I told you before, don't let nothing slide." When Mecca gave Dawn the paper, Dawn reacted with shock and disbelief on her face.

"This ain't true, Mecca! I swear, I . . ." she cried. "You were at your aunt's hearing! I didn't testify against her at the hearing when the grand jury indicted her!"

Mecca thought, *This bitch must think I'm dumb*. They don't need her testimony at the grand jury! As Dawn spoke, Mecca looked around the park. It was dark except for the few street-lights that lined the walkways and streets that went through the park. Mecca chose a spot behind the trees and brush, blocking them from the view of people outside the park.

"Why would my aunt make this up? Why would she choose you to make this up on?" Mecca asked, beginning to feel the tears form in her eyes. She was in pain, hurt from the betrayal at the hands of her best friend, the only person she trusted besides her aunt. Dawn was like her sister and she had betrayed that trust. Mecca hated the position that she was in. The position the game forced her in. She couldn't walk away from this now. She had to hold it down for Ruby.

"Even if I did, Mecca, I would have done it for you. For you to get out of this game! But I didn't do—"

Before Dawn could finish her sentence, Mecca let off three shots to the chest, silencing her forever. It hurt because they had been through so much together, but then Mecca remembered that you couldn't trust anyone in the street. Especially someone that who supposed to be your family.

"You were a monster, Mecca!" Lou yelled as Mecca snapped out of the vision of shooting Dawn in the chest with a black .22 revolver, and afterward running out of the park, where Tah picked her up in his Porsche. Lou laughed. "I love it!"

Mecca looked at him confused. "Why is it so funny? I thought you didn't like what I was doing." Mecca said.

"I never said I liked it or didn't. I just find it hysterical and rather strange that"—Lou held his hands making quotation signs—"God would create you human beings and allow you all to do these things to one another."

Mecca looked confused and finally asked, "Where am I? How long is this going to last?"

Lou grinned from ear to ear before giving an answer. Mecca had a dreaded feeling of what he was going to say, though she would have used a different term for "Eternity."

Chapter Thirteen

Everybody was making a lot of money. Within that year, Mecca's stash reached six kilos a week. Tah traded his '87 Porsche for the up-to-date one. Mecca copped the 1991 SL500, forest green with chrome Antera rims. Li'l Shamel copped a gold Land Cruiser and leased an apartment in the Sheepshead Bay section of Brooklyn.

Before Mecca made her move, she knew she had to get another connect once Ruby's connect was properly disposed of. Li'l Shamel was instrumental in providing Mecca with another connect. He introduced her to a Cuban cat he met on Rikers Island where he had been laid up for a few months for a gun charge before going "up north" to do a two-year sentence.

"This Cuban nigga got some shit, Mecca. He lives in Queens. They got that raw shit out there."

Mecca began to re-up from the Cuban who called himself "Heck," short for Hector. She wanted to establish a good rapport with Hector to be sure that she could trust him, because at the end of the day she didn't want to be totally assed out on a supplier. Tah, in the meantime, helped Mecca with her situation with the connect they would no longer be using. He had worked with him in the past, and knew this connect was always hungry for money.

"Papi, I need eight of them," Tah said on a pay phone in Brownsville Houses. Ruby's connect smiled on the other end of the phone as he stood on the corner of 156th and Amsterdam Avenue.

"Listen, Papi, I'm not trying to come uptown for it. It's been crazy hot up there lately. We can meet in Brooklyn; it ain't that hot out here like it is up there," Tah continued.

If it were someone else, Papi would have found the request truly out of line. Brooklyn wasn't the place a nigga in his right mind would bring three kilos of cocaine to sell to some nigga from out there. However, Papi trusted Tah because Tah made him a lot of money. He even gave Tah consignment and Tah brought him his money with no shorts. Tah even offered for Papi to come into business with him in Brooklyn. Papi thanked him for the offer, but he wanted no business dealings in the borough of crooks and killers. Papi asked Tah where he wanted to meet him after he agreed to coming to Brooklyn.

"Under the Brooklyn Bridge."

Papi showed up under the Brooklyn Bridge in a gold Lincoln Town Car, which was a cab driven by an old, fat, gray-haired Dominican man. To the surprise of everyone who lay in wait, Papi showed up by himself with no backup. He really trusted Tah. Niggas who ran with Tah didn't trust him, but Papi didn't know that Tah was from Brownsville, and was one of the neighborhood's most notorious stick up kids.

Not wanting to look suspicious, Papi wore a Yankee pin-striped jersey, tight blue jeans, and a pair of white Nike Air Max sneakers. Tah showed up in a Black Chevy Caprice with no hubcaps on the wheels; the crew's hooptie. The same one they used to go on missions with. He wore a sky blue Nautica sweat suit with a pair of white and sky blue canvas Air Force Ones.

Tah got out of the car with a black duffel bag. Papi carried a large brown paper bag that had the words in big print on it, "BIG BROWN BAG." He walked over to the Lincoln town car that parked behind the Caprice under the Bridge. The streets were empty on the cloudy day. The smell of garbage and human waste was strong here.

When he reached the destination he placed the duffel bag on the trunk of the town car. Tah and Papi turned quickly, hearing footsteps and the sound of metal smacking into metal. They saw a homeless man pushing a shopping cart filled with soda cans. The homeless man had a long, beige, filthy trench coat, and a dirty, red, yellow, and green wool Jamaican hat. He walked with his head down.

He picked up a can on the ground and threw it in the shopping cart, taking a short glance at Tah and Papi. Tah waived off the homeless man, and Papi turned back to him and put the brown paper bag on the trunk. Tah looked in and saw the eight kilos of cocaine tightly wrapped with duct tape.

Tah and Papi heard the footsteps of the homeless man stop behind them. When they turned to look, the homeless man was picking up a small brown paper bag that had something in it. The homeless man looked in the bag curiously. They turned their attention away from the bum again and didn't see him pull a .25-caliber automatic out of the bag.

The old man in the Lincoln looked at the homeless man and his eyes widened in shock when he saw the gun. "Mira Carlos!" the driver yelled, trying to warn them that the man had a gun.

The homeless man put two bullets in the back of Papi's head. Tah reached in his pocket, pulled out his .380 automatic, ran to the driver's side of the Lincoln, and pumped five bullets into the old cab driver's head and neck.

Tah and the homeless man jumped in Tah's Caprice and sped off. Two members of Tah's crew parked down the block in a blue Acura Integra saw Tah pull out from under the bridge, and they pulled out after Tah and the homeless man drove by them.

"You can take the hat and that nasty-ass coat off. That shit stinks." Tah snorted. When the homeless man took the hat and coat off, Tah smiled at the person who wasn't a man, but his pretty girlfriend, Mecca.

Tah stopped the car in front of an apartment building that had a green dumpster in the alley. He grabbed Mecca's homeless costume and the duffel bag filled with newspaper and tossed it in the dumpster. He jumped back in the car and with the tires screeching, he sped off.

Chapter Fourteen

*Lust not after her beauty in thine heart, neither let her take
thee with her eyelids.*

—Proverbs 6:2

Li'l Shamel, actually Shamel Jacobs, was twenty-one years
old in 1995 like Mecca. He got his name from Ruby. No one
called him that except her. He never knew why Ruby called
him that, but he always thought it was a joke because for his
age he was built like a thirty-year-old running back.

During his time in juvenile and adult prisons throughout
New York, Shamel did nothing but read books and work out.
He had been in and out of group homes and jails all of his
life. The coppertoned, wavy-haired, hazel-eyed Shamel was
born and raised in the East New York section of Brooklyn.
His mother and father were alcoholics who lived in Cypress
projects. He grew tired of their alcohol-induced abuse on him
physically, as well as watching his father beat on his mother,
so he chose to stay with his grandmother in Sutter Gardens.

Sutter Gardens was a two-story housing complex that was a
little cleaner and less dangerous than Cypress projects where
Shamel had lived with his parents. But Sutter Gardens was far
from safe. Already trained and equipped to brawl, Shamel had
to prove himself the same way he did in Cypress, and he did.
Shamel never lost a fight in Sutter Gardens and he gained the
respect from the neighborhood tough guys by beating all of
them one by one. Shamel always said he was no "stranger to
danger," and adjusted well to the change that took place in the
streets once crack hit the hood. That danger was guns.

Shamel got his first gun when he was fourteen years old. It
was a .38 Special he found in a vacant lot where he and a few
guys from the hood stashed their packages of crack. The first

time he used it was when he was fifteen. He went to Empire Roller Skating Rink in Crown Heights strapped with his .38. When he and a friend got to the rink there was a group of guys from the Heights Ebbets Field projects in the front and they didn't look like they just came to skate and have a good time. They looked like trouble.

Shamel wore a black Woolrich coat, and a black Champion hooded sweater with a pair of black Girbaud jeans and a white and gray pair of New Balance sneakers. He had a gold nugget watch on his wrist and the watch caught the attention of the Ebbets Field crew. Shamel's friend held the .38 in his beige Woolrich. There was a crowd of mostly females waiting to get in the roller rink and cars blasting music were pulling up in front trying to find parking. The music blasted from the inside of the rink so it was hard for Shamel and his friend to hear one of the guys say for him to give up his jewelry.

"Yo, money, run that watch!" Shamel and his friend kept walking and that angered the Ebbets Field guys.

"Yo, duke! You ain't hear me? Run that watch!" one of the guys ran up and yelled in front of Shamel and his friend. Shamel looked the guy up and down, noticing he didn't have a weapon in his hand. Shamel turned to look at the other guys and none of them had any weapons.

"What you say?" he asked.

"Nigga, run that watch," the guy yelled again, this time getting more pissed off.

Shamel looked at his friend who gave Shamel the "What you wanna do?" look. Shamel smiled at his friends who were still looking at the dude.

"I'ma give duke the watch, so we can bounce!" Shamel took the watch off and handed it to the guy who was smiling at his crew behind Shamel.

"Y'all good?" Shamel asked. "We ain't got no money," Shamel lied, tapping his pocket.

"Get the fuck outta here, pussy," the guy with the watch said while putting it on his wrist. Shamel and his friend took a couple of steps past the guy who was admiring the wath with his crew standing around him.

"Pass me the biscuit, son," Shamel whispered to his friend. His friend slowly pulled it out of his jacket and handed it to Shamel.

The Ebbets Field crew had their backs to Shamel. Shamel turned around and walked up behind the guy with the watch. The music blocked them from hearing his approach. It was dark outside except for the light around the skating rink.

Shamel placed the gun to the neck of the guy with the watch and squeezed the trigger. The loud boom and seeing their partner fall face-forward made the Ebbets Field crew take off like a flock of pigeons flying off when someone approaches. Being that Empire Roller Rink was down the block from where Shamel shot the guy, the line of people in front of Empire did not hear or see him shoot, then take his watch off of the now dead guy's wrist. Still standing over the guy, Shamel put his watch back on after tucking the gun in his coat pocket. He walked over to his friend and with no show of emotion they kept on with their night as planned.

"There's mad bitches in that joint. Let's go."

His friend shook his head. "You crazy, son."

From that point on, Shamel did not hesitate to pull the trigger on anybody who even slightly disrespected him or any of his friends. He caught his first body when he went to Cypress to visit his mother. The Ebbets Field guy didn't die; he was paralyzed from the neck down. When he got to his mother's apartment, he heard her screams from the hallway.

"Stop, Brian, you're hurting me!"

When he entered the apartment, his mother's face and naked body had blood and bruises, old and new, all over them. Shamel's father was standing over his mother—who was curled up on the couch covered with a dirty fitted sheet stained with alcohol and piss—with a two-by-four of plywood in his hand. Shamel immediately reached for the .38 he had on his waist and without saying a word he emptied all six shots into his father's head and body. When his father slumped to the dirty, brown carpet, his mother jumped off the couch on top of her husband and cried.

"Baby, no! Don't die, baby! He didn't mean it!" Shamel's mother cried while cradling his dead father's body. She looked up at Shamel with tears flowing down her face.

"Why you do that, you mu'fucka!"

Shamel realized his mother was drunk and decided he'd come back when she was sober. He left and went home to his grandmother, not even bothering to answer, and left her there, drunk and crying.

"Grandma, what's wrong?" he asked, hugging her. Her entire body was shaking like a leaf.

"Baby, your mamma called the police on you! She said you killed your daddy."

"She called the police?" Shamel asked, holding his grand-mother at arm's length.

"Baby, you gotta go somewhere because she told them you're here!" She nodded, pushing him toward the door. Shamel never made it out of Sutter Gardens.

The police were all over the place when he stepped outside. He gave up with no incident. He was a juvenile at the time and the courts were lenient because Shamel was emotionally dis-tressed when he saw his mother being abused. He was given eighteen months in a juvenile lockup in upstate New York.

Ruby and Mecca took a liking to Shamel. He was loyal and he was about making money. He treated Mecca like a sister and when cats in Sutter Gardens tried to approach her to get some play, Shamel would quickly scold the offender verbally and sometimes physically. After a while no guy in Sutter Gardens came within two feet of her.

Secretly, Shamel had the biggest crush on Mecca. Even though she thought Shamel was good looking and he was a "real nigga," she loved Tah, and off the strength of Mecca, Shamel showed Tah love when he came to East New York, even though East New York guys and Brownsville guys didn't get along.

Mecca suspected Shamel had a crush on her when her twenty-first birthday came around; Shamel bought Mecca a pair of Channel boots and a five-karat tennis bracelet. Then to put the icing on the cake, he threw a surprise pool party for her at the Paedergat in Canarsie. All the hustlers from Coney Island, Brownsville, and East New York attended.

When Mecca showed up, Shamel had a red carpet rolled out for her. She was impressed and at the same time sad because

Tah never did anything like that for her. His birthday gifts were predictable. He would buy her a pocketbook, take her to the movies and an expensive restaurant, then to the Waldorf or Plaza Hotel to spend a weekend having sex.

When Mecca arrived in her SL300, Shamel opened the door for her and walked her down the red carpet. He had one of his soldiers throw rose petals at her feet as she walked. She wore a full-length white mink over a white linen, one-piece dress by Giorgio Armani. The black, Gucci, five-inch-heeled shoes matched the black handbag by Christian Dior perfectly.

"Damn, Mecca, you're a star!" Shamel told her as she walked in.

"You look damn good yourself!" Mecca smiled, holding on to Shamel's arm. He wore a white linen suit by Armani, and a black Bossalini with a white silk band around it. On his feet, he matched the hat with a pair of black gators with a gold buckle. He adorned his wrist with an oyster perpetual Rolex with diamonds on the bezel and a four-karat pinky ring with a platinum setting. As they entered the pool area, where no one was because no one came dressed to get in a pool, Shamel looked around as if looking for someone in particular.

"Where your boy at?" Shamel asked.

"Who, Tah? Please, that nigga found it more important to be out of town than to be here for my birthday," Mecca replied, looking at the ballers and girls who showed up at her party. She recognized some of the guys from Brownsville and Coney Island, but the guys from East New York she didn't know personally. She knew who some of them were by face and reputation. Shamel knew all of them and they respected him. He impressed Mecca to the fullest extent when the big-name guys sent him over bottles of Cristal and some hugged him as he went by while wishing Mecca a happy birthday.

Shamel spent the whole night with her. He danced with her fast and slow. When Mary J Blige's "I Never Wanna Live Without You" song from her *My Life* album came on, Shamel hugged Mecca real tight while they slow danced. Mecca could hear his heart beat as she rested her head on his chest. His muscular chest felt good to Mecca and she wondered what he looked like naked.

What kind of nigga would be out of town for his girl's birthday? Especially a girl like Mecca? This nigga must not realize what he got. She is a bad mu'fucka, and her body is off the hook. To top it off, she a soldier! A nigga couldn't ask for better, Shamel thought.

The surprise Shamel had for Mecca didn't end at the pool party. He and his East New York crew all chipped in and copped Mecca a candy-apple red Lexus GS400. When he pulled up in front of his building, the Lexus was parked in front with a red ribbon around it.

It was four o'clock in the morning, and the crew was supposed to be there as part of the surprise, but they got tired and took off for the night. Still in all, Shamel pointed to the car and said, "Happy birthday, Mecca. That right there is yours."

Even though Mecca could afford to buy the Lexus herself, the thought that Shamel would go this far for her birthday made tears well up in her eyes. She hugged Shamel tight.

"Thank you, Shamel. Why you doing all of this?" Mecca asked, a little confused and hating that he wasn't her man. Shamel held Mecca back so he could look in her eyes. Mecca looked at him and thought this nigga looked real good.

"'Cause you deserve it. You and your aunt are like the family I wished for." Shamel looked away from Mecca out the front window of the car. "I don't understand how this nigga ain't around for your birthday. You deserve better, Mecca."

Mecca thought about what Shamel said all night. When Tah's birthday came, Mecca went all out to make his birthdays unforgettable. She cooked big dinners for him and his crew, and gave him the best sex he could ever come by, and he had the nerve to not even be around for hers.

"What's better, Shamel?" she asked, grinning. Shamel hopped out of the driver's seat, walked around and opened the door for her, and grabbed her hand.

"C'mon with me."

"Where are we going?" she asked as she held his hand.

"My crib. I wanna show you something."

"Ain't we going to wake your grandmother up?" Mecca asked, but didn't hesitate to follow him. Shamel kept holding her hand while walking to his building.

"My grandmother went down south two days ago."

Mecca had been inside Shamel's house before, usually to drop off packages for him to give the workers. She gave him consignment. If she picked up six keys, she would give Shamel two and charge him twenty thousand. She would profit two thousand off of each key.

Every time she came to his crib, he fought the urge not to make a move on her. His rationale was that he didn't want to put her in an uncomfortable situation with Tah. Shamel also didn't want to ruin their friendship and business venture. He figured he'd just wait until Tah fucked up. Now the opportunity presented itself and he wasted no time making the move he had wanted to make since the first day he laid eyes on her.

When he and Mecca entered the apartment, Shamel cut the light on and the nicely decorated two-bedroom apartment came into view with the smell of potpourri in the air. He got right down to business.

He held Mecca's face between his palms. She looked at him confused until he put his lips to hers and parted her mouth with his tongue. For a moment she hesitated, then gave into his advances. The kiss was sensual and Mecca felt the wetness begin to develop between her thighs. She acknowledged to herself that this nigga could kiss and his lips were soft. For the first time, she didn't have to taste cigarettes in her mouth. Shamel didn't smoke, while Tah smoked like a Navajo Indian.

Shamel lifted Mecca up with ease and carried her into his bedroom that had a queen-sized bed, a fifty-inch Sony television, a surround sound system along its side, and a *Ms. Pacman* arcade game in the corner with stacks of sneaker boxes lined up on the wall beside it.

Posters of the Notorious B.I.G. were everywhere along with pictures of guns torn out of a *Guns & Ammo* magazine. There were clothes thrown on a folded metal chair in front of his closet.

His strength turned her on. He made her feel special. She felt like a princess. Tah never carried her into the bedroom. The sex with Tah was good, but Tah was the only person she ever had sex with, so how would she know the sex was good when she never experienced sex with anyone else? This was her opportunity to find out if Tah's sex was indeed good.

She was surprised at her own feelings. The thought of giving herself to another man usually made her feel guilty, but for some reason she didn't feel that way with Shamel. Maybe it was because he showed her more attention in one night than Tah did in five years. On that note, she gave her full attention to Shamel and was willing to do whatever Shamel wanted to do in bed.

Shamel kissed Mecca softly on her neck, which made chills run through her whole body. He nibbled on her ear lobe. It tickled Mecca a bit, but she still moaned with a small chuckle. At the same time, he let his hand slip up her dress and rub her vagina outside of her laced Victoria's Secret panties. Mecca arched her back and inhaled deeply.

He felt the wetness of her on her panties. Slowly he slid her panties down while he kissed her on her lips. He lifted her dress up to her waist, got on his knees and removed her shoes, sucking her toes. Tah never sucked on Mecca's toes, and Mecca didn't know getting her toes sucked would feel so good.

While he did that, she lifted the dress over her head and threw it on the floor. She removed her bra while looking at Shamel suck each toe individually. He licked her ankles, then her calves slowly. Then he kissed her inner thighs until he buried his face between her legs. He opened her pussy lips with his thumbs and sucked on her clitoris. Mecca felt his warm tongue on her and almost flipped off the bed. She gripped the sheets as she came all over Shamel's face.

"Shamel, don't stop! Oh, Shamel, keep eating my pussy," she moaned.

Shamel ate Mecca's pussy for a half hour. Mecca came more times in that half hour than she did in a month with Tah. When he finished, his face looked like a glazed donut.

"You taste so good, Mecca," Shamel said seductively. He took off his linen suit and stripped naked down to his silk socks.

Mecca had fantasized about Shamel's body before. When his Sutter Garden basketball team played against other teams, most from other parts of East New York in high-stakes games, Mecca stared at the bulge in his shorts. Seeing him naked, she found that what she fantasized about was actually the way she pictured it. Along with his chiseled muscular frame, he had the biggest dick Mecca could have ever imagined. She thought Tah's dick was good to go, but damn. Shamel was holding!

She was almost scared. Before she let him stick his pole in her pussy, Mecca wanted to return the oral favor. She got up and pushed Shamel on the bed on his back. She wiped her juices off his face with her hands then she stuck her tongue in his mouth and they kissed for a few seconds. She sucked on his nipples and Shamel closed his eyes. His heart was beating fast. He couldn't believe he finally got the girl he always wanted, and she felt the way he imagined she would. He got to make love to her the way he pictured when he masturbated with her in mind.

Shamel didn't feel it was the right time to reveal to Mecca how he felt. He knew time would tell how she felt about him. He knew telling her that he had once had rough sex with her aunt Ruby back in the day would make him telling her he loved her unbelievable. He would never tell her that though, and hopefully, Ruby wouldn't either.

Shamel moaned as Mecca went south, gripping his dick. He could feel her tongue massaging his shaft while her lips moved up and down his dick. She massaged his balls while she sucked and Shamel started humping her mouth. At first Mecca gagged, then she handled all of him like a pro. Shamel held Mecca's head, stopping her.

"I wanna cum in you, Mecca, not in your mouth."

Mecca smiled. "We got enough time for that. You tasted me, so gimme a chance to taste you."

Shamel stalled and leaned his head back. In between the sound of Mecca slurping on his manhood, he felt himself about to explode. Mecca felt his hot cum splash against the back of her throat. She kept sucking as his juices flowed down her throat. Shamel gripped the bed and lifted his waist.

"Damn, girl, oh, shit," he moaned, looking at her while she was licking the cum off the tip of his dick.

"You good?" Mecca looked at him, smiling.

Shamel laughed, "No doubt, baby girl."

Mecca began to stroke Shamel's dick to get it hard again. She rubbed her palms to warm them, then started playing with his balls. "C'mon, big boy, get up," she said, looking at his semi-erect dick. She licked the head of Shamel's dick and it stood at full attention, hard and ready in no time. Mecca crawled on her knees, smiling seductively at him.

"Come here," he said, folding the pillow under his head lifting it.

Mecca climbed on top of him, reached behind, and grabbed his dick. She lifted herself and slowly slid down on him. She inhaled deeply and screwed up her face, feeling Shamel's dick fill her insides. Shamel palmed both of her plump ass cheeks while she leaned forward so he could suck on her light brown breasts with the dark brown nipples.

She rode his dick in a slow rhythm. Every time she moved, Shamel felt his dick tingle with pleasure. He fought back the urge of moaning out loud, and whispered, "Damn this pussy good. I want you, Mecca, all to myself!"

"You got me, oh God, you got me," Mecca responded in between moans, savoring the feel of his dick beating on her G-spot while she bounced up and down on the entire length of him.

Shamel turned Mecca doggie style, held her by her waist, and watched his dick go in and out of her dark pink pussy surrounded by golden brown skin and curly pubic hairs. He slapped her ass, sending chills through Mecca's body. Mecca moaned with every stroke and slap on her ass.

Shamel held her shoulders while he pumped, looking at her flawless skin. Her ass was smooth like a baby's ass. She turned her head, looking at him as he pumped. Her face was turning red and she held her mouth open.

"Oh, Shamel, fuck this pussy! Fuck me."

He pushed Mecca down so her stomach could touch the bed. He lifted her ass up and pushed himself deeper in her. Mecca felt herself cumming and it didn't stop. Her whole body shook as she came all over Shamel's dick. Cum dripped down her legs from her pussy.

After ten minutes in that position, he laid her on her back and put her legs over his shoulders. Mecca came three times before Shamel bust his second nut. Mecca felt his cum inside her and she pulled his waist into her.

Mecca and Shamel fell asleep in each other's arms. She woke up first and snuck into the kitchen to cook breakfast in bed at three o'clock in the afternoon. Forty-five minutes later, Mecca woke Shamel up with a steaming plate of French toast, scrambled cheese eggs, and home fries, with a glass of milk and orange juice.

"Damn, you can cook, too? That nigga Tah is crazy," Shamel said as he leaned his back against the wooden headboard while Mecca dressed in one of his T-shirts with nothing else on. She placed his plate on a pillow and set the pillow on his lap. Mecca went back into the kitchen and grabbed her plate, and went back in the room with Shamel and sat on the bed next to him.

"Speaking of that nigga, he has been beeping me all morning," Mecca said, grabbing her clear pink pager off the nightstand next to the bed.

"Where he beeping you from?"

"The area code is seven-one-seven. That's in Pennsylvania somewhere," she replied, putting the pager down on the stand.

"You should call. Something might be wrong," Shamel said. Even though he wanted Mecca for himself, and Tah out of the way, he knew that still didn't mean he could totally shit on the nigga. He might have been in jail, and Shamel didn't wish that on anybody. He wasn't about to go to war with no dude about his girl. He knew, regardless if it was Mecca, nothing was worth your freedom, and he refused to die over a woman.

Shamel handed Mecca his gray Motorola cellular phone. Mecca looked at her pager while she dialed the number. A voice answered on the first ring.

"Harrisburg Police Department. How may I help you?"

"Sorry, I dialed the wrong number," Mecca said, quickly hanging up. She looked at Shamel with her eyebrow raised. "That was the police in Harrisburg. I think that nigga locked up."

"Why you hang up?" Shamel asked.

"He might be under a fake name. I gotta call the ville and see what's what," Mecca answered. Mecca dialed another number, then pressed the send button on the cellular phone.

Chapter Fifteen

The labeling of a snitch is a lifetime scar/
You'll always be in jail . . . minus the bars.

—Jay-Z

Knowing it wasn't a wise move discussing the specifics over the phone of why Tah was locked up, Mecca decided to drive to Brownsville to get the full details on the goings-on that got Tah caged in Pennsylvania. She drove to the ville in her new Lexus. When she pulled up in the Brownsville Houses in the bright red Lexus, all eyes were on her. She spotted some of Tah's crew standing in front of his building. They stared at the car, not knowing who was driving.

When Mecca stopped and got out, she could see the crew mumbling to each other. Other people went back to their business while a group of girls with bad hairdos and cheap, ten-dollar dresses rolled their eyes and stared at Mecca enviously. Mecca called over one of the crew.

"Craig, come here." Craig, a short, purple-black-complexioned cat with a bald head dressed in camouflage fatigues and construction Tims skipped over to Mecca.

"What's up?" he asked, showing his chipped tooth and bottom teeth in gold with engraved letters saying "C-Money."

"What happened to Tah?"

Craig shook his head and sighed. "I told that nigga don't go down there with scary-ass 'Mika. He had to clap one of them Pennsylvania niggas, and both the dude and 'Mika told he did it. Now he locked up with a hundred grand bail."

"'Mika? You talking about Tamika with the scar on her face that he used to fuck with back in the day?" Mecca asked, surprised.

"Yeah, that 'Mika," Craig said.

Mecca was about to ask a thousand questions in regard to Tamika and Tah's dealing with each other, but there was no need in asking Craig because he would lie for Tah anyway. Mecca knew she had to ask him face to face.

"They got that ten percent shit down there. All he need is ten Gs," Craig said, snapping Mecca out of the thought of Tah dealing with Tamika behind her back. Mecca walked back to the car and opened the passenger-side door, reached in the glove compartment, and pulled out a blue and white Gap bag. She handed the bag to Craig.

"That's eleven; go get the nigga."

Tah showed up at Mecca's apartment the next day wearing a brown Pelle Pelle leather jacket and black Parasuco jeans, with brown and green Gore-Tex Tims known as "beef & broccolis."

"Yo, good-looking, boo! I had to get outta there, they be hanging niggas out there, for real!" Tah said, sitting down on Mecca's couch. Mecca rolled her eyes with a look that seemed to Tah like she wasn't happy to see him.

"What's up with you? Ain't you glad to see me?" Tah asked with his palms held out, shrugging his shoulders.

Mecca sucked her teeth. "Please, nigga, if I didn't want to see you I wouldn't have bailed your dumb ass out. What the fuck were you doing with Tamika?"

Tah put his hands on his lap and screwed up his face. "Who told you I was with 'Mika? Niggas got big mouths and don't be knowing what they talking about."

Mecca stood in front of him with her hands on her hips. "Niggas was talking about what happened to you and how you got locked up, stupid. How the hell else I was going to bail your dumb ass out?" Mecca shot back. "You in Pennsylvania with Tamika instead of with me on my birthday, huh?"

"It ain't even like that, Mecca. Don't go jumping to conclusions," Tah said, knowing how heated Mecca could get in no time. He didn't feel like her bullshit because he knew they would argue for the rest of the night.

"Like what, Tah? Fuck is you talking about? You weren't here with me, that's the conclusion."

"You saying it like I'm fuckin' her or something. That bitch a mule."

"So, what you was mule dicking her?" Mecca said sarcastically.

Tah sighed, not wanting to continue arguing about Tamika. He felt stupid even dealing with her again sexually and bringing her out of town with coke in her bra, girdle, and pussy. It was this bitch's fault he got locked up.

A guy from Harrisburg approached Tamika in a bar and asked her name. Instead of saying her name then politely telling the guy she had a man, she said, "Don't worry what my name is. Get your country ass out my face!"

The guy slapped the taste out of Tamika's mouth. She held her face then started swinging on the guy. Tah walked in the bar and saw the guy and Tamika throwing blows at each other. Tah ran over and tried to pull Tamika away. The guy kept swinging and mistakenly punched Tah in the face. Tah let go of Tamika, pulled a .45 from his pants, and shot the guy in his stomach and arm.

The bar cleared in panic. Tah and Tamika took off running toward the hotel they were staying in, but they didn't make it back to the hotel. The cops caught them three blocks from the bar. They had the ambulance with the shot guy in it come to where they stopped Tah and Tamika. Before the ambulance pulled up, Tamika started running her mouth.

"Officer, I ain't do nothing. I ain't shoot nobody. I ain't tell him to shoot him!"

Tah tried to tell her to shut up, but she kept yapping. They opened the back of the ambulance where the guy lay on a stretcher, holding his stomach, pointing at Tah.

"Please, Mecca. I ain't fucking her. I don't want to argue about this no more. I'm sorry I wasn't here for your birthday, and I'll make it up to you. I got to pick up some money first."

"I know you're going to run and get my ten Gs back," Mecca said while walking away.

"All right. A yo, who Lexus is that in front of the crib?" Tah asked, walking over to the window and moving the black curtains to look at it.

"It's mine. It was a birthday gift!" Mecca yelled from the kitchen.

"Damn, who gave you that for your birthday?" Tah asked curiously.

"Shamel and his crew chipped in and copped it for me!"

Tah felt the anger build up in his chest jealously. "Word? Niggas feeling you like that?"

Mecca walked back in the living room with her hand on her hip. "Please, Tah. At least niggas thought about me on my birthday. Niggas ain't trying to get with me. Niggas is family. Niggas is loyal."

Mecca lied about Shamel, but she told the truth about the other guys not wanting to get with her. Tah got up and walked toward the door.

"Where you going?"

Tah opened to door and without looking at her, he answered, "I'm going to get your money." Then, slammed the door.

Tamika walked around Brownsville like she had no worries. At first she figured Tah loved her and wouldn't hurt her. Plus, he was out of jail, and she knew Tah didn't expect her to take the fall for the shooting. She already brought drugs out there for him, what else did he expect? All of those thoughts changed when she realized he was avoiding her. She tried to speak to him on the phone. She tried beeping him and calling his cellular phone but when he heard her voice, he hung up. He erased her number off his beeper and told a group of her girlfriends to tell 'Mika she didn't exist to him anymore.

Then 'Mika stepped over the line when she went to Sutter Gardens and knocked on Mecca's door. Luckily for Tamika, Mecca wasn't home, but her emotions superseded her intelligence. She wrote on Mecca's door in black marker, *Tah, I'm sorry. I didn't mean to hurt you. I love you.* She could never catch Tah at home, so she knew for sure that he would see her note at Mecca's house.

Mecca was usually out of the city staying at Ruby's villa, which Mecca owned legally. The house was in her name and her SSI savings covered the mortgage. Ruby's lawyer helped Mecca secure the home. She happened to be in the city often since she and Shamel started creeping around. Tah spent most of the time in Brownsville doing stick ups and hanging with his crew.

He went to see Mecca twice a week, either to drop off money or spend a night after having boring sex. After the wonderful sex Mecca was having with Shamel, she seemed disinterested when she had sex with Tah. The sex she had with Shamel was always satisfying and they never did the same things. There was always something new when they got together. Mecca came to her apartment after spending time with Shamel and saw what Tamika wrote on her door.

"Oh, no, this bitch didn't!" Mecca grumbled, opening her door. She picked up her phone and called Shamel. "Boo, you won't guess what this bitch Tamika did to my door!"

Shamel rushed over to Mecca's Brownsville apartment to see what was going on. Shamel was shocked when he saw it and he knew that whoever this Tamika was, she done fucked up. He thought if he knew Tamika, he would have told her, "You don't wanna do that. Mecca is not the one."

"This bitch doesn't learn, huh? I cut this bitch face in school and she still don't get it!" Mecca said angrily. "C'mon Shamel, we going to find this bitch!"

Mecca drove her Benz with Shamel riding shotgun with the seat leaned all the way back. Mecca drove with her seat leaned back so far it looked like the car was driving by itself, if you looked from the outside.

Both of them had their guns on them. Mecca had a chrome .45 with a pearl handle that Shamel bought off a crackhead for her. Shamel had a MAC-11 with a shoestring tied around it that he put on his shoulder under his red and gold Avirex leather jacket. Mecca saw Tah and his crew standing on the corner of Mother Gaston and Dumont and pulled up on the corner. She walked straight over to Tah.

Tah saw the anger on her face and mumbled to his crew, "Now what?" Shamel got out of the car with her and that angered him even more.

"Where's that nappy headed-bitch of yours, Tah?" Mecca yelled.

"What is you talking 'bout, Mecca? What bitch?" Tah, asked confused.

"Don't play stupid! Tell the bitch she can tell you she love you in your face or on a postcard, not on my fucking door!"

"Fuck is you talking about?" Tah asked, then he pointed at Shamel. "Fuck is he doing here? He your bodyguard now?"

Shamel interjected, "Hold up, son. Mecca is my peoples. I'm holding her down. Ain't nobody trying to take what's yours. So leave me outta this, kid."

Tah looked Shamel up and down menacingly and so did Tah's crew, who began mumbling under their breath. Mecca pulled out her gun and cocked it. Tah's crew all pulled out their guns when Mecca brandished hers.

"Ain't nobody gonna front on my peoples. So y'all niggas don't even think about it!"

"Y'all niggas chill!" Tah yelled to his crew. He turned to Mecca. "Mecca, put the biscuit away, ain't nobody gonna do nothing." Tah smiled at Shamel. "I don't know what you did, son, but whatever it is, put me on, 'cause I doubt if she'll do that for me."

Shamel ignored Tah's sarcasm. "Son, she bailed you out as soon as she heard you got locked up, and . . ." He figured he should cap it off with what he knew was somewhat true. "She love you, son, you're all she talks about when she in the East."

Tah looked at Mecca, and then he reached out to hug her. Mecca pulled back. "Where's this bitch? She wrote on my door, Tah. She must think you live there or she lost her mu'fuckin' mind!"

"Mecca, I don't fuck with that bitch. Why would I fuck with a bitch who snitched on me?" Mecca started walking back to her car with Shamel in tow. Tah stood there with his crew, angry. "I'm saying, where you going, Mecca? Let me talk to you!"

Mecca looked back at Tah with the "yeah, right" look on her face. "Talk to that bitch of yours, because I ain't doing no talking."

Mecca drove around Brownsville looking for Tamika. Crews of guys hanging out on corners stared as Mecca drove down Rockaway Avenue and Mother Gaston Boulevard. Girls stared with envy when they realized it was a girl driving. Some recognized Mecca from going to school with her. Some of them waved to Shamel out of spite, which Mecca ignored. Mecca noticed Shamel shake his head when the girls waved at him.

"I'd rather die than be like them bitches," Mecca said.

"I feel you on that."

Shamel noticed Mecca's eyes widen when she looked at another group of girls on the corner of Pitkin and Belmont.

"There go that bum-ass bitch right there!" Mecca pointed.

Shamel looked at the group. "What you wanna do?"

Mecca pulled over. "This bitch ain't worth killing, I'll beat her ass." She put her gun in the glove compartment. "Just hold me down just in case these bitches try to front," Mecca continued.

"No question," Shamel replied.

They both got out of the car. Tamika saw Mecca coming and shock was all over her face. Tamika could have pissed her pants at the sight of her nemesis. The girl who cut her face back in junior high. The girl who took her man. Yet, Tamika had to save face in front of her crew, so she initiated the standoff.

"Bitch, you walking over here like you—" Tamika was cut off by the sound of Mecca's fist against her jaw. Mecca kept swinging and punching Tamika in her face. She tried to fight back.

"Bitch, don't you ever come to my crib." Mecca spoke after each punch. "Looking for Tah. You bum-ass bitch!"

Mecca held Tamika's head down with one hand and upper-cut her in the face with the other. Tamika's nose was bleeding and her jaw was dangling from Mecca breaking it with her first punch. Tamika's friends were yelling at Tamika.

"'Mika, beat her ass! Don't let her do that to you!"

One of them even tried to grab Mecca. Shamel held his hand out in front of the girl while putting one hand in his jacket. "Get the fuck back before I pistol whip one of you bitches!"

The girls saw the menacing look Shamel gave and backed up.

"That's it, Mecca, damn, you got it!"

Mecca threw Tamika on the ground and saw that a large crowd was watching. Most of them were shopping on the busy strip of Pitkin Avenue. Some people stood at bus stops watching the girls. Groups of guys watched to see if one of the girls' clothes were ripped off to get a flash.

Chunks of Tamika's extensions came out of her hair. Her tight blue Guess jeans had dirt on them from the ground and one of her sneakers flew into the street. Mecca stomped her face on the ground and Tamika mumbled inaudible words. Shamel saw Tamika on the verge of damn near dying and grabbed Mecca.

"C'mon, Mecca, let's boogie."

Mecca was out of breath, but stopped to look down at Tamika. "Bitch, don't ever come near my crib again!" Mecca spat on her and walked off.

"Now, was all that necessary?" Lou asked Mecca after showing her the vision of the fight.

Mecca laughed. "You damn right it was necessary."

Lou shook his head. "You don't have to use that language, Mecca."

Mecca sucked her teeth and replied. "Does it matter? I'm going to hell anyway! I beat that bitch ass," Mecca teased and chuckled. Then she pointed a finger at Lou like a parent or teacher scolding a child. "Plus, I know who you are. I read the Bible and I even read the Qur'an. You the uh . . ." Mecca snapped her fingers. "You're Satan! That's who you are! I figured it out when you said you don't know why God created people who were going to cause bloodshed among each other, and you wanted to prove Him wrong. I read that in those books!"

Lou began to clap his hands. "Hurray for Mecca, she finally got something right! You thought for a second, instead of just reacting!" Lou stopped clapping, then continued, "If you would have figured things out when you had the chance you would have had a better life."

Mecca sucked her teeth. "You make it seem like I was stupid or something."

"No, not stupid. You just made stupid decisions. Listen, Mecca, I've walked the planet since its creation and you're not the worst person I've seen or met. Wow! I've met people

like Hitler, Idi Amin, some of the pharaohs of Egypt. Liars like Columbus and others involved in the most treacherous treatment of human beings, the enslavement of your ancestors. All I did was watch."

"What does this have to do with me?" she asked, cutting Lou off from reminiscing.

Lou folded his arms and rubbed his chin. "Well, Mecca, for some reason I kind of felt sorry for you, and you were one of the few people who didn't blame me for the things you did. Honestly, I don't know why you did the things you did." Lou shrugged his shoulders. "Things happen that we have no control over. But a job is a job, so let us continue."

Chapter Sixteen

Even in laughter the heart is sorrowful.
—Proverbs 14:13

"My appeal looks good. I'll probably get offered a deal instead of going back to trial," Ruby said to Mecca in the visiting room at the Federal Correctional Center for Women in Ohio.

Ruby put on a few pounds since she'd been down. Her face was puffy around the cheeks with the beginning of a double chin forming on her neck. She tried to conceal the weight gain by wearing a large, beige, prison-issued shirt and pants. Her hair was pulled in a tight ponytail, but the wrinkles developing on her forehead and eyes told of Ruby getting stressed and older.

Mecca listened attentively to her, despite the noise in the crowded visiting room. There were kids running around while their parents, mostly black and Hispanic, engaged in sexual acts performed while guards turned their backs. The visiting room smelled like popcorn and cheap perfume.

"Hopefully everything goes good for you," Mecca replied.

"Yeah, this crooked mu'fucka convicted me on some bullshit. They had no evidence against me for no murders except for the Spanish cat because the police was right there, but there were witnesses that seen him come up behind me with a gun. I got an affidavit from one of the witnesses, some lady from Long Island. There's another witness from uptown, a black dude, but he act like who don't wanna help a bitch. I got his address. I'll send it to you to see what you can do!"

Mecca nodded while unintentionally seeing a black inmate getting oral sex from a fat white girl two tables away from where Mecca and Ruby sat.

Looking at Ruby saddened Mecca regardless of how many times she came to visit her, which was usually once a month, depending on where Ruby was located. The feds usually transfer inmates to different prisons throughout the country so an inmate won't get too familiar with the prison and area around it. Ruby looked powerless, which was something Mecca wasn't used to, nor Ruby. She conducted herself as if she were still running the show on the streets, though, because Mecca made her feel that way even though Mecca ran things and Ruby's name was forgotten.

Mecca made sure Ruby's commissary account stayed above $5,000. Money that Ruby had when she got locked up, she was spending on high-priced lawyers. She currently had three expensive lawyers working on her appeal. The cost was a little over $1 million.

Mecca kept Ruby updated often on what was going on in the streets. She told her about Dawn, and Ruby only replied, "People get what their hand calls for." Mecca spoke of Shamel so much and so highly that Ruby figured it out.

"You feeling Shamel, ain't you?" Mecca blushed. "Yeah, you feeling him," Ruby replied, already knowing the answer.

To Mecca's surprise, Ruby just smiled and said, "He's a good nigga, Mecca. Better than that Tah cat. I don't trust him. You know how niggas from the ville is. The grimiest they come."

Mecca told Ruby about the incident with Tamika.

"You should have cut her face again. What kind of nigga doesn't do anything to somebody who snitched on them? He a sucker-ass nigga! Leave his punk ass!" Ruby said sternly.

"I'm about done with this nigga." Mecca snorted.

After four hours, the visit ended with Mecca promising Ruby that she would see her next month and find the witness who didn't want to cooperate, and Ruby sending her love to Shamel. Before Ruby hugged Mecca she left her with a last piece of advice. Ruby held her face between her palms like Mecca was still a little girl. Mecca felt a little embarrassed but she just listened.

"Leave that clown, Tah. He going to fuck around and be your downfall."

On her flight home, Mecca thought about everything she and Ruby had talked about. Before she got to the airport she called Shamel and told him to pick her up in two hours at JFK. Mecca smiled at the thought of Ruby finally giving her a blessing when it came to Mecca dealing with boys. She had to admit to herself that she was falling in love with Shamel. She didn't have the heart to tell him because she didn't know if he felt the same way. He showed signs that he was in love, but with guys you never know. Some of them just want steady pussy.

When Mecca got to JFK Shamel was there waiting in his Land Cruiser. When she got in the Jeep, Shamel gave her a kiss on the lips and handed her a rose with a card. The card was a Hallmark card with a brown teddy bear on the front that had a red letter "I" on a white T-shirt. When Mecca opened it, the inside said "Love You." Mecca had butterflies in her stomach and she felt the blood rush to her face. She hugged Shamel tightly and replied, "I love you too, Shamel. No lie." She smiled from ear to ear and playfully slapped Shamel on his shoulder.

"You act like I was gone for a long time, surprising me like this."

Shamel drove, looking at the road ahead. "Five minutes away from you is like a lifetime."

Mecca knew right then and there that she had to leave Tah and commit herself to Shamel. During the ride to Brooklyn, Mecca told him about her visit with Ruby. Shamel smiled when she said that Ruby gave her blessing with dealing with him.

"Next time you go see her, I'm going," Shamel said.

"She'll be feeling that," Mecca replied. When Mecca relayed to him what Ruby had said about her appeal and the witness from Harlem, Shamel became angry at the witness and promised Mecca that he was gonna make sure this nigga do the right thing. Even if they had to pay him whatever.

"Matter of fact, we gonna make that a priority," Shamel said, already putting a plan into action. Mecca nodded in agreement.

Two nights later, as Shamel was exiting his Land Cruiser at a weed spot on Pitkin and Miller Avenue, two cars screeched to a halt and eight men jumped out. Shamel didn't have his gun on him this night and he cursed himself for it when he realized the masked men were not cops. Before he could run or try to fight, he felt something heavy and hard hit him on the back of his head, and everything went black.

When he came to, his vision was blurred for a few seconds and his head hurt like hell. When he was able to focus, he saw that the room he was in looked like hell. He could tell he was in an abandoned tenement by the smell of rotted wood mixed with human waste and whatever animals used the place as shelter. The windows were boarded up and the walls were covered with graffiti, chipped paint, and once-plastered holes. The wooden floor that also had holes was littered with syringes, empty crack vials, and garbage. The two men who stood in front of him had the black ski masks still covering their faces. Shamel looked around for the other men who had kidnapped him, but he couldn't see or hear the presence of any other people in the building.

"What's the deal, son, you all right?" one of the masked men chuckled.

"Fuck y'all niggas want? I ain't got no money like that," Shamel said wearily. Both men started laughing.

"And we're Spiderman and Superman, mu'fucka. We know you got money and the bitch you deal with got mad paper. We gonna see how loyal y'all li'l team is," the other masked man barked.

"Leave her outta this, son. How much you want?" Shamel said, angry.

"Damn, kid. That hit a nerve, huh? This nigga must be in love or something, son," one of the men said to the other.

The other one didn't laugh or join in with the other about Shamel loving Mecca. "I thought you ain't have money like that. Soon as we bring the bitch up you ready to peel, huh? Too late, we called her and told her fifty thousand or your ass is out."

The masked man who didn't laugh at the love joke leaned closer to Shamel. "She got a half hour to drop the money off where we told her or you a body, son."

Shamel recognized the voice. He knew if he let him know that he knew who he was he would definitely leave the building in a bag. There was a time and place for everything, especially revenge.

The other masked man took a cigarette out of a pack of Newports he pulled out of his black fatigue pants, and lifted his mask over his mouth, revealing his mouth. Shamel saw the gold teeth the guy had on his bottom teeth. The word 'Born' was engraved on them.

When Mecca received the call she immediately went to her safe she had hidden in an apartment she rented in Bushwick. No one knew about this apartment except her. She rented it just in case she needed to hide out and no one would be able to tell cops or her enemies where she was. The caller told her, "We got Shamel. If you think we lying, go pick his truck up on Pitkin and Miller where we picked him up from. If you want to see him alive, we need fifty thousand. Drop it off in the garbage bin on the corner of New Lots in a half hour." The phone clicked off.

Mecca drove to Pitkin and Miller with one of Shamel's soldiers and tears welled up in her eyes when she saw his truck. She knew something was wrong when he never returned from the weed spot. She told Shamel's soldier to take the truck back to Sutter Gardens and "get ready for war."

Mecca dropped the fifty thousand where she was told, then drove off. Back in the tenement, a third man wearing a mask appeared in the room and whispered in the other masked man's ear. The man whose voice Shamel recognized nodded his head, then bent over, putting his face close to Shamel. Shamel could smell the alcohol on the guy's breath through the wool mask.

"I guess that bitch love you or something 'cause she paid for your freedom and life nigga. Next time, have your heat on you, stupid!"

All the while, Shamel was trying to get his hands loose from the duct tape around his wrist and ankles. His hands were taped behind his back and he was sitting on a crate with his back against the dirty wall. One of the masked men pulled out an orange box cutter and it made a clicking noise as the blade was pushed out.

"Let's see if she'll be attracted to you or pay for your plastic surgery after this."

Shamel started struggling to get his hands loose. He knew what was next. Unfortunately, the tape was too strong and thick for him to break loose. The masked man without the box cutter began punching Shamel in his face and body with fast punches. He felt his eye begin to swell and blood flowed out of his nose. He could taste the blood in his mouth as the guy kept punching.

Fortunately, he was in shape, so the body punches didn't affect him, but the blows to the face were making him dizzy and the pain was excruciating. Then the worst happened.

"Hold his face, son, I'ma eat this nigga food!" the one with the box cutter yelled.

One of them held his face as Shamel tried to turn away. He felt a pinch, then a burning sensation. The masked men then put duct tape around his eyes. They picked him up under his arms and dragged him off the crate, down some stairs, which seemed like they went on forever, banging against his butt and legs.

"Open the door, son!"

The cold night air rushed in as the door opened. Shamel felt the air cooling the blood on his face, which was numb. In the distance, he heard cars driving by and police sirens. Then the men let him go, and his head hit the ground. Lying still, he wondered what the men were doing until he heard them open a car door.

"Cut the tape from his wrist, son!" one of them yelled. Hearing the sound of the box cutter open made his body tense.

"Turn around, mu'fucka!" someone said, tugging on his arm. With the strength he had, Shamel turned over on his side and let the guy cut the duct tape off his wrist. When his hand was freed, he pulled the tape off of his face at the same time he heard a car door slam and tires screeching.

By the time he got the tape off his eyes and pulled it from his ankles, his kidnappers were gone. Shamel looked around the neighborhood to see where he was. The block was filled with tenements; some abandoned, some not. The sidewalk was filled with piles of black industrial garbage bags and littered with garbage, baby diapers, and drug paraphernalia. He touched his face and felt the deep gash and the swelling. He looked at his hands and saw that they were covered in blood.

The block looked familiar; he knew he was in Brooklyn, but was unsure where. He looked at a street sign as the elevated train at the corner rode by, making a screeching sound. Shamel could see the sparks of electricity from under the train as he read the sign: HULL STREET AND BROADWAY. He knew he was in Brownsville. Shamel walked to a pay phone on Broadway and dialed Mecca's cell phone. She picked up on the first ring.

"Hello!"

Shamel never felt happier to hear someone's voice. "Mecca, it's me."

"Shamel, where you at?" Mecca screamed into the phone, sounding relieved.

"Come get me. I'm on Hull and Broadway. I know who did this."

"Don't move, I'll be right there. I'm sorry, Shamel," Mecca cried.

"Don't sweat it, Mecca. This ain't your fault. These niggas going to pay. Hurry up, though. Niggas ate my food, I'm leaking."

Chapter Seventeen

Revenge is like the sweetest joy
next to getting pussy.

—Tupac

The image of Lou was now dressed in a Catholic archbish-op's robe. The yellow and purple robe had gold crosses on the crest and Lou held a large, black Bible in his hands. He opened the Bible and looked at Mecca.

"Mecca, you ever heard the saying 'vengeance is mine saith the Lord'?"

"Yeah, I have been to church before. Damn, I wasn't always in the street," Mecca countered, sounding aggravated.

"I'm not a psychiatrist. I'm not going to ask you why you're so angry even in death, but," Lou said loudly, "you've been angry all your life so you carried it with you to the other side," Lou said, rubbing his palms together. "Now, I asked you about revenge. Don't you think it's rather odd that the creator says revenge is his, but he made it so humans would feel the urge to avenge themselves against their adversaries? Are you following me?"

Mecca looked at Lou confused and shrugged her shoulders.

"I figured you would do that," Lou said. He began to pace back and forth. "It's a catch-22, Mecca. It's not fair, where is the mercy in that? You create something to be able to do as it feels, but you punish them for the choices you gave him. Is that love? No, it's a game!"

"Why are you telling me this? If you have issues with God or whoever, take that up with Him, Her, Them, but leave me alone!" Mecca barked.

Lou put his hand against his heart. "I'm not bothering you, Mecca, I'm trying to teach you something," Lou replied.

"What good does it do me now? What is this knowledge going to do for me? I'm dead."

"Mecca, knowledge is infinite. You never know what will become of you. Who knows what His Greatness has in store for you?" Lou paused and smiled. "I'm just doing my job."

Mecca picked Shamel up in her red Lexus and took him to Kings County Hospital, where he was stitched up. He received a hundred and three stitches for his face, and was released from the hospital the same night.

Shamel's face was numb from the Novocain they used to put the stitches in. He could barely speak when Mecca drove back to East New York. He reclined in the passenger seat with a large gauze pad on the left side of his face. His whole face was swollen, and to anyone who knew him, he was unrecognizable.

"Who did this shit, Shamel? It was Tah, wasn't it?" Mecca asked with the look Shamel had seen on her face when she went after Tamika. It was a look that made her seem like a different person, like when Bruce Banner got angry and was about to transform into the Hulk.

To Mecca's surprise, Shamel shook his head and struggled when he replied, "It was those niggas Kaheem and Born."

"You can't be serious." Mecca's face turned into a look of disbelief.

"Yeah," Shamel replied in a groggy voice.

"Your own cousins? Why the fuck would they . . ." Mecca banged on the steering wheel. "Niggas is real shiesty, Shamel. You treat them niggas like your little brothers. You did everything for them niggas!" Mecca wondered why when she called Kaheem's house, his girl said she ain't see him in a few days. When Mecca told the soldier of Shamel's who came with her to pick up his truck what happened, he asked when the last time was that anyone had seen Kaheem and Born.

Mecca didn't think anything of it at the time because she was so worried about Shamel. She thought maybe they were at some chick's crib doing whatever. The last thing she would have thought was that they were involved in a kidnapping for ransom on their own cousin. *How grimy is that?* she thought.

The thought if it brought a lump up in Shamel's throat. He fought to hold back the tears. His mind flashed back to when his cousins Kaheem and Born, both twenty years old now, came from Brownsville to stay with Shamel and his grandmother after their house burned down, killing their mother and their little sister, who was two years old.

Shamel couldn't believe that his own flesh and blood would do him so dirty, but the situation would definitely be handled. He was thankful that he had a ride or die chick like Mecca by his side, and knew if shit got sticky he could always turn to her for help.

"Don't worry, Shamel, everything gonna be all right," Mecca said, rubbing his thigh. Mecca looked over at Shamel and could see the pain in his eyes. Well, the one eye that was open. The other was swollen shut from the punches he took to the face by his kidnappers.

Shamel looked at Mecca for a few seconds, and then looked out the passenger window. "Word to my grandmother soul, I'm gonna kill them niggas, Mecca."

Mecca put what she had to do for Ruby on hold to tend to Shamel while he healed. She drove over to his building every morning to make him breakfast in bed. She helped him dress and she cleaned his face and changed his gauze pad. To put him more at ease she would suck his dick and let him cum in her mouth. His ribs were sore so she laid him on his back and rode him.

Tah came over to her apartment twice a week and Mecca would treat him like a stranger. When he tried to have sex with her she would turn him down.

"I don't know what that bitch Tamika got. You ain't gonna be fucking me after you fucked her."

Tah would accuse her of fucking Shamel and say that was the reason she didn't want to have sex with him. Mecca would ignore him and Tah would leave. Eventually Mecca started seeing less and less of Tah, except when he collected money from his soldiers and copped coke off Mecca and took the consignment.

Mecca knew eventually Tah was going to be a problem. She figured Tah would eventually feel that if she was no longer his girl, he shouldn't do business with her or look over her other spots in Brownsville, and that's exactly what started to happen.

Mecca got the word that her spots in Langston Hughes and Tilden were constantly being robbed and no one knew who was doing the stick ups. When Mecca asked Tah about it, he simply said, "I can't be in three places at one time. I'm saying you should put your boy Shamel in charge of those spots. Ain't nobody doing it in my projects. Niggas respect who I be."

When Mecca spoke to Shamel about it, Shamel knew exactly what Mecca knew. "He knows because he's the one who got niggas doing it," Shamel said.

"I ain't been showing my face around the ville. Mu'fucka think that I'm on some high posty shit," Mecca replied.

Shamel shook his head. "Nah, Mecca. Niggas know you a female and even though you bust your guns, niggas still can't grasp the thought of a girl running a spot. Another strike is that you're not out there on the front lines. Niggas respected your aunt so off the strength niggas went with the flow, but how long will you last just off the strength of who your aunt is? Your aunt is not here so niggas don't give a fuck no more."

Mecca slammed her fist into her palm. "I'ma show these niggas I ain't no soft-ass chick!"

Shamel grabbed Mecca's hands in his, and then kissed her softly on the lips. "Chill, Mecca, you ain't got to do nothing. That's what I'm here for. I'm going to handle this. You my woman now and I ain't gonna have you running around getting into no shootouts with niggas. I got this."

Three weeks after the kidnapping of Shamel, as the swelling on his face disappeared, Shamel was back out on the streets. The scar on his face was still raw and pinkish, giving Shamel a menacing look. Shamel called Kaheem's girlfriend and Kaheem answered the phone.

"Shamel, what up, son!" he bellowed, sounding as if he were happy to hear from his cousin.

"Ka, what up. Where you been, kid?"

"A yo, son, me and Born was out of town in B-More trying to get something going out there. There's crazy paper out there, son," Kaheem lied.

Shamel kept his cool and talked as if he didn't know that it was his own cousins who kidnapped him and cut his face. "You heard what happened, right?" Shamel asked.

"Yeah, son. We gonna find out who did that foul shit and it's on!" Kaheem said, trying to sound sincere and angry about what happened to Shamel. Shamel could tell that Kaheem covered the phone with his hand. He heard him mumbling in the background.

"Where Born at?" Shamel inquired, setting his plan in motion.

"Still in B-More. He fucks with some bird out there. Nigga act like he in love or something," Kaheem chuckled.

"When he get back in town, y'all come see me, all right?"

"I'm saying if shit is back to normal. I'll be back on the block tonight," Kaheem replied while getting a stronger grip on his girlfriend's hair as she sucked his dick.

"That'll be good. Yeah, come through."

Dear Aunt Ruby,
I hope that by the time you receive this letter you'll be in the best of health physically and mentally. As for me, I'm maintaining and holding things down. A lot of shit has been going on and I feel like I'm going to have to go there. Shamel got kidnapped and niggas cut his face. I had to cough up paper to the cats who got him or Shamel would have made the column. Tah on some other shit. All of a sudden gates in the ville get held up and he dumb to who or what. I know he behind it all because I ain't fucking with him. Times are hard and I need you. Things ran smooth when you were home. Niggas and bitches think I got soft, but I swear I didn't. I'm going to prove to you that I didn't. When you come home, things will still be on the up. Aunt Ruby, write me back ASAP and let me know what you think and what I should do. I miss you and I'm coming up next month.
Love, Mecca

When Mecca went to her mailbox a week later, she kind of expected Ruby's response to be short and to the point, but Mecca wished Ruby would at least break things down more. Reading the response, Mecca knew her aunt was angry at her.

Dear Mecca,
Take care of what I asked you to do.
Ruby

Chapter Eighteen

Faithful are the wounds of a friend; but the kisses of an enemy are deceitful.

—Proverbs 27:6

"There's a proverb in the Bible, Mecca, that says, 'Hell and destruction are never full: so the eyes of man are never satisfied'," Lou quoted. He continued, "Never satisfied, how true that is," Lou snickered. "Greed, greed, greed. Humans are greedy! How did you put up with conniving, low-down people and still feel that it was worth it?"

"You just don't understand. I had to do what I had to do," Mecca responded with candor.

Lou howled with laughter. "You're wrong, I do understand. I understand that your whole life you've been surrounded by these types of people. Hate to have to say it to you, but your parents were those types of people too."

"I wasn't around them long enough for that," Mecca growled, angry at Lou's comment.

"That's so unfortunate. All I'm saying is that you were raised to think that what you were doing was right, but at some point with all you were going through, you should have realized nothing good would come of that life. Your family was the perfect example of why you should have stopped."

"Stopped and did what?" Mecca yelled.

"Let's see."

Shamel's grandmother returned from her trip down South. Before she could share the news of how good of a time she had, and advise Shamel and Mecca to save up some money, buy land down there, and get away from these treacherous streets, she was concerned about the scar on Shamel's face.

"Baby, what happened? How did you get that? Lord Jesus!"

"I was fixing a light at Mecca's apartment and one of those florescent bulbs broke and cut my face," Shamel lied, with Mecca cosigning his tale.

"You got to be careful. I bought you and your cousins some stuff back," she said, digging in her black leather suitcase. Shamel watched his bowlegged grandmother walk to her suitcase slowly, as if her bones hurt. He figured her arthritis was getting worse. He acknowledged that for her eighty years of living, her dark chocolate skin, though wrinkled a little, made her look twenty years younger.

She still had pretty long hair, now gray, that reached beyond her shoulders when she didn't have it in a bun. She always dressed as if she was going to church: skirts down to her knees, knee-high stockings with shoes that nurses wore, and a blouse buttoned up to the top. Shamel rushed over to help her open the suitcase.

"Thank you, baby. I brought y'all some shirts that are nice. They look as good as those expensive clothes y'all waste y'all money on. Y'all crazy with them ninety-dollar shirts and pants, and hundred-dollar sneakers."

Shamel looked at Mecca, shrugging his shoulders as his grandmother pulled out multicolored, flannel, button-down shirts and some blue and black jeans. The kind they sold in Sears or gave you in prison.

"Ain't they nice?" she asked, holding up a shirt, showing Shamel. "And look at these jeans. They just like the ones y'all wear and I only paid twenty dollars for the shirt and pants together! Clothes are cheaper in the south than up here! This city is so crazy I got to go, and so should y'all! Mecca, you're a pretty girl. Ain't no pretty girl like you need to be wasting her time in this crazy place. These guys have no respect for women up here. Down south they treat you like a lady, you hear me?"

"Yes, ma'am," Mecca replied.

Shamel's grandmother handed him the clothes. "Go try them on, and give these to those two knucklehead cousins of yours. Those two are up to no good. Where they been? I ain't seen them in a while before I left. Tell them I said don't be calling me from no Rikers Island asking for bail. I'll tell that judge to keep they little tails in there."

Shamel threw the clothing on his bed. "Grandma, I'll try them on later. I got to make a run!" Shamel yelled from his room. He walked out of his room and waved his hand to Mecca, signaling for them to leave.

"Okay, baby. Don't forget to tell those knuckleheads I wanna see 'em."

"I ordered the double cheeseburger, son!"

"Nah, nigga, I did. This your Big Mac!" Kaheem and Born argued in front of a McDonald's on Broadway and Kosciusko Street in Bushwick. Kaheem held the McDonald's bag in his hand while Born tried to reach in and grab the double cheeseburger.

"What difference does it make? Just come on!" Kaheem's Puerto Rican girlfriend yelled while she folded her arms, trying to keep warm from the cold night air. Her cream complexion was red from the frigid wind. The black and red North Face kept her upper body warm, but the tight-fitting Parasuco Jeans that gripped her heart-shaped, plump ass didn't protect her from the cold.

"It's cold as hell and you dumb-ass niggas wanna argue over some burgers. Kaheem, let's go!"

Kaheem and Born both looked at her at the same time and in unison barked, "Shut the fuck up!"

"Y'all niggas need to get a life, for real."

"Karmen, you get yourself a job and all of the sudden we gotta get our lives together. You got the nerve to ask Mecca to come work with you at this bullshit McDonald's!" Kaheem grumbled while Born laughed.

"Some people change. Unlike y'all dumb asses y'all want to be in the streets forever. This shit don't last forever, y'all gonna wind up in jail . . ."

Kaheem and Born finished the sentence with Karmen, "Or dead!"

"We heard it all before, Karmen. Come up with something new. Nothing last forever, man," Kaheem said.

Karmen thought Mecca would at least give it a try. She and Mecca became friends when Kaheem brought Karmen to Shamel's crib. They double-dated twice and Karmen and Mecca clicked. Karmen liked Mecca's style. She knew Mecca was real and not like the fake chicks in her neighborhood who smiled in your face and gossiped behind your back.

After Dawn, Mecca told herself she would never get close to another chick like that. In fact, Mecca kept her circle extremely small. Shamel and her aunt. Yet, she could not help but be drawn to Karmen. Karmen talked about a lot of things besides men and materialistic things. Karmen had goals. She wanted to save up money and open a restaurant that served soul food and Spanish food. She wanted to eventually leave New York after opening up a chain of restaurants. She loved to cook. She worked in McDonald's to save up money to go to culinary school to become a chef.

Mecca wondered why somebody like Karmen would be in a relationship with a low-life like Kaheem. She figured there was somebody for everybody. Karmen even suggested that she and Mecca go into business together. Mecca would agree with her, but she thought that Karmen was just a dreamer and it would never happen. As long as she was with Kaheem, he would do nothing but bring her down. A lot of times, Mecca wanted to tell Karmen about what she thought, but it wasn't her business. Maybe Karmen knew something she didn't.

"Whatever, Kaheem, I'm walking. Y'all can argue over some burgers all night if you want, I don't care," Karmen said, starting to walk up Broadway under the elevated train tracks that the J train ran on.

As the train rode by, Karmen looked back to see if Kaheem and Born were behind her. She sucked her teeth when she noticed them still arguing over the burgers. Karmen heard footsteps behind her when she turned. A man who appeared to be a homeless bum bumped into her.

"Damn, watch where you going," Karmen snapped.

"I'm sorry, ma'am," the man said gravely.

Karmen looked him up and down, studying his dirty, ripped-up jeans, old gray sheepskin that looked like a mangy dog, and some old beat-up New Balances that were caked in dirt. Karmen looked at the man's face. It didn't fit the way he appeared. His face looked clean, when he spoke he showed pearly white teeth, and he was clean-shaven. To her, he appeared to be attractive and no older than twenty-five. As Karmen walked passed him, the man turned around and grabbed her from the back in a bear hug.

"What you doing?" Karmen screamed as a car screeched to a halt and the man, who was too strong for Karmen, lifted her head and walked toward the car.

"Get off me! Kaheem!"

By the time Kaheem and Born heard Karmen scream and they took off running toward her, she was already in the back of a black MPV minivan that screeched off. Kaheem pulled his black .357 Magnum and shot at the vehicle until he emptied his gun. "Karmen!" he screamed, watching the back of the MPV disappear into the cold night.

In Mecca's East New York apartment, Shamel's cellular phone rang while he sat in front of Mecca's fifty-two-inch screen television playing Super Nintendo. He answered after the first ring.

"Yo!"

The voice on the phone answered indistinctly, "She said she'll meet you in Queens."

Chapter Nineteen

Open rebuke is better than secret love.
—Proverbs 27:5

"Welcome to the Baisley Park Houses," the orange and blue sign said as you came into the eight-story, brown brick housing project on Guy R. Brewer Boulevard in South Jamaica, Queens. It was a notorious neighborhood that bred one of the most infamous drug gangs in the city of New York; a project that filled the pockets of hustlers with millions. The people of Jamaica, Queens called it "The Baisley."

Shamel had a partner he met on Rikers Island from the Baisley, and he would let Shamel use the apartment to hide out from the police in Brooklyn if needed. He also let Shamel use it when he was creeping on Mecca.

"You think he would put up the money?" Shamel asked Karmen, referring to his cousin putting up ransom money for her.

"If he did that to you, I know he don't give a fuck about me," Karmen said to Shamel as she sat at the kitchen table eating four chicken wings and fried rice off of a Styrofoam plate from the Chinese restaurant. Shamel sat on the other side of the small wooden table eating a pastrami and cheese sub sandwich.

"I told you before, Shamel, he can't be trusted. Neither of them," Karmen continued.

Shamel pulled his cellular phone out of his black and red Avirex leather jacket and set it on the table in front of Karmen. "Call him and find out. You got to put the act on. You know, sound like you're scared and all that."

"C'mon, Shamel, you know I know how to act. I got this, watch the performance." Karmen smiled and grabbed the phone. Karmen dialed Kaheem's cellular phone, and he answered on the first ring.

"Who this?"

"Kaheem, come get me, boo, they gonna kill me!" Karmen said in a shaky and terrified tone. She hoped she sounded believable over the phone.

"Karmen, you all right, ma?" Kaheem asked, sounding concerned.

"Yeah, Papi, I'm fine, but they want thirty G's and they'll let me go!"

"Karmen, listen. You know where you at?"

"No. Just come—"

Shamel grabbed the phone and disguised his voice the way Kaheem and Born tried to do when they kidnapped him.

"A yo, duke, thirty G's. Drop it off on Linden Boulevard by the weed spot. Right on the block where the car lot is at. You got an hour."

Before Shamel hung up he heard Kaheem say, "A yo, hold up, son. Listen. That bitch ain't worth nothing to me. Do what you gonna do."

Shamel let Karmen listen to what Kaheem said by putting the phone between his ear and hers. Karmen was hurt by what he said, but not shocked. She shrugged her shoulders,

"Oh, well, we knew what to expect though," Karmen said, getting up and throwing the plate of Chinese food in the garbage.

"Damn, niggas ain't shit!" Shamel grumbled.

"You should know that. You ain't shit either, or is this pussy so good you can't turn it down?" Karmen said as she sat on Shamel's lap and ran a finger along Shamel's ear. He grabbed her ass and squeezed through the jeans, grinning.

"You want me to answer that?" Shamel spoke as he smiled in her face. Karmen grabbed Shamel's crotch and felt his hard dick under his pants.

"Damn, that big boy ready, huh? To answer your question, I want you to answer mines by fucking this pussy."

Karmen stood up and unzipped her jeans, pulling one pant leg down, exposing the red lace thong she had on underneath. At the same time Shamel pulled his pants down to his ankles, letting his dick poke out through the hole in his blue silk boxers. Karmen pulled her thong to the side and sat on his stiff dick.

"Ay, Papi, I know Mecca's pussy ain't better than this."

"I can't get involved in that. Those cops are going to harass me."

"So you're just going to allow a woman who was protecting herself from a man trying to kill her to sit in jail for life?" Mecca asked the eyewitness from Harlem who saw the Spanish man creeping up on Ruby trying to shoot her.

Mecca was dressed in an ocean green blazer with a white blouse underneath and a beige skirt that made her look like she was a businesswoman. Her hair was neatly pressed out to her shoulders, with a part running down the middle of her head. The witness looked like a nerdy computer wiz who lived alone, sitting at his computer all day, drinking tea and eating potato chips. He was a brown-skinned, frail-framed, twenty-five-year-old college student from Rhode Island attending Columbia University. He tried to close the door of the brownstone on 138th and Morningside, but Mecca jammed her foot between the door and the frame.

"Please just leave me alone. I'll call the police!"

Mecca sighed and put on a sad demeanor. "Please, man, she's my aunt, and she's all I have. Just please help her."

"I don't think I can help her anyway. From what I hear, she's in jail for other murders. She's not an innocent person I just seen protecting herself, she's a monster," the guy said, watching Mecca's facial expression change from a pleading one to a face of fury and rage. Mecca stared at him coldly for a few seconds, moved her foot, and let him close the door. Then she walked away.

The witness looked through the glass on the wooden door at Mecca's back and shook his head. "People are crazy these days."

If the man knew who Mecca was, he would have taken the $100,000 she had offered him and signed the affidavit. If he knew what that look in Mecca's face meant, he would have packed up and headed back to Rhode Island. Instead, he put it all behind him and forgot all about Ruby and that day. The witness remembered the look on Ruby's face when she emptied her gun. It was the same look he just saw on Mecca's face.

Later that night, the police dispatcher at the thirty-fourth precinct received a call that a black male was found dead on a Harlem sidewalk, apparently from jumping off the roof, committing suicide. The caller told the dispatcher that it happened on 138th and Morningside.

Lou closed his eyes and shook his head. Mecca wanted to scream, but she didn't. She would have never guessed that Shamel would cheat on her. Especially with Karmen, a girl that Mecca had grown to like. A girl she considered a friend. Shamel, the man she would have died for. A man whose ransom she didn't hesitate to pay to his own cousins. A man she loved with all her heart and left her man for.

"Let me ask you something, Mecca. If you knew or found out all this before you were shot, what would you have done with your life?"

"I don't know," Mecca answered in a low tone with her head down.

"I know. You would have killed them all. Wouldn't you?" Lou yelled.

Mecca simply shook her head. "I don't know!"

"There's no doubt in my mind you would have killed them all. Still in all, Karmen did offer to help you change your life. It's the least she could do even though she was having sex with your man," Lou grinned, then continued, "So sinister are you humans, but, Mecca, there's a lot more I have to show you. The worst is yet to come."

"How much worse could it get?" Mecca looked at him, astonished.

"Beyond your wildest imagination. Shall we proceed?"

Chapter Twenty

It is better to dwell in the corner of the
housetop, than with a brawling
woman and in a wide house.
—Proverbs 24:24

Karmen limped into her Bushwick apartment looking as if she had been raped and beat up. Her nose had dried blood on it, her hair was tossed, and her red and black North Face was ripped after Shamel promised to buy her new clothes.

"C'mon, Papi, why we gotta rip the North Face? I already let you punch me in the face. I like that coat."

"As soon as we do what we gotta do, I'm going to take you shopping, all right?" Shamel promised, pinching her cheek playfully and kissing her on the lips.

"You promise?" Karmen asked in a childish tone.

Shamel held up his left hand as if he were taking an oath in court. "I swear on everything I love."

Karmen limped into her bedroom where she found Kaheem sleeping.

Kaheem woke up when the light came on. Wiping the cold out of his eyes with both hands, he said in a groggy voice, "Hey, what's up, ma, you all right?"

Karmen took off her coat slowly as if she were in pain and rolled her eyes at Kaheem getting out of the bed. "Does it look like I'm all right? And what the fuck you doing in my house, you wasn't going to help me come home. Those mu'fuckas was going to kill me."

Kaheem walked toward Karmen and tried to hug her. Karmen pushed him away from her.

"Kaheem, get the fuck away from me. You ain't shit."

"Listen, ma, I knew if I acted like I didn't care they would let you go. They wouldn't have gained nothing by killing you." Kaheem tapped his temple with his index fingers grinning. "It was all part of my plan."

"So you gonna play games with my life? You rather risk me getting raped or killed than pay twenty or thirty G's. Money you have, mu'fucka? If you loved me, you would have done the same thing Mecca did!"

"How you think I know how to play this, Karmen?" Kaheem said. He stepped closer to her and whispered like someone else was in the house. "I wouldn't have killed my cousin. I knew Mecca would have paid though."

Karmen acted as if she were shocked to hear what Kaheem said. "You did that shit, Ka?" Karmen asked loudly.

Kaheem put his finger to his lip. "Shhh, Karmen. Damn, don't let the whole Bushwick hear you. Yeah, I did it. Me and Born."

"Why you had to cut his face, though, Ka? That's your cousin!"

"Man, fuck that nigga. He don't give a fuck about me and Born, all he care about is himself and Mecca. He lucky we ain't body his ass. The nigga got soft anyway. He washed up."

Kaheem heard the squeak of the bedroom door being opened, and before he could grab his pants to get his gun, Shamel already had his silver and gray .40-caliber automatic pistol with a red beam pointed at Kaheem's forehead. Shamel had tears in his eyes.

"All the shit I did for you niggas and it's fuck me, Ka? That's how it is?"

Kaheem held up protesting hands. "Son, it don't gotta be this way, for real!"

Shamel moved closer. "What way it gotta be then?" He looked at Karmen and spoke, "Karmen, go downstairs and wait for me."

Kaheem looked at her and Shamel, confused. Karmen did as she was told, angering him even more.

"Karmen, where the fuck you going? Stay your ass right here. He ain't your man!"

Karmen kept walking and shot back, "You ain't my man neither."

"Yo, Karmen! Fuck you, bitch."

Kaheem went to reach for his pants. "Son, don't move, 'cause the next time you do, I'ma squeeze," Shamel said, kicking Kaheem's pants away from him. Shamel felt the gun in it as he did.

"Why you snake me like that, Ka? I ain't been nothing but good to y'all niggas. If you needed some paper you could have asked me. You ain't have to do this. Then you gonna eat my food," Shamel said quietly.

Trying to sound as if he wasn't scared, Kaheem asked, "So you gonna kill me, Sha? I'll give you the money back, son. I just needed a quick buck and I figured Mecca would cough it up."

"So why you pick me for bait?" Shamel yelled.

Kaheem stood with his hands to his side. "Who else, son? Mecca don't give a fuck about nobody. Not Tah Gunz or nobody except you and her aunt. Her aunt ain't here so it's you."

"Nigga, we supposed to be family!" Shamel said with tears rolling down his face.

"I'm saying, son, I fucked up. I'm sorry, kid. What else can I say?" Kaheem pleaded.

"Nothing."

Shamel squeezed the trigger and the first bullet hit Kaheem in the stomach, making him bend over forward. The second bullet caught him on the top of his head, shattering his skull and sending blood and brains out, landing on Karmen's bed.

Karmen sat in Shamel's blue and silver Grand Am looking up at the window of her third-floor apartment. She watched as Shamel removed the sheet she used for curtains and lifted the window. Shamel looked out and then ducked his head back in, emerging with a black plastic garbage bag. He threw the bag on the fire escape, then climbed out. He leaned on the rail looking up and down the block to see if anyone was coming. The street was empty.

Karmen could see the smoke from the cold air coming out of Shamel's mouth fast. Shamel lifted the bag and threw it on a pile of garbage bags on the sidewalk in front of the building.

Karmen waited another fifteen minutes, and then Shamel came out the front door carrying her sheets and blanket. He walked over to the car and told Karmen to roll down the window.

"Hold these. I'll be back," Shamel said in a low tone.

Karmen grabbed the blanket and sheets then quickly rolled the window back up. She threw them on the backseat, then watched Shamel drag the garbage bag into the alley on the side of her building.

He went so far into the alley that the dark night engulfed him and Karmen could not see him. A few seconds later, he emerged and skipped over to the driver's side and got in. He pulled a cassette tape out of his glove compartment and put it in the tape player. He started the car up and sped off just as the Notorious B.I.G.'s voice barked, "Who shot ya?"

Shamel dropped Karmen off at Mecca's apartment and told Mecca he'd be back. Born was coming to see Shamel and his grandmother. Mecca was more than happy to let Karmen stay with her after Shamel told her what happened.

"Let her lay low here for a few days, then she can go back home."

Before Shamel left, Mecca asked him if he was going to take the trip with her that weekend to see Ruby. Shamel touched his scar and said, "I ain't ready to go see her yet. Not while I'm still a little bruised. Tell her I send my love and I'm definitely coming next month."

Mecca understood how he felt. She wouldn't have wanted to see somebody she hadn't seen in years with brand new wounds on his face, so she didn't press the issue. Shamel had a lot on his plate right now dealing with the betrayal from his own blood, and already killing one and preparing to kill the other. It was a pill Mecca found hard to swallow.

Shamel sat at the oval-shaped, black wooden table with his grandmother, with a plate of smoked turkey, rice, and garlic bread, waiting for Born to join them.

"Where them boys at? Didn't you tell them what I said?" Shamel's grandmother asked, setting two plates on the table for Kaheem and Born.

"I spoke to Brian (Borns birth name), but Kaheem I ain't hear from," Shamel lied.

"They so hardheaded, those two," his grandmother said, frustrated.

Just then, Shamel heard keys and the door opened with Born walking in.

He had on a Coogie sweater with red being the most outstanding color among the other colors that lined it. His Pelle Pelle jeans were pitch black and his suede Wallabee Clarks were died red. A red bandanna hung out of his back pocket.

Shamel shook his head. Shamel knew Born used to be a Five Percenter, but since this Blood thing came to New York, a lot of Five Percenters turned Blood, and Born jumped on the bandwagon. It angered Shamel that Born didn't at least put the bandanna away in the presence of their grandmother, but like his grandmother said, "Them boys are truly knuckleheads."

"Hey, Grandma. When you get back?" Born greeted his grandmother. He hugged her, then sat at the table and gave Shamel a low-toned, "What up, kid?"

Shamel looked at him while chewing his food and simply nodded his head.

Grandma tapped Born on his shoulder, "Go wash your hands, boy! What I tell you about that?" Born jumped up and bopped to the bathroom; all the while, Shamel watched him menacingly.

"What's gotten into you, Shamel?" Grandma asked, seeing the angry look on his face. Shamel forced a smile.

"Nothing, Grandma. I was just wondering why Kaheem ain't here."

"You boys like running the streets like it's something good out here. Ain't nothing but trouble out there and as long as you're out there . . ."

Shamel heard his grandmother talking but his mind was elsewhere. He watched as Born walked back to the table and sat down to start eating. Grandma slapped his hand.

"Boy, say your grace! If you and your brother would have come at the same time, we could have all said grace together for the love of Jesus. You two need the Lord. All y'all need the Lord."

Born acted as if he were praying, then said, "Amen." He knew not to argue with his grandmother about him not believing in a "Mystery God" or a "Spook." He knew he had no wins with her so he just went along with what she said.

"Where's your brother, Brian?"

"I don't know, he probably out looking for Karmen. She disappeared," Born said, looking down at his food.

"Shoot. She probably tired of his crap. He ain't got no job and he lay around on his tail all day. A woman ain't going to constantly put up with no lazy man. A real woman at least," Grandma commented.

After they ate the meal with pound cake for dessert, Grandma cleaned off the table and went in the kitchen to wash the dishes. Born took out a cigarette from a pack of Newports he had in his pocket. He was about to light it when Shamel said, "Don't do that, you know she ain't with that smoking in here, and neither am I."

Born put it down and looked at Shamel curiously. "What's up with you, son? You act like you ain't got no holla for a nigga. Ice grillin' me all night. I ain't the nigga who did you wrong. I'm family, kid." Born smiled.

Shamel chuckled, "Family, huh?"

Born stood up. "Grandma, I'll be back."

"Where you going now?" Grandma yelled.

Born walked to the door with Shamel in tow. "I'm going out to smoke a cigarette."

"Okay, baby!"

Shamel and Born went in front of the building and stood in the foyer, and Born smoked his cigarette while leaning against the building mailboxes.

"Sha, what's up, son? You chillin'?"

Shamel looked out the glass door entrance and exit of the building at passing cars and his Land Cruiser parked in front.

"I'm chilling, kid. Trying to get this paper."

Born blew out smoke from his mouth, nodding his head. "I hear that, son. Wassup with Mecca? I ain't seen her in a while."

Shamel looked at him out of the corner of his eye. "She chilling. Same shit. Yo, Born, let's take a ride to the weed spot real quick. I got a fifty bag."

Shamel knew Born wouldn't turn a free smoke down. He was a serious weed fiend. He smoked so much he would make Snoop Dogg, Red Man, and Method Man say, "Dayum!"

Born hopped off the mailboxes and followed Shamel to his Land Cruiser. Born was surprised when Shamel drove to the same weed spot he got kidnapped in front of on Pitkin and Miller Avenue. Quickly, he restrained his surprise on his face and looked out the passenger window.

As Shamel pulled up, Born kept his eye on the street, avoiding eye contact with Shamel. Born saw a person standing in front of an alley beside the weed spot disguised as a grocery store. The person had long dreadlocks down to his shoulders. Some of the locks covered the face of the brown-skinned short person wearing a camouflage jacket and pants, with his hand in one pocket.

"Born, duke got that smoke right there. Police raided the spot the other day," Shamel said, handing Born a fifty-dollar bill. Born grabbed the money and stepped out of the Jeep. He dug in his pocket and switched Shamel's fifty-dollar bill for a counterfeit fifty dollar bill he had.

"Dread, gimme fifty," Born said, holding the money out.

In a Jamaican accent, the dread asked, "You wan' chocolate or you wan' skunk, my yoot?"

Born tried to look in the dread's face who had his head down, looking in a sandwich bag that contained small plastic bags with weed in it. He thought the dread sounded as if he were trying to hide his real voice. When he asked Born what he wanted, it sounded like a female trying to deepen her voice. Born ignored the thought, thinking it's probably him tripping off the dust he smoked before he showed up at his grandmother's house for dinner.

"Let me get that chocolate," Born replied.

For a split second, Born took his eyes off the dread to look up and down the block for cops or an enemy. It was in that split second that he felt something slam into his temple after hearing a loud bang in his ears. Then everything went blank.

The dread stood over Born's body with a .357 Magnum Blue steel in his hand now pointed down at Born. The dread put five more bullets into his body before running off and jumping into a candy-apple red Lexus parked a few spaces behind where Shamel parked his Jeep. When Mecca jumped in her Lexus, she removed the wig and followed Shamel's Jeep happy, that everything went as planned.

Chapter Twenty-one

". . . stay civilised, time flies/ incarcerated, your mind dies."
—Nas

"Maybe you need to wear a suit more often," Mecca said to Shamel, who was dressed in a black double-breasted Italian silk suit. He smirked at her, watching the reflection in the full-length mirror in front of him.

"The only time you'll see me in a suit is at times like this."

"That was a good deal they gave us for a double funeral," Mecca commented.

Shamel's grandmother wanted funeral services for her two grandsons together. When she received the call about Kaheem, she didn't cry. She had mentally prepared herself for that call when they first came to live with her. Then the call came about Born, which caught her by surprise because they both got murdered a few hours apart from each other, but not together. She did eventually shed a few tears for her grandsons and prayed.

"Lord, I know those children were always up to no good, and some hardheaded ones, too. But I beg you, Lord, to forgive them and have mercy on their souls."

Mecca wore a black Chanel dress that reached her knees and hugged her curves. She complimented her dress with two-karat, princess-cut diamond earrings and a black Chanel pocketbook. Her black four-inch heels were by Gucci.

The men who attended the funeral, who were mostly friends of Kaheem and Born, simply stared at her as if she were the star of the show. The women, who were either girlfriends of the men in attendance or of the many girlfriends Kaheem and Born had, gave Mecca the evil eye. As a show of respect and honor to Kaheem and Born, the men who were their friends and associates showed up in red suits, and some wore red street clothing with bandannas around their wrists.

The funeral was held in a funeral home called Unity in Brownsville. Shamel, his grandmother, and Mecca sat in front while the others sat behind them in the wooden pews sectioned in two rows. The bodies of Kaheem and Born, dressed in black tuxedos, lay in two cherry wood caskets in front of the mourners. The mortician did a great job at covering up the scars and gunshot wounds on both bodies, and although it wasn't possible to piece Kaheem's skull back together, it was barely noticeable that the top of his head was sewn shut.

A preacher gave a speech about life and death and spoke a few good words about Kaheem and Born, which Mecca knew were lies. To her, there was nothing good about the two scoundrels. All they did was rob and shoot people and snake those close to them. Mecca looked at their bodies and thought, *There lie two no good niggas. The world is better off without them. They deserve to be wherever they are. See you in hell mu'fuckas.*

Mecca turned to look around the funeral home, wondering if someone heard her thoughts, and looked at some of the people, wondering how many of them felt the same way. She smiled at Karmen sitting behind her in a black, button-down, cotton Gap shirt, black Gap jeans, and a pair of black leather Timberland boots.

Karmen half smiled back at her, and she noticed the smile leave Mecca's face as she caught Tah and his crew come inside the funeral home. Tah and his crew entered all dressed in black. The four of them wore black butter soft leathers, baggy jeans, and Timberland chukkas.

Tah looked at Mecca, smiled, and nodded his head as he and his crew found seats in the back. She wondered what Tah was doing there. Did he know Born and Kaheem? Born and Kaheem were from Brownsville, but she didn't think they knew or even associated with Tah. If they did, then could it be that Tah was the mastermind behind Shamel's kidnapping? Mecca was willing to bet he was. How she would find out was another question she needed an answer to, and knew it would be hard to get.

The N.Y.P.D. set up shop outside of the funeral home. Some were on the roof of the building and across the street in marked and unmarked vehicles. They were investigating the murders and wanted to know who Kaheem and Born associated with. It was obvious to them that the two were Bloods, which to the N.Y.P.D. meant anybody could have killed these two.

"Mecca a grimy bitch, son. She know damn well her and duke did this shit and they gonna sit up there acting like they hurt. I like her style," one of the members of Tah's crew whispered in his ear.

Tah smiled and whispered back, "She ain't shit, right?"

Tah hated the fact that Mecca left him for Shamel. Not so much because he loved her, but his ego and pride couldn't deal with some nigga taking something from him. He didn't want people to look at him like he couldn't keep a girl and he had no control, or like she played him. He swore to himself that both of them would pay for their violation.

After the preacher finished his sermon and asked if anyone wanted to say something about the two men (and no one could or would say good things about them), everyone viewed the bodies. The Bloods left red bandannas, bullets, and weed in the caskets and threw gang signs as they passed by the bodies.

Tah and his crew were the first to walk out of the funeral home. They stood around out front hugging people they knew, and staring menacingly at guys they had beefs with in the past or guys they robbed. Tah hugged a girl he knew from Brownsville and his jacket lifted up as he did, revealing the black 9 mm Berretta he had tucked under his belt. A plainclothes cop noticed the gun and immediately spoke into his walkie-talkie.

"I see a gun. I'm going to walk toward the guy. When I get to him, back me up." The cop got out of his unmarked car directly across the street where Tah stood. He walked over to Tah from behind.

"Excuse me. Can I have a word with you?" the cop said, tapping Tah on his shoulder. Tah turned around and looked the white man up and down, curiously.

"Who the fuck is—" Before Tah could finish the sentence, he heard yells from a dozen cops.

"Freeze! Don't move!"

The cop in front of him showed his badge and grabbed Tah by the arm and patted him down. Tah's crew all began walking away as the other cops told the crowd to either walk away or go back into the funeral home. The guys dressed in red all walked away quickly. Some of them also had guns on them. The cop who approached Tah pulled the gun from his pants.

"What you got this for, buddy? Plan on shooting up the funeral?"

Tah grinned as he was cuffed. "Nah."

The cop searched his pockets while another took his arm. "You got anything in your pocket that will stick me? Did you come here to shoot these guys again?"

"Fuck you talking about?" Tah wiped the grin off of his face, puzzled by the officer's comment.

"The dead guys, you come to shoot them again?" The cop continued smiling at Tah.

"Fuck outta here, I ain't shoot nobody!"

The cop walked Tah to one of the marked police vehicles. "Yeah, right, wise ass. You're innocent, huh?"

"Did you ever think about taking up acting instead of selling drugs, Mecca?" Lou asked sarcastically after showing Mecca the funeral of Kaheem and Born. "'Cause you're good, you got Halle Berry beat for an Oscar!"

Mecca ignored Lou and thought about what he said. Everyone around her was an actor. Shamel acted as if he truly loved her. So did Tah. Karmen acted as if she was her friend, yet she was fucking Shamel and smiling in her face. Who else was acting? she asked herself. Mecca admitted she acted like she didn't kill Born and Kaheem, but they deserved it, and the only reason she had to act that way was to avoid suspicion. She didn't act like that with the people she loved. She was real and loyal to those who were supposed to be her friends and loved ones.

"You're like the jackal," Lou said excitedly. "You disguise yourself and everything. You're amazing!"

Mecca sucked her teeth, but kept silent. She was tired of Lou's antics and this game he was playing with her. She wanted it to end. If she knew that death was like this, and because you did wrong you would have to watch what you did and what others who were supposed to be your friends did, she would have changed her life. But death is the most unsolved mystery that exists.

"But Shamel, he's way better than Denzel Washington. Y'all were made for each other!" He chuckled. "I got to give it to Ruby, though, she is the best who ever did it. No one can compare to the diva, Ruby! That's right, I said it, Ruby is a diva!"

"My aunt is straight-up real," Mecca said sternly.

"You ever read in the Bible—"

"Fuck the Bible! I don't wanna hear that shit. Just get this shit over with!" Mecca yelled, cutting Lou off. Lou smiled and bowed as if he finished performing on stage.

Chapter Twenty-two

Federal Courthouse, Brooklyn, 1999

"Objection! Your honor, counsel is retrying the case. This is an evidentiary hearing."

"Counsel, what is your point?"

"Your Honor, with all due respect, I'm trying to show how my client was prejudiced by trial counsel's failure to call these witnesses. These witnesses would have provided that my client was defending herself!"

Ruby sat next to her lawyer dressed in a beige prison suit with her hair cut in a low Afro. She smiled hearing her lawyer argue the case. Mecca and Shamel sat in the spectators' seats, two rows behind the defense table where Ruby and two lawyers sat. Shamel and Mecca were the only spectators in the courtroom, along with court officers, who were standing at the entrance to the courtroom.

"I'm going to overrule the objection. Proceed."

After the two-hour hearing, Mecca spoke with Ruby's attorneys about Ruby's chance of getting a new trial or having the conviction vacated. Mecca dressed in a Dolce & Gabbana powder blue, button-down blouse, and butt-hugging, black khaki pants, with a pair of powder blue Gucci shoes. She held her black Coach bag under her armpit while listening attentively to Ruby's lawyer explain how Ruby's chances looked good, but the courts were unpredictable. The attorney promised to keep Mecca updated on the case; until then they would have to wait.

While Mecca spoke to the attorney, Shamel sat speaking to a shackled Ruby. The judge allowed an in-court visit. She looked Shamel up and down, smiling.

"I knew you were going to be a looker, but damn, I didn't think you would be this fine."

"Stop fronting like you into men again," Shamel joked. Ruby could see that Shamel kept himself in good shape. His frame filled in the gold and black Versace shirt, and Ruby felt a tingle in her pussy.

"When you gonna come visit me again? You in love now, huh? So I can't get no more of that?"

"You know since this shit happened, Mecca hardly lets me out of her sight," he said in a low tone, fingering the scar on his face.

Shamel remembered the last time he snuck off to visit Ruby. She paid the guard to let her sneak off into a bathroom in the visiting room that the staff used. When Shamel walked in, Ruby had her beige prison skirt lifted up to her waist, and was holding on to the sink, bent over.

"Hurry up, Shamel, we got ten minutes."

Shamel quickly pulled his Fila velour pants down and already erect, grabbed his dick and pushed it into Ruby's hairy pussy. Ruby felt Shamel's large dick fill her insides. She thought she felt him in her stomach when he rammed his pole in and out of her. She held her head down and tried to hold her moan in. She inhaled and exhaled loudly.

"Shamel, fuck me ! Fuck me harder!"

After about fifteen minutes, the guard knocked on the door and told Ruby her time was up. The shift was about to change. She fixed herself up before walking out of the bathroom and back to her seat. Shamel walked out a minute later and took his seat at the visitor's side of the table. He knew that dick was Ruby's weakness and he had no quarrels exploiting that fact. He knew if he gave her what she wanted he would get what he wanted. When he wanted her to give Mecca her blessing to mess with him, he gave her one of the best half hours of fucking she ever had on one of their secret visits.

When Ruby was on the streets, he would fuck her when she wanted to go heterosexual for a minute. Then she would reward him with cocaine for him to sell. It was on one of their creeping moments when Shamel suggested to Ruby that she put him in charge of Sutter Gardens by giving him five kilos on consignment and he would re-up from her. When she got locked up he promised Ruby that he would continue to re-up from Mecca and protect her. Ruby agreed.

"She's all I have, Shamel. I went through a lot to get where I'm at and I want to return to the streets the same way I left them!"

Mecca returned to the courtroom, where Shamel was speaking to Ruby. She sat next to Shamel and smiled at her aunt.

"The lawyers said it looks good," Mecca said, enthused.

Ruby shrugged her shoulders. "They been saying that for the last ten years, Mecca. They say whatever to keep that money coming in."

"You know it takes time when it comes to these appeals. You got all them other bodies thrown out. All you got now is this one," Shamel said, trying to lighten the mood. He knew Mecca was in a good mood after speaking to the lawyer. Ruby's attitude toward her possibly having the murder of the Spanish man overturned made Mecca's change.

He didn't want to be around her when she was in a bad mood. He already had to put up with her when she was on her period. Those were the worst three-to-five days to be in her presence. It was on those days that Mecca never second-guessed shooting or cutting somebody. When the marshals told Ruby her in-court visit was over, Ruby gave Mecca and Shamel a warning before they left the courthouse.

"Y'all be easy out there. Stay off them phones and hang them cron's up for a minute. They are looking to that witness who got hit uptown. They trying to link it to me."

When the marshal walked Ruby out of the courtroom, she smiled at Mecca, and without a sound coming out of her mouth, Mecca read "I love you" on Ruby's lips.

Mecca did the same. "I love you too."

When the visit was over, Ruby would return to her cell and cry herself to sleep. She hated the fact that her weakness was a man's penis, dating all the way back to when she was in love with Wise. She despised the fact that a man could control her if he made her orgasm. Her attempt to control her life was one of the reasons she turned to women for sexual gratification. She had no weakness for women.

Before she fell asleep, she got up from the bottom bunk and tapped her cellmate's leg. Her cellmate was a young, black woman who resembled Monique; same complexion, height, and build.

"Kima, I need some attention, baby," Ruby said in a commanding tone.

Kima rolled her eyes and put down a book called *Shattered Souls* written by Dywane Birch. She jumped off the top bunk. Ruby covered the cell door with a sheet then she pulled off her beige prison dress. She laid on her bunk after taking her white panties off. Kima put her knees on the floor and leaned between Ruby's legs and sucked and licked Ruby's pussy. Ruby held her head and closed her eyes and moaned.

"Lick this pussy, Kima."

Tah was back on the streets, and like most cats who returned from prison without plans of going straight, Tah had plans to take over Brownsville regardless of whose toes he stepped on. While he was up north, he got the word that all members of his crew were Bloods and that Brownsville Houses were being run by a Blood cat from East New York. The blood was getting his product from Shamel.

Tah blamed Mecca for everything that happened. Shamel was her boyfriend and he got his product from her. Tah found out that Mecca made Ruby's villa her permanent residence and transformed her East New York apartment into a weed spot. She was selling weed and crack. Word on the street was that Mecca's re-up was fifteen bricks and ten pounds of weed a week.

While Tah was up north, he became a Blood. He moved up in ranks quickly off his rep on the streets and while he was locked up he caught cuttings and stabbings that made him feared throughout the state system. It was the reason he served his whole sentence. By the time Tah served his sentence, he was a general. The word was sent to Brownsville that when Tah came home, he was the general over the ville, and anyone who didn't abide by that would be dealt with accordingly.

"I'm feeling this CLK right here." Tah grinned as he stared at a 1999 candy-apple red CLK 600 Benz.

"It's yours if you want it, son," replied Mo Blood.

He was the Blood from East New York who Shamel put in charge over Brownsville Houses. Mo Blood received the word from his higher-ups in state prison throughout the state that when Tah returned, he was under his command. Mo Blood was loyal to the U.B.N. (United Blood Nation) and had no quarrels with the order. In fact, he bought Tah a full wardrobe of all the latest fashion, and now they stood in a Benz dealership in Freeport, Long Island so Tah could have a ride.

Tah was feeling good! Tah was ready to handle business and was planning to disrupt the entire operation. People had to pay for the time he spent locked up and the money he lost while being away, and at the top of his list were Mecca and Shamel.

Chapter Twenty-three

*Wrath is cruel, and anger is outrageous; but who is able to
stand before envy?*

—Proverbs 27:4

Lou stood in front of a bright light. A light too bright for
human eyes. A voice spoke from the light as Lou kneeled
down.

"Where do you come from?"

"Your Majesty, I come from walking up and down the
earth, observing the bloodshed and destruction that humans
cause among each other," Lou replied.

"What about the girl?" the voice asked. Lou paused for a
few seconds before responding.

"Her ways, her lifestyle, and the people around her are a
perfect example of what I've told you from the beginning.
These beings you've created above us are unworthy of the
praise you give them. With all due respect, Your Majesty,
they are weak. I'm trying to understand their psyche. I'm
trying to come to terms with why you believe that these
animals would love you as I do, most glorified and exalted."

"This is why I cast you and those like you out. You question
things; you have no authority to question me. I know what
you know not. You're using this child Mecca as a guinea
pig for your silly games. You don't understand humans.
You walked the earth for millions of years and still can't
understand them. It wasn't meant for you to do!"

"I'm not playing a game with her at all, Your Majesty. I
actually pity her. Her life has been filled with turmoil and
betrayal by those she loves. I can relate to her plight, Your
Majesty. This is one I ask for you to show mercy on."

"Continue. What I have planned for her will manifest
through her will!"

***

The image of Lou returned in the eyesight of Mecca.

"What, you took a lunch break or something?" Mecca asked sarcastically.

"Mecca. I'll ask this question again. What would you do if you were given a second chance to live?"

Mecca thought about lying to Lou when she answered the question. She wanted to tell him, "I will start my life off fresh, get a job, and leave the streets alone," but she figured he would know she was lying, so she might as well keep it real.

"I don't know. It's hard to say now with all that you've shown me. Where would I begin? I have no real friends except my aunt."

Mecca couldn't see Shamel's thoughts of him having sex with Ruby when Lou showed her Ruby's court date. He withheld showing Mecca that for a specific reason. He wanted to see how mentally prepared Mecca was before he showed her the ultimate betrayal. Mecca already saw the infidelity that Shamel engaged in with Karmen, but how would she handle betrayal from the only person she trusted?

"Revenge doesn't change what's already been done, Mecca. You have to realize that. You can't remove the past, you can only work on the future. No one loves you more than you can or do. I know you heard the saying, keep your friends close, but your enemies closer. Most of the time your friends are your enemies. Even your family," Lou said, staring into her eyes, seeing if she could read his thoughts.

"Why did you say 'even your family' like that? What are you trying to say, Lou?" Mecca yelled.

Lou began to second-guess revealing to Mecca what he was going to reveal. It could either make or break her, but he hoped that it would make her realize that nothing good comes out of evildoers. So he decided to reveal to her what he called the "Ultimate Betrayal."

Chapter Twenty-four

*A continual dropping in a very rainy day
and a contentious woman are alike.*

—Proverbs 27:15

Langston Hughes Projects, 1982

"You like this dick, don't you!"

"Oh God, I love it! Don't stop! Please don't stop!"

"Whose pussy is this? Say whose pussy this is!"

"This is Darnell's pussy!" Ruby moaned as she was positioned in doggie style while Darnell rammed his large manhood in Ruby's vagina. After three hours of wild, sweaty sex, Ruby laid on Darnell's chest playing with his chest hairs.

"You got to promise me. Give me your word that you won't hurt anybody," Ruby said.

"C'mon, baby, you know my word is good. All I want is the stash of boy he got. I told you we're gonna get rich," Darnell replied, referring to the drugs he planned to get later that day.

Ruby turned over in the bed, and Darnell slapped her plump ass playfully as she reached on the floor and grabbed her blue Sergio Valente jeans and pulled out a set of keys. She rolled back over and handed the keys to Darnell. He kissed her on the lips and jumped out of the bed.

"Don't worry, ain't nobody gonna get hurt."

The next day, Darnell and his little brother wore masks and entered the Langston Hughes apartment using the keys Ruby gave him. He saw a little girl asleep on a bed in the corner of the living room. Well, he thought she was asleep, but the little girl saw the masked men enter the apartment. She closed her eyes and lay still, thinking they wouldn't see her.

The little girl thought her tactic worked when the two men walked past her and into her parents' bedroom, and she crawled under her bed. She heard the men talk loudly to her parents.

"Don't do anything stupid. Don't make us kill you. Get up slowly!"

Seconds later the little girl watched as her mother and father were led into the living room and made to sit next to each other on the couch. One of the men tied them up with duct tape on their mouths, wrists, and ankles. The little girl then watched one of the men walk to the refrigerator and remove a plastic bag with a gray powder in it. Then she heard one of the men say, "You got the shit, Darnell?" The look on her father's face made the girl assume that her father knew the man called Darnell.

Her father tried to speak through the duct tape but couldn't. The guy Darnell appeared angry that the other man yelled his name out. Darnell yelled at him and her father was moaning loudly at Darnell. The little girl heard Darnell, when he removed his mask, tell her father that his days working for Stone were over.

Silently praying, the little girl made no noise while roaches crawled over her face and inside of her footie pajamas. She watched the tears flow down her mother's face and then she let out a low scream as the masked men pointed the gun at her father's head and pulled the trigger. She let out another low scream when the gun was pointed at her mother and the trigger was pulled.

The men left the apartment and drove in a custom van. Darnell pulled over and ran to a pay phone on the corner of Mother Gaston Boulevard and Sutter Avenue. A voice picked up on the first ring.

"Darnell, what the fuck did you do, mu'fucka!" the voice yelled.

"Ruby, they knew who I was. My stupid brother said my name!"

"My niece saw that shit! How could you do this to me?"

After receiving the call from the little girl named Mecca, Ruby rushed over to her sister's house to get her niece. She didn't want her niece talking to the cops. On the way over to pick up her niece, Ruby banged on the steering wheel of her Camaro. She cursed herself for letting Darnell talk her into setting her brother-in-law up.

Ruby just wanted to take Stone's dope from Blast so she and Darnell could start their own spot. Darnell fucked Ruby so good she couldn't resist telling him no. She wanted to do anything he asked so he could give her dick when she wanted it.

Ruby didn't consider herself a nympho; she just had a weakness for a man who made her have multiple orgasms. She blamed Ron for her weakness. He was her first lover and her first sexual experience, which was unforgettable. She didn't realize the power of an orgasm. It wasn't just the orgasm that did it. The feeling of a man's hard penis touching her G-spot drove her nuts. Not too many men knew how to find her spot. The ones who did had Ruby at their mercy.

Ruby swore to herself that she would make Darnell pay for what he did. She didn't know who Darnell's little brother was but to this day, she wished she did know who he was. If she had killed him back then also, he would have never been able to kill Monique. The police got to him before Ruby could get her revenge. He was now serving twenty years to life for it.

Ruby also swore to herself that she would make sure Mecca had the best of everything. Mecca wouldn't want for anything ever. She was to never find out what Ruby did. So she made it her duty to hunt Darnell down and kill him so he could never tell anyone.

After that, the killing continued. Ruby killed her way to the top. She wanted to rid herself of all potential threats to what she was building for Mecca. She knew she wouldn't last long and eventually she would be killed or in jail, but before that could happen, she would make sure Mecca had all she needed.

"Nooo!" Mecca screamed at Lou. Lou held his head down and shook it back and forth.

Chapter Twenty-five

For jealousy is the rage of a mans, therefore he will not spare in the day of vengeance.

—Proverbs 6:34

Tah and Mo Blood crept around the villa that Ruby left to Mecca in the Hamptons. He knew the code to disarm the alarm system, and the two pit bulls Mecca had didn't bark when they recognized Tah's smell. He gave Mecca the pit bulls as a birthday gift when they were together.

Mecca was asleep naked while Shamel walked to the kitchen naked to eat some leftover baked macaroni and cheese and some cold chicken wings. He put the macaroni and cheese in the microwave and set the time for a minute and a half.

Shamel watched the macaroni heat up on a plate that spun around inside. There was a hissing sound a split second before his head exploded against the glass door. His body slumped to the floor after Mo Blood put the bullet in the back of his head from his black 9 mm Berretta with a silencer on it.

Tah crept into Mecca's room with Mo Blood behind him. When Mo Blood saw Mecca's naked body, he whispered, "Damn, she is thick, son!"

Tah tapped Mo Blood on his shoulder and put his finger to his mouth signaling for him to keep quiet. Tah pulled some rope out of a black Jansport book bag he had in his hand. He knew Mecca was a heavy sleeper, so tying rope to her headboard wouldn't wake her; it was tying her up that would be a problem.

Tah tied the rope to the oak wood headboard. He whispered to Mo Blood after he tied to rope to the board.

"Son, I'ma lay on top of her to hold her down; tie her hands to the headboard," Tah instructed. Lying on top of Mecca awakened her.

"Yo, what the fuck is you doing?" Mecca yelled, unable to see who was lying on top of her. Tah positioned his body horizontally across Mecca's stomach and chest. She recognized Mo Blood and figured it was Tah on top of her.

"Tah, get the fuck off of me!"

Mo already had one of her wrists tied to the headboard. She wouldn't let him get the other wrist. She was kicking and moving wildly. Tah had no choice, so he got off of her.

"Son, hold her feet!" With one hand tied, Mecca kicked and punched with her free hand.

"Tah, you bitch-ass nigga! Get the fuck outta my crib!"

Tah caught Mecca's free hand and held it. She couldn't fight against the strength of Tah. His time in prison lifting weights and taking supplements and eating protein bars had him strong and muscular. He put his arm around her throat and squeezed, putting her to sleep.

When Mecca's body went limp, he tied her feet with rope and tied the rope to the bedpost. He tied her other hand to the headboard. Mo Blood grinned and attempted to touch Mecca's private parts, but Tah swung his fist hard, landing a right hook on Mo Blood's jaw, knocking him unconscious.

After he tied Mecca to the bed, he slapped her on the face to wake her up. At first her vision was blurry, and then it became clear after a few seconds. Still a little disoriented, she stared at Tah. Slowly her eyes drifted to the chrome .50-caliber Desert Eagle he pointed at her.

"Tah, why are you doing this? What did I do to you?" Mecca pleaded trying to loosen the ropes by tugging on them.

"Why you think, Mecca?"

"Just because we ain't work out together, that don't mean we couldn't be friends," Mecca lied.

She knew she couldn't be friends with Tah because she couldn't trust him. He violated her by messing with Tamika behind her back. They could never be friends. Mecca remembered what Ruby told her about letting people mess up one time and no more. She fell in love with Shamel. He was the man Tah could never be and Shamel treated Mecca the way Tah didn't know how.

Tah laughed hysterically. "That's what you think this is about? I couldn't care less if you were sucking my dick. This ain't about me being mad because you stop dealing with me."

"Then what do you want from me? Money? You robbing me, Tah?" Mecca asked.

Tah shook his head. "You got in way over your head, Mecca."

"Tah, what are you talking about?" Mecca cried. She looked into his eyes and she knew he was high.

"You're not your aunt, Mecca. She's gone."

"Put the gun away, Tah, and untie me, nigga. You high off them pills!"

Mecca yelled, trying to sound authoritative, thinking it would make Tah listen. She remembered Tah would leave her alone when she got angry just like Shamel did. Most of her life people feared when she got angry, the same way her aunt made people fear her.

Those days were over and Tah couldn't care less about that look Mecca had on her face. The look that Mecca got when she was about to hurt someone. Tah thought, *This bitch still think a nigga her flunky or something. She outta her rabbit-ass mind.*

"Bitch, I ain't your damn flunky!" Tah yelled his thoughts out loud.

"Tah, who the fuck said you was a flunky?" Mecca asked. "You my man, nigga, not no flunky. You listening to them lame-ass niggas you be with and they put shit in your head. Be your own man mu'fucka!"

Tah knew when Mecca said he was her man she meant it as a friend. She was saying it like another nigga would say, "that's my man," but Tah knew that was bullshit. She didn't give a fuck about him. He wrote her from jail plenty of times and never got a reply. She sent him money one time and no letters. He poured his heart out in some of the letters, knowing she was lying up with Shamel. He vowed to himself that she would pay for his broken heart. No one treated Tah Gunz like a scrub. No one.

"Fuck you, Mecca!" Tah pulled the trigger.
When the bullet hit Mecca on her forehead, everything went black.

Lou and Mecca stared at each other for a few minutes. Mecca saw two silhouettes walking toward Lou from behind him. When the two silhouettes reached Lou they separated, and one stood on one side of Lou and the other on the opposite side. Their faces lit up and Mecca saw a male and female in long white robes, and then she recognized the faces of her parents.

The image of Lou and her parents disappeared and Mecca's vision was blurred. She saw a shadow behind a bright light. Her eyes were blinking rapidly. When her vision cleared, Mecca was looking up at Shamel's grandmother.

"Nurse! Nurse she's up!" Grandma yelled. A short, middle-aged, Spanish nurse rushed into the hospital room and smiled at Mecca.

"Hay Dios mio, she's alive!" the nurse said excitedly.

Shamel's grandmother held her hands and head up in prayer. "Thank you, Jesus."

November 6, 2001

Ruby received her mail from the corrections officer sitting at a desk on the cellblock. She rushed to her cell, anxious to open the envelope from the courts. She knew it was the decision for the appeal. When she got to her cell she ripped open the envelope and her knees almost buckled as she read:

AND NOW, on this 6th day of November in the year 2001 it is decided that the petitioner Ruby Davidson's motion to vacate a sentence of Life imprisonment is granted. The warden of said prison where petitioner is currently confined is ordered to release prisoner C024688 upon receipt of this order.

Ruby's heart leapt out of her chest as she read the order vacating her sentence. She was free. She handed the paper to her cellmate.

"I did it, baby! I'm out!" Ruby yelled enthusiastically.

"That's great, baby!" Kima said excitedly, but was secretly happy to be getting rid of her bully of a cellmate.

"Did you hear anything about your niece?" Kima asked, changing the mood. With the smile and enthusiasm gone from Ruby's face, a grim expression took over. Ruby took the paper from Kima's hand.

"They said she's out of a coma, but she might be a vegetable for the rest of her life."

Shamel's grandmother smiled at Mecca and rubbed her hand. Mecca's head was wrapped in bandages, but being in a coma for a month all the swelling went down in her face. Tah shot Mecca three times: once in her chest, one in the side of her face, and once in the forehead. When she turned her face simultaneously with the first shot that hit her forehead, it just grazed the front of her brain.

"Baby, your aunt's appeal went through. She's coming home tomorrow," Shamel's grandmother said, thinking the news would bring a smile to Mecca's face.

Mecca heard the news but couldn't speak. She wanted to yell at Shamel's grandmother about everything she knew about her grandson, her aunt, and everybody who betrayed her. Instead, she stared at Shamel's grandmother's eyes blinking, and a tear rolled down her cheek.

Chapter Twenty-six

A child represents a world from which
we have been forever exiled.
—Robert Greene, *The Art of Seduction*

The playful screams and laughter of the children in the playground surrounded by the towering, dingy brown buildings of the Brownsville, Brooklyn, housing projects harmonized with the sound of mothers yelling various commands to wandering, overly playful children. The sound of a bustling avenue, with its buses, cars, and always present roar of police sirens, served as a backdrop. One particular little girl, cute, with long silky hair done up in pigtails adorned with red ribbons at the ends, looked over to her mother, sitting on a bench with other young mothers, and waved with a huge smile. Though in a conversation filled with neighborhood gossip, her mother was always alert to the whereabouts of her only child.

"Be careful on those monkey bars," she yelled across the courtyard at her daughter and just as quickly turned back to the conversation at hand.

The little girl watched as her favorite relative, her aunt Ruby, entered the playground. She stood in front of the little girl's mother and talked using a lot of hand gestures. As usual, she saw her aunt remove a wad of cash from her pocket and hand it to her mother.

Climbing on the monkey bars, where other kids played, the little girl wanted to reach to the top like she saw other brave kids doing. She also wanted to impress her auntie. As she ascended the bars, she looked over to see if her aunt was watching. Disappointed that she didn't notice her, she called out to her. Just as she called, one of her feet slipped off the bar and caused her to fall down toward the black rubber mats placed under the monkey bars. Her small head and body banged off the bars as she fell. Her crying shrieks alerted her mother and aunt, who were seconds late to catch the girl's body, preventing her from hitting the mat.

Before the little girl's mother ran over to her, she felt herself being lifted off the mat. She was dazed, with temporary blurred vision, and it seemed as if the noise of the playground became muffled. When her vision cleared, everything moved in slow motion. That was when she looked into the face of the person who had picked her up off the ground. He was tall and wore a pitch-black trench coat. His Afro was the shiniest and neatest 'fro she ever saw. Even her handsome father's curly, perfectly round Afro couldn't compare to that of the man holding her hand. His bright smile reminded her of the keys on the piano in her music class. As she took in the glow of his dark, rich complexion, she realized that the pain in her head from the fall was gone. Then the man spoke, and his voice seemed to hypnotize her.

"Throughout your life you will fall. What's important is how you function when you get back up."

"Baby, are you okay?" The little girl heard her mother's voice. She was confused as to why she was now holding her mother's hand instead of the hand of the man who picked her up. She looked around the playground, once again hearing the familiar sounds of the ghetto, searching for the mysterious man, but he was gone. Her aunt's cheerful voice grabbed her attention right after that.

"Look, she ain't even crying. She tough like her auntie."

"Let's hope she doesn't follow in her aunt's footsteps," the girl's mother retorted flatly, attempting to deflate the air out of her sister's chest full of pride.

Suddenly the sound of gunshots erupted in the projects. All the parents ducked, running toward their children, who instinctively ducked down as they listened to their parents' yelled commands. The little girl clung to her aunt as the shots rang out for a few seconds; then it ended as quickly as it began.

***

Mecca jumped out of her sleep. The gunshots in her dream awakened her as her heart beat rapidly. She looked around, realizing she was lying in her hospital bed. After her labored breathing subsided and she could hear the beat of the heart monitor next to her bed, she mumbled to herself, "You were always there, weren't you, Lou? I remember you now." She took the time to get herself together and, after a while, realized that she could hear voices outside of her room. She could hear only a few words that were being said because their voices were low.

Since the fatal shooting at the hands of her ex-boyfriend, Tah, and seeing her entire life with the assistance of Lou, Mecca had to be institutionalized and treated with intensive therapy sessions. She couldn't get over the feeling of wanting to kill her aunt, and any remaining foes from the past that might still be alive. Since she chose not to talk, the doctors thought it would be best for her to stay, much to Mecca's dismay, of course.

"It's more mental than physical," a male voice murmured.

"It's been so long. When can I see her?" a female voice asked in a sad tone.

"I don't think she's ready yet. She hasn't even spoken yet."

When Mecca looked at the door after a face appeared in the entrance, she recognized the face of her once beloved aunt. Now a face she felt sick to her stomach seeing.

Seeing the smile on Ruby's face made Mecca want to jump out of her bed and choke the life out of her, but that was physically impossible at this point in her life. Even more disappointing, when Ruby walked into her hospital room, she walked in with Karmen. Both Ruby and Karmen smiled at Mecca. A song her father used to play when she was a child came to mind; it was The O'Jays' song about backstabbers. That was exactly how she felt about both of these women.

"Good morning, Mecca." Ruby spoke to her with a hesitant smile on her face.

Instead of responding, Mecca simply turned her face and closed her eyes.

Ever since Lou showed Mecca her aunt's betrayal, she couldn't even stand the sight of her. For Ruby, it was probably a good thing that Mecca couldn't move, because she probably would have already killed her by now. It hurt Ruby that Mecca wouldn't respond to her, but she kept coming back to check on her niece's progress. That was what family was supposed to do.

Lou had been visiting Mecca in her dreams since she'd been out of her coma. He was sitting behind a huge mahogany desk, in a large, burgundy-leather, cushioned office chair, while Mecca lay on a leather chaise lounge, when Mecca asked, "Why can't I get up, Lou? Why are you keeping me paralyzed?"

In a measured tone Lou replied, "Because the revenge you seek is not yours. You've done that half of your life, and it has gotten you nowhere. Be on your best behavior, and you will walk again, I promise."

Chapter Twenty-seven

The most eloquent expression of the unconscious is the
dream, which is intricately connected to myth. . . .
             —Robert Greene, *The Art of Seduction*

Joseph of the Bible was known for his ability to interpret
dreams. It was that ability that caught the curiosity of the
Pharaoh of Egypt, whose own interpreters were useless.
Joseph interpreted the Pharaoh's dreams and became a
powerful man in ancient Egypt. As Mecca Sykes attentively
gazed into the bright eyes of Lou, she wondered who could
she wake up and ask to interpret her dreams and tell her
exactly who Lou was.

"You do not know what vengeance is, because it is not
yours to give," said Lou, dressed in a white overcoat, as he
held a stethoscope to Mecca's chest. Mecca lay still on a stark
white linen hospital bed, with a preoccupied expression on
her face.

"You act as if I'm dumb or something. Mind you, Lou, I'm
grown. I'm not the child you visit in my dreams," Mecca
replied gruffly. Ever since Lou had snapped Mecca out of
her coma and had begun appearing in her dreams, Mecca
realized that she had become intrigued by his speeches about
her doing the right thing in life and letting go of the feeling
of getting some payback on all those who had betrayed her,
especially her aunt. Initially, she had found him annoying
and somewhat cruel for putting her through the grueling
task of viewing her friends and loved ones being betrayed
and herself as a victim of the double cross.

Mecca no longer had anyone in her life that she could talk
to about her issues. She used to talk to Ruby about them or
Ruby's lesbian lover, Monique, whom Mecca had confided in
more than anyone else. She could rely on Monique to give her

motherly advice about men, sex, and feminine issues. After Monique was shot down and killed in the projects Mecca felt like she had no one. She and Ruby had never had that kind of relationship, so she had to learn the hard way about life and trust. As for Lou, he had not only told her that the life she lived was one big lie filled with betrayal, lust, and greed, but he'd shown her how and why.

What could be more interesting than seeing your life played out in plain view, from your childhood to your adult life, and glimpsing things you didn't see at the time? Things like your so-called friends' and family's secret lives of treachery.

"Grown?" Lou questioned, removing the stethoscope from Mecca's chest and chuckling. "Is that what you all call fully matured adults now?"

"What makes you think I want revenge?" Mecca inquired, rolling her eyes at his sarcasm.

Lou looked at the stethoscope in his hands. "If only humans could make machines that could listen to what's in your heart instead of just its beat, then someone would be able to answer that," Lou replied, setting the stethoscope down on a bedside table and rubbing his hands together as if he had a big secret. "Unfortunately, they can't and I can, and your heart tells me revenge is what you seek."

Mecca looked away from Lou and wondered how she could be faulted for feeling angry about being snaked by people she would have risked her life and freedom for. How did he expect her to feel, knowing what they did behind her back? What world did he live in?

"You turn your eyes away so I won't read your feelings and thoughts. Very smart of you, dear," Lou said, snapping Mecca out of her thoughts.

"Huh?" she asked, dumbfounded.

"Revenge doesn't always have to be killing everyone that betrayed you. Karma is nature's form of revenge, and some-times you have to let nature take its course," Lou preached.

"That 'what goes around comes around' crap? Please!" Mecca said in a tone of disbelief. Lou shook his head. Then Mecca displayed a mischievous grin on her face before saying, "Is this one of those moments where you're gonna show me rather than telling me?"

"Don't tell me you're beginning to enjoy this?" Lou commented, shaking his head at Mecca. If only she could just see what he was trying to get her to see, she would be up and out by now. Mecca smiled. Lou shrugged his shoulders, then placed his hand on her forehead, as if he were checking her temperature. "So be it."

The rapper Juvenile's voice roared through the Brooklyn strip club as the naked strippers followed his orders to "Back that ass up," while ballers, gangsters, and average Joe nine-to-fivers whooped and hollered. Throwing money at big-booty women onstage doing acrobatic maneuvers on poles and erotic dances had them acting a fool. There were even women among the crowd of horny men who were cheering the dancers on and letting go of the cash in their hands, putting it into the G-strings and between the squeezed breasts of half-naked women. In a smoky haze, Mo Blood sat in a secluded booth, sipping on a shot of Belvedere, listening to one of his associates spill some news that made him nervous.

"They gave the green light on Tah. They know you was with him, but it's not certain how they going to play it with you," Mo's associate reported, afterward leaning back in the booth from yelling in Mo's ear over the loud music.

"Tah made an O.G. call and I followed. That can't be my fault, homie," Mo Blood yelled.

"I feel you," his associate said, blowing smoke out his mouth while staring at the girl onstage. "That's what niggas in the mountains is saying. It's the homies on the streets making it an issue with both of y'all."

"First off, that bitch and that cat Shamel had it coming. So what's the beef about for real?" Mo inquired, knowing the associate was just a messenger. Even he didn't understand why the heads of their blood set were angry about what Tah did to Mecca and Shamel.

Luckily for Tah and Mo, the cops were the least of their worries. The cops in the Hamptons made sure that type of news didn't go public, especially in an upscale area of that magnitude. A drug-related homicide in the Hamptons? Property values were more important than some dead drug dealers from New York City. Still that didn't stop the word from getting out on the streets of Brooklyn. When the word got to Shamel's friends, they weren't happy and they wanted heads.

"The dude Shamel had bulletproof love with the homies, and he made a lot of them rich," the associate continued in a somber tone.

"I heard he ain't respect blood. He rocked his own family, and they were blood," Mo countered, wondering if he should get out of Dodge.

Shrugging his shoulders, the associate replied, "I think it got more to do with the chick Mecca's aunt. You know, she was a real live bitch back in the day. She knew a lot of heavy hitters and players, and a lot of them respected her, gee. You feel me?"

"So, what that mean? This ain't the eighties!" Mo Blood responded tartly.

"She back on the streets," the associate revealed.

Just as he finished his sentence, a scantily clad girl wearing a G-string and a pink see-through bikini top jiggled her way over to the booth.

"Wassup, Mo? You ready for that private dance?" she asked with a forced smile.

Mo immediately felt his manhood come to life. Horny as hell and drunk off the liquor, Mo couldn't wait for this particular private dance. Mo regularly had private dances at the club, but not with the sexy Tasha. She wasn't into the "private dance" thing, because dancing was not what was meant by the word *private*. Tasha had fallen on hard times and had a two-year-old son to clothe and feed. Her reluctance to give "private dances" in secluded rooms in the basement was making her lose money she definitely needed. She had a choice to make, starve or eat. She chose to eat. So when Mo asked her if she was ready, she surprised him and said, "Gimme about an hour and I'll come get you." And wait Mo did.

"No doubt, ma, I'm ready," Mo Blood told Tasha an hour later. Grabbing Tasha's hand after jumping out of his seat, Mo gave his associate the Blood gang handshake, then spoke loudly over the music. "Yo, Meek. I'll holler at you tomorrow. Talk to them dudes, though. Let them know that was Tah's call, not mines."

"All right, my dude," he answered with a lustful stare at Tasha. "Tear that pussy up, homie!"

Mo smiled while Tasha led him toward the back of the club, to a door leading to the basement. Once in the small room that was decorated with a small bed and a full-length mirror in the corner, leaning against the thin wood-paneled wall, which vibrated from the loud music, Mo got undressed quicker than a New York minute. After Tasha nervously undressed, Mo pulled her on top of him as he lay on his back, dick harder than a baseball bat.

"Don't you got a vest?" Tasha asked.

"Ma, I ain't got no disease. Word to my flag," Mo replied gruffly, ready to go.

Tasha shrugged her shoulders, then straddled Mo. Reaching behind her, she gripped his bulging erection and placed it in her warm, soft middle. Mo held in the urge to moan from the way she made her walls clench his manhood.

Tasha moved her small waist slowly and rhythmically, as if she was moving to the sound of a slow jam. She bit her lip and closed her eyes, feeling Mo fill her insides. Mo squeezed her soft, plump ass as he dug in deep. She felt so soft, he thought his hands would melt into her skin. As Tasha sped up her thrusts, she began to moan.

"Yeah, Daddy, fuck this pussy!" Tasha said into Mo's ear. Her moaning and dirty talk excited Mo, who matched her rhythm with hard thrusts, banging her inner walls as if he was trying to break them down. He ordered her into the doggy-style position, wanting to see her from behind. It was Tasha's favorite position, and once in it, she put her back into it.

"Oh, shit, Mo! Yeah, right there! That's it, Daddy!"

Mo didn't want to release yet, but the feeling of her pussy was too much for him, and he couldn't hold it any longer. Tasha knew he was about to release his load from the change in his thrusts.

"Don't cum in me," she grunted. Mo heard her request but paid her ass no mind. Tasha felt his warm juices in her and tried to pull herself out from under him but couldn't due to his body weight.

"Mo, why you do that?" she wailed, pushing him off of her.

"My bad. It's just that pussy good, Ma," Mo replied nonchalantly, while trying to catch his breath. At the same time Mo was thinking, *Bitch, you knew you was going to start selling that ass. Why you ain't got no condoms on hand?* Mo paid her the buck fifty she asked for and left.

At the end of the month Tasha went to the clinic to get herself checked, which was the club's policy, as was using contraceptives. Tasha waited for the results in the clinic waiting room. A half hour later she was called to an office, where a counselor greeted her as she entered, closing the door for privacy. Tasha was a nervous wreck: the unprotected sex with Mo had her biting her nails for the past three weeks, and she couldn't get it off her mind. The counselor gave her a long speech about AIDS and how people with the disease could live a healthy life if they took the right medication and practiced a healthy lifestyle.

"Please, just gimme the results," Tasha snapped, tired of the anticipation.

"Miss Jackson, you are HIV-positive," the counselor responded.

Tasha fainted in the office.

Good for his ass, *Mecca thought as she looked at Lou with an amused smirk on her face. She didn't know Mo Blood personally, but she remembered him from hanging with Tah and had never liked him. Yet she was bored and wanted more.*

"Is that it?" Mecca questioned Lou, anxious to see what else was going on out in the world. She could have thought of a million other ways to get at Mo Blood, but what she just saw would do for now. At least until she got better and got out of the hospital.

"I see you're starting to get a kick out of this," Lou replied as he placed his hand back over her head. Silently he prayed for Mecca and hoped she would change her wicked ways.

Tamika heard banging at the door over the sound of the sexy, sultry voice of Aaliyah as she sang "Rock the Boat." That used to be her and Tah's jam, but ever since their son had got there, their favorite song wasn't the only thing they no longer shared.

"I'm coming!" she yelled out to let whoever was on the other side of the door know she had heard their knocking. In a pair of tight cutoff jean shorts and a long white T-shirt, with no bra underneath, she sang along with Aaliyah as she walked to the door, smiling with anticipation. When she looked through the peephole, the smile quickly disappeared. Her son's father was the last person she wanted to see, especially now that she was expecting the company of a dangerously cute guy she met in downtown Brooklyn.

"What now, Taheem?" Tamika complained after answering the door with one hand on her hip, showing much attitude.

"What you mean, what now? Don't play with me," Taheem *growled, pushing past her to enter her apartment. "Where my son at?"*

Tamika sucked her teeth, closing the door. *He always pops up at the wrong time, acting like seeing his son is the main reason he makes unannounced visits. Really, he shows up high and drunk, wanting sex and a place to crash when no one else wants his trifling ass in their house. Those days are over,* Tamika told herself, especially after he got his nose wide open off that bitch Mecca, who scarred her face for life. Even though Tamika didn't feel sorry for what had happened to Mecca, it still confirmed to her that Tah was no good.

"*Our* son ain't here, Taheem. He at my mother's for the weekend," Tamika said, watching Tah remove his Tims and plop down on her couch. Turning on her floor model TV, he looked as if he were planning on staying longer than she wanted him in her apartment.

"I got company coming over, Taheem. You got to go. If you want to see your son, walk your ass over to Tilden and spend time over there with him."

"Company? I know you don't be bringing no lame-ass niggas around my son." Tah chuckled, staring at the TV as he channel surfed. Tamika walked over to him and snatched the remote out of his hand.

"Nigga, please! I don't say nothing when you have all those nasty bitches in my son's face. Plus, this dude ain't no lame. You're not the only nigga with a gun, Tah."

"Who is he, then?" Tah snapped as he stood up, walking to the refrigerator.

"None of your business," Tamika snorted. "Plus, you don't put food in this house, so don't go eating everything."

Tah ignored her, pulled a gallon of milk out of the fridge and a box of Fruity Pebbles from the cupboard. To Tamika's annoyance, he used a pot instead of a bowl to eat the cereal. Before she reacted, a knock at the door grabbed her full attention, as it did Tah's. As Tamika walked to the door, she saw the grin on Tah's face and rolled her eyes at him.

"Let's see who Romeo is," Tah mumbled.

Tamika opened the door, smiling at the six-foot, caramel-skinned, big, brown-eyed cutie who favored the singer Trey Songz. He was wearing a tan Yankees fitted cap, which was leaning halfway off his head, and a tan Woolrich coat to match.

"Wassup, Dance?" Tamika greeted.

In a deep baritone voice that moistened Tamika's panties, showing an even white smile, he replied, "What's good, ma?" Once Dance entered the apartment, his smile vanished as he caught the grinning face of Tah Gunz with a mouth full of cereal. Dance looked at Tamika quizzically.

"Dance, this is my baby's father, Tah," Tamika said uncomfortably, knowing Tah would start trouble. He did that with every guy she dated or attempted to date. His friends in the neighborhood would alert him that she was seeing someone, and Tah would show up every day so that he could see who the guy was. Most of the time he would have his friends or flunkies rob the guy or beat him unmercifully. To this day none of the guys had come back to Brownsville for payback. Part of Tamika's nervousness came from the fact that she knew Dance was the type to come back, and not to fight, either, but to do some damage.

When Tamika met Dance downtown, he was surrounded by a mean-looking crew of thugs from his Lafayette Gardens neighborhood, called "L.G." by Brooklynites. It is one of the borough's most notoriously dangerous housing projects.

Dance and his crew were all decked out in the hottest urban fashion and diamond flooded jewelry. It was obvious to Tamika that Dance was the boss by the respect the others showed him and the way people went out of their way to greet him as he and his crew shopped heavily. After she gave him her number, her panties got wet when he walked to a milky white Cadillac Escalade. She told herself she had to have him.

Dance nodded his head toward Tah without saying a word. Tah's menacing stare didn't intimidate Dance, and he wasn't worried about a possible confrontation with Tah. Dance knew how to fight well and was known more for his itchy trigger finger. He also knew that coming to Brownsville, Brooklyn's grimiest neighborhood, meant that trouble was a possibility. So he had come prepared, toting a twenty-one-shot Glock 9 mm.

"Uh, yo, duke, where you from?" Tah blurted as Dance took a seat on the black leather couch, removing his black flight jacket, which he wore over a tan button-down polo shirt. Tah immediately spotted Dance's icy Piaget watch. Dance ignored Tah's question.

Tah was caught off guard by Dance's display of courage, especially since he was out of his own territory. Dance didn't believe in just being the man in his own hood, though. That made Tah think that either Dance was a good bluffer or he really was a gangster, most likely hiding a weapon on himself. Tah finished his cereal then put his boots and coat on while smiling at Tamika. She knew the look was a sinister one that meant the episode between him and Dance was not over. Tamika rolled her eyes, then Tah gave Dance a hard stare.

"You a real gangster, huh?" Tah grunted, opening the door. Dance stood up, with Tamika trying to hold his arms to pull him back on the couch.

"You wanna see how gangster?"

"Nah, playboy, I believe you. It's nothing. 'Mika, I'll see you later." Tah smiled.

Still holding on to Dance's arm, Tamika mumbled, "Bye, Tah." She knew he would be back, and he wouldn't be alone. He would come back with his goons. Dance knew that also. He was angry at the confrontation, but more angry at himself for not finding out more about this chick. He didn't know she had a kid. He should have gone with his first instinct and had her meet him at the hotel on Pennsylvania Avenue. Blinded by the fact that she had a banging body, he'd rushed to Brownsville to tear the pussy up.

"You wanna go out somewhere, instead of staying here?" Tamika asked, worried. Dance sensed her nervousness. This made him rethink his conclusion that Tamika probably was setting him up.

"Why you ask me that?"

"Dance, my baby father is a lowlife, and he is going to come back to start some bullshit."

Dance could sense the fear in her voice. He wondered whose life she feared for more, his or her kid's father. He knew most likely she didn't want her son to be fatherless, and he definitely wasn't playing stepdaddy. Damn, the things dudes went through just for a piece of ass.

"I'm not worried about dude. I got something for his ass if he wants problems," Dance responded matter-of-factly.

"Please, Dance, let's just go. I don't want anyone to get hurt," Tamika pleaded.

Hearing familiar voices in front of the building, Tamika looked out the window. To her dismay, Tah and his crew were out there, looking as if they were preparing for trouble. Dance got up to look out the window and saw the problem Tamika saw. Sighing, Dance took his cell phone off his waist and dialed a number.

"Yo, son, come to Brownsville Houses. These niggas wanna act up. Come now!" Hanging up, Dance turned to Tamika. "Let's wait here for a minute." Tamika grew more fearful. Dance's tone was calm but sinister.

"Dance, he's my son's father. I don't want anything to happen to him. Please, let's just go."

Her plea convinced him as to whose life was more important to her. Dance didn't know her reason for not wanting her son to grow up fatherless. Personally, she could care less about Tah. She just didn't want her son to grow up without a father in his life, like she did.

Tamika didn't want anything to happen to Dance, either. She was planning on giving him the best sexual experience he'd ever had, hoping he would become her sugar daddy. Tah always seemed to get in the way of her plan, and that was one of her reasons for despising him. The main reason for her disdain for Tah was the fact that he made a lot of money on the streets and gave her nothing. Once in a while he would give her money for their son, and that was only when she fussed about it. Otherwise, he was under Mecca's ass, strung out.

While Dance waited for his cavalry to arrive, Tamika tried to take her mind off the situation by attempting to unzip Dance's pants to give him what she called her "tongue talent" and some goodies afterward. With his mind on the drama about to unfold, Dance pushed her hand away.

"Another time, ma." Before she could protest, his cell phone's ring tone of the song "Niggaz Done Started Something" by The Lox went off, with him quickly answering it.

"Yo!" he barked into the phone. Tamika watched as Dance got off the couch and looked out the window. "Yeah, I see y'all. Yeah, that's them. I'm coming down now." Dance clicked off his phone and headed toward the door.

"I'm coming with you, right?" Tamika asked. Dance paused, with a thoughtful look on his face, before replying, "Yeah, baby girl, c'mon."

While Tamika got dressed, shots rang out from in front of the building, startling her and causing a smile to show on Dance's face. He recognized the sound of the AK-47 that he gave to his cousin going off. He was proud that his boys came through, representing L.G. Dance pulled out his Glock and cocked it back as Tamika came out, dressed, with a look of terror on her face.

"C'mon, shorty!" Dance commanded.

Tears welled up in Tamika's eyes. "Dance, they shooting. We can't go out there!"

"It's cool. They just wanted to get them dudes from in front of the building. My peoples ain't come to shoot nobody," Dance lied with a straight face.

When they reached the front of the building, Tamika screamed when she noticed that the person lying on the ground, in a pool of his own blood, was none other than Tah, moaning in pain.

"You don't look so gangster now, homie!" Dance taunted while Tamika got on her knees, cradling Tah's head in her arms.

"Taheem, get up. Don't die, nigga. Your son needs you!" Tamika cried as Tah's eyes blinked rapidly and tears flowed down his cheeks.

"Shorty, you coming? You can't help him," Dance said as his crew drove off and Tah's crew vanished into the Brownsville night.

"Dance, I have to get him help. He's dying!" Tamika yelled.

Dance shook his head. "Nah, ma, he dead."

While Tamika looked down at Tah, crying, Dance placed his Glock to the back of her head and pulled the trigger. The sound of the shot echoed through the hood as Tamika's body slumped on top of Tah's. Still alive, Taheem closed his eyes, unable to feel Tamika's body on top of his due to a bullet shattering his spine from the neck down. Dance walk to his truck, parked in the parking lot in front of the building. He didn't want to kill Tamika, but leaving witnesses wasn't his thing. Charge it to the game.

As sirens roared through the night, Taheem opened his eyes after playing dead. He could hear his own labored breathing among the sounds of the streets. He never thought that things would turn out like this. Why did he allow himself to get caught up in these situations over women who didn't care too much for him? Silly pride, he was told by an O.G., could get a man in deep shit. *How true that is*, Tah thought as he lay there, feeling his life slip away.

***

After being out for what felt like hours, and not satisfied with what Lou had shown her, Mecca woke up, staring into the face of her doctor, who was checking her blood pressure. He smiled at her, and then, after he was done, he left quietly. Mecca stared out the window at the rainy Brooklyn afternoon, thinking to herself, *Lou calls Mo Blood getting AIDS revenge?* Tamika getting killed meant nothing to her, and Tah should've been tortured, not just shot. Lou would have to do better than that to get her to change her mind about seeking revenge herself. She agreed that maybe she should move on, but her anger over how everything went down and what she found out still had her heated, and she wasn't ready to let it go just yet.

"Good morning, Ms. Sykes. Are we going to try and get up today?" the nurse asked her in a friendly tone.

Mecca shook her head no at the fat, redheaded, jolly nurse's irritating voice. It was going to be a long day. Mecca couldn't wait to go to sleep again so she could pick a bone with Lou.

Chapter Twenty-eight

Length of days is in her right hand;
in her left hand, riches and honor.
—Proverbs 3:16

There is a saying among convicts that when asked how much time they are doing or did, the answer would be two days: the day they went in and the day they get or got out. In between is nothing but a blur to some. For Ruby, those days were spent plotting and scheming how she would get revenge on the people who set her up, shot her niece, and killed Shamel. Most important was how she planned on getting rich again.

When Ruby's murder and drug convictions were overturned, and the case was dismissed due to the testimony of an eyewitness, she was given time served for the drug conviction, and began to map out exactly what she would do to get back on her road to riches.

Ruby had many associates and a few lovers in prison, but one person in particular became her confidant. Daphne, a five-foot-five, smooth brown-skinned woman with penetrating hazel eyes, was her favorite. Though no lesbian by far, she had "experimented" with sexual acts with a woman, but it wasn't to her liking. She always told Ruby there wasn't nothing like a hard dick banging up against your walls.

What Ruby did like about her was Daphne's likable personality and her ferocity when she became angered. Ruby saw herself in Daphne. She had a no-nonsense, take-charge attitude that screamed leader. The added bonus to Daphne's repertoire was that she was also from Brooklyn. The women met when Ruby was transferred to the women's federal prison in West Virginia. Daphne had already been there ten years on a fifteen-year stint for being part of a conspiracy to distribute large quantities of heroin. Her boyfriend at the time was a Jamaican-born, Bed-Stuy raised hustler who ran a crew out of Tomkins projects. He and Daphne met in 1984, when she moved into the projects with her mother, stepfather, and sister. Afterward, her mother married an abusive man from Bed-Stuy and moved them in with him.

Daphne loved her older brother and was always sad thinking about how much she missed him. There were rumors about his murder, but nothing ever came of them. He was a drug dealer, so the cops swept his murder under the rug like so many other murders in the ghetto. His presence was greatly missed because he was the man of the house after Daphne's real father was sent to prison for two murders, with a sentence of fifty to life. It was her brother who really took care of the family after making lots of money on the street, which he also used to spoil his baby sister.

He was barely home because he lived mainly with women blocks away from where Daphne and the family stayed. She was protected by the family because she was the baby. Often, she wasn't allowed out to play with kids on her block, and she went to an all girls' school. Extremely smart and an avid reader, she knew things about various topics, from romance novels to black history. Most of all she loved to read the dictionary, because she was determined to learn the meaning of a new word every day.

When she did see her brother, he would give her money to buy candy and toys, and he would make sure she wore the latest style of clothing. Her brother was only about five years older than her, and although she was a teenager, he wanted her to remain innocent. He encouraged her to play jump rope and jacks, and when she got clothes, he made sure they didn't make her look too grown up. The only time she got to show off the clothes was when she went out with her mother to shop for food or visit relatives far away in Queens.

Daphne hated her stepfather, who would get high off ecstasy and cocaine. He also got drunk on hard liquor and abused her mother physically and verbally. Once she was old enough to get out of the house, she began to hang out in Bed-Stuy more than she did in Brownsville. No longer did anyone pay attention to her, like they had when her brother was alive. She figured that the only reason why her mother and sister had been protective of her was to please her brother, because he was her favorite, and if Daphne was happy, then he was, and when he was happy, he gave money to the whole family. Now that he was gone, Daphne could run the streets, and run the streets she did.

Kids growing up in the ghetto tended to get into trouble because of the lack of anything constructive for them to do. With the city's non-caring attitude toward its poor inhabitants and the city's politicians' frequent mishandling of the city's budget, no decent after-school programs existed for the children. The playgrounds were unsanitary due to addicts using them as a place to get high and dump their syringes. The people were too poor to buy things to keep their children's minds from the activity on the streets, so the kids ran them and got into trouble.

Daphne was no exception to this phenomenon. She hung out with the kids in the projects and became amazed at ghetto life, especially at the older guys and girls wearing the expensive clothing and jewelry, like her brother did. The guys reminded her of him; and the girls, of the women he'd dated. These women were the stars of the neighborhood, and she wanted to be adored just like them. By the time she was fourteen, she was well developed and was mistaken for a nineteen-year-old. Still, even people knowing her actual age didn't deter some of the neighborhood hustlers from trying to make her one of their conquests.

At the tender age of fourteen, Daphne lost her virginity when her and a boy from the projects cut out of school and went to his house to do the nasty. It took place on an old, dusty, uncomfortable couch, which made the experience for her unsatisfying. The couch was covered in plastic, and as the boy pumped his dick into her, she stuck to the couch from sweat. It was irritating, and the boy was simply just hurting her. After that she never had sex with him again.

Everyone in the hood liked her, though. She was the nice girl who always smiled. That was a mechanism she used that was taught to her by her brother. She was told by her older brother that regardless of what you were going through, you never showed anger. He told her that when people knew what got you angry, they would use it against you. So, Daphne always smiled. However, when her brother died, she stopped smiling altogether and began to wear her emotions on her sleeve. Her brother was her greatest joy, and with him gone, what did she have left to smile about?

It was her pretty smile that attracted a young Jamaican guy everyone called Marley to her. They called him that because he was Jamaican and he smoked a lot of weed at an early age. His father was one of those Rastafarians, but his real name was Donovan. His almond brown complexion and high cheekbones gave him an exotic look that the girls loved. His eyes were hazel, just like Daphne's.

He was her dream man. He dressed like her brother and made money like him, selling weed for his father. At the age of fourteen he had more jewelry than all the kids in the projects, often wearing diamond rings and necklaces. Nobody dared rob him because his father was ruthless, and so was his crew, made up of family members. All of them were members of a Jamaican crew called the Shower Posse. They got the name because if anyone ever got out of line, as a reaction they would be showered with bullets.

Instantly, Marley fell in love with Daphne and made sure she was the flyest dressed girl in the projects. By the time Marley was seventeen, he was driving a Benz and had his own weed and heroin spots down on Franklin Avenue. Daphne worked out of Marley's uncle's Jamaican restaurant, where they secretly sold weed and heroin. She couldn't have been happier. Soon afterward, both of them moved out of the projects into a two-story home in St. Albans, Queens. They traveled to Jamaica a lot to visit his relatives. No matter what, Marley always treated her the same, like when they first met, and Daphne swore she would never love another man like she did him. She never did.

Her world came crashing down in 1987, when federal authorities raided Marley's spots on Franklin Avenue and their home in Queens. Daphne was working in the restaurant when the raids were being carried out, while Marley was home. She, along with the others, were all arrested and taken to the federal building in Brooklyn.

The next day Daphne received the most heartbreaking news: she found out about her lover's murder. Marley was gunned down by agents during the raid. He was shot a total of forty-one times and died instantly.

After a lengthy two-month trial, Daphne and fourteen other defendants were convicted on various charges under the RICO statute. The only evidence they had on her was her voice on the phone with Marley, talking about orders of beef patties. A government witness lied and said she was referring to drugs.

Daphne was given fifteen years. She knew the feds were being hard on her because she refused to cooperate. The time did not matter to her. It didn't matter if she got out of jail. As far as she was concerned, life was over. Life without Marley was something she did not want to face. Many days and nights she thought about taking her own life, but she just did not have the courage to pull it off. Even though she was depressed, she tried to take her brother's advice and smile but couldn't. Then she met Ruby.

The two women were inseparable in the prison, except for when they were locked in their cells. Daphne didn't cell up with Ruby, because she celled up with only her lesbian lovers. She respected Ruby because she reminded her of her brother and Marley in certain ways. Ruby was bossy like her brother and laid-back like Marley.

At first she was skeptical of Ruby. All the women in the prison were scared of her, so Daphne stayed away. Ruby was in great shape, with a muscular, well-toned body that was still distinctly feminine, like Serena Williams, the tennis star. However, Daphne was sure that she did not want to get into a confrontation with her, so she avoided her.

It was inevitable that the two would meet due to their being from New York. In the federal system, it was customary for inmates from the same cities to clique up. They sat at the same tables in the mess halls and shared space in the rec yard. In the prison they were at, it was a little different for New York inmates. There New York inmates cliqued up with people from their own borough of the city. Ruby and Daphne being from Brooklyn made it more likely that they would cross paths.

After meeting Ruby, Daphne had a different opinion of her. She understood Ruby's rough exterior was a defense to ward off people who would take her kindness for weakness. Growing up in Brownsville, Ruby learned to take that approach at an early age. Daphne could identify with her, and they quickly bonded, with Ruby nicknaming her "Smiley."

In January 2000 Daphne was released, two years before Ruby's conviction was overturned. They kept in contact with each other, and Daphne made sure that Ruby's commissary account stayed full. Every month she would send Ruby five hundred dollars. Though Ruby didn't need that much, holding down a job as a cook in the prison mess hall, she saved the money Daphne sent her. The only thing she would spend some of the money on was phone cards to call and talk to her niece and her niece's boyfriend, Shamel, who was also her secret lover and who also kept Ruby's commissary full.

Daphne was on the street when Ruby received the news of Mecca lying in a coma after being shot and Shamel's death. Ruby also got the news that two days before she walked out of prison, Shamel's grandmother passed away. To say Ruby was ready for war was an understatement. She already held the guilt of being responsible for Mecca's parents being murdered, and now her niece sitting up in a coma because she couldn't protect her was too much. She had watched Shamel grow from a boy to a man, and even though they were sneaking around behind Mecca's back, she still cared about him. Shamel's grandmother dying was the icing on the cake. They always said tragedy came in threes, and those three events put Ruby on edge. Once she got out, she would have business to take care of. Daphne joined her at the funeral, and afterward, Daphne laid out the beginning of her and Ruby's plan to rule Brooklyn.

"Weed is really popping now. Marley's family in Jamaica gave me two hundred and fifty grand when I came home. I opened a restaurant in Crown Heights, which served to quadruple the money I invested in a short amount of time. I got a weed contact from them also in Texas. If you want, you can fly with me out there this weekend and see what kind of stuff they got. You want the best so you can make lots of paper."

After Daphne gave Ruby fifty grand to go shopping, she smiled and asked, "You ready?"

"You know it!" Ruby told her while they embraced.

They drove from the Brooklyn cemetery in Daphne's 1999 pistachio green 750iL BMW. When they stopped at the restaurant, the rays of the sunny day gleamed off a candy-apple red, two-door convertible Benz with a big purple bow on the hood.

"Somebody about to get a big surprise around here," Ruby said, looking out the passenger window at the Benz.

"I know." Daphne smiled.

Ruby looked at her holding a key in her hand. Puzzled, she looked at the key as Daphne held it out to her. Then she noticed the Mercedes-Benz insignia on the key.

"Welcome home, Ruby."

"Get out of here. No, you didn't!" Ruby screamed out.

"Yes, I did! Now, get in it and go see your niece."

At the mention of her niece, Ruby's smile quickly vanished. She knew she would have to toughen up and face what she felt she couldn't. Her mind was filled with guilt: she blamed herself for Mecca's condition. Every thought made her regret bringing her into this game. It had cost her years of freedom and almost the life of her beloved niece.

"It's not your fault, Ruby. It's about get back. Now it's your time," Daphne said in a measured tone of reassurance.

Ruby simply nodded her head and grabbed the keys.

Immediately, she got in and inhaled the fresh smell of the beige leather interior. When she started the car, she became more excited at the sound of the engine. She hit a button, and the convertible roof mechanically drew back. All the while Daphne kept a smile on her face, happy that her friend was home and excited for her.

Ruby looked over at Daphne, as the cars were parked parallel to each other. "You coming with me?" she asked while Daphne tossed her a CD.

Ruby stared at the Alicia Keys CD while Daphne answered, "Spend time with your niece, and call me when you're done. I'll show you where you're staying."

Ruby nodded. She placed the CD in the system and pulled off. It didn't even matter to her that she didn't have her license. It was the Brooklyn way!

Karmen lay on her back, unsatisfied, as a casual sex partner of hers humped like a rabbit, dripping sweat on her dry skin. This was the last time she'd be giving this dude some pussy. He fucked like he had just lost his virginity! Even his grunting was irritating to her.

"This pussy good, ma. Who pussy is this?"

"Are you done yet?" she asked instead of responding to his question, her tone filled with irritation.

With his eyes closed, he held on to her thick hips and mumbled. After he released his fluid into the condom, Karmen quickly got up and walked to the small motel room bathroom, slamming the door.

"It's hard to find a good dick these days. All these cats think about themselves," Karmen said to herself while standing in front of the mirror, fixing her long hair into a ponytail.

Karmen had yet to find a man that could bring her to orgasm. Most of the men she dated were men she dealt with in her new hustle. Credit card scams.

More often, the men in the scam were African immigrants, who were usually in the country illegally and used American women. They would take the women all over the country, getting thousands of dollars of merchandise with other people's credit cards, then selling the merchandise at a cheaper price. Karmen was under the impression that these African men, with their Mandingo dicks, would be good lovers in bed. She was sorely disappointed. A lot of them were a waste of big dicks, and even if they were decent lovers, Karmen couldn't get into it, because the guy didn't believe in deodorant. She held her breath most of the time in bed.

With the credit card scam, the money she made with her partners in crime was decent, but not enough to satisfy her thirst for the hottest and latest in fashion and a means of paying the bills. Gone were the days when her boyfriend, now dead, would give her money and Shamel, after dicking her down, would do the same.

So her choice was easy. At Shamel's grandmother's funeral, Mecca's aunt had offered her a job at a grocery store she was opening up, where groceries weren't the only thing being sold. Karmen didn't hesitate to take the offer.

Meeting Mecca's aunt felt like meeting a celebrity. Karmen had heard so much about her from Mecca and Shamel that she could barely believe it. She was a legend in Brownsville and East New York. She even noticed the resemblance between Mecca and her aunt, and she could also see where Mecca got her swagger.

When Karmen first met Mecca, she immediately took a liking to her. She had style, and she commanded respect from men and women alike. At first Karmen didn't feel guilty about having the affair with Shamel. They had known each other before Mecca met him. She was always at their grandmother's house when she dealt with one of his two cousins, Kaheem and Born.

The more she got to know Mecca, the more she felt guilty, but the good sex and money she was getting erased most of the guilt. Still, she was deeply saddened when she found out that Mecca had been shot and was in a coma. She visited her in the hospital often with Shamel's grandmother, who also loved Mecca like her own. Mecca had tears in her eyes when she came out of it and Shamel's grandmother told her that Shamel was dead. Her eyes just blinked. Now Karmen wondered how she would react when she was told about Grandma's death.

Karmen walked out of the bathroom, naked. The short charcoal black African guy who looked at her with lust in his eyes sat on the hotel bed, stroking his manhood, as if he was ready for another round of skin smacking. His look of lust turned into a gaze of disappointment when Karmen picked up her black thong and clothes and began to dress. He hated to see her cream-colored, gorgeously built body disappear in her clothes.

"You want to leave already?" he asked as his manhood shrunk.

Karmen rolled her eyes. "I'm outta here. Oh, I need that money, too." She pulled her purse strap over her shoulder and placed one hand on her shapely hips, with the other held out.

"We still have three hours left," he sulked in his thick accent.

Karmen walked over to his brown slacks, which were lying on the brown carpet, and went in his pockets.

"Wait. I will get it for you." He jumped up off the bed, but Karmen already held a wad of cash in her hands. She quickly counted a thousand dollars, then dropped the slacks and the rest of the cash on the floor and walked out of the room.

Growing up on the rough streets of Bushwick, Karmen learned at an early age that you couldn't wait around for things to just drop into your hands. You had to go out and take them with no fear. Fear was a hustler's worst enemy. And Karmen, who grew up poor, living in a crowded tenement with four sisters and a mother and father strung out on dope, knew if you let fear take over, you would starve.

Karmen hopped in a cab, smiling. Tomorrow she would head downtown to buy that Dolce & Gabbana blouse she had seen at Macy's. She reminded herself that she would go to a sex shop, too. It was time for her to get a vibrator. If you couldn't find someone to make you cum, might as well do it yourself. Nobody would treat you better than you would.

When she got to her Bushwick apartment building, she rode up in the elevator alone. Once at her floor, she got off and noticed two suited white men in front of her door. Confusion was written all over her round, pretty face.

"Can I help y'all?" she asked. It didn't take a rocket scientist to figure out that they were police, but suited cops usually meant major problems.

"Is your name Karmen Santiago?" one of them asked in a calm and even voice.

"Yes, that's me. What's up?" Karmen asked, nervousness filling her thick Brooklyn accent.

Both men flashed their badges. "Ms. Santiago, we are from Brooklyn North Homicide. We would like to ask you some questions concerning the murders of Kaheem and"—the cop speaking quickly looked at his pad—"his brother, whom they called Born. Can we come in, or would you like to take a ride to the station?"

***

"I sense you're not satisfied with the karma the people who've betrayed you are receiving," Lou said while sitting with his feet propped up on a large oak wood desk in what appeared to be a doctor's office.

"Lou, how many times do I have to tell you I'm not thinking about revenge? I just wanna move on with my life," Mecca replied, trying to sound sincere as she paced the office, staring at the paintings on the walls. She would say whatever she needed to say to Lou for him to release his hold on her and let her out of the hospital. Intrigued by the paintings, she skipped right by some, while others she stared at a little longer. Some of them, Mecca realized, were of her as a baby, her at eight, then her as a teenager, and finally there was a painting of her as the adult she was.

"Mecca, Mecca, my dear Mecca. Just how am I supposed to believe that after all you have seen and know about your so-called friends and family? That you just forgave and forgot?" Lou asked, sitting up, with his feet on the black carpeted floor.

For a moment, she stood in front of the painting of her at eight, hiding under a bed. "I've always been a grateful person, and now that I have a second chance at life, I want to show my gratitude. And you're just gonna have to take my word for it."

Lou walked over to Mecca. Standing next to her, he stared at the painting. He shook his head before saying, "Childhood is a golden age for mankind. So innocent and full of misunderstanding of this cruel world. To think it was Sigmund Freud who said that childhood is a time of uninterrupted bliss. Don't you wish you could have it back, Mecca?"

Suddenly, her dream state switched to the painting on the wall. Eight-year-old Mecca remembered hiding under the bed, with tears running down her face. She looked back and forth at her mother's and father's eyes, which held fear. Their voices were muffled due to the tape around them. Two men with guns barked menacingly at her father, while her mother cried.

The words the men said couldn't be heard in the dream. One of them removed the tape from around her father's mouth and was talking intimately with him. For the first time in her eight years she saw fear on her father's face. She remembered him as a fearless man who would stand up to anyone. He was their *protector, their hero. No one messed with her or her mother because they were Bobby Blast's family.*

Her father's fear heightened hers. Seeing the tears in her mother's eyes made her cry even more. She hated to see her mother cry. She could still remember the first time she saw it, back when Mommy and Daddy were arguing and her father stormed out of the apartment, yelling that he would never come back. Mecca cried as she lay in bed with her mother, until the middle of the night, when she felt her father hug both of them. She heard his voice mumble, "I love you. I will never leave y'all."

Then the only sound Mecca heard in the dream was the gunshots that took her mother's and father's life. Little Mecca stayed under the bed, and the two men left. She heard the door slam, then the footsteps. It took a while for her to look out from under the bed when a person's black, shiny shoes and the hem of his long trench coat came into view. She knew who it was. Then his face appeared, and he stretched out his hand.

"Come out from under the bed, Mecca. I will protect you. I will never leave."

Mecca awoke from the dream as the sun shined through the blinds over the hospital window. The rays beamed in between the slats, making lines of long triangular light appear across the walls of the room and on the bed. For a moment, she looked at the print of her feet under the white sheets.

Slowly, she pulled the sheets off of her body and placed her feet on the cold tiled floor. Instantly, she noticed the metal walker in front of a bedside table.

Taking hold of it, she stood slowly. Her first steps after lying in bed almost six months were shaky and wobbly. Her legs responded slowly as she took baby steps, eventually moving quicker toward the window. Parting the blinds, she stared out at the sunny Brooklyn streets and smiled.

"Mecca?" The voice made her turn and face the door. Ruby stood next to Karmen, who covered her mouth in shock. Her eyes watered, just as Ruby's did. The smile left Mecca's face, and she turned to stare back out at the Brooklyn scenery. Her only thought as she looked at the familiar streets was a simple one. These streets are mine.

Chapter Twenty-nine

For they eat the bread of wickedness,
and drink the wine of violence.
—Proverbs 4:16

Daphne hired five trusted women among Donovan's relatives to bag up pounds of weed. She instructed them to put the different types of exotic weed in small glass jars, small twenty-dollar bags, and sandwich bags, which she would sell as weight broken down into quarters, ounces, and halves. After showing Ruby to a furnished brownstone apartment in the Clinton Hill section of Brooklyn, she drove her to a gutted, abandoned store in Crown Heights.

"I bought this place six months ago," Daphne told her as they stood on the sidewalk, observing the bodega with its dirty yellow sign.

"The money clean?" Ruby asked with her hands in her black Enyce velour jacket.

"Of course. You know the feds still watching."

Both women entered the store after Daphne opened it up. Ruby looked around at the dusty interior. With nothing special standing out, it appeared to be an average bodega, which almost every corner in New York City's neighborhoods had. Taking another step, Daphne crushed glass under her foot.

"With your friend Karmen working here, it will look like any other bodega."

Within a month, the store had been up and running. Karmen had two of her sisters, Maria and Tina, help her run the place. They quickly got a lot of business. Guys in Crown Heights began to frequent the store just to try to kick it with the three Puerto Rican cuties that worked there. Karmen was kind to all the guys and was flattered by their compliments, but she gave none of them the time of day. Her sisters were another story. Not only did they flirt with the guys, but they even left the store at times for quickies in a guy's car or apartment.

Karmen scolded them about their activities, but she knew it fell on deaf ears. She realized they would have to learn how to deal with the opposite sex the way she did. Eventually, she thought, they would get burnt out spreading their legs for everyone that paid attention to them, leaving them with sore pussies and broke pockets. Karmen knew she had to pay attention to business and also the illegal business being run out of the store, in the back. Ruby gave Karmen bagged-up weed to sell with these instructions.

"A person has to buy something like potato chips or a twenty-five-cent juice if they want some weed. Believe me, they will do it! This is some high-quality shit, better than any other spot in Brooklyn. I won't have a lot of it in the store at one time, but before you run out, always call this number," Ruby had instructed, handing her a small white card. "Just say, 'Wassup, shorty? You coming over?' and somebody will bring the next batch."

In no time, the word spread that the store in Crown Heights had some of the best smoke in town. Karmen and her sisters were enjoying the money they were making. The more money Ruby made, the more money she paid Karmen and her sisters, who did little with their money but shop for clothes and jewelry.

"Stack your money. There will always be rainy days ahead," Ruby had informed Karmen one day. Karmen knew that she was referring to her possibly going to jail. Karmen hated to think of that, and she really thought that the day would never come. It was just weed, but the thought of those homicide detectives still bothered her in the back of her mind. The cops found out from the landlord that her boyfriend, Kaheem, was killed in an apartment that was leased in her name, and right after the murder she moved.

"I couldn't sleep there anymore. It reminded me of him," Karmen cried. However, what the cops did not know was that her tears were from fear of them thinking she had something to do with the murders, and were not for her dead boyfriend.

"Where were you?" one of them asked while sitting on a wooden stool in her kitchen.

"I was at a friend's house in East New York," she lied as the scene played in her mind. She hadn't actually witnessed the murder. Shamel had ordered her to wait outside while he took care of his cousins, who were snakes. Murder, Karmen felt, Kaheem and Born deserved.

"Who might that friend be? Can that friend verify that?" the other cop grunted.

"She is in a hospital. She can't talk at this point," Karmen replied, referring to Mecca.

The cops finally left the apartment, telling her that they would more than likely be back to talk to her and giving her their cards, with the usual, "If you find out anything that will bring the killers to Darnell, give us a ring."

"I'll definitely do that."

Karmen figured they wouldn't get anything. Shamel was dead, and the only other person that knew about it was Mecca, and she couldn't talk. Even if she could, Karmen doubted she would talk to the cops about it. Then she figured that, hopefully, that bullet to the head had taken her memory. She was damn lucky that that bullet had only cracked her skull, just barely grazing her brain.

Still, she was shocked when they entered Mecca's room and saw her standing at the window with the aid of a walker. It seemed like a miracle to her. For months now, Mecca had lain in a coma, only to come out of it and not talk or move out of the bed. The doctors said that she wasn't paralyzed, that it was like a person coming out of a mild stroke, and that it would take time for the brain to recuperate from the trauma.

But she was still beautiful. Her hair grew back from when the doctors cut it to operate, but it wasn't long like it used to be. Her skin was no longer too pale and had gained some of its natural color back. Now all she had to do was gain her weight back and the old Mecca would emerge.

Still, this was the hardest time. During the following weeks, Mecca went through physical and speech therapy. She quickly got her swagger back, and though she talked, it was slow and low. Most of the time, she barely talked; she just glared at people. Karmen could swear that every time Mecca looked at her and Ruby, there was a look of anger or hate in her eyes. It was like she wanted to lash out, but something was holding her back. When Karmen brought it up to Ruby, she waved it off.

"She's just stressed and frustrated. That therapy could stress a person out. Can you imagine being a grown person having to learn how to walk and talk again like you're a baby?" Ruby tried to explain to Karmen so that she could understand. Though it made sense to Karmen, the look still left her shaken.

"Watch. The Mecca we know will be back. Did you hear about Tah Gunz?" Ruby asked as she drove her Benz through Manhattan traffic after a day of shopping for clothes with Karmen.

"Yeah, they say he in a wheelchair. That's messed up that Tamika got caught in the middle of that," Karmen replied, knowing that Ruby had never seen Tah face-to-face and couldn't wait to get her hands on him.

"Good for his ass," she growled, "and that little bitch Tamika had it coming too."

Looking over at Ruby, Karmen saw the same facial expression on her face that Mecca had had when she looked at her and her aunt. What was it?

"I have to make a stop uptown before we head back to Brooklyn," Ruby said, snapping Karmen out of her thoughts, but another quickly came to bother her. Now that Mecca could talk, would those cops question her about her alibi the night Kaheem got killed? All Karmen could do was hope Mecca didn't remember, or was she still the same Mecca before she got shot?

Thirteen years ago Alejandro Torres was a thirty-five-year-old Dominican with a medium build. At the time, he was a middleman on the Harlem drug scene. Now forty-eight and weighing close to three hundred pounds, he was an ex-convict fresh off a five-year bid for the sale of a kilo of cocaine to an undercover narcotics cop. His once curly black hair was now gray and cut short. His youthful appearance had gone, leaving a man with a deeply lined face who looked older than forty-eight years.

His Bronx parole officer had explained the conditions of his parole when he was released. The one rule that made him a loner on the streets was not to associate with known criminals or convicted felons. All his associates were criminals, and most were convicted felons. So on any given day, you could spot Alejandro in his everyday attire of Sergio Tacchini sweats suits, either playing dominoes in front of a bodega in the South Bronx or sitting on a park bench, feeding pigeons and ducks in a Central Park pond.

Today, though, Alejandro was in Central Park, lighting a cigar before he began feeding the pigeons. Suddenly a whole flock descended in front of the bench. He looked up from lighting his cigar and saw a black woman throwing down pieces of bread. The shades on her face hid her eyes, but he could tell she was a pretty dark brown lady from her profile.

"For a minute, I thought they were gonna come snatch the bread crumbs out of my hand," Alejandro said.

The woman simply smiled. Her sweat suit couldn't hide her firm, pointed breasts or her shapely body. During those five years in jail, Alejandro had collected a lot of porno magazines, and his favorites were the ones that featured thick black women. This stranger reminded him of one of those fantasies.

"I like the ducks better. They don't fly in crowds like these guys," Alejandro continued, trying to strike up a conversation with the woman.

"And they definitely don't bite the hands that feed them. Right, Al?" the woman said after looking at her Jacob watch. Her tone had a bite to it, which caught him off guard.

Alejandro stared at the woman quizzically, wondering how she knew his name. Since she had called him Al, she had to have known him for many years. Yet the woman didn't look familiar to him. It was the large shades that covered most of her face.

"If you're the police, there is no reason for you to be following me. I've been clean since I've been home. I'm done with the streets."

The woman took note of how well he spoke English now and laughed before pulling out a handgun with a silencer. Then she removed her shades. Alejandro thought he was looking at a ghost.

"I thought you had a . . ."

"Life sentence?" The woman completed the sentence for him.

Alejandro sighed, then proceeded to finish feeding the pigeons. He accepted the fact that she was there for one reason. Revenge. He realized that she must have gotten her sentence thrown out on appeal. Trying to show a brave face, he spoke to her with a surrendering tone.

"Ruby, so many years have gone by. I'm out of the game now. Why don't you let bygones be bygones?"

"I was straight up with you, but you tried to have me killed, like I would rat you out one day. I will never be a rat," Ruby answered.

"How did you find me?"

"I know people in high places," Ruby replied.

Alejandro had no idea that his parole officer, a black woman he sometimes flirted with, was the sister of Daphne's older sister, who had a different mother. In 1998 she became a parole officer after marrying a corrections officer who encouraged her to get into law enforcement. One thing she didn't want to be was a cop, so she chose parole so that she could help criminals stay out of jail by helping them attain employment and stay out of trouble. She was known to parolees as "the people's PO."

Daphne had convinced her sister to give her Alejandro's information by telling her that Alejandro was a friend of Donovan's whom she was trying to get in contact with. Daphne lied and told her that he gave Donovan a good deal on his first car, and she wanted to see if he was still in the car business. Her sister was reluctant because she could lose her job by divulging such sensitive information. Besides all that, it was against the law.

"You're about to visit that high place," Ruby said to him just before squeezing the trigger, sending bullets into Alejandro's chest.

He fell from the bench in a bloody heap, causing the pigeons to scatter from his sudden movement. She slipped away as the birds flew over her head, and no one in the area witnessed anything. Ruby walked out of the park to where Karmen was sitting, waiting for her in the Benz. When she reached the car, she smiled.

"Nothing like a walk in the park to get your blood flowing," Ruby said with a smile as they pulled off. She was cool with the way everything went, and was even happier to learn that Mecca was getting discharged from the hospital the next day.

Mecca found it hilarious that Lou was dressed in plaid pants, white patent leather shoes, and a bright yellow sweater.

"Church?" Mecca asked, surprised.

"Why are you surprised that I said church?" Lou paused from tapping a golf ball into a paper cup to stare at Mecca's back while she stared at a painting of herself as teenager, wearing big gold door-knocker earrings, a small rope chain around her neck, and a green Gap sweat suit.

"Because you're like a demon or something. The devil, right?" Mecca turned her head, looking at him with a grin.

"If I'm the devil, then what are you, Mecca?"

"I believe in God," she answered.

"And I don't?" Lou asked. "The devil does evil deeds, as you were taught. So what do you call selling drugs, killing other humans, stealing, extorting, and all the other commandments that you violated?"

Mecca sucked her teeth and waved Lou off. "Heard it all before, Lou. It's overrated now. I'm not the church-going type, anyway. I can pray at home."

"Prayer means nothing if after you pray, you go out and do the evil deeds again that you asked forgiveness for. Are you that shallow, Mecca?"

Mecca ignored Lou and looked back at the painting of herself in her teens. Then her dream switched from Lou's office to her and her former best friend, Dawn, hanging out at the Albee Square Mall in downtown Brooklyn. They were dressed stylishly eighties as they roamed the crowded mall. Then Mecca came in eye contact with a girl who, she'd noticed, had been staring at her since she and Dawn entered the mall. For some reason, every time they would cross paths during their two hours in the mall, the hazel-eyed girl would glare at her as if she knew her.

"Why is that bitch down your throat?" Dawn asked, noticing the girl staring at Mecca.

Mecca knew it couldn't be jealousy. The girl was dressed twice as nice. She saw the girl's jewelry and knew she couldn't compete with this strange girl, and she had to admit the girl was pretty. So what was her problem? Oddly, the girl would then turn away and walk off with an older girl that looked like her sister or mother.

When she and Dawn left the mall, they spotted the girl. Mecca couldn't tell if the girl was her age or older, but if she guessed, the girl was older. Again, the strange girl glared at Mecca as she and the other woman entered a burgundy Jeep Wrangler. Mecca couldn't read the look, so she simply watched the girl take off a Louis Vuitton coat, place it in the Jeep's backseat, get in, and take one more look at her as the driver pulled off.

"Girl, I know you ain't get another chick's man to like you like that bitch we had to cut," Dawn blurted.

"Can't help it if I'm beautiful. It ain't my fault." Mecca grinned.

A week later Mecca was watching TV in the Coney Island apartment she lived in with her aunt. A woman's face flashed across the screen while the news reporter was talking about a large drug bust in Bed-Stuy. She was sure the woman's face was that of the girl she'd seen at the mall. It just had to be her. Those piercing eyes, she recognized. By the time Mecca turned the TV up, the report of the bust was over. Then his face appeared on the screen. It was the guy with the leather trench coat and neat Afro. He smiled.

Mecca awoke in her queen-sized bed. She looked around the spacious bedroom with all the "welcome home" balloons, cards, and flowers spread around. Just then she remembered she was at Ruby's brownstone apartment. She got up, washed, ate a bowl of Cinnamon Toast Crunch cereal, and dressed.

Realizing that Ruby wasn't there, Mecca decided that she would take Lou up on his advice and go to church. At least that was what she put on the letter she placed on the refrigerator. Mecca had other plans.

Chapter Thirty

If you seek her as silver, and search for her as for hidden treasures, then you will understand the fear of the Lord and find the knowledge of God.

—Proverbs 2:4–5

When Ruby introduced Daphne to Mecca, Mecca's heart skipped a beat when she saw her eyes. She could not believe how much her eyes resembled the girl's in her dream. Those same penetrating hazel eyes. Mecca wondered what the significance of it all was. Who was she? She could not remember her when she was a teenager; she never saw that girl in her life. But those eyes! Mecca simply stared at Daphne as she smiled, a beautiful display of even white teeth. It was Daphne's smile that made Mecca feel as if she was a kind, cool person who had an inviting personality. She found Daphne's voice soothing and easy. Not loud and ghetto, but confident, with a swagger to her, which made Mecca begin to like her.

Over a soul food dinner that Ruby and Daphne had cooked, Daphne told Mecca all about herself. Mecca could tell she wasn't telling everything, but Mecca respected that. You never put all your cards on the table. Always be mysterious; keep people guessing and off balance. That was what she had learned from her life in the game. When people had you figured out, then they began to plot and scheme how to remove you. When you were mysterious, they didn't know how to plot on you.

Yet Mecca liked the fact that Daphne was loyal and a hustler. Qualities she wished everyone around her could have. Still, she would never put her full trust in anyone again. At the same time, Daphne grew fond of Mecca. She reminded her of herself. She could tell that she listened more than she talked, and she also noticed that Mecca was very observant. Mecca wouldn't open up to her, and like Mecca, Daphne respected her for that. She knew you had to feel a person out, measure them to see what they were fit for. A lot of people put on acts like they were fit for the game, but when things got bad, people put their tail between their legs like scared dogs.

Daphne was a good reader of people, but she couldn't read the look in Mecca's eyes. Especially when she looked at her aunt Ruby and Karmen. She had not known Mecca long enough to read the gaze, but her instinct told her something was not right. Still, the women bonded. They had the same taste in style. Daphne put micro braids in Mecca's hair so her real hair could grow quickly. The scar from her operations was barely visible and was covered by the braids.

One afternoon, as they drove through Manhattan after they ate at a downtown restaurant, the three women silently stared at Ground Zero, where the World Trade Center used to be. They were in their own thoughts at what they were seeing.

Thinking to herself, Mecca realized that in the few months she'd been in a coma, the world had changed quickly. Daphne simply thought about how crazy it must have been for the people who got caught in that mess. Ruby realized that was why the price of weight went so high and there were so many cops. Bin Laden got shit hot!

Daphne showed Mecca her restaurant, gave her a tour, and then drove over to Ruby's grocery store that Karmen ran. Once in the store, she noticed the look again when Mecca saw Karmen behind the bulletproof glass Ruby had installed. Ruby knew that the stickup men would think the spot was sweet, being that it was run by young women, so she wanted Karmen and her sisters to feel secure. Also it would give Karmen time to toss the stash of weed in a secret compartment under the cash register that led to a barrel of acid in the basement. If the cops raided, there would be no evidence.

"Hey, Mecca!" Karmen said excitedly, coming from behind the bulletproof glass.

"What's up, Karmen?" Mecca simply nodded with a forced smile.

Karmen and Ruby showed Mecca the store and how the whole operation was set up.

"Weed is really poppin' now, Mecca. It's like crack in the eighties," Ruby told her.

"It's cheaper, and you don't get a lot of time in jail," Karmen added.

"That's what's up," Mecca responded but was really thinking how she wanted to put both their asses in a casket.

After the tour of the store, Ruby and Daphne surprised Mecca by taking her to a Queens car lot. As soon as they walked in the showroom, a tall, tanned white man in an expensive suit walked up to Daphne with a hug and a smile.

"Daphne, I was expecting you yesterday. Everything is ready. Here are the keys." He handed the keys to Daphne, who then turned and handed them to a confused Mecca.

"On behalf of me and Ruby, welcome home!" Daphne said.

"What are you talking about, Daphne?" Mecca asked.

"Let's show her," Ruby chimed. They walked out into the lot and pointed to a silver, fully equipped 4.6 Range Rover.

"It's yours, baby!" Ruby pointed to the truck. Mecca loved it, and immediately, she climbed in the driver's seat, took in the smell of the black leather interior, and scanned the features.

"You ready to pull out?" Daphne asked from the passenger-side window.

"I think so."

"I'll ride with you just in case. Ruby, drive my car," Daphne said as she threw the keys. "I'm riding with Mecca."

At first Mecca drove slowly and cautiously. Then the feeling of familiarity set in, and she shed the nervous feeling and cruised to the sounds of Jay-Z's *The Blueprint* CD. Daphne looked at Mecca's expression and smiled. Her spirits seemed to be up, but Daphne knew there was something she had hidden deep within her soul, something she wanted to let out, but she seemed not to have anyone she could trust. That made her confused because in prison, Ruby would be elated to receive visits and letters from her niece. They seemed to have a sisterly relationship. Daphne knew that Ruby took her in after Mecca's parents were killed and raised her like her own. So why the look of scorn? Daphne knew she would have to get to the bottom of this to learn more about her new friend Mecca.

Later that night, while Ruby and Daphne went to a WNBA game at Madison Square Garden, Daphne's restaurant was robbed by two armed, masked men. Marley's sister was closing the place when someone placed something hard against her back.

"What you gonna do is open the place and take us to the safe. If not, you die here," the voice said in a skin-crawling, menacing grunt. She did as she was told. Marley's sister, Andrea, found it kind of strange that the men knew exactly where the safe was and where they had stashed some weed. In no more than five minutes, the two robbers left with two pounds of weed and fifty grand in cash.

Still shaken from the ordeal, Andrea locked the door from the inside, sat on the floor by the cash register, and called Daphne. Sitting courtside, Daphne felt her phone vibrate on her hip.

"Hello?" she yelled.

"Da . . . Da . . ." Andrea stuttered.

Daphne covered one of her ears. "Hello? Who's this?"

"Daphne, it's Drea!" she managed to yell.

"Drea? What's up?"

"I just got robbed!" she cried. Daphne did not hear her clearly and asked her again. This time, she heard every word.

"I'm on my way, Drea. Don't go nowhere!"

"You can't front, Lou. I'm doing good, despite the fact that they didn't receive their karma for what they did to me," Mecca said while they walked through a children's ward at a hospital. Glancing in each room, Mecca saw children suffering from various ailments and injuries. They stared at Mecca as they walked by, reminding her of the hazel-eyed girl she saw in the mall.

"So, all the time your aunt did in jail, you don't consider that a consequence of her acts?" Lou asked, checking the security guard uniform he wore.

"Yeah, I guess so." Mecca shrugged.

"And Karmen has her own problems. Her life isn't peaches and cream, and she is playing with fire by what she is doing

right now," Lou said as he walked into a room where a doctor was standing, holding a long needle filled with clear liquid. The sight of it simply frightened Mecca.

"What is he going to do with that?" She looked at Lou quizzically. Lou had a smile on his face.

"Don't worry. You won't feel a thing. You're dreaming, Mecca." The doctor approached her and took a firm hold on her arm. She tried to pull back, but she couldn't move as Lou held her tightly from behind.

"Mecca," he said, "trust me, it won't hurt. Have I ever lied to you?"

"I don't want no needle, Lou. I'm not sick!"

"It's just a truth serum. It will be quick."

He held the needle up before her face and pressed on the plunger, watching as the liquid squirted out of the sharp tip. The pinch of the needle caused her dream to switch back to her teens. She was sitting in Gershwin Park with Dawn, watching a basketball game between a Brownsville and an East New York team. They were cheering for their neighborhood team when a voice from behind startled her.

"Take the necklace and watch off. Don't turn around, or I'll clap you."

Mecca felt the gun against her back. From the corner of her eye she saw Dawn reach over to her and remove the earrings and necklace. Confusion spread in her mind as to why Dawn was helping them rob her.

"You always thought you was all that," she said with a smile.

Then Mecca heard a shot. She ducked as the crowd scrambled and screams could be heard everywhere. When she got up, Lou stood in front of her with a spent casing in his hand. He looked at the bullet and simply said, "A few more inches to the left and it would have pierced your brain. Don't play with death, Mecca."

Mecca awoke with Ruby shaking her arm.

"Mecca, get up, girl. You got to see the doctor today."

"What time is it?" Wiping the cold from her eyes, she yawned and responded in her groggy morning voice. Ruby took a quick glimpse at her watch.

"It's nine o'clock in the morning. C'mon. Your appointment is at nine thirty. Whoever this guy Lou is you're dreaming about must got some good sex," Ruby continued as she walked out of the room.

Mecca was shocked.

The very same morning, Karmen opened up the store, and he walked in. He wore a black, sleeveless Sean John sweater over a white, short-sleeved, collared shirt. Karmen stared at his black jeans from behind, admiring his physique. He was one of the finest men she had seen in a long time. His creamy complexion was smooth and flawless; his jet-black hair was silky and curly, with a sharp line up from his forehead to his five o'clock shadow. His eyes were a pretty brown, and when he approached the glass partition, his voice was harmoniously deep and sexy.

"Do you have any eggnog?" Miguel Sanchez asked. Karmen snapped out of her infatuated daze and answered.

"Yeah, all the way in the back. I'll show you."

She quickly came from behind the glass and walked Miguel to the freezer, making sure she walked in front of him so he could get a glimpse of her voluptuous measurements. It didn't take long for him to assess Karmen's goods. Her blue denim jeans hugged her frame like a leotard on a ballet dancer.

Opening the freezer, she grabbed the eggnog and turned to hand it to him. She almost bumped into him as they came face-to-face. She could smell his cologne, and Karmen felt herself become wet between her thighs. His six feet made his chest come almost near her face, and she could see he was in good shape.

"I'm sorry," he said, stepping back and taking the eggnog.

"It's nothing." She blushed.

She knew she had to say something to him. She would kick herself in the ass if she let him get away. That was her motto in life. "Don't let a good opportunity pass, because you will regret it." The last time a man made her wet just by the way he looked was a long time ago, and he was no longer alive. She had to have this one.

"Are you from around here?" she asked as she was walking back toward the door that led behind the counter.

"Yes, I am. I just returned from overseas, playing basketball," he replied. "By the way, my name is Miguel."

"I'm Karmen."

She was satisfied, she had accomplished her goal. She got him to stay awhile and talk. She learned that he was originally from the Bronx. He was of Panamanian descent, and he lived by himself in an apartment around the corner from the store.

"I heard a lot about this store," he said, giving her a grin.

"Yeah? What have you heard?" Karmen asked curiously. She hoped that he wasn't one of those guys who looked down on a woman for hustling to get a dollar by any means except for degrading herself by selling her body. Though, Karmen didn't knock the hustle.

Miguel's smile grew wider. "I heard good things, and I'm wondering if I can get a sample." His dimples made her melt. She gave him a jar of the best weed they had in the store. "When do you get off of work?"

"Later tonight," she answered.

"Cool. Here's my address. . . ."

Later that night the two of them couldn't wait to rip each other's clothes off in Miguel's simply decorated apartment. They didn't even make it to his bed when they kissed each other passionately, removing their clothing at the same time, stopping only to pull shirts over their heads. Karmen rubbed his ripped abdomen and felt the harness of his athletic body. He picked her up off her feet, kissing her while she guided his thick manhood inside her creamy walls.

"Ay, Poppy!" she moaned as he put her back against a small closet door and slowly moved his hips, feeling the warmth of her insides grip his shaft. The tightness made him grit his teeth. He walked over to a couch, still holding her, and then laid her on her back, pushing himself deeper in her middle.

"Shit, Miguel! I'm coming, baby!" Her juices soaked his pole and pubic hairs. She scratched his back as orgasm after orgasm pulsed through her body.

In every position from doggy style to her riding him, she felt as if she no longer owned her body. It was his to do as he pleased. To spice up the sex, Karmen even let him give her anal pleasure, which she hollered all the way through. After three ejaculations from him and countless orgasms from her, they finally rested in each other's arms on the carpeted living-room floor, with Miguel staring at the ceiling fan.

"Do you have a girlfriend?" Karmen asked while catching her breath.

"No. Why?"

Karmen smiled. "You do now."

Chapter Thirty-one

With her enticing speech she caused him to yield, with her flattering lips she seduced him.
—Proverbs 7:21

"Has that ever happened before, Daphne?"

"Not since I been home. The thing is, if it were a random robbery, I would take the loss. But these people knew exactly where the stuff was at," Daphne replied angrily as she and Ruby sat at Ruby's kitchen table, discussing the holdup. Daphne was convinced it wasn't Andrea who had set it up, because when she arrived at the restaurant, Andrea was too shaken for it to be an act. Plus she trusted her. Andrea was extremely loyal to Daphne due to Daphne's loyalty to her brother and family. After seeing Andrea like that, Daphne told her to take off as long as she needed, while she got to the bottom of things.

Immediately word went out around Crown Heights that whoever had information on who pulled the heist would get a hefty reward. The loss was nothing to Daphne; however, it was a matter of principle. A lesson had to be taught.

"Can you think of anybody who would do this? A past enemy or jealous hater that would take it there?" Ruby asked, sipping a hot cup of coffee. Her question reminded Daphne of a lesson Marley had always reminded her of when he said, "There are no friends in the game, baby. Matters of the heart have no place with matters of greed." Once again, Daphne had a feeling that his words would prove prophetic.

"None that I can think of."

Mecca walked in, sliding her slippers across the tiled kitchen floor, wearing a black silk two-piece pajama set and scarf on her head. Instantly, both Ruby and Daphne stopped discussing the robbery.

"Wassup, Mecca?" Daphne asked, happy to see her. "What you doing tonight, girl? You got to go out on the town and hit a club with me! You with it?"

Mecca thought about her invite while looking in the cupboard for a box of cereal. Then, as if someone had cut a light on in Mecca's head, she turned and smiled. "Yeah, let's do it."

That night, while Mecca and Daphne went to the club, Ruby drove over to Crown Heights to drop off a package to Karmen at the store. Listening to Heather Headley's voice bang through the car's sound system, Ruby was in deep thought about the robbery of Daphne's restaurant. The whole thing reminded her of the time her spots in Brownsville were being robbed daily. At one time, she thought it was just random, but she found out it was Stone.

The last thing Ruby wanted to think was that Daphne could be behind the setup. Ruby knew you couldn't control the way someone might think, but if you took control of the situation, then you could persuade people to see things your way. She knew that she had to find out who was behind the robbery, for her sake and Daphne's. If Daphne started showing any signs of mistrust toward Ruby, she would act first before Daphne made a move. Damn! It was never a smooth ride in the game.

Ruby walked in the store with a plastic shopping bag containing the package of weed Karmen called for. The store was unusually empty, and Karmen stood behind the glass partition with a strange look on her face. Her sisters weren't chatting in front of the store with a group of guys, as was their normal routine, nor were they standing around inside the store, watching the small TV they had installed behind the cold-meat counter.

The sound of a gun being cocked was all she heard, followed by, "You want to drop the bag and put your hands up, and don't try to be a superhero, or you'll end up super dead."

Ruby did as she was told.

"Turn around," the voice commanded.

Slowly, Ruby turned around, and she saw Karmen being led out from behind the counter by a man in a black mask, leather peacoat, holding a shotgun to her back. Out the side of her eye, she saw Karmen's two sisters being brought out from the back of the store by another masked man, holding what looked like an AK-47.

"Boss lady, you gonna open up the safe in the back and give us what we came for," the guy holding the gun to Ruby said in a low growl.

Listening carefully, she tried to recognize the voice, but after thirteen years of being off the streets, how could she? Knowing where the safe was hidden was an indication that these guys knew either her, Karmen, or her sisters. They had to know them, because only they knew there was a safe hidden inside one of the freezers, covered by juices and milk. Ruby didn't believe in coincidences. First, Daphne's restaurant, then the store. She ruled out Karmen because she knew nothing about Daphne's restaurant. *Who are these people?* she wondered as she walked to the safe.

As Ruby walked, she mumbled to the guy, "I'll pay you double the amount you're getting out of this if you tell me who sent you."

The guy chuckled and then put the gun to her ear. "Listen, bitch, live or die. That's the only options 'round here right now."

Since Ruby just got out of jail, she was nervous about carrying guns. She wished she had hers on her now. These guys didn't even bother searching her. Just another indication that this was an inside job.

When it was over, the guys made out of the store with ten thousand dollars' worth of weed that Ruby had in her bag and thirty thousand in cash from the safe. Not to mention the thousand in the cash register from the sale of groceries. Karmen and her sisters were crying and shaken up, just as Andrea was. Ruby was infuriated.

"Y'all stop bitching! You're alive! Go home and sleep it off. I'll call you tomorrow, Karmen."

Walking out of the store, Ruby hopped into her whip and sped off. She didn't know where she was driving to; she just drove in deep thought. She guessed it was a natural instinct of hers from the time she ruled the rugged streets she grew up on, but her aimless driving had her wind up in her native Brownsville.

When she looked at the street signs that read Rockaway Avenue and Livonia Avenue, she asked herself, *What am I doing here?* She knew she would need to buy an arsenal, and what better place to get something hot than Brownsville? Someone referred her to an apartment in the Brownsville Houses where a person could buy any kind of gun they wanted. That someone was Mo Blood.

Being back in Brownsville brought back so many memories for her. The thugs on the corners, the loud young girls on project benches, the kids in playgrounds, and the sight of police cruisers speeding down avenues reminded her of the good ole days.

When she entered the building, a blunt-smoking crew of young, do-rag- and oversized-clothes-wearing guys paused from their animated conversations about the hottest rapper out to stare lustfully, skeptically, and questionably at the thick, sexy Ruby in a pair of form-hugging jeans and a black and blue North Face. The Halle Berry haircut fit her facial features, but to some of the young cats, it spelled *dike*.

Ruby knocked on the door. The sound of music blasted from apartments. The familiar project hallway smelled of customary old urine, paint from a freshly painted elevator door, and burning garbage from the incinerator. Yes, the good ole days. A frail, shirtless teenager answered the door. Looking at him, Ruby thought he was probably five years old when she got locked up.

"What's good, ma?" the rotten-toothed kid asked, sticking his nappy head out of the door and looking around skeptically.

"I need some steel," Ruby stated.

"You police?" the kid asked.

Ruby smirked. "If I was, I would have been ran up in there. No, I'm not police. Ask an older person in that crib about Ruby from Langston Hughes."

Upon hearing the name, the kid's eyes lit up. Everyone in Brownsville had heard of the notorious female gangster Ruby, and everyone had heard she was back on the streets. He stepped back, holding the door open to invite her in.

"Yo, Mo!" the teen who answered the door yelled.

"Yo, what's up!" A tall, lanky guy entered the living room, looked at Ruby. He immediately recognized her from back in the days when he ran with Tah's stickup crew. He remembered they would stick up her spots, until Tah Gunz fell in love with her niece. She was a legend, but only in the eighties. Those days were gone. Mo Blood wondered what she was doing here. Did she know who he was?

"What you looking for, ma?" Mo asked, hiding his nervousness with a cocky appearance.

"I'm looking for some guns. I was told this is the spot."

Mo lit up a cigarette. Inhaled and then spoke. "And who told you that?"

"That's not here or there. Y'all got what I need or not?" Ruby replied with a cocky tone of her own. She knew she could have gone to Daphne to get guns, but her pride wouldn't let her depend on Daphne for everything. She was used to being independent and in charge. So she decided to get what she needed on her own accord.

"Any kind in particular?" Mo asked.

When the purchase was final, Ruby, with the help of Mo Blood and two other goons, carried two duffel bags down to her Benz. Mo Blood admired the car enviously and realized that she didn't waste any time doing her thing. Niggas been hustling for years and couldn't even cop a decent set of wheels. Ruby spent ten thousand in cash on two AK-47s, an AR-15, three .50-caliber Desert Eagles, and a .40-caliber handgun.

"If you're with it, I can get you the best weed in Brooklyn. My prices are good," Ruby told Mo before she got in the car.

"We'll talk. You got a way I can reach you?"

Ruby reached in the glove compartment, removed a pen, and wrote her cell phone number down. As she was handing the number to Mo, a man in a second-floor apartment had a camcorder aimed at both of them. Their every movement was captured and recorded on tape. He even caught her speeding off.

"I ain't never been that scared in my life, I swear," Karmen said as she sat in Ruby's living room, telling Mecca the details of the robbery, while Miguel sat beside her on a brown suede couch.

Mecca simply acted like she was listening enthusiastically, but she couldn't get how good-looking Miguel was out of her mind. Being in a coma and recovering from it had definitely put a dent in her sex life. And with so much on her mind, she hadn't had the time to think of a man's company. Yet seeing Miguel made all those feelings of wanting to be held and made love to by a strong man surface.

Even though she was lusting over Karmen's new boyfriend, Mecca didn't feel guilty. Images of Karmen and Shamel sleeping together kept entering her mind, and that made lusting over Miguel all the more justifiable. Now she was thinking of the challenge of getting him in bed.

Her glares didn't go unnoticed by Miguel, either. When he first laid eyes on her, he found it hard to believe that she had just come out of a coma after being shot in the head. She was absolutely beautiful. Yes, Karmen was, too, but in an "around-the-way girl" way. Mecca, on the other hand, had an aura of sexy classiness. When she looked at a person, it was as if she were staring into the person's soul. He admired her ability to listen more than she talked. He couldn't say that about Karmen: she babbled all day long about things that didn't interest him. Sure, the sex was good, but her personality became boring. She wasn't a challenge.

Mecca, on the other hand, reminded him of his mother. Same golden complexion, same sexy eyes. The graceful manner in which she walked and talked. At the same time, she wasn't a pushover. A man had to tread carefully with her. She reeked of independence.

"It's all part of the game, Karmen," Mecca said.

Karmen excused herself to go to the bathroom, while Mecca and Miguel remained in the living room. She pulled out a deck of cards from her pants pocket and looked at him. "Do you play tunk?"

"I'm the best," he bragged.

Mecca grinned. "How much money you got?"

Miguel returned the grin. "How much you willing to lose?"

"Oooh, cocky. There's nothing sexier than a confident man," she cooed.

"Likewise with a woman." Miguel gave her his sexy smile.

In that little exchange both of them knew they wanted each other. With money Ruby and Daphne had been giving her to do as she pleased, Mecca removed a stack from her pocket and held it up before his face.

'That's three stacks. I could afford to lose more, but I doubt I will. You be easy on yourself now," Mecca taunted.

Miguel smiled. He removed a small stack of bills from his wallet. "Not much cash, but I got this." He showed her his platinum Visa card. "I got an idea. Whoever wins the best of five, the loser treats to dinner."

"Y'all playing cards? What y'all playing?" Karmen asked as she entered the living room.

Mecca rolled her eyes. "It's a bet."

A week later Mecca snuck off to a Manhattan restaurant. The place was elegant and exquisite. It was definitely a place where the rich and famous dined. The menu was made up of Italian cuisine, and everything looked or sounded just as good.

After plates of veal Parmesan, pasta in a delicate cream sauce, a bottle of Krug champagne, and a conspiratorial plan to hang out again a few days later, Miguel told the maître d', "Check please. I'm paying by card."

"Why the truth serum, Lou?" Mecca asked while being strapped down by her wrists and ankles to a hospital gurney.

"It's self-explanatory, my dear." Lou, still wearing the security guard uniform, stood over her in the brightly lit room and smiled.

"Truth about what?" Mecca looked at him quizzically as she struggled with the restraints.

"About what you're up to. Do you think I am a fool, Mecca?"

"I swear, Lou, I don't know what you're talking about," Mecca whined in a pleading tone.

Lou leaned closer to her face and stared into her eyes. It felt as if his eyes pierced her flesh. What was he talking about? she wondered. Was it her lustful thoughts of Miguel? Or was he angered that she wouldn't discuss what she'd been doing while awake? Was Lou feeling left out? Then she realized that he knew only about things that happened, not what would happen, and her silence angered him.

"I thought you knew what was in my heart," she snapped.

"I do," Lou said, turning his face from hers. "Your intentions and actions sometimes conflict. That is human emotions."

Mecca smiled assumingly. "Lou, I've done nothing immoral. I will not lie to you. You have truly been a friend, and I know you care about my well-being."

Lou believed her. He nodded to the doctor, who administered the shot of truth serum. "Release her."

When Mecca's dream switched, she was lying naked on her bed in Ruby's old Hamptons home while gripping the sheets in ecstasy as her lover's face was buried between her thighs.

"Please don't stop," she moaned in euphoric pleasure.

He continued to please her orally, orgasm after orgasm. She felt heavenly as the tension and stresses of her life lifted from her body with every orgasmic release. She held his head as his tongue danced in and around her middle. He squeezed her bottom as she arched her back off the bed. It was too much for her, and she pulled away from his mouth. When his face came into view, she felt sick to her stomach. Tah Gunz smiled at her.

When Mecca came out of her sleep, she wiped her eyes, then stretched. She could feel her satin panties were soaked. Her wet dream was a signal that she needed a tune-up, and fast.

Chapter Thirty-two

A gracious woman retains honor,
but ruthless men retain riches.

— Proverbs 11:16

"The crazy thing about it is she doesn't know who I am."

"Still, be on point, though. She is a vicious broad."

Mo Blood pushed the wheelchair up a ramp in front of the project building and stopped before the elevator. Tah Gunz was paralyzed from the waist down after spending months in the hospital, recovering from bullets to his stomach that traveled to his spine. The doctors informed him he would be paralyzed for the rest of his life.

For the first two months in the chair, Tah was frustrated and depressed. He hated having to depend on family and the few friends he had to help him with the basic things, like using the bathroom, showering, and getting out of bed in the morning. He woke up every day still in disbelief at his condition. Then there was the responsibility of raising his son. With Tamika dead, it was now his time to be a full-time father. He felt helpless, wondering how he could raise his son when he could barely help himself.

After a while, Tah became accustomed to being in the chair and learned how to get up in the morning, climb in it and the tub. The city paid for the installment of bars in the bathroom to accommodate his condition.

He put the word out about who had done the deed after learning from one of Tamika's girlfriends where the guy Tamika had been seeing was from. The word he put out meant nothing to his homeboys. Unbeknownst to him, high-ranking Blood members had stripped him of his status. He lost points with the gang when word got out that he had shot Mecca and

Shamel out of jealousy. He was considered a sucker unworthy of general status.

"Yo, but the weed is official, my dude. We got all the spots in Brownsville beat," Mo boasted as they rode the pissy-smelling elevator up to the fifth floor of Tilden Projects. "We doing like ten Gs a day."

Despite the fact that Tah had lost his status, Mo still treated him with respect.

Mo Blood made sure Tah's appearance stayed up. He kept him in the latest gear and took him out to parties and clubs with him and the crew. Tah accepted his demotion in rank like night and day. It came and went. The guys he grew up with still treated him with respect. Who cared what some guys in jail that were never getting out thought? Brownsville still belonged to him and his crew.

"Nobody found out nothing about this dude from L.G.?" Tah asked as they entered the small apartment.

Though his crew still respected him, no one was going on a hunt for some guy that shot Tah. There was money to be made, and Tah shouldn't have been at Tamika's in the first place. What was the purpose of starting problems with a dude just trying to get some pussy from a girl that shouldn't have meant nothing to him? Pussy had no face; that had always been the code.

Not to crush his pride, Mo simply said, "Not yet. The homies in L.G. ain't really saying too much."

The sound of a cell phone ringing caught Mo's attention. It was his.

"What's poppin?" Mo blurted into the phone. Tah watched as Mo's expression changed from something the caller said. "What! When?" Mo roared. "I'm on my way now!" Mo slammed the phone shut and rushed to the door.

"What's the deal?" Tah asked.

Opening the door, Mo turned to Tah and answered, "Niggas ran up in my spot and robbed it."

Mo slammed the door shut, rushing off to Brownsville Houses.

***

Daphne's Jamaican restaurant was practically empty as she and Mecca sat at a table by the window, eating plates of spicy West Indian food. The more they spent time around each other, the closer they got. They truly adored each other. Ruby didn't mind, because she had a lot of things of her own going on, and to relieve her stress, she frequented lesbian hangouts for casual sex.

As tempting as it was, Ruby would not go near a man sexually. She knew what a piece of good dick could do for her. She had to think straight and sensible when it came to the game, and she did not need any emotional distractions. She wanted to remain in control at all times, and that was what the lesbian lifestyle afforded her. She was the dominatrix. Not to mention that she had an assortment of sex toys to play with also.

"No word on those robberies yet?" Mecca asked, sipping on a Kola Champagne.

Daphne sighed. "Nah. Not even a rumor."

Mecca still couldn't get over how much Daphne's eyes resembled those of the girl from her dreams. She still could not figure out why the girl in her dreams had stared at her as if she wanted to hurt her. Changing the subject, Mecca buried her head in her hands.

"I'm bored, Daphne. My aunt doesn't want me working or nothing. I'm used to ripping and running."

"You know your aunt still partly blames herself for what happened to you. So she is being protective, and I understand that," Daphne replied.

"So I'm supposed to just sit back and take an allowance from you and her? I sold the house in the Hamptons. I don't need an allowance."

Ruby hadn't argued with her when she informed her about selling the Hamptons villa. Mecca wanted no part of it. It reminded her of a bad time in her life, just like the projects she lived in when her parents were killed. That was the spot where Shamel was murdered. Even after finding out about his betrayal, it still hurt how everything went down. There was no possible way she could sleep in that house with the memories of Tah shooting her constantly on her mind. Selling it was the best thing to do.

"You know what you should do, Mecca?" Daphne asked, as if something suddenly came to mind.

Mecca looked on with anticipation.

"You should travel. Go everywhere. The islands, Africa, Paris. Just travel."

"By myself?"

"Girl, you need a man. Find yourself a good man and see the world," Daphne proclaimed.

Mecca knew she spoke from experience. She recalled the conversations they had had about Marley, Daphne's dead boyfriend, and all the traveling they had done together. The stories of their love life made her envious. Mecca wished she had a man like Marley to treat her like a princess and remembered that Shamel had treated her as if she were his one and only. But she knew now that he was a cheating dog. She watched as Daphne's attention wandered toward the window.

"You miss him, don't you?" she asked consolingly.

Daphne replied sullenly, "Like hell."

"Girl, you need you a man, too!" Mecca joked to bring cheer to the moment.

They both laughed.

"What do you think about Miguel?" Mecca asked.

"Girl, he is fine!" Daphne answered with a grin. "And I see the way he looks at you! Oh, yeah, and I see your looks, too. Let me find out."

Blushing, Mecca looked down at her food.

"Oh, no, you didn't, Mecca!" Daphne snorted.

"What?"

Daphne waived off. "That girl Karmen is a bird, anyway. Do you, ma!" Pausing for a moment, she looked at her with a serious expression. "Speaking of Karmen, let me ask you something. There's this look you give her every time you see her, I noticed. And the look isn't the one that says y'all have good history. What's up, Mecca?"

"Isn't it obvious I hate the bitch?"

There was no way Mecca would or could explain to Daphne seeing Karmen having sex with Shamel in a vision showed to her by Lou, the devil, or whoever he was. How would that sound? Yeah, I hate the bitch because a man in a vision showed me her fucking my dead boyfriend?

"She's an ass kisser. A flunky. I can't stand flunkies," Mecca answered.

Then Daphne stepped on dangerous territory when she asked, "Why do you give your aunt the same look?"

Mecca was stunned. After inhaling deeply, then exhaling, she replied, "It's long story. Let's take a ride to Coney Island."

That night, while Mecca and Miguel ate at a City Island restaurant, Mecca couldn't get the conversation she had earlier with Daphne on the Coney Island boardwalk out of her head. Men had stared at the two sexy sisters with the glittering diamond earrings, expensive designer clothes, and perfumes that gave the fishy-smelling beach a mixture of good and bad scents. Daphne was shocked and angered by what Mecca had revealed.

"On the visiting floor, she would sneak in the bathroom and fuck my man," Mecca had told her.

"She's into woman, though. At least that's what I thought," Daphne had murmured.

Still, Daphne couldn't understand why Ruby would do such a thing to her niece. As much as Ruby claimed to adore and love her niece, how could she backstab her like that? Now Daphne began to doubt Ruby's loyalty. She couldn't imagine how she would feel if one of her friends or family members had betrayed her like that with Marley.

"Mecca . . . Mecca!" Miguel snorted.

"Yeah."

"Where you at, ma? You were in a zone. You must have a lot on your mind."

"Let's go to your place and help me take my mind off of things." Mecca smiled.

"Check please!"

Later, as Gerald Levert's "My Kind of Love" played, Mecca and Miguel locked lips and tongue kissed passionately.

"God, I want you so bad," Miguel whispered as he lay in the bed, watching Mecca do a striptease out of her red lace thong and matching bra. Miguel couldn't believe how in shape she was after coming out of a coma. Her tight stomach went perfectly with her small waist and rounded hips. Her breasts were the perfect handful, with pointed nipples of a golden brown hue. She crawled between his legs, taking his stiff manhood in her soft hands, softly stroking him while giving him a seductive smile. "You're so beautiful," he mumbled.

"You are too," she replied seductively.

They began to kiss again. The taste of cinnamon-flavored toothpaste invaded Miguel's mouth as she straddled his stiffness and let herself down slowly. So many months without sex had made her vagina tight, and looking at his size, she knew she had to be easy. A sharp gasp slipped out of her lips as she slid down his pole. She rubbed his chest, biting her lip as she felt herself become filled with Miguel and a pleasant feeling. She couldn't believe how quickly she began to orgasm.

"Miguel, it feels so good," she moaned. He laid her on her back and explored her gorgeous body with his tongue. When his tongue introduced itself to her clit, she lost control.

She squeezed his head and tried to get up. It was too much, but Miguel held her down firmly and continued to please her. She felt so good, she thought she would faint. Once again, he entered her while she lay on her stomach. Miguel kissed the back of her neck, then nibbled on her ear as he stroked slowly, letting himself go deeper within her confines.

"I'm cumming, Miguel!" Mecca moaned as she released her cream all over Miguel's dick. Miguel also couldn't hold back any longer, and he felt his balls tighten, pushing the baby-making fluid through his shaft into Mecca. Afterward, they lay in each other's arms, exhausted and satisfied.

"I'm coming to see your first game," Mecca said while looking into his eyes.

"My first game is in Italy."

"I know, Miguel. I wanna travel with you."

When the hunger built within them again, they made love into the wee hours of the night, until they both fell asleep in each other's arms.

"Idle time is the devil's workshop."

"You should know,"' Mecca said sarcastically to Lou while she sat in his office lounge chair, watching him pace back and forth behind his desk.

"Ha-ha, very funny," he snorted. "On a serious note, this is a time to find out what your talents are. You ever thought about finishing school?"

"For what? I got enough money to live a comfortable life," she answered.

"Oh, I forgot you sold the villa. Money isn't everything, Mecca," Lou growled.

"It is when you come from nothing. And I don't just have money from the villa. I'm getting SSI from the state for the shooting."

"So that's it. Sit around, collect money, and do nothing? Sounds like heaven in the Bible. You do good on earth, then sit around in heaven, doing nothing forever."

"Take your frustrations out on someone else, Lou. I have heard these sarcastic Bible complaints before," Mecca retorted.

Lou cleared his throat. "Anyway, love . . ." Lou pointed at the wall. "Look at that picture."

Mecca did as she was told and turned to see what Lou was referring to. Her eyes went wide in shock as she looked at a picture of her and Miguel making love.

Then she awoke out of her sleep, staring at a sleeping Miguel. For some time she watched his soft breathing and smiled to herself. He was definitely a keeper.

Chapter Thirty-three

I will also laugh at your calamity;
I will mock when your terror comes.
                                        —Proverbs 1:26

Karmen knew the signs well; she's been through it before. When a man started messing with another woman, he started becoming distant. He started making excuses as to why he didn't call or why he stood you up. He became less talkative, and his mind always seemed to be somewhere else. She just wished it wasn't Miguel. For the first time in her life she thought she'd found a good, honest, loving man. He was everything a woman could ever want: sexy, successful, and good in bed.

Karmen knew the odds were against her. The ratio of men to women was ridiculous in her city and, she imagined, all over the world. Men were outnumbered at least ten to one, and that meant competition. Karmen wasn't about to get bent out of shape, lowering her self-esteem over a man. She would just confront him and tell him to keep it real. The truth of him messing with another woman would hurt, but it beat being lied to and treated like hand-me-down clothes.

She told herself over and over again that if he was messing with another woman, or several, for that matter, she would either have to step her game up and make him want her more or just walk away. She wished she had another option, because she didn't want to take the latter.

"Just tell him it's you or her. Let him feel like he's losing out. If you let a man feel as if you're in need of him, he will step all over you," Mecca explained while Karmen removed the micro braids out of her hair. Daphne was out of town, handling business, so Mecca had opted to go to Karmen's Bushwick apartment to get her hair done.

Talking to Karmen about her problem with Miguel made Mecca feel in control. She felt as if she had Karmen's emotions in her hands. She couldn't have been more elated about it. It made her secret affair with Miguel much more exciting. She couldn't wait to travel with him to Europe, where he was a star, to be seen in photos taken by paparazzi, and to send them back to Ruby, who would probably show Karmen. Mecca laughed inside.

"Anyway, what's up, Mecca? You trying to hit Speed up tonight? I'm putting my 'fuck 'em, girl' gear on and enjoying myself," Karmen uttered. Mecca knew it was a front. Women that were hurt usually tried to hide the pain by hanging out with the girls, getting drunk, and sometimes waking up hungover in some strange man's bed, feeling disgusted at themselves. To watch Karmen act a fool over her broken heart would be entertaining.

"Yeah, why not?"

Later, they showed up at Club Speed, fashionably late, of course, and Karmen had definitely thrown her "fuck 'em, girl" dress on.

As they danced with a couple of guys, Mecca quickly grew uninterested in dancing and went to the bar to have a shot of Belvedere. Karmen joined her and quickly made the night much more interesting. Shot after shot of various drinks were bought by men trying to leave the club with her, and she drank each one of them. Mecca even warned her about how much she was drinking.

"Karmen, you're overdosing on the liquor. Slow down, before you pass out."

"I can hold my liquor. Don't be such a party pooper. Enjoy yourself," Karmen responded in a drunken slur, which made Mecca want to slap her. Instead, Mecca shrugged and watched her dance with a bunch of different men, letting them grope on her. She took out her phone and put in a text message.

Minutes later she watched Karmen being led into the men's bathroom by two men. Mecca followed. Once inside, the two athletically built men led her to one of the stalls. Karmen lifted her dress up, and while one guy sat on the toilet, she took him in her mouth, while the other went in her from behind. No more than ten minutes into their X-rated action, the stall door flew open. Karmen was too drunk to even hear it. She kept on performing orally on one guy.

"Karmen, what the fuck!" Karmen stumbled to face the voice that had called out her name. She wiped the saliva from her mouth and smiled. Mecca stood behind him, shaking her head.

"Miguel, you came to join us?"

"C'mon, Karmen. You going home," Mecca said as she grabbed her by the hand and pulled her out of the stall.

After dropping her off, Miguel and Mecca drove to his apartment.

"Damn, I didn't know she was that type of girl, Mecca," Miguel said while driving Mecca's truck.

"Me neither," she lied.

"Well, at least I don't have to worry about breaking her heart any longer. I was definitely about to cut her off," Miguel said, shaking his head.

"And why were you going to do that?" Mecca asked to see if he would answer truthfully.

Miguel looked at her and smiled his sexy smile. "Because my heart belongs to someone else, and I'm about to show her how much of my heart, mind, and body she has."

"Wow, she must be a hell of a woman." Mecca continued to act as if she didn't know who he was talking about.

"You sure are one hell of a woman."

Mecca thought about the two hundred dollars she had paid to those two guys to take Karmen into the club bathroom and smiled before adding, "Yeah, I sure am a hell of a woman."

Karmen woke up the next day, in the afternoon, feeling like someone had run over her head with an eighteen-wheeler truck. Her mouth was dry as sand, and her jaw was sore, as well as her pussy. Lying on her stomach, she realized she was still dressed. When she lifted her head, she could see the vomit stain on her black satin sheets.

"Karmen, why are you still in bed? Ruby's been calling you all day, and you ain't answer the phone. She is pissed."

Her sister's loud voice made the pounding in her head worse. Karmen had to pee bad, so she got up and dragged herself to the bathroom, walking past her sister.

"We opened the store, anyway, so don't worry, but it sounds like you got more to worry about with Miguel. Tell me it ain't true!"

Karmen sat on the toilet with the door open and groggily asked, "Tell you what ain't true?"

Her sister appeared at the door of the bathroom. "He came over here and got his clothes, and he left. He told me it was over between you and him because you were at Speed last night, getting doubled by two dudes in the bathroom!"

"What?" Karmen barked. Though she tried hard, she realized she could barely remember last night. She did remember going to the club with Mecca, but she didn't remember seeing or going with Miguel.

"That's what he said," her sister continued.

She hoped she hadn't blacked out and done anything stupid. It began to make sense why her pussy and jaw were sore.

"Karmen, how did Miguel know you were at the club last night? Who did you go with?"

"I went with Mecca," she responded while getting off of the toilet and looking at her face in the mirror. She looked a wreck.

"That's strange, because she's the one that drove him here to get his clothes."

"Oh, no, that bitch didn't!" Karmen's eyes opened wide with a sudden jolt of sobriety. She realized at that moment that she had been played, and payback was definitely coming in the near future.

"The guns, the weed, everything. Nobody knows who did it," Mo Blood explained to Ruby while they sat on a park bench in Brownsville as a basketball tournament was under way. The roar of the crowd and the whistles of referees blocked out their conversation from any possible ear hustlers. While Mo explained what had happened when masked gunmen entered the spot, Ruby sipped on a strawberry shake from

McDonald's. Her clothes were unusually feminine, a pair of black capri pants, a white halter top, and a pair of Jimmy Choo pumps. Ruby nodded as he ran down the details that were given to him by one of the workers.

"Mo," she said abruptly, "take a ride with me downtown."

Mo couldn't read the tone in her voice. It was flat, and he couldn't tell what type of mood she was in. That made him nervous.

"Downtown? For what?" he asked. Sensing his nervousness, Ruby tried to make him more comfortable.

"Listen, two other spots of mines got robbed, and I think I know who it is. I want you and your team to handle it for me. I'm going to show you who it is."

Mo shrugged his shoulders. He knew she wouldn't try anything crazy in busy downtown, or so he hoped. Plus, he was holding heat, so if anything got funny, he wouldn't hesitate. He was sure she had no idea that he was involved in the shooting of her niece and Shamel. The only names that came up in that in the streets were Tah Gunz and them. The "them" could be anybody. Mo coughed violently as he walked to Ruby's car.

"You need to check that cough. It sounds crazy," Ruby warned.

Mo waived it off, continuing to cough. In between, he murmured, "Too much of that weed, that's all."

Mo never saw the girl Tasha from the strip club again after that night he went up in her raw. Nor did he go get himself checked out. Tasha quit working at the club once she got the results of her HIV test. She just left without notice to anyone.

At first, she'd wanted to confront Mo about her status, because he was the last person she had unprotected sex with since her last HIV test. She couldn't believe that she let him hit it without a condom. She realized that confronting him wouldn't change her status, and it probably would cause him to blame her if he was positive, and she knew Mo and the guys he ran with were a bunch of cowboys. She would let the disease take revenge for her.

Ruby and Mo drove downtown to the sounds of "Wanksta" cranking out of the car's sound system.

After a minute or so Ruby turned the sound down and said, "Let me ask you something, Mo."

"What's up?" he replied from the reclined passenger seat.

"You grew up in Brownsville projects?"

Pushing his blue Yankee fitted cap up from over his forehead, he replied, "Yeah, lived there all my life."

Ruby nodded, with a thoughtful expression on her face. "Do you remember a dude they called Wise that used to work out there? This was in the eighties."

Mo tried to recollect. "Yeah, that name rings a bell." A moment passed. Then his memory cleared, and he continued, "Matter of fact, yeah, I remember now. He used to live in Langston Hughes. Yeah, I remember dude."

"Do you know any of his family?"

Again Mo tried to recollect. "I know he had sisters, but they didn't live in the PJs. I heard they lived somewhere far out in Brooklyn."

Ruby nodded her head, then turned the music back up. While the *Get Rich or Die Tryin'* CD played, Mo wondered why she was questioning him about a dead old-school gangster and his family. Figuring Ruby out was like trying to answer a calculus problem in Chinese.

Ready for something to eat, she pulled over at a pizza shop on Fulton Street. "You want anything?" she asked before exiting.

Mo began reaching into his pockets. "Yeah, let me get a slice with extra cheese."

He held out money to her, but she simply opened the door and said, "It's on me."

Mo shrugged, putting the money back into his pocket. While she walked away, he stared at her backside, and just imagining getting a piece of that bubble made him hard. Then his thoughts shifted back to the questioning about Wise.

Mo remembered the rumors of who Wise was killed by and why.

Ruby got back in the car and handed Mo his pizza. "I got you some grape juice with it," Ruby said, placing their juices in the cup holders between their seats. Mo immediately devoured his pizza due to him having the munchies from all the weed he'd smoked earlier. After eating, he reclined his seat back as Ruby changed the CD to the radio. Jaheim's voice leaked out of the speakers.

The last thing Mo remembered before falling off into a deep sleep was Ruby looking over at him, smiling. He could no longer fight the heaviness in his eyes. He barely heard her voice.

"You think I don't know. . . ." he thought he heard Ruby say, and then everything went black.

Mo felt something cold on his face when he came to. He coughed and blinked his eyes, trying to clear whatever fluid had been thrown in his face. He couldn't move his arms and realized they were bound behind his back, as were his feet. He knew he was seated in a chair, though, and when his vision cleared, he didn't know where he was. The first thing he saw was Ruby's grinning face.

"Glad you can join us, Mo," Ruby snorted.

"Ruby, what's the deal? What's going on?" he asked with fear in his voice. The dim room appeared to be a basement. The concrete walls, with boxes stacked against them, and the floor gave him that impression.

"I'm sure you know what's going on," Ruby said, walking behind Mo and turning him in the chair toward her. The sound of the wooden chair scraping against the cement reverberated through the basement. Mo was shocked when he was now facing a bound and gagged figure in a wheelchair. He focused his eyes on Tah Gunz.

"Allow me to introduce you to the infamous Tah Gunz. Tah, this is Mo Blood. Does he look familiar?" Ruby smiled and grunted tauntingly. Tah's voice was muffled from the gag. Mo immediately began sweating and pleading.

"Ruby, I swear on everything I love, it wasn't me who did your niece."

"Damn, Tah, this is the type of dude you had in your crew?" Ruby asked in a chuckle.

Ruby had found out about Mo's involvement when she visited the East New York neighborhood of Sutter Gardens, where Mecca had once lived. It was Shamel's old neighborhood. She was a legend in that part of the borough also.

Everyone knew that Shamel ran the area, selling drugs that he got from her.

When she got out of her Benz in front of one of the buildings, a group of guys playing dice all stopped what they were doing to gaze at the car and the thick, stylish woman getting out of it. Most of them were too young to know who she was. They figured she was coming to see relatives that she had in the Gardens. One of them, the oldest in the crowd, smiled when he recognized his former boss.

"Oh, shit! I know that ain't the boss lady herself," the chubby, Rocawear-jean-suit-wearing guy barked as he walked toward Ruby.

Ruby recognized him even though he had put on weight. "Breeze, what's up, baby boy?" she asked excitedly.

They embraced in a warm hug. "When you get home, Ruby? I thought they threw the book at you, ma!"

"You ain't know I got that overturned last year? I've been home almost a year now. We need to talk," Ruby told him.

Breeze told his crew that he would be back after Ruby asked him to take a ride with her. During the ride, Breeze updated her on what had been going on in East New York since she'd been absent. They talked about how the September 11 attacks put a serious dent in the crack game, but weed became the new crack.

"It's like it was in eighty-eight, Ruby, but with weed."

When the subject turned to the murder of Shamel and Mecca's shooting, Breeze became sullen as he told her, "I miss my nigga, Ruby. I'm sorry about your niece. How she doing?" Ruby told him about Mecca being back to her old self, which made Breeze smile. Afterward, he told her about what he'd heard about the incident, and the names responsible.

"A lot of my homies are Blood. They let me know that some Bloods out of the Ville did it. Some dude named Tah Gunz and his flunky Mo Blood. They from Brownsville Houses."

Ruby couldn't believe what she was hearing. She almost broke the steering wheel, she squeezed it so hard. She was actually helping a guy get rich who had something to do with her friend and niece being shot. She looked at Breeze's brown, pudgy face and said, "I know who they are. You want some payback?"

***

Breeze smiled. Mo Blood stared at Breeze as he leaned against the stack of boxes for recognition. When Mo realized he didn't recognize who Breeze was, he looked back at Ruby. He wouldn't look at Tah, because he couldn't stand to look at the guy who had got him caught up in this position. Mo remembered advising Tah that he should forget about Mecca.

"Dog, she ain't all that to be going all the way out to Long Island for," he'd warned through a smoke-filled haze as he sat back in Tah's car, but Tah was adamant about making her and Shamel pay for trying to make him look bad in the eyes of everybody in Brownsville. "Nobody takes nothing from Tah," was his motto. Not even women.

"Breeze, which one you want?" Ruby asked as he straightened up off of the boxes while rubbing his palms together. Breeze poked Tah Gunz with his index finger, making his head move backward.

"This nigga here," he growled.

"Hold up, Breeze. I wanna play a game," Ruby said with childlike excitement. Pointing to a wooden staircase that led up to a door, she continued, "Untie Tah, and if he can make it up those stairs to that door in thirty seconds, we won't kill him. If he can't, he has to kill Mo here, then kill himself."

Breeze laughed at Ruby's proposal. He knew there was no way a paralyzed Tah would be able to crawl ten feet to the stairs and then pull himself up to that door in thirty seconds. But if Ruby wanted to play . . . so be it.

Breeze pulled a thick wad of cash out of his pocket and began counting some. "I got five hundred he doesn't make it."

Ruby pulled out her wad of cash from her jeans pocket. "I got five on it."

Breeze untied Tah, looked at his Oyster Perpetual Rolex, and barked, "Your time starts now!"

Tah leaped out of the chair by pushing himself to the floor. He began crawling frantically toward the staircase. With money in their hands, both Ruby and Breeze roared as if they were at a horse race.

"Go, boy! Go!" Ruby screamed.

"Ten, eleven, twelve . . ." Breeze counted.

Tah's mouth was still gagged with a red bandanna, which was Breeze's idea of a sign of Tah's affiliation with the Bloods, yet he still mumbled inaudible words. Sweat dripped from his face; his black Akademiks jeans were stained with dirt. He stopped a few times to catch his breath and looked longingly at the door.

"That's five hundred for Breeze, baby!"

Ruby howled, "C'mon, Tah! Do it for Brownsville, baby!"

"Thirty . . . Time's up!" Breeze barked.

Ruby removed the clip from her silver and black .40-caliber Smith & Wesson after cocking it and placing one in the chamber. Then they dragged Tah Gunz back into his wheelchair, while Mo Blood shit his pants, pleading with them.

"Word to Blood, Ruby. I didn't do anything to your peeps. I had to come with him. He is the general. If I didn't go, they would have put the green light on me!"

Ruby looked at Breeze, who shrugged his shoulders.

"You damned if you do and damned if you don't. You caught a bad break, Mo," said Ruby. Mo sighed as Ruby removed the gag from Tah's mouth.

"Ruby, listen. I'll work for you for free if you let me ride," he wailed.

"I can't believe these are the niggas that had everybody shook. Yo, y'all niggas, man up!" Ruby barked as she handed Tah the gun. "You got one shot in there. Now, you can get stupid and shoot me or Breeze, but you can't shoot both of us."

Breeze cocked his Desert Eagle .357. "All you gotta do is shoot Mo. It should be easy for you because he gave you up immediately. This boy would definitely snitch on you."

Breeze pushed the wheelchair directly in front of Mo Blood. He and Tah looked at each other, their eyes filled with tears. Mo was taking deep breaths as his life replayed in his mind. Then he thought about seeing his dead homies once he was dead. Tupac's words played in his head as he wondered if his homies had saved him a place in Thugs Mansion.

Boom!

"Whoo! Now, that was some shit!" Breeze roared after Tah pulled the trigger, hitting Mo in the forehead. The back of Mo's head exploded, and blood and brains spilled down his shirt.

Tah sat there with the gun in his hand, his arms down on both of the wheelchair's armrests. He stared at the lifeless body of his dead homie. His thoughts were blank. Then Ruby took the gun from his hand, put the clip in, and cocked it. One thought surfaced.

"I'd rather you kill me, instead of doing it myself or this dude." Tah nodded toward Breeze.

"What difference does it make if it's me or him?" Ruby asked.

"'Cause you're from Brownsville," Tah replied.

Breeze chuckled. "Any other dying wish?"

Tah kept looking at Ruby. "You're a Brownsville legend. That's why I want it to be you. Another thing . . . Can you place my body on Rockaway Ave.?"

Ruby smiled at Tah. "Yeah, sure." She nodded to Breeze. "Go 'head."

Breeze put the Desert Eagle to Tah's temple and squeezed the trigger.

Afterward, they crept out of the abandoned warehouse in East New York and walked to Ruby's car. The block was empty except for the rats rummaging through the vacant lots and streets. There were no other buildings on the block, so more than likely Tah's and Mo's bodies would be devoured by vermin before they were ever discovered. And by that time, they would need dental records to identify them.

"Don't forget my five hundred." Breeze held his hand out as he sat in the passenger seat of Ruby's car.

"You don't forget nothing, huh?" Ruby grinned as she pulled the five hundred dollars out of her pocket and handed it to him.

"Never that. You see, I never forgot your pretty face," Breeze flirted. Ruby took the remark for what it was and simply shook her head.

"I guess your memory ain't that good, 'cause you would have remembered I like pussy."

They both laughed as she turned up the car's system and Donell Jones began to sing.

The breeze blowing through the open sliding glass door cooled Mecca's and Miguel's sweating bodies as they lay entwined on the ocean blue satin sheets, listening to Mary J. Blige's voice serenade their lovemaking. The ocean waves could be heard crashing against the shore just outside of the beach house that Miguel rented during his off-season.

Mecca squeezed Miguel's tight ass while pushing him deeper within her gash. Just as she moaned, she heard footsteps enter through the glass door. Immediately, they turned to see a distraught Karmen standing there with a gun in her hands.

"I thought you loved me, Miguel. I thought I was your Puerto Rican princess," Karmen cried, pointing the gun toward them.

Miguel jumped up, while Mecca covered herself with the sheets. Karmen had the gun pointed at Miguel, who stood in front of her, with his manhood wet and dangling between his thighs. Sobbing, Karmen looked down at his pole, then back at him.

"Why, Miguel?"

"Karmen, put the gun down and let's talk. You don't have to . . ." Miguel was suddenly cut off as something hit him in his chest. He fell backward, landing on the plush white carpet. Mecca jumped out of bed immediately.

"Miguel! Oh God, Karmen! What did you do?"

"He's my man, Mecca! Just like Shamel was my man before he met you!" Karmen growled. Miguel was trying to catch his breath as blood seeped though a small hole on his chest. Mecca could see the carpet under him begin to turn red.

"Is that what this is all about? Shamel and me? Why didn't you tell me that you and him were dealing with each other?" Mecca asked, rubbing her fingers through Miguel's hair.

"I love you, Mecca," Miguel whispered.

Karmen snapped out. "Fuck you, Mecca!" Then shots went off.

Mecca's dream switched to her sitting in Lou's office, with him folding his arms across his chest, looking at her as if he were waiting for an explanation.

"I'll be honest with you, Lou. My intentions at first were to get even with her, but as I get to know him, I'm falling hard for him every day."

"Will you be honest with him and tell him the same thing?" Lou asked.

Mecca was taken aback by the question. "For what? Why do that? All that matters now is how I feel about him at this present moment."

"I guess it's all fair in love and war, huh?" Lou shook his head in disbelief. Standing up from behind the desk, Lou walked around to Mecca. "Can I show you something I didn't show you before, when you were in your coma?"

"How much worse could it get? You gonna show me, anyway, Lou, so get on with it," Mecca sighed.

Nervous at what Lou would show her, she told herself that it could not get any worse than it already was. He'd already shown her how her aunt had set her parents up to be murdered, so if he'd held it back from her, it had to be deep. Lou placed his hand on her head, and the vision began.

Flashback, 1974

"Ever since you got pregnant, you act like having sex with me is a terrible thing," Bobby Sykes yelled at the woman everyone in Brownsville called Big Mecca once she gave birth to her daughter.

"Bobby, it's not like I don't want to, but, baby, I'm eight and a half months pregnant. My back hurts, and sex isn't helping," she told him in a low voice, trying to conceal the argument from the rest of the projects.

"I got needs, Mecca, and you're supposed to fulfill them, like I do yours," Bobby growled.

"You make it sound like you're my pimp or something. Bobby, go on with the bullshit."

Angered, Bobby simply shook his head. He grabbed his suede jacket and keys off the kitchen table.

"So you're just going to leave? Every time we get into an argument, you quick to run outside. What you going to see another woman?" Big Mecca screamed.

"I don't have time for the bullshit. I'll be back," Bobby replied, walking out of the door. A porcelain ashtray crashed into the door, shattering into dozens of pieces.

"Don't come back, you bastard!"

Bobby made his way out of the building, and when he got to Rockaway Ave., he spotted a friend of Ruby's. She was a fine sister who always gave Bobby a flirtatious look. It was no secret that all the girls in Brownsville found Bobby "Blast" Sykes to be the finest brother in the neighborhood, and he did not hesitate to cash in on his sex symbol status.

"Hi, Bobby," said a voluptuous, thick woman wearing her hair in two Afro puffs. Her tight blue jeans revealed how thick her thighs were. The three-quarter black leather jacket tied at the waist with a belt hid the plumpness of her bottom, but Bobby knew from seeing her in the summer what she was hiding under the jacket and clothes.

"Hey, baby. How's it holding?" Bobby flirted. He was already sexually frustrated after two months of getting no sex from his girl. It was time he made his move.

"I'm fine. Not as fine as you, though," the woman replied seductively.

That was all Bobby needed to hear. Minutes later, after some liquor and some lines of cocaine, Bobby and the girl were sucking and fucking savagely in a seedy motel on Pennsylvania Avenue. After four hours of sweat-drenched fucking, it was time to check out. As they both dressed, Bobby turned and looked at the girl.

"Damn, baby, I forgot your name. I always see you with Ruby, but I forgot."

The girl rolled her eyes at Bobby as she put on her clothing. "Bobby, you know my name is Monique."

A month later Bobby ran into Monique on Mother Gaston Boulevard, at a grocery store. He nodded to her as he paid for a pack of cigarettes. She had a sad look on her face as she said, "I need to talk to you outside."

Bobby stepped outside while removing a cigarette from the pack and lit it. He deeply inhaled the smoke while Monique blurted that she was pregnant, causing Bobby to choke.

"What? What you telling me for?"

Monique placed her hands on her hips, sucked her teeth, and rolled her eyes. "I'm no whore, Bobby! You're the last person I fucked. It's yours."

"You know I got a newborn baby girl and I love my woman. I don't need no controversy now. If you're gonna have the kid, I'll help you out, but please keep this between us," Bobby sighed.

"I want this baby, Bobby. I just wanted to let you know. Don't worry. It's between us."

When Monique gave birth to a healthy, seven-pound-two-ounce baby girl, she put the baby's name on the certificate and listed the father as unknown. A nurse placed the baby in Monique's arms and asked what her name would be.

"Her name is Dawn." Monique smiled.

The baby looked just like Blast. Not too long after she got out of the hospital, Monique moved out of Brownsville and relocated to Coney Island. Still, the word spread through Brownsville of who the father was. When the vision was over, Lou sat back at his desk while Mecca cried.

"Is it fair that Monique and your father told no one?" he asked while Mecca's mind flashed back to the time she sat on the park bench with Dawn and shot her in the head.

"Baby! It's okay! It was just a dream!" Miguel said, holding Mecca in his arms. He could feel her heart thud against her chest as they lay naked in his bed. After she calmed down a bit, he got up to use the bathroom and get a facecloth to wipe the sweat off of her. When he came back in, Mecca was getting dressed.

"Where are you going? I thought we were having breakfast together," Miguel said, confused.

"I have to go home," Mecca said while dressing quickly.

"I'll drive you, but why do you have to go?"

"You don't have to drive me. I'll catch a cab," Mecca said, fully dressed and grabbing the phone from his bedside table.

"What's wrong? Did I do something?"

"No, Miguel. I just need some time alone, that's all," she replied as she listened to the phone ring. She responded to the operator's question once her call was answered. "Yes, I need a cab. I'm at . . ."

Chapter Thirty-four

Can it be that it was all so simple then?
—Raekwon and Ghostface

Junior McLeod sat on a white plastic chair in his lush garden, chopping a pineapple he had just picked from a tree. His long dreadlocks with sprinkles of gray hung loosely down the side of his face, down to his stomach.

"So many years have passed since my son's murder, yet you still hold on to the pain. This is the life chosen by so many youths, and the consequences are known," Junior said in a heavy Jamaican accent. His voice was a raspy sort of whisper. Every time Daphne looked at him, she thought of how Donovan would have looked if he hadn't been murdered by the police.

Marley, as he was called, had looked just like his father. Junior McLeod left the streets of New York after making millions, returning to his native Jamaica and living a simple, but comfortable life in the mountains of the island. He had had a large house built that was straight out of a *House Beautiful* magazine. The mini mansion overlooked lush green hills. Daphne loved the peaceful surroundings. It was a relief from the concrete chaos of New York City.

After his son was murdered by FBI agents, Junior sought to find out who was responsible for snitching on him. If the person had been hidden by the government, he wanted their family dead. There was no room for mistakes, and plenty of people paid with their lives. When word got out on who the snitches were, the murder rate in New York City reached unbelievable numbers. The city was under siege.

Members of the Shower Posse and their rivals were being slaughtered. It was nothing for a kid playing in a vacant lot to stumble upon a corpse with some of its limbs missing. Junior was finally convinced by his wife that enough was enough. If things continued the way they were, Junior would be dead or would be sent to prison—with so many numbers, his sentence would sound like a Social Security number. When Daphne was convicted, Junior went to Jamaica.

Before leaving, he made sure that Daphne wouldn't spend a day in jail wanting for anything. He loved her like she was his own flesh and blood. She was one of the most loyal people he had ever met, and he knew she loved his son to death. To this day, he could see the pain in her eyes from the loss.

"It was a piece of my life that made up half of my soul. The other half was Donovan," Daphne said in a measured tone as she stared off into the valley. She watched the wind gently blow through the trees from behind her D&G shades.

"Your other issue is trust, I assume?" Junior asked while cutting pieces of pineapple with a small knife and popping the juicy fruit into his mouth. "Has she shown signs of mistrust?"

Daphne folded one leg over the other and straightened the wrinkles in her linen capri pants. Her matching sandals revealed peach painted toenails to match her halter top.

"Not exactly, but something in her niece's eyes when she looks at her tells me there is something I don't know about her. Something evil."

Junior was a very wise man, well learned in all aspects of life, the streets, and politics. It was well known that the Shower Posse, being an organization that was a political force that opposed the Jamaican government and its treatment of the poor natives of the island, at one time influenced many of his ideas and gave him a broader look upon the world. This, together with his dedication to the Rastafarian religion, gave a mystical aura to Junior's person.

Thinking deeply, he responded, "And you have grown close to this niece of hers?"

"Close, yes," Daphne answered in a tone that spoke of the lingering doubt deep within. "But not close enough for her to reveal what's really the core reason I sense her resentment toward her aunt."

"You Yankees are so paranoid of each other. Trust is so hard to come by in the States, especially among our black people." Junior chuckled, and then he asked, "Are you sure yet about your brother's murder? And if not, will you trust your instincts?"

Junior's words were a sad reality. Daphne couldn't even count on two hands how many people she had trusted throughout her life. She couldn't trust her mother, because she was easily influenced by an abusive man that made their family's life miserable. She and her sister were close, but not as close as she was with her brother. She had total trust in her brother. Then there was Donovan. She had trusted him with all her heart. She knew that he would never cross her, that he was a loyal man, and that this was in his blood. That was why Junior was another person she trusted. She knew that she had to earn his trust, and she did that by not snitching when she got locked up. It was clear that if Junior had had the slightest inkling that she was going to cooperate, he could have had her erased, even in jail.

"The answers will come soon, Daphne. What's on the inside of a person will eventually come to the surface. It's a guarantee," Junior said while standing up. "Until then, take a trip with me into town. I have some people for you to meet."

Daphne stood and stretched. "And I have someone I want you to meet," she said with a smile.

Before Daphne and Junior drove into town to meet the people he spoke about, they stopped at the airport in an onyx-colored, chauffeur-driven Rolls-Royce Phantom with tinted windows. Daphne ran into the terminal and minutes later walked back, carrying a Louis Vuitton duffel bag, accompanied by Mecca.

"Junior, I want you to meet my good friend Mecca," Daphne said as they entered the backseat of the car.

"It's a pleasure to meet you." Junior extended a soft, slightly wrinkled hand.

Mecca smiled. "It's nice to meet you."

Gazing into her eyes, he immediately saw the pain in them. It was a deep pain that, if not diffused, would eventually explode to the surface and cause a lot of damage to others as well as to herself. Immediately, she could feel his gaze and knew that he wasn't just looking at her physically; he was studying her. It didn't make her uncomfortable, because she would do the same whenever she met a person. She could also tell that he was a man of deep wisdom. In an odd way, he reminded her of Lou.

"So, you're from Brownsville?" Junior asked, cutting the air of silence in the car.

Mecca looked directly into his gray eyes. *What is it with these eyes?* she wondered. "Yes, I am."

Junior smiled and shook his head. "When I lived in Flatbush, I remember people were very skeptical about going into Brownsville. It was a dangerous place in the late seventies, early eighties. I never had a problem there. I was always welcomed."

Mecca nodded her head while looking out the window as they passed a shantytown where small children played around shacks and adults stood in groups, staring at the Phantom. Realizing they were in the slums, she finally understood what poverty really was.

Eventually, the graveled road turned into well-paved streets, and the slum faded away, replaced by a South Beach replica. The Phantom came to a stop in front of a luxury hotel, where a uniformed valet approached. The driver of the Phantom waived him off as he got out, opening the rear doors for his passengers.

"Greetings, Mr. McLeod," the doorman said warmly.

Junior simply nodded and smiled as he led Daphne and Mecca into the hotel's foyer. It was easy to tell that it was a five-star establishment simply by looking at it. The foyer itself reminded Mecca of the Waldorf Astoria or Le Parker Meridien in New York, and there were a lot of American and European tourists present.

While Daphne and Junior went up to the luxury suite to have a meeting, Mecca was treated to a full day of pampering in the hotel's spa. She enjoyed a full-body massage by a handsome masseur, a facial that made her skin look expensive, and both a pedicure and manicure, courtesy of Junior. Afterward, she felt totally relaxed. The tension built up in her from her dream about Dawn being her sister, Miguel, and from all that had transpired in the past few months, since coming out of the coma, lifted off of her, making her feel rejuvenated and refueled.

She felt bad about how she treated Miguel, though. Since the Dawn dream, she'd been avoiding him. She told herself that she needed the space from everything, and when Daphne asked her to accompany her to Jamaica, she quickly accepted. Now she wished Miguel was with her, enjoying the island.

As bad as she didn't want to fall in love with him, she found herself falling hard. She didn't want to repeat what she found out about Shamel, so while she soaked her feet, she made a long-distance call to him.

The phone rang a couple of times; then Miguel's warm voice answered, which made her smile. Yes, she realized, she was in love. Again.

While Mecca and Daphne soaked up the sun in Jamaica, Ruby was roughing out a cold New York winter, hanging out in clubs and bars and collecting money from the grocery store Karmen ran and from Breeze, who was now pushing weed in his Sutter Gardens neighborhood.

Even though Ruby was still trying to find out who was responsible for the robberies of her spots and Daphne's restaurant, there hadn't been any other robberies committed, and there was still no word about them on the streets. Ruby found that strange and suspicious.

Did those involved hear that both Ruby and Daphne were on the hunt and wanted them dead? Maybe that scared them off. Or were they waiting for another opportunity to strike? It stressed her out trying to figure out their angle.

Things were flowing smoothly, except for Karmen's attitude. Ruby figured she was suffering from a broken heart, because she didn't see Miguel around anymore, but Karmen was letting her emotions get in the way of making money. She opened the store late a lot, and she let the product run out before calling for more, resulting in lost sales when customers wouldn't wait around for the next supply of weed. When Ruby

spoke to her about it, she would apologize and say it wouldn't
happen again, but it did. When Ruby asked one of Karmen's
sisters what Karmen's problem was, she told her that Miguel
had broken up with her. He'd caught her in the club with
another guy.

Neither Karmen nor her sisters dared to tell Ruby that
they suspected Mecca of stealing Miguel. They knew how she
felt about her niece, and if Ruby thought that Karmen had ill
feelings toward Mecca, that could spell trouble for Karmen. So
Karmen did the "scorned woman" thing and slashed Miguel's
tires and left notes on his door.

When Miguel walked in the store, angered by the tire slashing and notes, Karmen was glad she had got his attention. Her
plan was to confront him, then apologize, hoping he would
take her back. Her plan backfired.

"If I had known you were this immature, I would have
introduced you to one of my little cousins. They're some horny
twelve-year-olds." Miguel threw the notes on the floor and
stormed out of the store.

Karmen stood there, embarrassed and humiliated. It was
then that Karmen started thinking of ways to pay Mecca back
for taking her man. She had already realized that it could
only have been Mecca who called him to the club, and she
remembered how Mecca would stare at him. For a moment,
she'd been blind to the facts, but no longer. They both would
pay.

However, Karmen underestimated Ruby's ties to the streets.
So when she hollered at a guy she knew from Bed-Stuy, where
the store was located, about robbing it, word quickly got back
to Ruby.

"Do the job," Ruby told the guy that Karmen was conspiring
with. "That will be part of the pay for getting rid of her. Wait
till after Christmas, though."

"Why after Christmas?" he asked.

"I like her sisters. I don't want to spoil their holiday."

They both burst out laughing.

"Nah, seriously. Wait."

***

Back in Jamaica, Junior brought Daphne and Mecca to the shantytown they had passed on their way to the hotel. The area was dark and loud, with reggae music blasting from some of the shacks. The pungent odor of dead animals filled the air. Mecca followed them inside a small shack where a skinny old man sat at a wooden table, wearing African garb, including a beaded necklace made of wood, with what looked like the teeth of some animal connected to each bead.

The small house was decorated with wooden African sculptures, various potted plants, and a small bookshelf, which held books on healing, African black magic, and medicines. In the middle of the house, in a makeshift living room, sat a table covered with what looked like lamb's wool. Surrounding that were candles on shaded lamps that made shadows dance across the cement walls.

"Ladies, I'd like you to meet Doc Benjamin," Junior said as the old man stood up and bowed slightly.

Doc Benjamin smiled, showing his missing teeth and soon to be missing ones. He twisted his gray chin hairs, which grew from his lined, dull black skin. Mecca had noticed that the majority of the people she met in Jamaica had bloodshot eyes. Doc Benjamin was no exception.

"I am honored," Doc Benjamin responded in an accent that wasn't broken like that of the native Jamaicans. He spoke clear English. His words were pronounced as if he were an English professor at a prestigious college.

When Doc offered his company tea, Mecca knew it was customary to accept the offer. When you were a guest in someone's home, turning down the offer was a sign of disrespect, so she reluctantly accepted.

They sat at the table while Doc poured tea into small glass cups out of an old teakettle. He gazed into Mecca's eyes as he poured her tea, and unlike the gaze she had received from Junior, Doc's gaze made her nervous.

"What are your names?" he asked.

They told him their names, and Mecca noticed that Doc kept looking at her strangely. Sometimes it appeared as though he was looking around her head, as if something was on it or floating over it. Nervously, she found herself looking up and around. Doc gave her the creeps.

Turning to look to see if Daphne felt the same way, she was puzzled that she did not seem to be affected by the strange old man. Junior talked to Doc about what he'd been up to living up on the mountains and about mutual friends that they had not seen in a while. Doc then turned and studied Mecca again.

"Don't hold on to the grudge. They will have their day."

Mecca looked behind her, then at everyone in the room, only to find they were all looking at her as if she was onstage, ready to perform.

"What . . . what do you mean?" she asked nervously. How was he able to read her thoughts? How did he know the words Lou told her in her dreams?

"I mean, you are angry at people who can't cause you any more harm than they're doing to themselves," Doc said.

As he spoke, Mecca became dizzy. Her head felt hot, and the room seemed like it began to spin. All she heard was Doc's voice as she felt her body being lifted, and she was floating in the air until her body touched something soft and flat. Her vision blurred, and she felt as if she were sinking into the soft surface she was lying on.

"Let it go. You don't need him no more," Doc's voice echoed as her blurred vision went dark. "You are stronger than it."

Then Mecca saw him. He was drowning in a vast ocean, while she stood on the deck of a yacht. He held out his hand from the strong black current.

"Mecca! Help me! Don't listen to him!"

Mecca cried as she looked for a life jacket. She found one and threw it to him. "Lou, grab the jacket," she yelled.

"You can make your own decision, Mecca. God has given you a choice," Doc's voice echoed somewhere in her mind.

"Mecca, please don't leave me. I love you. All I want is what's best for you!"

Mecca held out her hand to grab Lou's. "Hold my hand!"

Lou grabbed on, but the current was strong. He struggled to pull himself up on the deck, but Mecca was losing her grip.

"Lou! Hold on!"

"Don't drink any more tea!" Lou yelled.

"What?"

Lou increased his grip on Mecca's arm and pulled himself up on the deck. Mecca immediately hugged him.

"Lou, go hide in the boat. People are trying to get rid of you. Go!" Mecca ordered.

Lou did what he was told.

"He is gone. I don't need him anymore!" She yelled into the darkness.

Her vision went black; then it blurred, and she was able to see the shapes of people. When it cleared, she looked up into the smiling faces of Doc Benjamin and Junior. Junior held out his hand to lift her off of the table.

"What happened?" she asked, confused. She could not remember how she ended up lying on the table. She felt light-headed. She sat up and saw Daphne walking toward her.

"You fainted, Mecca. Doc said it's probably the humidity in the air. Plus, you're not used to that kind of tea. It's marijuana tea mixed with spices," Daphne said, pulling Mecca off the table.

"We're ready to leave now," Junior said, shaking Doc Benjamin's hand.

Doc then shook Daphne's and Mecca's hand. He looked into Mecca's eyes and in a soft voice said, "No one can show you what you don't want to see."

Inside Junior's Phantom it was silent as they rode back to his home. Mecca stared out the window as the slum villages turned into postcard countryside. She still couldn't believe she'd fainted. She felt so embarrassed, despite Daphne telling her that it had happened to her also on her first trip to the island.

"I passed out longer than you did. I had a big cup of the same tea," Daphne had told her while walking out of Doc's home to the car.

Mecca remembered feeling hot from drinking the tea, but not to the point where she felt a fainting spell coming on. It had happened so quickly, though, and that Doc guy was a strange man. She didn't even get that creepy feeling from Lou that she got from Doc Benjamin. One thing for sure, she thought, she never wanted to see the likes of him again.

Her thoughts switched to Miguel, and she smiled thinking about their talk on the phone. She was glad that he wasn't offended to the point where he didn't want to see her again.

"I understand if you don't wanna be involved with me. I just want you to know that I'm sorry for the way I acted," Mecca had told him.

"Mecca, I want to be involved in every aspect of your life. Talk to me. That's what I'm here for. You can tell me anything. I won't judge you or look at you differently. I promise."

Miguel knew how to make someone feel at ease. His voice was soothing, and to Mecca it was an aphrodisiac. His voice made her wet and horny. She wanted to pull his lips through the phone just to taste them.

"There is so much to talk about Miguel. It's hard to explain."

Mecca knew that she would have to share personal things with Miguel, but what she would tell him was something she found hard to figure out. She couldn't tell anyone about Lou. No one would understand. Telling him about Ruby and Karmen wouldn't change anything. The hurt from Ruby's betrayal would still be there, and as far as Karmen was concerned, she couldn't tell him that she was with him initially as a get back for her having an affair with Shamel. She would have to figure it out someway, somehow. Then she wondered if Lou might have the answer. She couldn't wait to go to sleep that night.

Flashback, 1976

"Look at you. You're a big girl now, huh?" Big Mecca announced while standing at the open bathroom door, smiling at her daughter on the white potty. Little Mecca simply looked up at her mother and smiled.

"Bobby, come look at your daughter. She's using the potty!"

Bobby Blast appeared at the door, also smiling. "That's Daddy's girl. She can do things on her own. She's just like her daddy!"

Mecca's dream fast-forwarded to six years later, with her coming out from under the bed after witnessing her parents' murders. She ran to the telephone and dialed her aunt's house. A half hour later police arrived at the apartment. Mecca was left with her aunt's friend down the hall.

"What's her name?" the female detective asked Ruby's friend as she bent down to her.

"She can speak," the neighbor answered. Tears ran down her face.

"Mecca."

"Can you tell me what happened here?" the detective asked.

"My mommy and daddy are dead. I won't see them again until I'm dead," Mecca responded.

When the detective tried to elicit more information, Mecca fell silent. She began to look around for the man with the neat Afro. She did not see him and was confused. Then Ruby walked in.

The vision disappeared, and Mecca found herself sitting in Lou's office. He faced away from her in his large swivel chair, and though she could not see him, she heard his voice.

"You didn't need help making those decisions, Mecca. You used the potty all by yourself. You knew without anyone telling you that you wouldn't see your parents again. You can and will decide your own destiny. Making mistakes is all part of being human. You're not perfect, and no one should expect you to be perfect."

Though the voice sounded like Lou's, Mecca wasn't sure. What he was saying was something Mecca knew Lou would not say. It was like Lou expected her to walk a straight line, or he would be angry. This voice she was now hearing was a voice of reason, pleading with her almost. Then the chair turned, and Mecca's eyes widened at the sight of Doc Benjamin.

Mecca awoke out of her sleep in the guest room inside Junior's home. The room was dark, and you could hear the sound of crickets and other night creatures talking to one another. The canopy bed she lay on had a netted covering to keep out mosquitoes or any other creeping night creatures. As she struggled to control her labored breathing and bring it back to normal, she mumbled to herself.

"I've had enough of Jamaica." With or without Daphne, she would be on the next flight back to New York, as far away from Doc Benjamin as possible.

Chapter Thirty-five

*Do not trust in a friend; do not put your
confidence in a companion.*

—Micah 7:5

Daphne's and Mecca's flight arrived at Newark International Airport. Once there the women separated. Mecca was picked up by Miguel, and Daphne's BMW was in long-term parking. Daphne drove out to an eatery on Long Island called Jillian's to meet Ruby. During that drive, Junior's take on Mecca kept repeating in her mind.

"She has been betrayed, and it was a betrayal that left a deep wound. She is loyal. That's why she clings to you. But whatever pains this woman, it's a pain that's been there for a long time."

Daphne needed to know what it was, and if she couldn't get it from Mecca, she had no choice but to confront Ruby. When she'd called her after landing, Ruby had quickly warned Daphne to call her from a public phone and gave her the number to one on Long Island. When she finally called her from a phone, Ruby sounded excited.

"Daphne, where's my niece?"

"She's at a duty-free shop. Why? What's up?"

"Tell her Tah Gunz and his homie are washed up," Ruby answered, as if she was telling Daphne she had just won a lottery jackpot.

"I'll tell her," Daphne said. "But I need to see you now. We have to talk."

"What's up, Daphne? Something happen?" Ruby asked, not liking the tone of Daphne's voice.

"No. I just have to discuss some business with you. We haven't talked in a while," she lied. She did not want to put

Ruby on the defensive. She wanted to catch Ruby unaware so that she would not make up answers about Mecca's situation. That way, she would be able to detect the lie.

Without question, she knew that when it came to Ruby, she would have to use all of her cunning to illicit the answer from her. Ruby was no one's fool, and she knew her well enough to know you couldn't game her. Being friends with her in prison had allowed Daphne to see how easily Ruby could talk another inmate into believing that they were the best of friends or lovers, only to have Ruby con her out of money and drugs.

"Meet me at Jillian's," Ruby told Daphne.

Jillian's had been a favorite of Ruby's since she'd been home. They served traditional American cuisine, and you could also enjoy bowling and shoot pool. Ruby loved to eat and then bet on a game of pool.

When Daphne arrived, Ruby was deep in a game of pool against a tall, handsome man who looked like a young athlete.

The basketball star laughed while eyeing Daphne. Those eyes of hers could really make a man weak on resisting. He had noticed her when she walked in like every other guy in the place. Her confident swagger, blended with the beautiful face and sexy physique, was a sight for sore eyes.

"You gonna introduce me to your friend?" His voice was Kobe Bryant deep.

"I'm not here to socialize with strangers. If you could be so kind and leave me and my friend to talk, that would be appreciated," Daphne blurted, placing her Hermès bag on the table and not even looking at him. The basketball star shook his head and walked off.

"Damn, girl, that man is fine," Ruby said, laughing, before turning her attention to Daphne. "Are you okay?"

"I'm no one's groupie, and I don't have time for headaches," Daphne shot back. Ruby looked at her for a moment and could tell by her tone and body language that something was on her mind. Something that seemed to be eating at her.

"So what's up, Daphne? What's good? Tell me about Jamaica."

"It was a good trip for me, but I'm not sure it was for Mecca," she responded, looking directly into Ruby's eyes. She always noticed that the mention of Mecca's name made Ruby's facial expression change. Mecca was a sensitive topic for her. The guilt was still an issue for Ruby because she had not stopped blaming herself for what happened to her.

"Why do you say that? Did something go wrong?" Ruby asked in a low voice.

For a moment Daphne looked into her eyes and knew that she did not want to hear sad news about Mecca. Ruby was tired of blaming herself for Mecca's downfall.

"Nothing went wrong. Something is wrong. Very wrong," Daphne stated.

Ruby stiffened, ready to go on the defensive. "What do you mean?"

"Something is eating at her, Ruby. What do you think it is?"

"The girl just came out of a coma—"

"She's been out of the coma for a year now. That's not it," Daphne said, cutting her off.

"Why are you asking me, Daphne? Ask her!" Ruby shot back as she began to feel the anger rise within. Daphne seemed to be cross-examining her, as if Mecca's attitude was somehow Ruby's fault.

Daphne was tempted to tell her that she did question Mecca about the look she gave Ruby and Karmen, but Mecca's answer about both women sleeping with her boyfriend didn't convince her that that was the root of the problem.

"I asked you because you're her aunt. You know her better than anyone else. Talk to her, Ruby. It's like you've been around her, and maybe that's the problem. Y'all were close before you went to jail. Maybe she feels your time away made y'all grow apart."

Ruby looked away, as if her attention was diverted to something else in the restaurant. She wouldn't tell anyone that the guilt she felt was deeper than just Mecca being shot. That was just the surface of the matter. Ruby felt that if she hadn't set Bobby Blast up to be robbed and both of them hadn't got killed, Mecca would have grown up living with her parents, who would not have allowed her to run the streets and get knee-deep into the game.

Ruby's time in jail had made her reflect on the mistake that she'd made raising Mecca the way she did. What kind of person would do that to her own flesh and blood? She told herself she had to accept who she was, but not what she'd made out of Mecca. She wouldn't allow her to be involved in street life ever again. It would be over her dead body. Ruby sighed.

"You're right, Daphne. I'll have a talk with her. Where did she go?"

"She's with Miguel."

"With who?" Ruby's eyes widened. Daphne looked dumbfounded. She'd forgot that Ruby wasn't aware of Mecca and Miguel. She'd let the cat out of the bag, so she decided that she would tell all.

"You didn't know they were messing with one another?"

"No, I didn't know that. And when was I going to find out?" Ruby grumbled.

Daphne took a sip of her chocolate milkshake and shrugged.

"That's why this bitch Karmen been acting up lately," Ruby said, shaking her head. Now Daphne was confused.

"Acting up? What did she do?"

After Ruby explained about Karmen's plot to have the store robbed, Daphne growled in anger. "I'm not too enthused about all the killings, but on this one, do what you see fit."

Four days after Christmas, the snow blanketed the streets. Christmas lights blinked on and off in houses and storefronts, lighting up the dark streets. Yet something contrary to the holiday spirit was being plotted. Three men in dark apparel sat in a black Lincoln Town car on the side block that Ruby's store cornered.

"All y'all gotta do is climb the fence and go through the back. The door is open," the leader of the three-man gang said to his comrades. The leader, who was the one Karmen had conspired with to rob the store, never told his crew that it was more than a robbery, that it was a hit. He didn't feel it necessary to tell them, because he didn't plan to split all the spoils.

"I'ma walk in like a regular customer. They about to close, so it won't be anyone in there," he said while taking a look at his watch. "Let's move."

"I want you to cum in my mouth, *Papi*," Tina moaned as she took her new friend, whom she'd just met earlier, in her mouth while he sat on a crate in the back room of the store.

The young Spanish guy held her head as her neck moved up and down and she bent between his knees. His eyes were closed, and Tina never saw the two masked men enter the room. They became aware of their presence when they heard the sound of the gun being cocked.

"Hey, *Papi,* fun time is over." A masked man pointed the shotgun in his face.

"Don't shoot please!" The Spanish guy's face went pale with fear.

The other gunman pointed his Heckler & Koch MP5 at Tina. "Put homeboy dick back in his pants and lay down on the ground."

Out front, where Karmen and Maria sat on crates, watching a small color TV, a customer walked into the store.

"I forgot to lock the door," Maria said, looking at the face of the guy, whom she recognized from Bed-Stuy. "We're closed, *Papi!*"

"Nah, bitch, I'm just opening up for business." He smiled at Maria, then quickly brandished a nickel-plated .50-caliber Desert Eagle from the inside of his black leather trench coat. Maria froze in her tracks. Her heart pounded in her chest as she raised her hands.

"Lay on the floor." He pointed the gun at Maria and then looked at Karmen, who was slowly walking toward Maria. "You do the same, sexy."

Karmen and Maria did as they were told. At the same time, Karmen was wondering why he was showing his face. *My sisters aren't supposed to see him! He must be drunk! Dumb-ass nigga!*

Two shots rang out from the back of the store. Maria let out a short scream, and Karmen looked up at the man with the gun.

"What the fuck was that? Why are they shooting?" Karmen yelled frantically. She knew it was a setup, but had the plans changed?

"Shut your ass up, bitch! It's warning shots," the man spat back sharply. The two masked men came from the back of the store, holding trash bags.

"It's done," one of them said to the leader.

"What's done? Don, what the fuck is going on?" Karmen yelled again, confused as to when the plans had been switched up.

The two masked men looked at Don, confused. How did she know his name? Then they realized he wasn't wearing a mask. Maria looked at her sister, confused, too. How did she know this man?

"Oh, you remember me?" Don asked, trying to play dumb in front of his partners.

"Don, don't get all—" Karmen's words were cut short when he pointed the Desert Eagle at the top of her head and squeezed. Blood and brain matter squirted all over Maria's face upon impact, but before she could scream, Don put a bullet in her skull, shutting her up forever.

"Yo, son, what the fuck you doing?" one of his partners asked.

"C'mon, we going out the back," Don replied as he started off, with his crimeys in tow.

When they got in the back, Don saw Tina and her new lover, still alive and tied up, with tape around their mouths.

"Meet me in the car," Don told his partners. They looked at him as if he were losing his damn mind. "Fuck y'all waiting for? Go ahead!"

Once they did as they were told, Don went to the stash spot Ruby had told him about. It was a small door underneath the small refrigerator. He opened it and removed four pounds of weed inside of a shopping bag. Tina had tears running down her face and held a fearful expression, which got Don off a little bit.

Both of them were mumbling inaudible words right before Don put bullets in their foreheads.

He bent down to pick up the shell casings, like he did when he killed Karmen and Maria, and then exited the store. When he got to the car, where his partners waited, he popped the trunk and placed the shopping bag in it.

"What's in the bag, Don?" one of his crimeys asked as he got in the passenger seat.

"I got my mom some groceries," Don lied. He started the car, and the hard beat and lyrics of Beanie Sigel filled the interior as Don sped off.

Mecca tried to open the office door, but it was locked. Confused, she decided to knock instead.

"Lou, you in there? Why is the door locked?"

As she put her ear to the door, she heard movement inside. It sounded like a scuffle was going on and someone was choking.

"Lou, what's going on? Open up!" Mecca grabbed the doorknob while banging her shoulder against the door.

"Mecca, go away. I will deal with him myself," answered Doc Benjamin's voice.

Mecca was infuriated. "No!" she screamed, and then, with two hard kicks, the door flew open and Mecca watched as Doc Benjamin had Lou down on the desk, choking him. Mecca reached into her Louis Vuitton purse and removed a nickel-plated, pearl-handled .380 automatic. She pointed the gun at Doc Benjamin's back and grunted, "You let him go, or I'll kill your ass."

"Mecca, those days are over. Plus, you don't love this man." Doc Benjamin howled a throaty laugh. He squeezed harder, and Lou's eyes rolled in his head.

"Let him go!" she yelled as she squeezed the trigger, emptying her gun in Doc's back.

"It's okay, baby. No one's here. You had a nightmare," Miguel said, holding Mecca's head against his bare chest as they lay naked in his bed. Miguel could hear her heart beat. He figured her nightmares were from her being shot and going into a coma. However, recurring nightmares of being shot by Tah Gunz weren't even close to what Mecca was experiencing. Mecca knew that Miguel wouldn't understand. Nobody would.

Chapter Thirty-six

A whisper separates the best of friends.
—Proverbs 16:28

Club Opium was jam-packed with people from all walks of life as the Las Vegas club hosted a "welcome home" celebration sponsored by the famous *Don Diva* magazine. A who's who of the famous and infamous was in attendance, from athletes and entertainers to politicians and gangsters. With this high-profile gathering, law enforcement from government and local agencies were also strategically roaming the premises, eyeing targets of criminal investigations and their associates, potential targets themselves. Against Daphne's advice, Ruby attended the event, because she was invited to welcome home her former cellmate, friend, and lover after a ten-year stint.

"Why don't you and her celebrate it privately? That place gonna be crawling with feds," Daphne had warned, only to have her words fall on deaf ears.

There was no way Ruby was going to miss it. She would not just see her lover, but she didn't tell Daphne that the people from Don Diva wanted to do a story on Ruby's life in the eighties, up until her arrest and conviction. When Ruby had shared that news with Mecca in an attempt to reach out to her and rekindle the bond they had prior to her imprisonment, Mecca simply stated that she didn't think that would be wise. In fact, she thought it was plain stupid.

"I know what and what not to say. Plus, double jeopardy is against the law," Ruby had replied, taken aback by Mecca's tone. Mecca shrugged while she read an *Essence* magazine while sitting in Ruby's kitchen.

"It's your life."

Thinking to herself, Ruby realized that she didn't have time to keep trying to be nice to someone who got an attitude for God knows what. *If that's the way Mecca wants it, then fuck it.* Truth be told, Ruby was saddened by the way Mecca treated her, but she sucked it up.

"I love my niece," she'd explained to Daphne, "but I'm no ass kisser."

To Ruby, it was a good thing Daphne had helped Mecca find an apartment of her own, because Ruby hated feeling like she was living with a stranger. In the meantime, Ruby had got a call from her friend Tashera from Harlem, stating that she was coming home and that her father was throwing a celebration in Vegas, sponsored by *Don Diva,* who did a story on Tashera "Tashy" Williams.

Ruby stepped out of her rented baby blue X5, handed her keys to the valet, and walked the red carpet into the club. She was definitely a head turner when she appeared wearing a skin-gripping white catsuit under a waist-length chinchilla and a pair of Jimmy Choo heels. Ruby walked and looked like money. Before entering the party, she gave her name to a man standing at the podium, checking a list. The party was exclusively invites only. The man checked the list and smiled at her.

"Ms. Davidson, Ms. Williams told me when you came to call her so that she could walk you in herself."

The man dialed a number on his cell phone and spoke when a person answered, informing them that Ruby was there. He looked at Ruby with a smile that was becoming annoying to her. Ruby hated a kiss ass. No more than a minute later, a short, deliciously dark-skinned female ran toward Ruby excitedly. Ruby opened her arms to embrace her friend. Both women were overly excited to see one another; it was a much-awaited reunion for both of them.

"Tashy, what's good, ma?" Ruby asked while hugging Tashy, then releasing her to look into her eyes. They weren't used to seeing each other in clothing that wasn't prison issue.

Tashy knew from Ruby's letters that she was doing well in the world. She didn't send Tashy pictures, because they weren't allowed to correspond with former inmates in the prison, so they stayed writing every month.

"Damn, Ruby, you look good, baby," Tashy said, grabbing Ruby's arm and walking her into the club.

"All this is for you, Tashy? Your father loves his baby," Ruby responded as she scanned the club, which was decorated with "welcome home" banners, noting the live entertainment from the hottest hip-hop and R&B stars, the free food, and drinks of the most expensive kind.

"Daddy's little girl, even at the age of thirty-seven," Tashy giggled.

They met before Ruby was transferred out of the women's federal detention center in Virginia. Tashy came to the prison in 1992, after being convicted of money laundering and federal tax evasion. The initial investigation was directed at her father, a one-time member of a heroin-dealing organization headed by the notorious kingpin Frank Matthews, who had disappeared from sight after posting a two-million-dollar bail.

Tashy's father, Tommy "Scooter" Williams, was allegedly a lieutenant in the Matthews organization, but the government couldn't prove it. Tashy owned a hair salon in Harlem, which Scooter had bought her and which he used to wash his money. When Tashy started living a lifestyle that owning a hair salon couldn't provide, the government was watching. Informants told the government that dope was sold out of the place, so the feds felt that arresting Tashy would put Scooter in a bind. They figured he would give himself up to save his only daughter. They knew how close they were and figured they had Scooter at last. They were wrong.

They had no idea how much of a trooper Tashy was and how far she would go for her father. Even against Scooter's wishes, Tashy fought the case. She knew they had no solid proof that heroin was being sold from the salon. Her customers were longtime friends from the neighborhood and wouldn't dare snitch on her.

The government could not prove that heroin was being sold, so they convicted her of other charges. Since she was a first-time offender, the judge gave her ten years, instead of the twenty she could have received. The loyalty and honor she showed made her loved even more in Harlem. She did her time with the same attitude she had on the streets.

Her fellow convicts loved her just as much as people on the streets. Inmates that were without family and friends to come visit them or send money would receive some of her joy. Tashy would have someone send them money, and during family outings she'd invite the inmate to sit with her family. Tashy became good with the law and helped others with their cases without charging, unlike your average jailhouse lawyer. Many hated her for that but wouldn't dare let it be known. Despite her efforts to help, a hater or three always lurked in the background. There practically wasn't an inmate in the jail that wouldn't attack you for even saying a bad word about Tashy. Especially Ruby.

"C'mon, Ruby, there's some people that I want you to meet. The two most important people in my life," Tashy said, pulling her by her hands and passing tables with white coverings and candles placed there for the event. Seated all around were people old and young. Most of them were friends and associates of Scooter and were there to celebrate the release of his daughter, whom some had known since she was a child, and some had never met her but had heard about her. Because it was Scooter's daughter, they came from far and wide.

Ruby was rushed to the VIP section by an overexcited Tashy, to a table that seated two people, a tall older man, unmistakably her father, and a young, pretty woman who looked like Tashy's twin. A woman that Ruby had seen in pictures and had heard so much about during her time in prison.

"Daddy, Simone, I would like you to meet Ruby," Tashy announced, standing aside so her father could stand and shake Ruby's hand. Ruby noticed how handsome Scooter was up close. His skin had a copper tone and a rich glow. Scooter, now in his early sixties, was a well-respected old-school hustler with deep pockets. For a man in his sixties, Scooter held on to a well-built physique due to his daily workout of jogging and exercise and a strict no-red-meat diet. The only signs of age on his tall frame were the graying short Afro and matching mustache.

"Wow, you're beautiful, just like your mother," Ruby complimented.

"Thank you," Simone said to Ruby after embracing her and sitting back down.

Ruby remembered the days when they shared a cell and Tashy would stare for hours at pictures of her now twenty-two-year-old daughter. She was twelve then, but Tashy had pictures of every special event in Simone's life. Scooter made sure of that. Birthdays, graduations, proms, and all. Scooter taped and photographed everything for her. Every month Scooter would have someone bring Simone to the prison to see her mother. Tashy cried for long hours after every visit.

When Ruby asked about Simone's father, it was the only time Tashy's jovial aura would become dark and somber. Ruby figured the topic was a sensitive issue. Still, Tashy explained it to her.

"I was sixteen, and he was twenty at the time. I really liked him, Ruby. His name was Shane, and he was from Washington Heights. It wasn't meant for me to get pregnant, but it happened, and when my father found out, he blew a lid something crazy. He found out about Shane, whose father was a Dominican hustler my father knew. A week later I find out Shane was sent to the Dominican Republic forever. He was told to never speak to me again. Last I heard, he's married with kids."

"I've heard so much about you, Ruby. It's good to finally meet you." Scooter spoke in a deep bass voice.

Ruby wondered if Tashy had told her father that they were lovers who had spent nights in a small cell, having lesbian sex, using lotion bottles as dildos and melting commissary candy bars to lick chocolate off of each other.

Scooter cut his eye to Tashy with a smirk. "I wish Tashy would have told me you've been home. I would have made arrangements to meet you. So what have you been up to?"

Even though Ruby knew Scooter was an old gangster, she didn't think telling him that she was getting rich off of selling exotic weed in Brooklyn was a good idea. She didn't think he wanted Tashy around the criminal element anymore.

"I've opened up a business in Brooklyn. A grocery store. I'm about to open a restaurant," she answered, straight-faced.

Scooter nodded. "That's wonderful. I was hoping Tashy would get back into the spirit of running a business."

A maître d' brought over two chairs so Ruby and Tashy could sit at the table with Simone and Scooter. Ruby noticed Simone had a serious look on her face. She didn't inherit the constant jolly mood of her mother. Her face was oval shaped, like Tashy's, and surrounded by shoulder-length, dark, shiny hair and a bang that was slicked back, revealing a long forehead. Her eyes were elongated and a flat brown. Ruby figured she was a deep thinker.

"Can I enjoy my freedom first, Daddy, before you start on me about running a business?" Tashy spat with a playful grin.

A photographer from *Don Diva* approached the table. "Excuse me, Ms. Williams?" the photographer said humbly. "May I get a picture of you and your family?"

Tashy smiled. "Of course." She grabbed Ruby's hand and tried to pull her from the table to join her in the photo.

Ruby grunted between clenched teeth, "Tashy, she said family!"

"You are family. Now get up." Tashy smiled to the photographer. "This is my friend Ruby."

The photographer raised her eyebrows. "Are you Ruby Davidson from Brooklyn?"

"In the flesh," Tashy answered excitedly. "C'mon, take the flick. You can holler at her later on!"

Scooter, stood between his daughter and granddaughter, with Ruby next to Tashy, and posed for the picture.

Afterward Tashy, Ruby, and Simone danced, ate, and talked, while Scooter rubbed shoulders with the black politicians in attendance.

A lot of politicians had grown up in Harlem and had known Scooter coming up. They never forgot their friends when they made it in politics. So when the government began targeting him, they stood by him, and when Tashy was convicted, they rallied for her freedom. Though their cries went unheard, Scooter's name was cleared of drug dealing when the government couldn't prove the heroin was being sold out of Tashy's hair salon.

"How's your niece, Ruby?" Tashy asked while catching her breath after dancing with a famous R&B singer. Tashy knew everything about Mecca from Ruby's correspondence with her after she was transferred to the prison in West Virginia. Two years later Tashy was transferred to the same prison, and she and Ruby wasted no time becoming cell mates again.

"She's good," Ruby answered, avoiding eye contact. While Ruby had no problem sharing her personal issues with Tashy, this wasn't the proper place to talk about her concerns about Mecca. Even though they were lovers, they acted like sisters. They had sat up plenty of nights in the cell, sharing their life stories. They had bonded because they had a lot in common. When Tashy had told Ruby that she never had a mother, because she died giving birth to her, Ruby shed a tear.

When Tashy saw that, she knew that Ruby was her friend. Ruby hardly showed her feelings or emotions. The only time she showed any was when she was beating someone up. That was the first time she saw Ruby cry, and the second and last was when Ruby found out about her niece.

"When do I get to meet her?" Tashy asked with a wide smile.

"Whenever. Right now she's in New York, hanging with Daphne," Ruby said, knowing that simply mentioning Daphne's name would get her to change the subject.

Everyone in the West Virginia prison had known the two women had it in for each other. Though Daphne didn't need to hustle in jail, hustling was in her blood, so with her knowledge of the law, she became a jailhouse lawyer. Tashy was transferred to the prison, and word got out that she was also good with the law and she wouldn't charge an inmate for help.

It didn't upset Daphne that Tashy was helping inmates free of charge; what got under her skin was Tashy supposedly told inmates that Daphne didn't know what she was doing. So a confrontation between the two women was inevitable. Daphne didn't appreciate anyone talking behind her back, assassinating her character.

One sunny afternoon in the rec yard, while Ruby and Tashy sat on a bench, playing cards, Daphne walked up and sat next to Ruby, turning to stare at Tashy. Tashy was no punk, but she wasn't a fighter, either. She had grown up spoiled and protected by her father and her neighborhood. She never had to lift a finger at anyone.

That couldn't be said about Daphne. She'd grown up on the rough streets of two of Brooklyn's roughest neighborhoods: Bed-Stuy and Brownsville. She'd had to fight either in school, when girls would pick fights with her, out of jealousy mostly, and in the Tompkins projects. Tashy was no match for her.

"I hear you got a sweet tooth, Tashy." Daphne scowled while cracking her knuckles. Ruby looked at both women, confused.

"Daphne, what's up?"

"What are you talking about, Daphne? What is that supposed to mean?" Tashy snapped.

"It means you have my name in your mouth when it shouldn't be."

Tashy rolled her eyes and sucked her teeth. It was the first time that anyone ever saw her come out of character.

"Ruby, get this bitch before I—"

Daphne reached across the table and tried to choke Tashy, but Ruby grabbed her behind her waist. "Daphne, chill! Leave it alone!" Ruby ordered.

Tashy was on her feet, ready to rumble. "Let her go. I'll fight her. She don't scare me."

"Tashy, shut up. Nobody's fighting. Y'all both my peoples, so off the strength of me, squash this bullshit."

Both women knew that if they didn't respect Ruby's wish, they would have to face off with her, and neither one of them wanted that. Ruby was a ferocious fighter and wouldn't hesitate to use any weapon she could get her hands on. So both women went their separate ways. From that day forth, they disliked each other with a passion.

Tashy rolled her eyes. "You got your niece hanging around Miss High-and-Mighty, huh?"

"Tashy, you're a grown-ass woman," Ruby replied as she watched Simone, who sat quietly next to her mother. "Your grown mom's had a petty beef with this girl in jail over nothing, and she acting like a teenager. That is over. That is all behind us, Tashy."

Tashy waived Ruby off. "Yeah, whatever. Just don't have that bitch around me."

Ruby simply shook her head. "Grow up." When Simone got up to go to the restroom, Ruby inquired, "She seems uptight. What's up?"

Taking a sip of Dom Pérignon, Tashy replied, "I can't call it, Ruby. These young chicks these days are spoiled. Plus, she isn't the party type." She looked around and lowered her voice as she changed the subject. "I'm glad you came when you did. My father tried to hook me up with one of his politician friends' son. Girl, this man is so ugly, it looked like his face hurts when he smiles."

Ruby giggled. "How rich is he?"

"Who cares? A billion dollars couldn't make him cute," Tashy spat.

After the celebration, and after everyone emptied the club to do things in Vegas that stay in Vegas, Tashy snuck off to Ruby's suite in the Palms for a long-awaited episode of sucking and touching. Once they entered the luxurious suite, the women wasted no time coming out of their clothes.

As they kissed, passionately exploring each other's bodies with roaming hands, Ruby asked in a husky whisper, "Does your family know about us?"

Tashy moaned in her ear, "Don't ruin the moment," and pushed Ruby on the bed.

With a seductive grin, she parted Ruby's thick thighs and placed a warm, long tongue against her erect nipples. Ruby groaned and closed her eyes. To her, Tashy was the best lover she'd ever had. Tashy knew how to please her in ways Ruby couldn't resist.

She knew exactly where to touch Ruby, making her go nuts. When Tashy placed her tongue between her thighs, Ruby arched her back while holding on to Tashy's ponytailed head. The silk sheets felt smooth under Ruby's skin as they changed positions to eat each other out in the sixty-nine position, as well as using the doggy style and missionary. Their faces were wet with each other's juices, while their dark, voluptuous bodies glistened with sweat. When they were done, they both leaned up against the headboard, smoking a joint of potent Mexican bud.

"So does your family know?" Ruby asked, blowing smoke circles toward a ceiling fan.

"No, and it's none of their business." Ruby knew that wasn't Tashy's real reason for not telling them about her lifestyle. She knew how much Tashy tried to please her father, and hearing that she was a lesbian might not sit right with him or Simone.

"Don't you think they'll start to question and wonder why you're not with a man?"

"Shit," Tashy grumbled while passing Ruby the joint. "I'm a grown-ass woman. I don't have to explain my lifestyle to no one. I just did ten years for my father, so I'll be damned if he judges me. Simone, I think she'll understand. I mean, a lot of women are into it."

Putting the joint out in an ashtray on the bedside table, Ruby changed the subject. "So, what's your plan?"

Always the hustler, Tashy chimed right in. "I hear that weed is really popping. I know where to get it real cheap. I got a Cali connect, and you don't have to do a lot of traveling. I got a hookup at this FedEx joint back home."

"So you wanna sell strictly weight?"

"No doubt. You can get it from me cheaper than what you're getting it for. One hand washes the other." Tashy grinned.

Ruby knew that Tashy loved the idea of cutting Daphne's throat. Daphne's connect in Texas had good prices, and when she brought him other customers, he looked out for her by giving her a pound for free. She knew that if she stopped coppin' from the connect, he'd lose a customer and Daphne's commission would get shorter. She figured that Daphne would be angry if Ruby decided to switch connects, and hearing that Tashy was the reason would probably piss her off even more. Yet Ruby was about money, and no one got in the way of her making money. She owed no one an explanation. So the decision was easy for her.

"Give me a hundred pounds next week."

"It's a done deal." Tashy smiled.

Grabbing Tashy's face between her hands, Ruby smiled. "I'm so glad you're home, baby."

For another two hours, the women made love. Tashy left a sleeping Ruby to return to the hotel room she shared with Simone. As Tashy tiptoed through the hotel room so that she would not wake Simone, she couldn't remove the smile on her face. After a shower, Tashy climbed under the Versace quilt on the king-size bed. In the dark, she did not notice Simone sitting halfway up, leaning her head on a large down pillow.

"So are you and Ruby lesbians?"

For the past few months, veteran detective Thomas Caldwell had been vigorously investigating the triple murders of Karmen and her sisters. Tall, athletically built, with a stubbled chin, hooded blue eyes, and a weathered face, he resembled Brett Favre, except for his jet-black hair. Frustrated, he knew that he desperately needed to solve this case. It would be the biggest case of his career and could mean a promotion to captain with a conviction.

Sitting behind his desk cluttered with paperwork, family photos, and a mug of coffee, Caldwell read interview after interview of witness statements, trying to see if he had missed anything of value. Tapping a pencil on his desk, he scanned the office that he shared with four other homicide detectives. Being thirty-eight, he was the youngest of them all. His thoughts were interrupted by the ringing of his desk phone.

"Am I speaking to Detective Caldwell?" the voice on the line asked, with a vintage New York accent.

"Yes, this is he. Who's speaking?"

"This is Detective Mike Levy. I'm down at the Seven-three. I'm working a double over here in East New York, and I think there might be a possible link to your triple."

The news made Caldwell sit up in his chair, as the hairs stood on his neck. "Fill me in."

"The owner of the bodega where your bodies were is a resurrected problem out of prison, after putting in a little over a decade. Been home for a few years now, and bodies start dropping where the circumstances surrounding the murders make her a possible suspect."

"You said her?" Caldwell asked with a bit of surprise in his voice.

Levy sighed. "You heard right. Her name is Ruby Davidson out of Brownsville. This ain't your average mademoiselle we're talking about here, pal. She makes some of these male thugs look like the pope himself. Real evil broad, buddy."

"So where's the link?" Caldwell asked, anxious to hear the promising lead that would crack the case wide open.

"My double over here were guys rumored to have an involvement in the shooting of her niece, who recently came out of a coma, and the murder of her boyfriend. Her boyfriend's cousins, who were also murdered, one of them was romantically linked to one of your corpses. I think her name was Karmen," Levy said.

"Yeah, that's one of mine."

"She was questioned about the murder of her boyfriend and his brother due to suspicion that she was involved. I interviewed the detective working on that case, and he said after talking to her, he felt she knew more than she was letting on. What I'm saying is, all these murders someway, somehow, could be the result of dealing with Davidson and her niece."

Though not overly excited anymore over the lead Levy had given him, Caldwell tapped his pencil on the table a few times before responding. "What's the intel on her niece?" he asked.

"From what I heard, she ran Davidson's organization while Davidson did time. Now she's out of the game. I guess the coma was a wake-up call that she answered when she woke up."

Caldwell thanked Levy and promised to follow up and share intel relating to Ruby and Mecca. Hanging up the phone, he tapped his pencil against the desk, in deep thought. He leaned back in his chair and thought out loud. "If it was a robbery homicide, why would Davidson rob her own store and have the workers killed?"

Shaking his head, he rose from his seat and put the tan cotton blazer on over his stark white dress shirt. "Police work," he mumbled. Checking his police-issue Glock .40, he made a mental note to find Ruby Davidson for an interview.

More and more, his thoughts drifted back to the pretty Spanish girls murdered in cold blood. He felt a sadness for their family and friends. So young they were, with their whole lives ahead of them. He had nieces their age, who were full of life and promise. Their lives were cut too short for material things that could easily be replaced. Now all that was left of them was memories and faces painted on the metal gate of the store, saying, IN LOVING MEMORY OF KARMEN, MARIA, AND TINA.

***

"I'm not a baby. I'm a grown woman who can figure things out." Tashy avoided eye contact with Simone after she turned on the light to face her mother.

"Please, Mom, don't lie to me. I'm tired of living a lie."

Tashy looked over at her daughter, the spitting image of her, with traces of her father in her complexion, and sighed.

"It's true. Please don't be disappointed in me, Simone. I just don't want to embarrass you. I want to be the perfect mother and make up for all the lost time."

Simone's eyes filled with tears. "I'm not disappointed in you, Mom. I'm proud that you're my mom. I'm so happy that you told me the truth. It's okay with me, because I understand."

"Oh, Simone, come here, honey." Tashy cried as she embraced her daughter.

Afterward she wiped the tears off of her daughter's face and asked, "Why did you say you were tired of living a lie? What did you have to lie about?"

"I have a girlfriend, too." Simone shook her head, looking down at her hands.

Tashy's eyebrows rose. "Get out of here! You kidding, right?"

Simone gave her the "do I look like I'm kidding" look.

"Your grandfather know?"

"Yeah. That's why I wound up going to school out on corny Long Island, living in a corny neighborhood, surrounded by corny people, and having to lie to my friends about liking boys and playing girlfriend to this corny guy Scooter practically made me date."

Simone called her grandfather by his nickname at his request. He thought "grandpa" made him feel too old. Facing her daughter, Tashy folded her legs under her and sat upright in the lotus position. Simone did the same. Feeling like a teenage girl all over again, Tashy started the girl talk.

"What's her name? Tell me about her."

"Her name is Mona. She lives on Twenty-ninth and Frederick Douglas. . . ."

They sat up all night, catching up on each other's lives. Tashy listened attentively, learning what Simone's life had been like after her incarceration. Sometimes, Tashy teared up, feeling that she had missed some of the important moments that Simone told her about. Secretly, she vowed never to miss these moments in her daughter's life again.

At the same time Simone couldn't be happier. She felt free from the burdens that she carried, talking to her mother. Scooter had sheltered her and locked her away from the real world. He had plans for her to be married to the son of a football star, whom she was currently dating, to live in a big house and produce great-grandkids he could spoil like he did her. She never talked to any of her friends like she did to Mona and now to her mother, and it felt good. Scooter had forbidden her to go to Harlem to see Mona, and she knew that he had lots of people on watch for her. All she could do was call Mona on her cell phone and talk for hours. Otherwise, she dug deep into her schoolwork and classes at LIU.

"When was the last time you and Mona were together?" Tashy asked.

"It's been two months now."

"Guess what? You're coming to live with me in the city as soon as we get back." Tashy grabbed her daughter's hand and held it tight. Simone's face lit up with excitement.

"What about Scooter?"

"What about him? You're my daughter. He can't tell me what to do with my child. Girl, please! And guess where my crib is at?"

"Harlem?" Simone cooed.

"You know it. Right on 140th and Lenox."

"Ruby seems like a tough chick. Tell me about her. She must be somebody if *Don Diva* wants to do a story on her."

With a grin and a sigh, Tashy rolled her eyes. "Girl, I don't know where to begin. Ruby is more than a magazine article. She's a book."

Simone giggled. "What would you call the book?"

After briefly thinking on the title, Tashy smiled. "*Hell's Diva.*"

Chapter Thirty-seven

When I lie down, I say, "When shall I arise, and the night be ended? And I am full of tossings to and fro unto the dawning of the day."

—Job 7:4

Tears rolled down ten-year-old Mecca's face as she made her way from her bedroom, down the carpeted hallway of her aunt's Coney Island duplex. The pain in her head made her attempt to sleep fruitless.

Making it to the closed, locked door of Ruby's bedroom, she heard Luther Vandross's voice and smelled the strong odor of weed coming from the other side of the door.

"Auntie!" she squealed as she banged on the door.

After a few more tries, the door flew open and a naked Ruby, with bloodshot eyes, stood before her. Mecca looked in at the bed, where Monique sat, leaning on the brass headboard, smoking a joint.

"What's wrong, baby?" Ruby asked.

"My head hurts bad."

Monique quickly grabbed a pink terry-cloth robe and held Mecca by the hand as they made their way up the stairs to the kitchen.

"I'll give you something for the headache. You want some warm milk and cookies?"

Mecca nodded. Monique crushed an aspirin with a little water on a spoon. While the milk and cookies made Mecca forget all about the headache, Monique slipped her the spoon. Afterward, she wiped the milk off of her lips and took her to her room to tuck her in.

She kissed Mecca on her forehead once and whispered, "I'll see you tomorrow, okay, honey?"

Mecca smiled and nodded. Without question, Monique was one of Mecca's favorite people in the world, only after her mother and father and, of course, Aunt Ruby. In a way, Monique reminded her of her mother. Nothing seemed to bother her. With all the things Mecca saw living in Brooklyn, she wondered how Monique could be that way.

Sometimes, she wondered if it was seeing them making love on the couch one day that had made her that way. Then she realized that she would probably never know. Monique was probably just a happy person, because to Mecca, whatever it was they were doing on the couch, it bothered her, almost made her feel sick. Either way, Monique was happy. In the middle of the night Mecca awoke, crying, because of the throbbing pain in her head.

"Shhh . . ." she heard from the darkness. "Sleep comfortably, Mecca."

She recognized the voice of her friend and smiled, happy that he was present again. She thought he didn't care for her anymore, because he'd been gone for so long. Now he was back, and she could feel his touch on her head, which made the headache go away. Then she fell asleep. As soon as Mecca walked into the office, Lou wasted no time snorting.

"You think 'cause you saved my life that I'm supposed to ignore what you're up to?"

"You welcome. I'm fine. Nice to finally have you back," Mecca said sarcastically as she stood with her hands on her hips, eyeing Lou. Lou leaned back in his chair and folded his arms across the desk.

"You lied to me, Mecca. Why?"

"I have no idea what you're talking about, Lou," she replied, confused.

Lou shook his head. "You're better than I thought. Pulled one over on me. Could you believe that? Me!"

"Are you okay, Lou? Did that Doc guy give you some of his tea?"

"Cut the crap," he snapped. "I know you're plotting to start a war between Daphne and your aunt. I'm no fool!"

Mecca shook her head in disbelief. "You're kidding, right? Do we have to change positions? I'll be the one to enter your dreams and attempt to get you to see the reality of things, because you're tripping, Lou, for real!"

Lou rose from behind the desk and walked up to her. Though she took a nervous step back, Lou was face-to-face with her and grabbed her cheeks with his large, warm hands.

"Lou!"

"Shhh . . ." He cut her off, and then he softly kissed her forehead.

In a flash, the office and Lou disappeared, and Mecca stared at a vision of herself getting out of her Range Rover at Sutter and Hendrix in Sutter Gardens at night. Looking both ways, she entered the hallway of a building, with her face and head covered by a large black and gray North Face hood.

"What's up, ma?" Breeze mumbled, standing in the hall, with his tan Woolrich hood over his head.

"Wassup, nigga? What's poppin'?" Mecca blew into her hands, warming them.

Breeze pulled out a brown paper bag that was stuffed and handed it to her. "That's from the Jamaican restaurant. I got the loot from the Brownsville spot in my crib. I ain't wanna be out here with all that change on me," he replied.

Mecca looked in the bag and fingered the thick wad of cash. It was her half of the money Breeze passed off for putting him onto robbing Daphne's restaurant and Ruby's spot in Brownsville run by Mo Blood. Breeze and Mecca were the best of friends from when Mecca and Shamel were an item. Breeze and Shamel had been friends since they were kids, and when Shamel introduced him to Mecca, he immediately dug her style. To him, they were the perfect match. Mecca was a classy hood chick who had more heart and drive than most dudes Breeze knew. So, he didn't hesitate to act when she came to him, asking him to rob the spots. He did wonder, Why her aunt's spots, though?

"She's a snake, Breeze. I can't go into details now, but you know me, and you know how I operate. I'm loyal to the bone, but if you cross me, it's on," Mecca had simply growled.

He'd nodded. "I can dig it. You know I'll ride with you anytime."

"What you doing? Let's go get something to eat," Mecca suggested, stuffing the brown paper bag in her coat. Breeze put his arm around her and smiled.

"Your treat?" he asked as they walked toward her Range Rover.

"You know, you've always been a stingy nigga."

As they drove away, they concocted the idea that Breeze would move weed for Ruby and devised another scheme to make her business in East New York crumble like the Brownsville one.

"You tryin'a start a war with your aunt and homegirl?" Breeze inquired as he reclined in the Range Rover's plush leather seat. *"I thought you liked Shorty?"*

"I do. She good people. Plus, there's no way my aunt will come out on top if they go to war. Daphne's connected to the Shower Posse. My aunt has no army."

Breeze shook his head. *"You'd be a hell of a chess player."*

What Mecca didn't realize was that Ruby would partner up with Tashy, and Tashy's connections through her father were just as dangerous and powerful, if not more so, as the Shower Posse's. Sometimes, things didn't always go according to plan.

Mecca drove, smiling to herself. Revenge was definitely sweet. She thought of the pictures she had of Ruby conversing with Mo Blood outside a building in Brownsville Houses. When she gave them to Daphne and explained that those were the guys who shot her and robbed the restaurant, Daphne would realize why Mecca held something against her aunt and why Daphne should also. Wicked.

Mecca was awakened by a blond, bulimic stewardess with a nasal voice. "You'll have to fasten your seat belt. The plane is about to land."

Excited about her trip to Italy to spend a weekend with Miguel, who had returned overseas to start a new season with his basketball team, Mecca half smiled and fastened her seat belt.

The thought of seeing him made her horny and moist. When her thoughts drifted back to the dream in which Lou showed her the plot on her aunt, she shrugged and smiled. *Deal with it, Lou.*

A week after they returned from Vegas, Tashy could see why Simone was infatuated with Mona. She was New York sexy. Her eyes were big, brown, and full of life. She had a smooth bronze complexion that complemented her catwalk-lean body on long, toned legs. She walked with a confidence that oozed seduction, which many women just did not have. She was charismatic, street-smart, and worldly. These were the things that Tashy noticed the day she met her.

During the time Simone was in Mona's presence, the skin-stretching smile never left her face. Tashy knew they were truly in love and was a little envious of their relationship. Hers wasn't an emotional, spiritual intimacy; it was pure lust. She wished Ruby felt the same way she felt about her, but Ruby was a strong, independent woman who knew how to take care of herself. She didn't sit around looking for handouts; she was a go-getter. And she knew how to please a woman.

Still, Tashy knew that Ruby was the type that didn't become emotionally attached. Sure, she was a friend you could count on, but Ruby treated relationships like clothes. Wear them, and when it was time to buy new ones, put the others in the closet until you wanted to wear them again. Ruby's only loves were money and power.

Mona and Simone made a cute couple. While Simone was the listener, Mona was a talker. She wasn't a boring talker; she had lots of interesting stories and gossip. Living in Harlem made it possible for her to hear stories and gossip that would put the tabloids out of business. When Tashy noticed a scar on Mona's jawline, she inquired about it.

"That scar makes you favor Sanaa Lathan. How you get it?"

"I'll take the Sanaa Lathan comparison as a compliment," Mona replied while rubbing it. "I take it that Simone didn't tell you, but this scar is the reason we met."

Tashy folded her arms on the table and raised her eyebrows, waiting to hear the story. "Simone never told me exactly how you met. . . ."

Mona burst off into a fast-talking, excited narrative, which had become her trademark. It was after a house party thrown at a brownstone two blocks from Mona's house, where a group of neighborhood girls with too much liquor and weed in their system decided to cause some trouble. They were jealous of Mona's fashionable appearance and happy-go-lucky attitude. However, unknown to them, that was only a facade. Mona suffered internally. She was a hurt soul from losing both her parents in a fatal bus accident years ago, and she was never able to come to terms with the loss.

But the girls weren't aware of that, and they decided to pick a fight with her outside of the party. At the same time, Simone, who was there, after lying to Scooter that she was going into the city to buy some expensive-looking bag for her collection of books in college, partied it up. The downside to the lie was that Scooter had Wayne, Simone's fake boyfriend, escort her to the city. When she told him about the party, he gave Simone the corny speech she expected from him.

"Do you think it's wise of you to disobey your grandfather, then try and have me condone it?"

Simone sighed, wondering how this dude could be so lame. "Listen, Wayne," she began. "Loosen up a little. Live your own life, not the life your parents want you to live. Get your thumb out of your ass. Now, I'm going to this party, and you're coming, too, and if you keep your mouth shut, I might give you some tonight."

While they were dating, Wayne had begun to sense that she wasn't really interested in him. He figured that with his charm, she would come around; however, six months had already passed. Now his eyes widened. "Since you put it that way, I guess we can live it up a bit."

Wayne actually enjoyed himself. Simone tried to dance with him, but he looked like a stiff white boy. He reminded her of the character Carlton from the show *The Fresh Prince of Bel-Air*. After a while, she left Wayne to chat with friends she grew up with to catch up on what was going on in the old neighborhood.

A few blunts later and loads of gossip, Simone was ready to leave. She found Wayne dancing with a round girl in tight clothes that made her look like an overstuffed suitcase. It would figure that the two people in the party no one wanted to be seen with dancing would find each other. And Simone had to be with one of them. When her friends asked who the weirdo was who'd come in with her, she quickly answered, "My father sent him to bodyguard me."

When they got outside, Simone spotted a crowd of girls stomping and kicking someone on the ground. She knew it was another girl they were jumping when she heard the girl cry out.

These were the same girls that she'd noticed staring at her in the party and whispering to one another. She knew they were jealous of her clothes and real diamonds, because they looked raggedy as all hell, but she didn't really care. Now they were jumping some helpless female. She knew they did not like her, and she didn't really care for them, but they knew their place and would not try anything, because they knew who her father was. She walked toward the crowd.

"Simone, that is none of your business. We have to get back to Long Island!" Wayne squeaked.

"Shut up, Wayne!" Simone parted the crowd. "That's enough. Y'all get off of her!"

"Simone, mind your business. This ain't got nothing to do with you!" one of them grumbled.

"Don't y'all see she's had enough? Damn, it shouldn't take all of y'all to beat on one girl. Real women fight their own battles!"

Simone helped the girl off the ground. Blood leaked from a gash on her face. Her blouse and Italian-made pants were ripped and dirty, and her hair was out wild. She looked wrecked. Even with everything out of place, Simone could tell that the girl was beautiful, and the way she was dressed with her Manolos let her know she was fashionable and on point. These bitches were probably jealous. When Simone held the girl up, they both walked away toward busy Lenox Avenue. She could hear the girls mumbling under their breath, but they said nothing. Wayne followed.

"Where do you live?"

"Two blocks up. Thank you so much," Mona said, limping.

"Why were they jumping you?" she asked.

"I got too much attention from their boyfriends, and I'm new around here. Crazy thing about it"—Mona chuckled while holding a bloody hand on her open wound—"I don't like boys."

Mona then passed out. When she came to, she was lying in a bed in a Harlem hospital with twelve stitches on her swollen face and Simone holding her hand.

"Where am I?" Mona asked groggily.

"The hospital. You passed out."

Mona remembered the girls jumping her after the party, but she couldn't remember anything after that.

"My name's Mona. What's yours?"

Simone visited Mona in Harlem every weekend afterward. They had the same taste in fashion, TV shows, books, and the same feelings for the same sex. They were inseparable until Scooter found out that Simone was still seeing Mona against his wishes.

"That's it. That's the start of our relationship. Every time I see this scar in the mirror, it no longer makes me sad. I think of my honey, and the scar becomes like my lucky charm." Mona smiled at Simone.

Tashy had to hold back the tears. Afterward, Mona became a regular at Tashy's apartment now that Simone was back in New York City. At first Scooter protested, but when Tashy demanded that she be able to get reacquainted with her daughter, Scooter surrendered. Then, one day, Mona was introduced to Ruby.

At the first sight of each other, Ruby and Mona were attracted to each other. Mona was the type who liked to live life on the edge, the wild side . . . and to her Ruby seemed like the one who could provide that life.

For Ruby, Mona's aura was a seductive elixir that stirred the pure lust within her. Mona knew the more time she spent around Ruby, the more the temptation would grow, but she didn't want to hurt Simone. She loved her with all her heart, but love and lust were two different things. As far as Ruby was concerned, she had no commitments to anyone and she barely knew Simone. Tashy knew better than to try and lock Ruby down, because she had already tried in prison and couldn't do it there. So in the free world, that would be impossible. Still, Mona avoided being in Ruby's presence at all cost. If she saw her car outside Tashy's brownstone, she wouldn't stop by. She would call Simone and ask her to come to her apartment.

One thing Mona was sure of was that if she crossed Simone, it could be bad for her health. And from what she'd learned about Ruby, there would definitely be hell up in Harlem if a confrontation started between them. What she did not know about her was that when Ruby wanted something, she usually got it.

One night Mona answered a knock at her door, believing it was Simone coming over, and received a big surprise. Ruby stood in her doorway with a horny expression written on her face. No words were exchanged, but they both understood their silent communications and wasted no time devouring each other in a long night of passion. Mona had never experienced such pleasure before with a woman. It was as if everywhere Ruby touched or licked was a trigger for sending orgasms throughout her body.

In return, Mona explored every part of Ruby's curvaceous torso. The firmness of her body excited Mona. But to Ruby, Mona was okay in bed, but not as good as she'd expected and nowhere as good as Tashy. She decided that it was nothing worth repeating. But Mona was hooked.

After they concluded their lust making and Ruby left, Mona awoke in the morning with a huge smile, picturing the next time she and Ruby could sneak off and get into it again. She would soon find out that Ruby had no intentions of ever getting in bed with her again. The lust was gone.

Chapter Thirty-eight

Your secrets are safe with me. . . .
—Alicia Keys

Mecca leaned on the terrace of her hotel bedroom overlooking the streets of Rome, holding a glass of champagne. She inhaled the Italian air, smiling to herself and thinking about how well her plans were playing out. The manila envelope sitting on the king-size bed reminded her that the final part of her plan would soon be put into motion. Life was good.

While she awaited Miguel's return from a game, she toured Rome in her rental, using the navigation system to find places in the city. Thoughts raced through her mind as she took in the sights. The city was beautiful in an old, but rich way. It looked nothing like the buildings in Brooklyn and made her feel like she was in another world.

She was happy that she was financially comfortable to enjoy such pleasures and travel the world with the man she loved, who loved her back. Yet not all her thoughts were joyous. Occasionally, she would drop down into a depression as she remembered the things she'd seen on the mean streets.

It saddened her because it was all she knew. Even now she was using what she knew to pay back those who had wronged her when all she was trying to be was loyal. She thought about Daphne, those eyes, why she was in her dreams, and everything they had experienced since meeting. She hoped that her plan would make Daphne come out on top, because she really liked her. However, personal feelings had to be set aside in order for her plan to be successful. Too much was at risk.

When she stepped out on the town, she adhered to the saying, "When in Rome, do as the Romans do," and dressed in the finest Italian clothing and made sure Miguel did, too. They dined at outdoor restaurants, and they even played a game of boccie with a group of older Italian men and took in an opera.

Mecca hated the opera. For Miguel, Mecca's declarations of love weren't etched in stone until one morning, when he awoke and went to the bathroom. There he found her sitting on the toilet, defecating, with the door wide open. She smiled at him and wiped. That was when he knew they were in love.

For Mecca, Miguel's love was proven when she finally decided to tell him about her vision while in a coma and Lou. Once she began, everything came out like a flood, and she could do nothing to stop it. She cried when she told him about the murder of her parents and her aunt's involvement and how Lou had exposed all the lies in her life told by people around her.

Miguel simply listened, and when it was all over, he hugged her. "It was a vision, Mecca. How can you be so sure they are true?"

"A lot of the circumstances made it obvious," she replied.

Miguel didn't know how to take her revelations. All he knew was that he loved her and he wanted to spend the rest of his life with her. So he left it at that. The coma was behind them, and life was moving on. Realizing she'd been through a lot, he was determined to fill the rest of her life with happiness.

While they toured the ruins of the Colosseum, Miguel removed a small box from his silk white slacks and got on one knee. Mecca lost her breath when he opened the box, which held a four-carat diamond in a platinum setting.

"Mecca Sykes, one day isn't worth living if you're not my wife. Marry me."

"Yes!" Mecca yelled before he could even finish.

"Damn, what a brother gotta do to be more than just a fuck?"

"Don't ask to be more than just a fuck is what he gotta do," Daphne answered with a smile as she rushed one of her casual sex partners out of her apartment. Men practically begged for her to be their woman. She received so many flowers at her restaurant so often, people were starting to think it was a florist/restaurant. She didn't even read the cards. Andrea would amuse herself reading them to her, but she never paid any attention.

Daphne used men that she met on occasion like men used women. Purely physical. She wanted no attachments to any of them. To her, no man could replace Donovan. Everyone tried telling her to let go and open her heart, even Junior, who advised, "You will never be happy if you don't love again. What is life if you have no legacy to leave behind? You will achieve happiness from raising a family." While she listened and nodded, her heart said otherwise. There were big shoes to fill to receive her heart, and so far all the men she dealt with had come up short.

Shutting the door of her brownstone after the inadequate plumber left, she had a moment to think. Wrapped in a black silk robe that reached her toned thighs, she grabbed the manila envelope that had a bunch of stamps on it, had been postmarked in Italy, and had no return address, and opened it.

Daphne smiled as she saw photos of Mecca and Miguel posing in front of various European landmarks. The Eiffel Tower, Westminster Abbey, the Louvre, Buckingham Palace, the Leaning Tower of Pisa, and the Colosseum.

The smile vanished as she eyed the photos of Ruby smiling with Mo Blood, with Tah Gunz in the background. There was even a photo of Ruby and Breeze in front of his Sutter Gardens building. Daphne was confused. She had no idea who these people in the pictures with Ruby were, or why Mecca had sent them. She looked back in the manila envelope and took out a letter from Mecca.

Daphne,
First, let me say, I took your advice and traveled the world. What makes it more exciting is that I'm doing it with the man I truly love and trust. (You should give love another chance. You deserve it!) And guess what? I'm engaged! There are pictures of me there with the four-carat rock on my finger. Can you say bling-bling? I'm happy now, Daphne, and it feels good having people

around you that care about your happiness. That brings me to the pictures of Ruby and those men.

I told you once before that at one time my aunt was my idol. She was everything I wanted to be. She is courageous, independent, self-sufficient, and business minded. At the same time she is a ruthless, self-centered, "it's all about her" snake! She is the reason why my mother and father got killed. Her greed made her help set up my father to be robbed. She did it because she was strung out on dick. A man's good dick is her weakness. That's why she lives a gay lifestyle, so she can remain in control. She killed the men responsible for the murders so they wouldn't expose her.

She let me fall in love with a man who she was having sex with behind my back. He worked for her, but in reality, he called the shots because she was weak for the dick. Those men in the photos (the one in the wheelchair and the one with him) are the guys who shot me, putting me in a coma. She had them selling weed for her in Brownsville.

They are dead now. She killed them for the same reason she killed the men who killed my parents. Not to be exposed. She uses people for what she needs, and when she's done, she kills them. She's a black widow. The other man in the picture with just him and her, his name is Breeze. He is the guy who robbed your restaurant, and she staged the robbery of her store.

I'm telling you these things because she doesn't deserve to have the opportunity to do what she does to another person who has been loyal to her. What you do with this info is all on you, but I assume you will move wisely. I don't think I'm coming back to New York. As much as I love it, my heart belongs to my man now. Hopefully, we will see each other again. We gotta do Paris and Italy together. I met Donatella Versace!

Take care, Daphne. Oh, did you like my tearful act at Karmen's funeral?

Peace

Mecca

Daphne put the letter down, infuriated. Donovan's words played in her head as she contemplated her next move. "The longer someone stays in the game, the more likely they will slip up and show their hand. And most people bluff, as if they have a good hand, until the cards are shown."

Looking at Mecca's picture, Daphne mouthed, "Thank you, Mecca. We are definitely the last of a dying breed."

Daphne reached for her multicolored Louis Vuitton pocketbook and pulled out her Nokia cell phone. When the person she called answered, she spoke.

"Junior, I'm going to need an umbrella. A storm is brewing."

"Can you come out of the rain without getting wet?" Junior inquired.

"No. I was locked out of the house," Daphne sighed.

The line went dead. In their coded language, Daphne made it clear that a war was inevitable. There was no other way of dealing with Ruby that would leave her on top, and she would have to deal with the storm head-on. Junior wanted to know if it could be avoided, and from what Daphne said, it couldn't. Ruby had to die.

"Happiness is short lived when you enjoy making others unhappy."

"And what is that supposed to mean? Are you about to give me another one of your speeches? Because I got better things to do," Mecca announced to Lou, who sat on a bench, reading a newspaper, with his legs folded.

In this dream they were both dressed in eighties apparel, sitting on a bench in the Langston Hughes projects, which she'd grown up in.

The streets were empty, and a cold breeze flowed through the dark night. Mecca pulled the earflaps of her gray sheepskin hat over her ears, shivering at the cutting cold. As she looked up, she could see movement in the lighted apartments above.

"What do you have to do that's more important than being here with me?" Lou asked jealously. Mecca held her hand in front of her, showing her engagement ring off.

"I'm engaged, so what I have to do is be a good fiancée." Mecca smiled. "And travel the world."

"Just don't forget where you came from," Lou murmured.

"How can I?" she asked as she gestured at her surroundings with her hands. Afterward, she folded her arms across her chest and said, "You never told me why, out of all places and all people, you chose Brownsville and me."

Lou smiled. He smiled because he loved showing Mecca answers instead of telling her. He snapped his fingers, and suddenly the neighborhood came alive with sunshine and people. They watched as a group of children stood over a syringe that sat on the ground, among the litter of broken glass, crack vials, soiled pampers, and the other filth that ghetto streets are adorned with.

One boy, about nine years old, picked up the syringe to show the rest of his group that he was brave. At the same time, Lou said, "You're not the only one experiencing the likes of me, Mecca. There are Meccas and Brownsvilles everywhere, so there are Lous everywhere."

Mecca watched the boy with the syringe and wondered if he knew what it was. The boy acted like he was about to shoot dope, an action that he'd probably seen someone do before, because he knew exactly how to hold the needle. He grinned and spoke to the other kids, but Mecca could not hear him. Then he plunged the needle into his arm.

"No! No! Don't!" Mecca jumped up and ran toward him.

Mecca awoke out of another dream, feeling cold from the open hotel windows. The white curtains blew in gently, giving the room an eerie feel. She knew she didn't scream, because Miguel was still sound asleep next to her. Slowly, she got up and closed the double windows. She crawled back into the bed and cuddled up next to Miguel, who had his back to her. Feeling warmer, she wrapped her arms around him and held on a little tighter.

She watched as the colors of the sky began to change slightly as dawn approached. As Miguel turned, he tugged on the blanket in a way that exposed his nudity. Mecca felt his hardness and smiled. The sun wasn't the only thing rising up this morning.

Chapter Thirty-nine

If you cause opponents to be unaware of the
place and time of battle, you can always win.
—Sun Tzu, *The Art of War*

Ruby was nervously puzzled. For a week straight, she had had no idea where Daphne was. It was as if she'd ceased to exist. The Crown Heights restaurant had been shut down, and when she went to Daphne's house, a strange woman with a Haitian accent answered the door.

"I know no Daphne. I bought this house last week from a real estate agent representing the owner," the woman yelled over the sound of music that Ruby could not recognize. When she tried her cell phone number, the robotic voice told her that the number was disconnected.

She wanted to explain to Daphne that she'd got a better deal with another weed connect. She hoped that Daphne would understand and believed she deserved at least an explanation. Ruby had a lot of respect for Daphne, but business was business. Plus, she was hoping she could squash the animosity between Daphne and Tashy. Having the animosity exist between her two friends made her feel uncomfortable, and Ruby hated being uncomfortable.

In prison, she'd tried to bring the women together, but it wouldn't work. On the streets, she needed it to work, because such animosity could be bad for business, and she still planned on being in business with Daphne. Everybody was useful. That same week when she drove to Brooklyn, she received news that she was in no mood to hear.

"They raided the joint and took everything," Breeze told her while they walked up and down a rainy, empty block in Sutter Gardens.

Ruby stood under a large black umbrella, while Breeze wore a black rain suit. She didn't care about getting wet, but she found that her paranoia grew each day, and that prevented her from speaking in cars or houses about anything illegal.

"Everything?" Ruby asked, surprised.

"The safe and all. Luckily, my dudes ran out in time. Nobody got knocked." Breeze nodded.

"Why was everything in one crib?" she inquired, suspicious of the circumstances.

"We were just about to switch cribs because the other spot was hot. Some cat tried to rob the joint, and my man Kap had to clap him."

Ruby and Breeze stood silently watching as a black Caravan drove by slowly. The two white faces made it obvious that they were cops. The stocky cop in a flannel shirt on the passenger side smiled at Ruby and Breeze as they kept on driving. That smile made Ruby nervous.

"Come check me tomorrow, Breeze," Ruby said, walking toward her Benz.

"Where you gonna be at?" he asked as he began backpedaling into the building.

"I'll call you," Ruby roared as she jumped into her car.

She didn't like the way things were turning out. She was having a bad week, and she knew the police could make it more than a bad week. They could make it bad years. Brooklyn was becoming bad for business, with too many setbacks occurring. First, the robberies of her and Daphne's spots, then Karmen plotting against her, now the raid on the Sutter Gardens spot. A spot that was bringing in good money. In fact, all the money Ruby was making was coming from Sutter Gardens. She had closed the store after Karmen and her sisters were murdered. She had considered keeping it open to let Mecca run it, but Mecca was in her own world. She wouldn't sell weed out of it if she let her run it, because she did not want to put her at risk again. She finally decided to keep it closed when the cops came snooping around, until she could sell the place.

Breeze pulled his hood off his head after he came out of the rain. He grinned, thinking to himself that she fell for it. The cops had never raided the spot; it was still up and running. It was his and Mecca's now.

When Mecca had offered him the deal, he couldn't refuse. She'd told him that once Ruby was out of the way, she could get him weed and coke cheaper than he'd ever seen and that they could split it down fifty-fifty. He'd agreed, but he really had no intentions of doing business with her. He knew she was washed up and wanted to make money, but she didn't realize that she was cutting her own legs from under her by separating from her aunt. Mecca had no power without her aunt. It was a win-win situation for Breeze.

What he did not know was that Mecca had no intentions of partnering with him, either. He was Shamel's best friend, and Shamel had betrayed her. She knew Breeze was down with what was going on and said nothing. So he was on the list for payback, too. Plus, he proved that he couldn't be trusted by plotting against Ruby. They were supposed to be tight. It was another reminder to Mecca that no one in the game was your friend.

Breeze lit up a blunt before walking up the steps of the building. Taking his time, he stepped to the side as a tall, dark-skinned female with long dreadlocks down her back in a ponytail descended. He gave her a quick glance, thinking that she was coming from a friend's apartment, being that he never saw her before, and chuckled to himself after noting the strange clothing she wore. Her black-and-white Chuck Taylor sneakers looked weird with yellow spandex under a tan cotton trench coat. He shook his head as she passed.

"Excuse me, sir, can I get a light?" the woman said with a deep Jamaican accent.

Breeze turned to look down at her. She held a beedi cigarette in her hand, made of small brown paper. Taking a lighter out of his pocket, he walked back to her and lit it. He didn't notice her slide a machete down her sleeve and drop it into her hand. In one swift movement, she swung.

His eyes widened in fear just as the sharp blade connected with his neck, severing his head. When his headless body fell to the bottom of the staircase, his head landed beside it, etched with his stunned expression.

The war was on and popping.

***

"That's the Davidson broad," Detective Mike Levy mumbled from the passenger seat of the black Caravan he cruised the street in. Levy smiled as they drove past Breeze and Ruby, recognizing that they now saw them. He already knew who Breeze was from the neighborhood and his clashes with police and had decided to torment him a bit by keeping an eye on him.

Feeling this was his lucky day, he turned to his partner when Ruby got into her car. "She's taking off. Let's tail her."

The Caravan pulled over behind a parked car, waiting for Ruby to pass. Inside it was silent, except for the sound of the windshield wipers and cars passing over the wet streets.

Ruby noticed the Caravan as she drove by. When they began tailing her, she became nervous. "What is these crackas up to?" she mumbled to herself, nervously looking in her rearview mirror.

She drove slowly down Sutter Avenue with them on her tail, and her heart almost jumped out of her chest when she saw the light flash from the Caravan's dashboard. Then a voice over a loudspeaker roared, "Pull the car over to the right!"

Ruby sat still while she waited for the cops to get out of the Caravan with their hands on their side holsters. They approached the car from both sides, with bright flashlights beaming through the windows and right in Ruby's face.

"Turn the car off, and roll the windows down," Levy said after tapping the driver-side window. Ruby calmly did what she was told, well aware of trigger-happy cops in the city.

"What's the problem, Officer?" Ruby asked, trying to remember if she had run a stop sign or red light.

"I'll ask the questions, Davidson."

Him saying her last name without her giving him identification sent red flags up. She knew this wasn't a routine stop. Playing the confused role, she looked at Levy with a surprised expression.

"You know my name, so I guess there is no need to show my license, huh?"

"I don't think you're foolish enough to drive around without papers and a license, so we'll skip that. I need to ask you some questions about some particular murders out here in East New York. Would you be willing to come in for questioning, or are you going to play hardball?"

"Am I under arrest?" Ruby asked with a serious face. Rain dripped off the bill of Levy's Giants cap and splashed Ruby's cheek. She resisted the urge to wipe it off.

"No, you're not. Just some questions is all I want, and hopefully some answers."

"Give me your card. I'll come to the precinct with my lawyer. Until then, I'm on my way home. So, if you'll excuse me, I'll be pulling off." Ruby rolled her window up and turned the music in her car up to the max so that the cops could hear 50 Cent's voice sing, "Many men wish death upon me." The Benz's tires screeched, leaving Levy frustrated in the rain.

Ruby could not believe it. Murders . . . How the hell did her name come up in that conversation? She knew it could only be Tah Gunz's and Mo Blood's murders that the cops were talking about. The only person that knew anything about them besides her was Breeze. Could he be talking? she wondered. One thing for sure, she wouldn't risk her freedom by not tying up loose ends. Her freedom far outweighed a friendship or business association. Breeze had to go.

Detective Levy was unaware that he would be Ruby's alibi witness when Breeze's murder came to light. Just as he and his partner were driving off after pulling Ruby over, the call came in over the radio.

"All available units report to Sutter and Hendrix. Report of a homicide by decapitation."

Levy looked at his partner, wide-eyed. "Let's roll!"

When they arrived on the scene, there was only a marked squad car there. They were patrolling the area, and as they passed the building, a young woman wearing a robe, with her head wrapped in a scarf, and under an umbrella waved them over. The uniformed cops were apparently rookies, Levy noticed. Their young faces were ghost white as one of them patted the other on the back while he vomited on the sidewalk.

"You fellas okay? What we got?" Levy asked.

"Someone chopped a guy's head off in there. It's the most gross thing I ever saw," the cop doing the patting said.

"This is Brooklyn. Believe me, fellas, you'll see worse." Levy smiled back at his partner, who just shrugged. They walked into the hallway, and Levy shook his head at the bloody scene and headless body. Then he recognized the face.

"Ain't this a bitch?" Levy grunted.

"Holy shit! That's the guy the Davidson broad was just with," his partner grunted as he looked at the face.

"Fucking A right it is. Can't say she committed it, either," Levy sighed.

"Death just surrounds her. What a broad," Levy's partner replied while shaking his head. "I guess I'll call my old lady. Won't be home for dinner tonight."

Once in the comfort of her own home, Ruby decided to take a hot bath.

After the bath, Ruby went into her kitchen, wearing nothing but her own skin, to fix a meal. She was one of those people who could eat breakfast all times of the day and night. So she fixed a cheese omelet and toasted some Eggo waffles. Her cell phone rang as she was flipping the omelet over. Reading the caller ID, she knew it was Tashy.

"Tashy, what's up? Please gimme some good news, because it's been a terrible day." Ruby told her about the spot being raided in Sutter Gardens, then about the cops pulling her over and asking about some murders.

"Murders?" Tashy barked. "God, Ruby, you just got to lay low, ma. You got too much to lose."

"Don't I know it? I got things covered, though."

Tashy sighed. "I hope so. Anyway, Simone is really getting on my nerves."

"How? Already? She just moved in!"

"This Mona chick got her stressed out. She thinks Mona's cheating on her."

"Why she thinking that?" Ruby asked, picturing the rendezvous they'd had. Though Mona's performance wasn't memorable, it was nothing to be strung out over. Simone must be new to the lesbian experience. What Simone needed was a woman to rock her world, and she'd forget about Mona.

"She say's Mona's been acting different. Mona's been avoiding her. I try to tell her not to get all bent out of shape over her. If she's acting funny, let her go. Just now she went out, looking for her. She using that GPS they got on these cell phones to find her. Girl, the technology they got these days," Tashy rambled as Ruby's doorbell rang.

"Someone's ringing my door. I hope it ain't no damn cops," Ruby said, putting on her whorehouse kimono and walking to the door.

She unlocked the door leading to the brownstone's vestibule; then she looked through the curtain of the building's front doors and couldn't believe who was standing there, soaking wet from the rain. Mona. Ruby sighed. How the hell did this child know where I live?

To Tashy, Ruby said, "Tashy, I'll call you back."

"Who is it?" she asked.

"One of my peoples I got on the job," Ruby lied, ending the call and opening the door, frustrated.

"Mona, what the hell are you doing here, and how do you know where I live?" Ruby snapped.

Mona stood there with a sad look on her face as drops of water fell from her soaked hair. "I need to talk to you, Ruby. Can I come in?"

Reluctantly, she let her in. "Take those sneakers and those clothes off. I'll get you some dry ones. Why don't you have an umbrella?"

"When I got on the train uptown, it wasn't raining," Mona said, quickly stripping out of the wet Baby Phat sweat suit and Nike Air Max sneakers.

"Simone is looking for you as we speak. She knows you're in Brooklyn with that GPS stuff on your phone," Ruby said flatly.

"How do you know that?" Mona asked, staring at her. Ruby turned to walk into the bedroom while Mona stood in the living room in a pair of lace panties and matching bra.

"I just got off the phone with Tashy. How else would I know?"

"I don't care. I just wanna be here with you," Mona replied with a shrug. Ruby came out of her room with a robe for Mona. She placed her hands on her hips and looked at Mona with pity on her face.

"Mona, we're not going to be together, so get that out of your head now. Put the robe on. I'm gonna put your clothes in the dryer and when they're dry, you're gonna get a cab uptown to be with Simone."

"I don't want Simone. I'm in love with you. You should have never made love to me, Ruby. I didn't want to hurt Simone, and I tried to avoid you, but no. You had to come and make me feel better than I've ever felt in my life. "

"Listen, Mona, I don't want to hurt your—"

"Then don't . . ." Mona cut Ruby off. Leaving her robe open, she walked toward Ruby with a horny look on her face.

Ruby looked at her pussy through her panties and at her tight stomach, which served only to highlight her perky breasts, and almost entertained the thought of having one more session of mediocre sex with her. Maybe she could teach her something to use on Simone later on. Then she thought better of it, knowing she would never be able to get rid of her after that. Moving closer to Ruby, Mona was stopped by an outstretched hand that took a firm grip on her arm.

"You're young, Mona, and you got a lot to learn. If Simone ain't the one for you, you'll find someone that is. That person ain't me."

Mona's eyes began to tear up. Ruby wanted to snap, but the doorbell rang. Ruby threw her hands up in disbelief, wondering who the hell it could be now. She had just hung up with Tashy, so she didn't think it was Simone that fast. She also hadn't inquired about what time Simone left, but at that point she was already at the door.

"If you don't want to be bothered, I'll answer it. I'll tell whoever it is you're not here," Mona said while wiping the tears from her face.

"Good idea. In fact, tell them a Ruby doesn't live here. Tell them you own the place now," Ruby directed. While she went to put Mona's clothes in the dryer, she wondered what had happened to Daphne. Did the feds get her? Loud screaming broke her thoughts, and Ruby paused to see what was going on.

"Who the fuck lives here, Mona? Is this your secret lover's house? Move! Let me in this bitch!"

Ruby didn't immediately recognize the voice but knew it could be only Simone. That damn GPS! When Simone finally saw Ruby standing in her living room, in a robe, like Mona, she figured she'd walked in on a lovemaking session in progress or one that had just finished.

"Ruby?" Simone said, not believing her eyes. "How could y'all do this to me? How could you do this to my mom?"

"Hold on, Simone. There's nothing . . ."

"Don't fuckin' lie to me. You know what? Fuck this and fuck y'all. I hate y'all scandalous bitches."

Simone rushed out of the house, not giving either of the women a chance to speak. Ruby was vexed. She walked into her bedroom and returned with one of her own sweat suits. She couldn't believe how this shit was going down.

"Put this on, and get the fuck out now!" Ruby threw the sweat suit at Mona, who was about to say something, but Ruby cut her off. "Mona, don't make me beat your young ass up. I said go!"

Mona dressed quickly and left. Ruby didn't even give her cab fare. Exhausted, she plopped down on her couch and looked at a portrait of her sister. *I miss you, sis,* she thought as her eyes watered. She really needed someone she could talk to about her life. If only she were here. The portrait over the brick chimney and mantel was next to a picture of Mecca and Monique from 1984, standing in a Coney Island project hallway. Ruby smiled. She reached for her cell phone and dialed Mecca's number. Ruby's smile vanished when she heard the mechanical voice announce that the number was no longer in service.

Meanwhile, at a Jamaican restaurant in the Tremont section of the Bronx, Daphne sipped an Irish Moss out of a plastic container with a straw while sitting in a small office in the back. Engrossed in a card game with a young, light-skinned Jamaican guy who looked like a double for Spragga Benz, she checked her cards and smiled. The room was filled with marijuana smoke, which made her eyes water a bit. Then a dreadlocked woman walked in.

Daphne looked up and saw the huge mole on her nose that looked like a raisin sitting on a chocolate bar. Her dark skin was smooth and shiny. Her face was long and sculpted like that of an Ethiopian beauty queen. The woman smiled at Daphne and the Spragga Benz twin and then made a cutthroat gesture, which Daphne understood.

As the dreadlocked woman was walking away, Daphne murmured, "Just him?"

The woman shook her head and closed her eyes for a moment before opening them and saying, "The man's family, too." And then she walked out.

Daphne stared at Spragga's twin for a few seconds, imagining the carnage left behind. She didn't want innocent people getting caught up in the war she was bringing to Ruby and her associates, and hearing that the woman had killed Breeze's family was something that she didn't want. Especially considering that the woman did not like using a gun.

"Daphne, you all right?" the Spragga twin asked in a heavy Jamaican accent.

She snapped out of her thoughts. "Yeah, I'm good. I was just thinking." She knew she would have to accept the fact that innocent people would get caught in the middle. It was called collateral damage, she reminded herself. *Charge it to the game.*

A pool of blood flowed from under the door of apartment 2A in the Sutter Gardens building. Neighbors peered and came out of their apartments after hearing a woman scream in the hallway. A few minutes afterward, a ten-year-old boy wearing an oversize G-Unit T-shirt pointed to the floor in front of apartment 2A.

"Mommy, look at the blood," the boy called out as noisy neighbors gathered in the hall. The revelation caused other neighbors to look. A middle-aged man, home only an hour from work at a construction site, looked at the blood and walked to the top of the staircase to called down to police.

"Officer!"

"Yeah, how can I help you?" A balding, short man in a suit and long raincoat looked up the stairs. The man pointed to 2A.

"There's a whole lot of blood coming from that apartment!"

"Levy!" the cop yelled toward the front of the building.

Detective Levy entered the hall. "What's up, Joe?"

"Guy says there's blood coming from the deceased's apartment. Let's have a look."

Levy and the suited Joe Pesci look-alike walked up the flight of steps to Breeze's door. Once there they looked at the pool of blood and shook their heads. Calling back to another cop, Levy waited until he brought him a pair of latex gloves, put them on, and then tried the doorknob to the apartment. It opened. What they saw was a scene out of a horror film. There was blood everywhere. It even dripped from the ceiling fan. The decapitated and mutilated bodies of Breeze's seventy-eight-year-old grandmother, his twenty-two-year-old sister, whose eighteen-month-old baby's headless corpse lay beside her, along with his five-year-old son, were all inside.

"Holy shit!" the Joe Pesci look-alike wailed. Levy shook his head as his partner walked up next to him, looking at the gruesome scene. "Fucking animal, whoever did this shit!"

Levy looked at his partner. "This is bigger than the Davidson broad."

"Yeah, this is the work of foreign organized criminals, Colombians, Chinese, or some Caribbean gang," his partner commented.

"Hate to say it, but we may have to rub shoulders with the government dicks." Levy shrugged.

He walked out of the building, welcoming the drizzling rain on his face. It made him feel like God was looking out for him and washing away the sight and smell of death.

Reluctantly, he removed his phone and made the call. When a voice answered, he simply asked, "May I speak to Agent Doyle?"

Levy was put on hold. Putting his hand in his tight blue 501 Levi's, he grunted, "Fucking feds."

Chapter Forty

If everything in a dream were realistic,
it would have no power over us. . . .
—Robert Greene, *The Art of Seduction*

"So this was your plan? Lie to me, cause trouble between all the people you hate, and watch them kill each other off, while you live happily ever after away from the mess you've created?" Lou asked as he and Mecca sat on a worn couch in what she recognized as a project apartment Ruby once lived in with an ex-boyfriend.

"Smarter than you thought I was, huh, Lou?" Mecca responded, then swung her small legs back and forth without them touching the floor. Mecca was shocked at the sound of her own voice. It was the voice of a young child, about nine years old. It was the first time she realized she was in the body of a small girl.

"I never denied your intelligence, Mecca. I felt that you didn't know how to use your smarts. You could have been anything you wanted, besides a contributor to the death and destruction of your community. You could have—"

"Blah, blah, blah. Damn, Lou! You can't show me any kind of appreciation for saving your life, can you?" she interjected.

"You haven't shown me appreciation for saving yours," Lou replied.

Mecca fell silent. Lou's comment made her feel a tinge of guilt. He was right. Lou did save her life. She could have died in that coma, but it was Lou who wanted her to live. Yet all he expected in return was for her to fly straight. Nobody in her life besides her parents had wanted that for her. Then she thought about Monique. She wanted Mecca to do good, but Monique had lied to her.

She could have gotten any man she wanted, but she chose Bobby Sykes to sleep with and disrespected Mecca's mother by not telling her everything. Lou never lied to her. All he did was tell and reveal the truth.

"Lou, I am sorry for lying to you. Please understand I'm human. Everything I've ever loved wasn't real. It was all a sham. The people, the life I lived, were all nothing. It wasn't my fault, Lou." *Tears dripped down her face.*

Removing a silk handkerchief from the breast pocket of his white linen blazer, he wiped away her tears and then hugged her around the shoulders. "Do you remember me telling you that you didn't have to do anything to the people who betrayed you, because the laws of nature would deal with them?"

Mecca nodded.

"Mecca, even the most coldhearted people have a conscience. They hide it from others, but they can't hide it from themselves."

"What do you mean?" *Mecca asked, hating that he was beating around the bush.*

"Come with me." *Lou grabbed her hand and walked to the bathroom door.*

"I want you to open the door, walk in there, and close the door behind you," *he said.*

Mecca was confused.

"Trust me, Mecca. You will see what I mean."

Mecca opened the door slowly and stepped into the small beige tiled bathroom. She looked back at him before closing the door and saw that he was smiling and nodding his head reassuringly. When she closed the door and turned around, she saw her aunt Ruby sitting on the toilet, crying, with a razor blade in her hand, holding it to her wrist.

"Auntie, what are you doing?" *she screamed, but Ruby could not hear her. Mecca looked to the floor and saw a folded piece of paper with writing on it. When she picked it up and read it, she realized it was Ruby's suicide note. Tears fell as she began to read.*

My dearest niece,
Baby, I'm so sorry for the pain I caused in your life.
I wish I could rewind the clock and go back to the day

*you were born. The family has never been happier than
the day you were brought into the world. Me and your
mother's lives have been extremely hard and stressful,
but you eased that stress and made life worth living. I
never meant for your life to turn out this way. I hate
myself for things I've done. I'm no good for you, and if
I can't be good for you, then life ain't worth living. I left
enough money with Monique for you to live comfortably
until you get a job and straighten your life out.*

*The game ain't where it's at. I played it because it was
my way of surviving without parents to hold me and
your mother down. I hate the life, though. Understand,
Mecca, it's all I know. I love you so much, and I'll carry
that love with me to the hereafter.*

Loving you till death . . .
Auntie

*Just as Ruby put the blade to her wrist, a knock came at
the door.*

"Ruby, what's taking you so long? We got to go!"

*Mecca recognized Monique's voice. Thinking for a moment,
Ruby placed the razor blade back into the medicine cabinet
and ran cold water on her face.*

"I'm coming. Hold on. I'm peeing. Don't rush me!"

*After drying her face, Ruby examined herself in the
mirror, making sure there were no signs of the depressed
state she was in.*

*Mecca threw the note on the floor and opened the door.
Lou stood there with a blank look on his face. She turned her
head to see if Ruby was still standing there and saw nothing.
Feeling her eyes water, she wiped away the first of the form-
ing tears. She never would have guessed how deeply affected
Ruby was by her sister's death and how it would affect
Mecca's life. She couldn't imagine her going out like that. She
figured Ruby would rather go out in a hail of bullets.*

"You seem nervous, Miss Davidson. I assure you that you
have nothing to be nervous about. I understand that your

situation, coupled with the stresses of prison life, can sometimes become unbearably stressful. And we sometimes need someone with a good ear and open mind to vent those stresses to. That's what I'm here for. I assume you've never talked to a psychiatrist before."

Ruby shook her head no.

"Okay, well, I will explain some things about psychiatry and let you know my opinion, then give you options on how to deal with them. I can make recommendations, but it's all up to you. What's said in this room is strictly confidential. Only me and you will know," Dr. Clark said reassuringly.

After explaining psychiatry and her job at the prison, Dr. Clark asked, "Can you tell me about Ruby? Not Ruby, the convicted felon, but the Ruby that no one knows about but you."

For the first time in her life, Ruby totally opened up about how depressed she was about her life. As she spoke, she surprised herself at the things she revealed to this strange white lady. Mecca listened to her aunt say things she never would have imagined her saying to anyone.

"I'm a lesbian by choice, but the reality is that I hate being one. I want to have a family, get married to a good man, but I hate to show weakness," Ruby announced as she began to cry. Dr. Clark handed her a Kleenex tissue.

"So men are your weakness?"

"That's why I stay away from them." Ruby nodded.

"Why do men make you weak? What is it about them that makes you succumb to their power?"

"When they fuck me good, I can't control myself," Ruby responded through her tears.

Dr. Clark's eyes grew wide. When the doctor changed the subject to Ruby's relationship with her family, she noticed Ruby's facial expression change. The doctor knew from the look that it would be a topic she would have to approach lightly.

"You told me about your parents and how you and your sister had to go through life without them. Your sister's death affected you more than any other death in your life, I assume."

Ruby looked away from the doctor and toward a framed portrait of the doctor with a tall, medium-built, silver-haired man in a tuxedo. The doctor wore a long black dinner gown. Tears ran down Ruby's face.

"I miss my sister so much, it's killing me. Now my niece is out there on her own. She was unable to protect herself and got shot. She's in a coma!"

Dr. Clark came around the desk and rubbed her back. "It helps to talk about the pain. Don't hold that in, because you'll go crazy and do something irrational. You don't want to do that. You don't want to carry all that pain and anger around. You want to release it. It will take time, though. Time will heal the wounds." Handing Ruby more Kleenex, Dr. Clark sat back down behind her desk. "Did they find the people who shot your niece?"

Ruby shook her head. "No. I don't really know all the details."

"How does that make you feel?"

Ruby gave the doctor a gaze that bordered pure menace. It was one that made Dr. Clark nervous. She had seen the look before in the blank glares of sociopaths and psychotic killers. She would make a note of it in Ruby's files, she told herself.

"Like getting revenge on anybody responsible."

"Come now, Mecca. I think you saw enough." Lou opened the door, bringing the vision to a close. The office turned back into the bedroom, without Ruby or the doctor. Lou grabbed her hand and led her back to the couch while she sobbed.

"Why, Lou? Why didn't you show me this before?"

"What would have been different, Mecca? Do you honestly think that your aunt was happy about your mother's and father's murders? Do you think that she enjoyed hearing you were in a coma? You know your aunt, and you knew she would seek revenge. She didn't have sex with Shamel to hurt you. She was having sex with him because she's weak. He was just a symbol of her weakness. Your aunt doesn't know love, because she doesn't know what love feels like." Lou's words made Mecca sob harder while she held her face in her hands.

"What did I do, Lou?"

"What you did is take things into your own hands. What you did is start a war for revenge. But what you did not know . . ." Lou lifted Mecca's face to his by holding her chin up and continued, "The war was going to happen regardless."

Mecca awoke to the bright sun shining on her face. She squinted her eyes, looking at Miguel placing a tray of food on the table on the terrace. The food smelled lovely to her, and her stomach growled its agreement. She could pick out the various aromas of scrambled eggs and cinnamon French toast.

"Good morning, pretty girl," Miguel said while walking bare chested, with just a pair of black boxer briefs on. "I made you breakfast. I want to eat on the terrace with you before I leave."

Mecca got up and made her way to the large bathroom. She looked in the mirror and saw remnants of the dream. She wondered what Lou meant when he said that the war would happen regardless. One thing was for sure, she knew she had to get back to the States and try to stop what she'd started. Ruby deserved a second chance. She just wanted to be loved, and Mecca loved her aunt. She wanted Ruby to know that. When she sat down to eat with Miguel, he noticed the sad look on her face.

"You wake up to your man cooking you breakfast in Rome and you got a sad look on your face? What's up?" he asked while helping her sit in her chair. "Did I do something to depress you?"

"No, Miguel. It isn't you at all." She placed her hand over his to reassure him. "I have a lot on my mind, that's all."

"Talk to me, Mecca. What's bothering you?"

Mecca sighed. "It's my aunt. I have to get back home to see her."

It rained for two days straight in New York, and like the weather, Ruby's head had a black cloud over it that wouldn't go away. The episode with Simone and Mona had put her in a bad mood. It lasted even into the next morning, when she awoke, and then throughout the day. She cursed the rain as she jumped into her Range Rover and drove to a diner in the Sheepshead Bay section of Brooklyn to meet Breeze to discuss her next move. The raid Breeze had mentioned had put a big dent in her business, and she planned on using the money he was to give her to buy a hundred more pounds of weed to set up shop in a spot in Harlem that Tashy had established for her. The spot was in the perfect place to make lots of cash.

A young Dominican guy would sell the weed on consignment out of a car-repair shop. Ruby was paying fifteen hundred a pound from Tashy's connect and selling the pound in New York for four thousand. Her deal with the Dominican she dealt with in New Jersey was for him to give her thirty-five hundred for each pound to make it appear as if he was getting a great deal.

To calm her nerves during the drive, Ruby listened to her Anthony Hamilton CD. Yet, for some reason, even his soul-soothing voice couldn't calm her restless nerves, which were jumpier than a fleet of Chevy Impalas with hydraulics at a Cali lowrider contest.

To make matters worse, when she got to the diner, Breeze's black Charger on double deuces was nowhere in sight. She looked through the rain-soaked windows of her truck for any sign of him as she pulled into the diner's parking lot. It was packed with morning diners grabbing a bite on their way to work, those coming from a club, and those on their way to a motel to get freaky.

"Where the fuck is this nigga?" Ruby grumbled as she fit the truck in between a beat-up, multicolored station wagon and a dull white minivan. Putting her hood on, Ruby jogged into the diner, which smelled of a mix of culinary odors, cigarettes, perfume, and wet hair. Ruby made her way to a booth far in the back that gave her a window view. A young, thin white girl with an apron on over faded jeans and a black T-shirt placed a menu on the table.

"Are you ready to order?" she asked, popping gum in her raggedy-tooth mouth. Ruby removed her wet leather bomber and placed it on the leather-cushioned seat.

"Yeah, let me get some scrambled eggs with cheese, home fries, and bacon, with a toasted cinnamon raisin bagel."

"Anything to drink with that?" The anorexic wrote down the order, still popping her gum.

"Orange juice, fresh squeezed," Ruby ordered.

The girl grabbed the menu and walked with a strut, trying to show off a body that just wasn't there. Looking out from her window, Ruby saw no sign of Breeze or his car. Once again, she pulled out her cell phone and dialed his number. The house phone just rang. Ruby spotted the pay phone by the diner's bathroom and went to use it. She dialed Breeze's cell phone; on the second ring she heard a voice answer.

"Who dis?"

"Who dis?" Ruby asked with attitude.

"You looking for Breeze?"

"Give Breeze the phone, whoever this is," Ruby commanded.

"Sorry. Can't do that. Maybe you can come down to the Seventy-third Precinct and . . ."

Ruby quickly ended the call. If the police had Breeze's phone, she knew Breeze was locked up. Damn!

"Is there a problem?" the long-faced, skinny, greasy-haired waitress asked, holding a cup of orange juice in her hand.

Ruby shook her head and glared at her. "Nothing you can help me with except getting my order."

The girl placed the cup down in front of her, rolling her eyes. She wanted to cuss Ruby out but thought the better of it. Ruby looked like one of those ghetto girls who could fight and probably carried a box cutter in her purse. She walked away without saying a word.

Ruby dialed Tashy's number. When Tashy answered, Ruby said, "Girl, I got problems."

"Yeah, I heard," Tashy responded.

Ruby paused, hearing attitude in her voice. "What did you hear?"

"Simone came in here last night, calling you every name a mother doesn't want to hear coming out of her child's mouth."

Ruby sighed, rubbing her forehead. "It was a misunderstanding. She didn't give me a chance to explain why Mona was at my house."

"And the reason was?" Tashy spat in disgust.

"Hold on, Tashy. Don't give me attitude. I don't know how that girl got my address, first off. She shows up at my door, soaking wet from the rain, after I got out of the shower. I give her a change of clothes, while I was going to wash her wet ones. Then your daughter pops up and throws a tantrum."

"Did you do something with Mona, Ruby?"

"Tashy, please with the bullshit. The girl is obsessed, and I don't know why. I got a lot of shit going on in Brooklyn. I got no time for no little girl. Tell Simone to get rid of the crazy little bitch."

"Mona says y'all did something and she's in love," Tashy said flatly.

"Fuck, Mona." Ruby grimaced. "I need to get some stuff. Brooklyn is shut down. I'm moving uptown. I'll be there in an hour."

Ruby ended the call. When the waitress brought Ruby her food, she suddenly no longer had an appetite. She pulled out a wad of cash from her coat and counted out two hundred-dollar bills, throwing them on the table.

"I'm not eating. Here's two bills for your trouble." Ruby snatched her coat, put it on, and jogged to the Range Rover. She drove uptown in a rage. Things had to be put back in order. She had to find Daphne. When she turned the car on, Anthony Hamilton sang, "Sometimes I get lonely coming from where I'm from. . . ." That was exactly how Ruby felt.

Chapter Forty-one

So it is said that victory can be made.
—Sun Tzu, *The Art of War*

Detective Levy's eight-hour shift had turned into a twenty-hour one by the time the last body was taken out of the apartment. The crowd and media representatives, with their vans and equipment, dispersed, leaving the rainy East New York block eerily silent, with the exception of the sound of passing cars.

With a faintly stubbled chin and bags under his eyes, Levy came alive sitting in his unmarked car as Breeze's cell phone rang. It was like he'd just won the lottery.

"That was definitely Davidson's voice," he announced when the call ended.

"Sure of it? I haven't heard it in years," replied FBI agent Phillip Doyle from the backseat. Agent Doyle had agreed to drive from his Long Island home to Brooklyn after hearing about the open investigation on a woman he'd helped put away, supposedly for the rest of her life. That was until her conviction was overturned.

Doyle was a twenty-eight-year vet of the FBI's New York office. He became part of the investigation into the "Davidson Organization" when she shot and killed a Dominican drug dealer the FBI had targeted. He'd learned from other agents' investigations about a drug ring in the Brownsville section of Brooklyn of which Davidson was the boss. The word was, she was one bad bitch.

"I just finished talking to this broad right before the corpses pop up," Levy said.

"So, you're saying she has an alibi?" Doyle asked, reaching in his tan camel-hair trench for a lighter. When he spoke, his double chin shook.

"She was definitely at the scene, but when she left, the headless guy was alive."

Levy's young partner, who favored Johnny Depp, interjected, "I assume the guy's family was alive also. Most likely got it right before he was caught on the staircase."

"Police work doesn't call for assumptions, young man. We need facts," Doyle sermonized. He did everything by the book.

"So what do you think?" Levy cut in before Doyle gave one of his "how to be a good cop" speeches.

"It's definitely not her style. Did you contact the cop investigating the triple over in Bedford-Stuyvesant?" Doyle asked.

Levy sighed. "Yeah, I did. The guy is hard pressed for more details than I have. He said her owning the store where the murders took place ain't enough to go chasing her around."

"And he's right," Doyle barked, lighting up the cigar. "You mind?" He cut an eye at Levy.

"No. Go ahead," Levy said, immediately regretting his decision once Doyle lit up the foul-smelling cigar. Doyle spoke while smoke came out of his mouth.

"No sense in chasing ghosts. I think maybe Davidson has aligned herself with some real cowboys. Probably met some connections in prison and planned a takeover, once they got out. Looks like the work of some Middle Eastern syndicate, which I doubt would go into business with an American black girl from the ghetto. Has to do with trust issues, or the work of the Jamaican posses or other islanders, like Haitians, Trinidadians, that sort."

Levy rolled his window down, then looked at Doyle through the rearview. "So where do we start?"

"We can start by grabbing some breakfast," Doyle murmured, rubbing his rounded gut. "Then we go to the prison Davidson was housed at for thirteen years and find out who she was affiliated with. Plenty of rats in the federal joints that will gladly share information with us."

Levy nodded his head as he began to start the car. Doyle opened the back door to get out and get in his black eighties-model Lincoln Town Car. He pulled the collar of his trench coat around his neck, ducked his head back in the car, and growled, "Where do you Jewish guys grab a bite at this time of the morning?"

"I forgot Brooklyn has never been a place for the micks," Levy joked. "Just follow me, pal."

Doyle chuckled. "Brooklyn humor. Brutal as the streets."

The cool air that blew in from the Miami River was a welcomed act of nature for Daphne after temperatures reached ninety degrees in the shade during the day. Daphne, wearing a peach tank top, white capri pants, and white open-toe sandals, removed her Chloé shades while sitting on the porch of her beach home to read an article in *Don Diva* magazine her sister had referred her to.

Miami was Daphne's second best getaway spot, after Jamaica. To Daphne, Miami had the pace of New York, with its trendy boutiques and "party till the sun burns out" nightlife, and the tropical feel of Jamaica, with its lovely beaches and resorts and kind, courteous natives, while a mean, ruthless, murderous drug-culture underworld was in its belly.

When Daphne was relaxing at her white stucco, wood-framed, one-story beach home with two bedrooms, she felt at home. The master suite had glass sliding doors with an ocean view, while the whole place was decorated in an African motif, with carved wooden stakes imported from the Ivory Coast, bamboo woven chairs, African pottery, and portraits of the African grasslands. Miami was definitely one of Daphne's favorite places because it so often reminded her of Donovan. It was he who had shown her the city, which, he'd once said, "America didn't deserve."

When her sister brought the Don Diva magazine to her, she'd opened it up to the article and handed it to her. "Your homegirl done got herself famous."

The title of the article caught Daphne's attention. In big, bold black and gold letters it read, "Brooklyn's Bosstress."

She stared at Ruby's picture for a few seconds, looking into her eyes. She could see the sadness there and realized that she was the type of person that made it appear as if everything was cool on the outside, but on the inside were confusion, pain, sadness, and a desire to cry out for help. She was one of those people on a search for answers to their problems, knowing that no one had the answers but themselves. Daphne continued on.

For those who thought that New York City's eighties crack era was ruled by ruthless, violent drug gangs led by black or Hispanic men, think again. The tough streets of Brownsville, Brooklyn, have a secret. A true story of a Don Diva who was just as ruthless as, if not more ruthless than, some of her male counterparts.

After serving thirteen years of a federal life sentence, it was overturned in 2001. The government alleged that Ruby Davidson of Brownsville, Brooklyn, murdered a Dominican drug dealer in broad daylight on a busy Manhattan street. She is believed to have ran a criminal enterprise out of several Brownsville housing projects, grossing two hundred thousand a day in crack sales. Ruby Davidson is now a free woman, giving Don Diva an exclusive first-time interview from Club Opium in Las Vegas, where she and others are celebrating the release of one of Ruby's prison homies, Tashera "Tashy" Williams of Harlem infamy.

Daphne looked at a few pictures of Ruby posing with Tashy and what appeared to be Tashy's family. The words under the pictures confirmed who the people were. Daphne looked at Simone and saw the unmistakable resemblance between mother and daughter. Daphne had heard about Scooter Williams, Tashy's father, from the streets, prison, and the *Don Diva* story, but now everything seemed to fall in place.

She turned the page and saw small pictures of Ruby in eighties fashion standing next to a black 300 Benz. Another picture was of her standing next to a Sterling and some chick named Kima in beige prison clothes. Kima was one of Ruby's cell mates and lesbian lovers from the South Side of Chicago. There was even a map and pictures of the dilapidated Brownsville streets. The article continued.

Ruby was sometimes called "the Black Widow" due to the rumors around Brownsville that she was responsible for the murders of two men she was allegedly romantically involved with. The two men were members of the Five Percent Nation and went by the names of Darnell (a Brownsville hustler and stickup kid) and Wise (another Brownsville hustler, who served time for murder and was allegedly the man who introduced Ruby to the game).

Daphne swallowed hard before reading on.

After allegedly ridding herself of these men, it is said, and was confirmed by Ruby, that she became a full-time lesbian. Word on the street was that Ruby's lesbian lover, a girl named Monique, was gunned down on a Brownsville street as revenge for the murder of Darnell. There was no retaliation for Wise's murder, and Ruby denied any involvement in both.

When Daphne turned the page, she was shocked when she saw a picture of Ruby, Monique, and Mecca sitting on a couch in someone's apartment. Mecca appeared to be around thirteen years old. She wore her hair in a bang and ponytail, had on a pair of large door-knocker earrings with *Mecca* encrusted in diamonds, and a white sweatshirt. Daphne could see the same pain in her eyes that she'd seen just recently. The article continued with questions.

DD: Ruby, how does it feel to be free after thirteen years?

RD: I can't even put the feelings into words, but it feels good.

DD: I bet. So you grew up in Brownsville?

RD: No doubt. Langston Hughes projects.

DD: What was it like growing up in Brownsville?

RD: Growing up in the Ville, you learn how to mind your business, to fight and never be scared to lose. Just fight . . . and you learn to duck and stay low when the guns blast.

DD: The things you've heard, the rumors about things you did, which ones are false and true?

RD: I won't answer that on the grounds that I won't incriminate myself or others.

DD: Answered like a true G. People say that once you were locked down, your niece took over your dealings and that eventually got her shot and out of the game. That would make y'all some very unusual women. Y'all would be like the Candaces of Brooklyn. (Reporter's note: Ruby's face turns serious.)

RD: None of that is true. My niece had nothing to do with the game.

Daphne could imagine the look on her face. Mecca was still a sensitive issue with Ruby. Daphne looked up when Andrea walked onto the porch, wearing a long, flowing, one-piece cream cotton dress with a plunging neckline.

Andrea carried two glasses of sweet carrot juice in her hands and placed them on the small, white, round table Daphne sat next to. She was a strict vegetarian.

"Why not bring this thing between you and her straight to her? Why prolong it?" Andrea asked, sitting across from Daphne and looking her in the eyes. To her, Daphne was a unique object, because the sun always made her eyes appear to be different hues.

"She isn't even aware that I'm after her," Daphne said as she broke eye contact and looked away at the distant river. "I want her to suffer the loss of close friends like I suffered the loss of my best friend and heart."

"You said she is a selfish woman who only thinks of herself. I assume it is unlikely she will be affected by the loss of a business partner and his family."

Daphne turned back to Andrea. "She loves money. If she can't make money, she becomes miserable. This is why I made sure she had money when she came home. I wanted her to get comfortable and then snatch it all away. Then I'll kill her."

It was Andrea's turn to look out over the blue water. "Are you having doubts that she is responsible for your brother's death? You know it's just rumors, she never spoke about it to you, and you said she was pretty open with you about her business in the streets."

"Yes, she is pretty open about street stuff, but not personal business. From what I hear, her and my brother had some-thing personal going on."

"What about her niece? Isn't she close to her? Wouldn't losing her deeply affect Ruby?"

Daphne sighed. Explaining Mecca and Ruby's relationship was complicated. She wouldn't know where to begin. The fact that she liked Mecca also played a part in leaving her out of the war. Mecca had suffered enough.

Andrea read her expression. "You're fond of her niece, aren't you?"

Daphne avoided Andrea's gaze, causing her to smile.

"That's a good sign that you have not lost the ability to feel compassion. I almost thought you were becoming a monster." Andrea got up and walked into the house but paused before disappearing from the door. "I read the *Daily News*. Two children were in that house. Don't become what you want to destroy. You'll wind up destroying yourself."

As Ruby gripped the sheets and arched her back, a deep moan escaped from her lungs. It was a much-needed multi-orgasmic release from the stresses she had been experiencing lately. The tension just melted away with the flow of juices that creamed Tashy's face.

When she drove to Tashy's apartment, she went there expecting a verbal confrontation from her about Mona. However, when Tashy answered the door, wearing her silk kimono robe with nothing on under it, nipples harder than tire caps, and a seductive, "come fuck me" look on her face, Ruby grinned and gave Tashy what she wanted, and what Ruby needed her damned self.

Afterward, they lay naked on their backs, breathing laboriously, staring at the ceiling. Tashy grabbed one of her overstuffed pillows and hit Ruby on the stomach with it.

Ruby flinched. "Tashy, what the fuck are you doing?"

Smiling, Tashy responded, "I can't believe you tried to turn that young girl out. You got her obsessed."

Ruby grinned. She knew there was no sense lying to Tashy. She knew her better than a lot of people. She knew from experience that Tashy wouldn't be hurt by her habit of testing the playing field.

"You got to admit the chick got it going on," Ruby said, amused. Then she straightened her face out and became serious. "I didn't do it to hurt Simone, though. It was a one-time thing. The girl kept giving me googly eyes."

Tashy nodded. "I will keep it real. She's a cutie, but too young for me, and I won't do that to my daughter. I have seen her giving you the eye."

Ruby got up to go to the bathroom. Her once tight buns were now a bit jiggly. Tashy watched them with great interest as they bounced and realized that Ruby wasn't working out like she used to in jail. Plus, she was getting older now, and time was starting to take its toll. Still, she had a body to die for.

"So, how is Simone doing? Did she get over it?" Ruby asked from the bathroom.

"I hope she did. She's over my father's. I spoke to her yesterday, and she sounded like she was okay."

On her way out, Ruby grabbed a newspaper that sat on top of Tashy's entertainment system. "What about Mona?"

Tashy sighed. "Still wondering if you will give her a chance. The girl is crazy. I saw her on the Ave., and she came to me, apologizing, while at the same time asking if me and her could share your love. Ain't that—"

"Oh, shit."

Tashy was startled at Ruby's sudden outburst.

"What?"

Ruby slammed the paper down on the bed and began dressing quickly. Tashy looked down at the headline in big, bold letters on the front page. BROOKLYN BLOODBATH. Underneath it continued, "Three adults, two children, slain by decapitation. Story on page three."

"Ruby, what happened? Do you know about this?" Tashy asked while getting up and putting on her robe.

Fastening the button and zipper on her pants, Ruby answered, "That's my boy Breeze and his family! I was just with him last night. He was telling me how the cops raided the spot I had up in Brooklyn. The article said it happened last night. That had to be right after I left him. I got to see what the hell is going on!"

"You want me to come with you?" Tashy asked.

As Ruby walked toward the door, she turned to face Tashy. "Nah. What I need is for you to get that work for me so I can pop the spot over here. I'm really done with Brooklyn."

"I'm on it. Call me."

Ruby walked out the door.

A young Mecca and Dawn, who Mecca had thought was a friend but who was her sister, stood on the corner of Rockaway Avenue and Dumont, watching a funeral procession of luxurious and average cars following a hearse. The day was bright and sunny. The streets of Brownsville were alive at their usual pace. The corners, Chinese stores, liquor stores, and bodegas hosted the usual street corner congregations. People froze to watch the procession, as if it were the West Indian Day parade going through Brownsville.

It was common to see funeral processions come through the neighborhood. The dead were always driven through the place they lived before being buried. It was a way of letting the deceased and the deceased's neighborhood say good-bye to each other. Unfortunately, Brownsville was a place where death was a common occurrence. Mostly because of drugs, AIDS, and murder.

Mecca watched as a couple of guys on the corner across the street from where she stood poured beers on the ground. Some threw up peace signs with their fingers toward the hearse. Another guy walked up to the corner where Mecca and Dawn stood and placed his fist against his chest, then held up his own peace sign and said, "Peace, Wise."

Mecca looked at the hearse and thought about what the guy had said. She exchanged a glance with Dawn, who wore the same expression on her face. They remembered.

Nothing could erase the memory of Mecca and Dawn mistakenly walking into the scene of a murder. They'd rounded the pissy, graffiti-littered hallway steps after hearing the sound of something tumbling down the steps. They were startled when the body of a man landed in front of them, faceup, with eyes open. For a moment Mecca didn't recognize the man, because she had not seen Ruby's ex-boyfriend in a long time. He had been in jail and had just recently gotten out. When she looked up, she saw Ruby with a gun in her hand, standing next to Monique.

Back on the corner, Mecca looked at all the cars in the procession and admired the Benzes and other European sedans that drove by. She watched as a wood-brown Chevy Nova cruised slowly by.

The car meant nothing to her, but the person in the front seat did. Once again, she stared at those hazel eyes that shined like wet crystals when in the sun's light. It was the same blank stare Mecca had got from the girl in the mall. When Mecca looked closer, she saw the girl was crying. Obviously, Wise was somebody close to her.

"Mecca!" Mecca's attention was broken by a call coming from behind her. When she turned, she saw Ruby walking up the block with Monique. She waved her over. "I got to talk to you. Come here!"

Mecca turned to look at the hazel-eyed girl one more time and was shocked to see the girl out of the car, with a gun in her hand. She was no longer staring at Mecca, but her eyes were focused on Ruby and Monique.

She pointed the gun and started walking toward them while they were distracted by a group of women sitting on a project bench. When Mecca realized Ruby and Monique were the intended target, she yelled, but the sound of the gunshots overpowered her scream.

The scene disappeared. Mecca found herself sitting in Lou's office, on a leather-cushioned chaise lounge. Lou had his feet propped up on his desk, hands folded across his lap, watching her.

"Are you ready for the answer?" Lou asked.

"The answer to what?"

"The girl with the eyes. Aren't you curious as to who she is?"

"You figure?" Mecca said sarcastically.

Lou pointed to the wall, where framed pictures hung. Mecca turned to look at a picture of the same funeral proces-

sion. The girl's face in the Chevy Nova was different from the one in her dreams. Her jaw fell into her lap.

Awakened by the shaking of the Alitalia plane during a flight to New York, Mecca looked around, confused. A white woman in a blue business suit sat next to her, rapidly pressing letters on her laptop. Mecca noticed the woman had a *New York Daily News* folded beside her.

"Do you mind if I look at the paper?"

"Sure," the squeaky-voiced woman answered.

The bold letters on the front page immediately screamed out to her. After seeing the BROOKLYN BLOODBATH front page, she turned to page three and read. Her heart fluttered after she realized what she'd started. Guilt set in.

She didn't think mailing those pictures and that letter to Daphne would cause something like that to happen to Breeze's family. Especially those children. Mecca put the paper down beside the lady.

"You can keep it. I'm done with it," the woman said.

"No thank you." Mecca half smiled, then excused herself to go to the bathroom. Once inside the small, disinfectant-smelling bathroom, she vomited in the toilet. She rinsed her mouth out and stared at her reflection in the small mirror. Her skin was darker than usual from her days in Italy.

Leaving the bathroom, she made her way back to her seat and sat down, looking out the window at the New York skyline. She began to regret trading the Roman winter for the brutal New York winter. Was warning her aunt about what she helped put into play between Daphne and her worth leaving behind her wonderful fiancé, traveling, and relaxing in places of romantic bliss? She took a deep breath and rationalized. She would just have to find out.

Chapter Forty-two

For he comes out of prison to be king,
although he was born poor in his kingdom.
—Ecclesiastes 4:14

The federal prison in West Virginia looked more like a college campus or retirement community surrounded by a barbed-wire fence than a prison. The clean, cemented pathways cut through manicured grass and led to a red and tan two-story, brick, cottage-like building.

Agent Doyle, accompanied by Detective Levy, paid the prison an official visit. Both men came dressed like underpaid public defenders, with their cheap suits that resembled Salvation Army giveaways. They had spent the previous night in a motel in Ohio, after spending the day at the women's federal prison, interviewing guards, a prison psychiatrist, and inmates who knew and associated with Ruby while she was an inmate.

Doyle knew some of the inmates there either from previous cases or from them being informants. The ones he'd put there that associated with Ruby were happy to tell him to go fuck himself; the informants, on the other hand, had no valuable information, because, as one of them put it, "She was usually a loner, and when she talked, she never got personal."

Doyle felt that they would get lucky at the West Virginia prison. It was a less secure jail than the one in Ohio. The inmates in the West Virginia prison were mostly short timers there for white-collar crimes, and a lot of them were snitches. Ruby had been brought there when her court hearings started, and Daphne had been there when her time was getting short. Another plus for Doyle was that he knew the psychiatrist at the prison on a personal level.

She was a former agent at a New York field office with whom Doyle on occasion cheated on his wife. When she'd become tired of chasing criminals, she'd put her degree in psychology to use and got into the minds of criminals. The FBI used her expertise from time to time, when they needed the profile of a potential suspect, usually a multistate serial killer.

The mention of Ruby's name to certain staff members caused them to sigh, shake their heads, and grimace. Only a few of them smiled. A captain, who was an overweight redneck, said Ruby was a real cocky bitch with a stink New York attitude. Then he added a wink and said, "No offense, fellas."

The interview with the inmates did not go as expected, until a Spanish girl from Washington Heights, who was being held for cocaine distribution, overheard Doyle ask another New York girl about Ruby. She managed to maneuver her way over to Doyle and Levy when they were in the receiving area.

"Can we talk?" Doyle asked the five-foot-two, black-haired, light-brown-skinned girl.

Levy immediately noticed the three parts in one of the girl's eyebrows. Her eyes were chinky and brown, and she had a full set of lips and a pretty oval face. Though she was petite and was covered with baggy prison clothes, he could see the nice legs, plump rear, and tight, flat stomach that were her body. She spoke with a tough, cocky New York accent.

"About Ruby? What's in it for me?"

"What do you expect?" Levy inquired.

The girl rolled her eyes. "Look around. Does this look like a place I want to spend another ten years in?"

"Is the information that valuable?" Doyle asked.

"Depends on what's valuable to you," she spat.

"Who were Ruby's closest associates?" Levy asked.

He didn't want to play games with the girl. He knew these convicts would tell them anything they wanted to hear to get them out of jail. It didn't matter to them if they were lying; it was part of the deal.

It was up to the cops to sift through the tall tales to find the truth. Doyle could tell that the Spanish girl was most likely one of those jailhouse snitches who would sell her own children to get out of her situation. Knowing Ruby, there was no way in hell she would share anything incriminating with this girl.

"She hung with Daphne and Tashy the most," the girl announced.

"You wouldn't be talking about Tashy Williams, would you?" Doyle asked, wide-eyed.

The girl looked around to see if anyone was close enough to hear her, then continued. "Yeah. Tashy from Harlem."

"And who else did you say?" Levy asked.

"Daphne. She's from Brooklyn."

Before going to see the psychiatrist, Doyle had the records of all inmates named Daphne in the jail at the time Ruby was there pulled by the prison administrators. Doyle found out there had been fifteen Daphnes in the jail. Five from New York. There was only one from Brooklyn. Daphne Carter. After reading her file and finding out why she was convicted, Doyle had a big smile on his face.

"Looks like our dear Davidson made some interesting connections here."

"Shower Posse." Levy read the file. After a minute of reading, he looked up at Doyle with the same smile.

"You got it," Doyle blurted.

"Who is this Tashy Williams chick?" Levy asked.

"You've heard of Scooter Williams? Big fish uptown, rubbed shoulders with Frank Matthews back in the day?" Doyle shook his head no when Levy shrugged. "Before your time. Plus, you were confined to Brooklyn. Listen, I'm going to make some copies. I'll explain it on the way back. First, let's see this shrink."

Margaret O'Connely's office looked like the office of a CFO for a Fortune 500 company rather than a prison psychiatrist. On her mahogany desk a gold-plated nameplate stood out amid the neat clutter. Tiffany floor and table lamps, upholstered gold silk sofas and chairs, and other French furniture sat on top of a beige carpet by Edward Fields. Her floor-to-ceiling bookshelf was filled with leather-bound books and occupied a whole wall in the spacious office.

Directly behind her large desk chair was a wood-paneled wall with her many achievements on display. Degrees in psychology, behavioral science; awards as an FBI agent; photos of a younger O'Connely with J. Edgar Hoover and former president Jimmy Carter.

When Doyle and Levy entered the office, they no longer felt like they were in a federal prison. The office was warm and cozy. Margaret O'Connely's light-scented perfume permeated the air. She sat at her desk, in a tan business suit, which Levy immediately noticed. The woman's curly reddish brown hair reached her bony shoulders, and he reasoned that it had to be a wig.

Her penetrating blue eyes caught everything that went on and spoke volumes of confidence under the rimless spectacles. With an erect posture, she gave no illusion of who was in charge. Though her skin was pasty and showed signs of a few face-lifts, Levy figured she'd been one of those classic New York debutantes.

"Miss O'Connely, I would like you to meet—"

"Cut the crap, Phil. You never called me Miss O'Connely in your life. Don't start now," she said with a strong Irish/New York accent.

Doyle cleared his throat. "Marge, this is Detective Levy. Brooklyn Homicide."

Levy reached over the desk and shook her hand. Her pale, vein-filled hand was swallowed in his massive paw. To him, it felt like he was holding four cold French fries in his hand.

"Strange. I swear I had a premonition that you guys would be coming to me, asking about Davidson," she announced, shaking her head. Doyle and Levy exchanged curious glances.

"I don't understand," Levy announced.

Folding her arms and hands across the desk, Margaret spoke frankly. "When Phil called me and said he wanted to speak to me off the record about an inmate named Ruby Davidson, I thought maybe the FBI had a hard-on for this woman. I mean, she threw their conviction right back in their face. That her name came up in some Brooklyn homicides didn't surprise me, and I'll explain why."

Margaret reached in her desk and pulled out a yellow folder with black letters written in Magic Marker and handed it to Levy.

"You know you owe me, Phil. You know this is against the law and unethical. This is privileged information." Margaret took back the file and opened it on her desk. Before reading it, she removed her glasses and looked at Levy.

"Detective, I grew up in Hell's Kitchen when the neighborhood lived up to its moniker. I saw treachery at its worst. I grew up vowing to one day return to that kitchen and clean it up. When I joined them, that's exactly what I did. I put some mean sons of bitches away. I psychologically evaluated some crazy people. Some of them scared the crap out of me. I'm saying this to say, Davidson didn't scare me. She's tough, no doubt about it.

I know what those Brownsville streets can turn a good kid into, or anyone, to say the least. Al Capone grew up on those streets. Davidson is hard on the outside but would melt in your hands on the inside. She is controlled by emotions, and her emotions get the best of her. From what Phil told me, you are investigating some pretty brutal murders. What was it? A beheading and stuff like that?"

"A whole family, children included." Levy nodded.

Margaret bowed her head slightly, shaking it in disbelief. "Do you suspect Davidson is the murderer?"

"No. We suspect she is involved. We know she is not the actual killer," Doyle answered. Margaret sighed. To Levy, it seemed like a sigh of relief.

"Well, if it would help, she once told me that she wanted to get revenge on the people responsible for shooting her niece." Margaret put her glasses back on. "If any of those people were responsible, you may have your motive."

"From what I gathered, there was only a rumor of who was responsible for that. It happened out on the Island," Levy stated.

"Out of your jurisdiction," Margaret said abruptly.

"They never named suspects, anyhow." Levy acknowledged that fact with a nod.

After the meeting, while Doyle and Levy were preparing to leave, Margaret walked them to the door. She grabbed Doyle by the arm and stopped him.

"Why haven't I heard from you? You don't even return my calls."

"My schedule has been hectic and—"

"Don't lie, Phil. I can tell when you're lying. You can't look me in the eye," she growled and waited. When Phil was not forthcoming, she continued, "I understand. You can't afford a scandal before you retire. Just remember, I'm always a phone call away." She grabbed his hand and squeezed. He returned the squeeze and smiled.

During the ride back to New York, Doyle explained to Levy, who was driving, who Scooter and Tashy Williams were.

"This Frank Matthews guy was the largest heroin dealer, well, black one at least, in the country during the sixties. The guy was big. The government busted him for trafficking and other charges related to drug distribution, gives him a quarter-million-dollar bail. It gets posted, and he disappears, never to be seen again."

"A quarter million?"

"Cash," Doyle replied.

"Who brought that type of cash to bail him out?"

"Scooter Williams. Matthews's partner. The partner the government could never touch. The man is well connected at all levels. This guy could run for mayor of New York City with campaign money financed by drug proceeds that everyone knows about and win. They paint this guy as some type of Robin Hood of Harlem. He even let his daughter take the fall in a case of money laundering."

"That's this Tashy Williams?" Levy asked as he swerved as a deer ran across a stretch of the Pennsylvania highway.

"Correct," Doyle answered. "Now, this Daphne Carter. This is interesting." Doyle opened the copy of Daphne's file. "I don't know how dangerous she is, but the people she's involved with are extremely dangerous. I haven't seen this name in years." Doyle pointed.

"Who is that?"

"Junior McLeod."

"Daphne is Wise's little sister."

"What! Wow, do you know that?" Ruby asked Mecca over her cell phone while driving on the FDR Drive on her way to Brooklyn.

Mecca had rented a blue Dodge from the airport and was on her way to Ruby's house.

"I just remembered while I was in Italy. Trust me, it's true. Auntie, you have to be on point. She's after you, and she'll start by attacking anyone or anything close to you. I found out about Breeze and his family. Daphne is behind it," Mecca warned.

"Where are you?" Ruby asked nervously as she was contemplating Mecca's words. She thought about how, out of nowhere, Daphne had just vanished. Then these murders had occurred. Ruby also had a feeling about Daphne's background. Ruby only saw Wise's family in a picture he had in one of his dresser drawers in an apartment she'd once shared with him. That was why she'd asked Mo Blood if he knew Wise's family.

Daphne had told Ruby while they were in prison together that she was originally from Brownsville but her mom moved to Bed-Stuy when she was young. When Ruby had asked what part of Brownsville, Daphne told her a house off of Rockaway and Newport. Now Ruby remembered Wise mentioning his family living over there. She wondered how Daphne knew Ruby was the one who had killed Wise. No one knew for sure that it was Ruby except Mecca and Dawn, and none of them had known Daphne at the time.

"I'm on the Belt Parkway, on the way to the crib," Mecca answered while exiting off Pennsylvania Avenue.

"Don't go there," Ruby commanded. "Meet me at Prospect Park."

"Auntie?"

"What's up?"

"I love you." Mecca ended the call.

Ruby made a call after Mecca ended hers. Tashy picked up on the first ring.

"Ruby? What's up? You okay?"

"We're going to have to lay low for a while. That bitch Daphne is taking me to war."

"Who? That light-eyed bitch?" Tashy yelled.

"Yeah."

"For what?" Tashy inquired, ready to say "I told you so," but opting not to.

Ruby sucked her teeth. "'I won't discuss that now. Just stay low until I figure out the next move. Put that other thing on hold, too." Ending the call, Ruby tightened her jaw in anger, then banged on the steering wheel. "This bitch don't know."

Simone closed her eyes and leaned her head back on the headrest of Wayne's green Mustang convertible while her legs rested on the dashboard and his head was in between her legs. She imagined that it was Mona's tongue exploring her shaved middle and clit. She had to give it to Wayne when it came to his ability to please her with his tongue talent. It was the only way she was able to cum with him. When it came to his pipe game, he was a dud.

They were parked in a heavily wooded area in a Long Island park where a lot of young lovers came to do things they weren't able to do at their private schools and expensive Hamptons homes. The sun was setting, and the sound of crickets and other insects could be heard, along with Simone's low moans.

"Yeah, eat this pussy. That feels so good, Mona."

Wayne suddenly stopped and looked up at Simone with a glazed face, sporting an angry expression. "Mona?" He got up from off his knees, climbed over Simone, and sat in the driver's seat, wiping his mouth with the back of his hand. "My name is Wayne, Simone."

"What are you talking about? I know your name, boy. Now, finish, because I'm 'bout to cum again. C'mon, baby!" She added a seductive tone while rubbing his crotch, hoping to make him forget. It worked.

His angry expression changed when the blood rushed back to his penis. He grinned. Something moved in the bushes. Startled, they looked around but saw nothing. When they heard nothing, Wayne started to move to reacquire his position between her legs. In a quick motion a gloved hand appeared in the cracked window of the driver's side, holding a gun with a silencer. Before Simone could scream, the window was broken out and another gloved hand was placed over her mouth.

Blood, skull, and brains exploded on her legs as Wayne's body slumped against hers. She felt herself being pulled out of the car as she closed her eyes and tried to scream. When she opened them again, she was being held and pushed from behind.

In front of her was a person in all black. A leather three-quarter coat, black slacks, and boots to match. She saw the back of a van and couldn't tell if it was black or blue. When the man dressed in all black opened the back of the van, she was pushed in the back and landed on a carpeted floor.

"You scream, you die," a masked man said before closing the back door of the van.

Simone recognized the Jamaican accent as her body shook from fear. Why was she being kidnapped by Jamaicans? Ransom? Maybe they wanted Scooter to pay a ransom. He was rich and famous, and everyone new she was his granddaughter. Tears rolled down her face at the thought, even though she knew that he would pay the ransom. She just prayed that a ransom was what it was all about. Her body jerked as the van pulled off.

She could hear voices, but she couldn't see who was driving or who was in the passenger seat. There was a solid black wall dividing the back from the front. The people spoke in deep Jamaican accents, so deep she could barely understand them. Her heart almost burst when she understood one of them when he said, "Me wan feed er to me blood clot pirahna seen."

Then they laughed. Suddenly the ransom idea became questionable.

Scooter was tipsy and exhausted. Sitting in back of his emerald and black chauffeur-driven Rolls Royce Phantom, Scooter had a "love of life" smile on his face. He always felt that way after a sexual encounter at a five-star hotel with a twenty something model/actress who was the daughter or niece of one of his associates and who looked at him as her sugar daddy. Scooter had no problem spending money on women just as long as they filled his voracious sexual appetite.

"How was this one, Scoot?" asked the driver, who was a childhood friend from his old Harlem neighborhood. Scooter smiled at his old pal with the close-cropped beard, speckled with grays, on dark, weathered skin, the puppy dog eyes, and inviting smile. But Charlie "Big Gee" Thomas's humble disposition was contrary to his infamous reputation as a strongman/enforcer from the days of Frank Matthews. Not only was he employed by Scooter as his driver, but he also doubled as his bodyguard, and Scooter trusted him more than anyone he knew . . . even Tashy. The big, cuddly Charlie would literally jump in front of a bullet for Scooter.

"She was a workout, Gee. Young, energetic, and built like a thoroughbred," Scooter said, grinning.

The aspiring model he'd just bedded at the Plaza Hotel flashed in his mind. He wondered what his Ethiopian ambassador friend would think if he found out Scooter was banging his almost twenty-year-old daughter. It really didn't matter what the guy thought, Scooter told himself. He was probably one of those African guys who married his daughter off to some guy she had never met or didn't like who paid a herd of cattle to him for his daughter's hand. What better than to have a handsome, successful black businessman fuck her brains out for a shopping spree at Neiman's, Saks, and Tiffany?

"I need to just lay down in my bed now and recuperate from that episode. That dame almost gave this sixty-two-year-old heart a wipeout," Scooter added, putting his hand to his chest, emulating Redd Foxx on the classic TV show *Sanford and Son*.

"I tried to tell you, Gee, we ain't the same cats we were back on Lenox Avenue. We can't have two dames in one session, then go a few blocks up and bang another broad in one night. Those days are behind us," Big Gee said, glancing at Scooter through the rearview mirror.

Loosening his silk tie from his Italian shirt, Scooter stared out at the Long Island Expressway as he headed home. He realized that he had come a long way from the rough streets of Harlem. He was the son of Collin "Skins" Williams, who was called Skins for his love of shoes with different reptile skins, and Bernice "Bee Bee" Johnson, the niece of the infamous Harlem gangster/street legend Bumpy Johnson.

For Scooter, growing up was like waking up to a party every day where people gambled, hustled, got high, and lived like there was no tomorrow. Life in the Williams brownstone was just that. Skins was at first a numbers runner for his girlfriend's uncle and made a lot of money working for him. He always told Scooter, "Bumpy was the best black gangster this country ever had. He made sure everybody around him got rich. Nobody could complain with Bumpy."

Scooter wasn't schooled by Bumpy; he learned the street
life in another way. In fact, he never caught a glimpse of him
and didn't really care. He chose to emulate his father, who was
the coolest man that he ever saw. Skins never dressed down; it
didn't matter where he was going. He would dress up to run to
the supermarket. Then, when Scooter turned ten, Skins taught
him about the "policy," as the numbers racket was called.

Skins would drive Scooter around in one of his shiny
Cadillacs, collecting policy slips and money and sometimes
paying clients who hit the number. Scooter loved driving
around Harlem with his father. Skins was a celebrity, and
being the son of a celebrity made Scooter feel like one.

People in Harlem definitely treated him like one. The
hustlers, pimps, and gangsters acknowledged him with the
nickname "Little Skins" whenever they saw him on the street.
They would give him money, or they would call him over to
one of the corners or pool halls they hung out at and let him
shoot pool, dice, or listen to music. One pimp even got one of
his prettiest hoes to pleasure Scooter orally in a bathroom.

When the chick was done with Scooter, he practically fell
in love with her. Scooter snuck to that pool hall almost every
day to see if he could see the chick again. Though he never
saw her, he did see her pimp. By that time, he was a numbers
runner for Skins, who ran his own operation when Bumpy
Johnson was off the scene. While Scooter was collecting a
policy slip from the pimp, he asked, "Say, where is that dame
you introduced me to a few ticks back?"

The pimp looked at him, puzzled. "Who you talking about,
Little Skins?"

"My name's Scooter," he quickly corrected. He had earned
the nickname by outrunning a cop who rode on a small
scooter, trying to catch him after spotting him with a handful
of policy slips.

"Okay, I can dig it," the pimp acknowledged with a smile.

"I'm talking 'bout a dame you was with 'bout a year ago in
the pool hall on Lenox. You had her take me in the bathroom."

"Oh, you talking about Leslie," the pimp replied. "Leslie
back in Detroit. That's where she was from. I got her from a
player's ball when I was out Chicago. The dame chose me and

came back to the Apple. Told me she had to go back to see family." The pimp dropped his voice down. "You ain't tell your old man 'bout that, right?"

"No way, I'm no tattletale," Scooter said pompously, which made the pimp smile.

Saddened by the news, he knew one thing for sure: he would never forget her face. She was the most beautiful woman he'd ever seen. Detroit was so far away, and he hated it. He hated it more now because he felt like Motown took a piece of him away. When Skins died of lung cancer, Scooter was fifteen and he was devastated. By that time, he was partnered with his father in the numbers racket and he had a good amount of money to play with. He dressed as sharp as his father and emulated his walk and talk.

At the funeral for Skins it was as if the president of the country had died. The whole of Harlem showed up to pay their respects to one they deemed a gentleman gangster. During the sixties and seventies, the streets of Harlem changed for the worse. Scooter still operated the numbers spots his father left behind, but when a man named Frank Matthews showed up, Scooter's life changed also. Heroin found its way into Harlem during the Vietnam War, but Frank Matthews brought even more with him.

When Scooter saw how rich guys were getting from the sale of "H," or "Boy," as it was called, he quickly cashed in. When he met Matthews, he quickly agreed to move product out of the numbers spots. It was a good cover because the cops turned their heads when it came to numbers. Of course, they were receiving payoffs. In no time, Scooter was rich.

He never forgot the woman who gave him his first head job. In 1965 twenty-one-year-old Scooter traveled to Detroit with Frank Matthews. He was a known gangster all over the country. They attended a dinner party for a notorious Detroit gangster celebrating the release of one of his sons, who was a pimp, from prison. Pimps from all over the Midwest were there, and, of course, they showed up with their stable of women. There were well-dressed people from all walks of life at the party. The pimps wore colorful suits and shoes with diamond-flooded jewelry. Their women came in full-length fox and mink coats. You definitely had to be somebody to be there.

Though it was a celebration for a pimp returning from prison, Frank Matthews seemed like the focus of everybody's attention. Hands down, he was the richest gangster in the dining hall. He and Scooter were dressed to impress. Both men were in tailor-made suits. Scooter's was bloodred, and Matthews's was a canary yellow. They both wore ostrich shoes and diamond pinkie rings. Just being in the company of Frank Matthews brought Scooter the same attention. Then Scooter saw her face.

It was a face he would never forget. She looked as if she hadn't aged a bit. She had to be at least ten years his senior, but she looked the same as she did in the pool hall in Harlem. She walked in the hall with a full-length white fox, diamond earrings, followed by two other women on both sides of her.

Fortunately for Scooter, the women were seated at a table next to him and Matthews. A table directly in front of a makeshift stage, where A-list entertainers were due to perform. She smiled at Matthews as they were seated. Matthews nodded his head.

"You know her, Frankie?" Scooter asked.

"Who? Leslie? Who doesn't know Leslie? She's one of the biggest pimps in the Midwest!"

Scooter went wide-eyed. "Pimp?"

"Yeah. Why? You wanna meet her?" Matthews asked.

"Sure," Scooter responded. "Yeah, why not?"

The rest was history. When Leslie found out that Scooter was second in command of the Matthews organization, she didn't hesitate to start dating him. Scooter would fly her into New York for weeks at a time, staying in a luxurious suite at the Plaza or Waldorf Astoria Hotel. He would visit her sometimes in Detroit, on business trips. Scooter started lots of businesses across the country under different names of people who were willing to help him go legit.

Leslie was one of those people.

That same year, in the winter, Leslie gave birth to Scooter's daughter at a Harlem hospital. Leslie named her Tashera. Scooter was the happiest man in the world until, hours after giving birth, Leslie died.

By the time Scooter snapped out of his thoughts of the past, the Phantom was entering the driveway of his Long Island home. Pulling into the five-car garage, Scooter noticed Simone's sky blue two-door, drop-top Mercedes parked next to his caramel brown 1975 Cadillac Fleetwood. The Benz was Simone's twentieth birthday present. Scooter remembered the ear-to-ear smile on her face when she woke up that morning and he walked her to the front of the house, to the awaiting car with a large red bow on the trunk. Simone meant the world to him.

"Long night, Scoot. I'll see you in the morning," Big Gee said as he and Scooter exited the car.

Big Gee lived in Scooter's guesthouse, which was larger than the average suburban middle-class home. Even though he had two other homes, a condo in Queens and a Manhattan penthouse, he preferred the guesthouse built behind Scooter's Hamptons mini mansion. The house sat thirty yards away from the mansion on five acres of land. Gee loved the privacy.

"I'll probably be asleep through the day. Wake me up in the afternoon," Scooter said as he took careful steps entering the house through the garage.

As Scooter entered the spacious, ultramodern kitchen, he was immediately approached by his short, bubbly, extremely dark-skinned Haitian housekeeper. She was a middle-aged woman who had worked for Scooter close to twenty years now, and she could never seem to wear her wigs right. They always seemed to lean to one side more than the other.

The worried look on her face made Scooter nervous.

"Scotty, Simone hasn't come home, and Wayne's parents are looking for him," Lillian said with a heavy Haitian accent, which she'd had for the twenty years Scooter had employed her. Scooter looked at his Oyster Perpetual Rolex.

"Did you call her cell phone?"

"I keep getting her voice mail," Lillian answered.

Scooters forehead wrinkled as he raised his eyebrows in surprise. It wasn't like Simone or Wayne to be out past midnight, especially Wayne. His parents were strict disciplinarians. Lillian jumped at the sound of the cordless kitchen phone ringing. She quickly answered. Scooter stared at her face as she spoke to the caller. As the time passed, he became more and more nervous when she covered her mouth with her hand and her facial expression turned from worry to shock. She handed the phone to Scooter.

"It's Mr. Farrow," she mumbled.

"John?" Scooter boomed.

In a tearful, panic-stricken voice, Wayne's father spoke. "Scooter, they found my boy dead. Someone shot him in the head."

"What! Where?" Scooter asked on the verge of panic.

"In the park."

"Did anyone see Simone? She was supposed to be with him," Scooter asked as his heart raced.

"No. No one has seen her."

"John, where are you?"

Scooter then realized that the question was answered by the background noise. Police radios and people talking could be heard. They were obviously still at the crime scene.

"The park."

"I'm on my way." Scooter hung up the phone and suddenly felt sober. As he was walking out of the same door he'd entered, he turned to Lillian and grumbled, "Get her mother on the phone. See what she knows about where Simone is. Then call me right after."

"Yes, sir."

Scooter jumped in the Phantom, not bothering to call Big Gee. The big guy needed rest, and Scooter needed to sort things out on his own. These types of things didn't happen in the Hamptons. He had a feeling that this was not a random act. There was something deeper going on.

Scared and confused, Simone still realized there was no use in screaming for help. After driving for what appeared to be an hour, the van stopped. The back door opened, and one of the masked men placed a black bandanna over her eyes and tied it. Her captors then led her into a building that resembled a large, empty factory.

When they removed the blindfold, Simone studied her surroundings more. With the ceiling reaching at least three stories and thick, cubed windows at the top of the linoleum walls, the large space looked to her like some type of hangar, except there were no planes in sight.

They were tying her to a thick, chipped painted pipe when one of the hangar doors opened and a pistachio green BMW 750il entered. Two men wearing black ski hats at the top of their heads came out of the door and walked toward the car. Simone figured those were her captors. Why did they now feel it was okay to reveal their faces to her?

They were evil-looking men. Both dark skinned, with a red, blank, evil glare in their eyes. One was bowlegged, and Simone, despite her circumstances, found his walk sexy. Both had long, shaggy beards.

The occupants of the Beemer emerged. This took Simone by surprise. The driver was one of the prettiest women she'd ever laid eyes on, and the other woman, with long dreadlocks, reminded her of Erykah Badu. But the real pretty one, her eyes were like crystal balls, with a grayish silver gleam. It was like you could almost see through them. To her, she didn't look like the type of woman that would be involved with these dangerous-looking men. There was a kind of aura to her face that spelled innocence. As the women approached, they were followed by the men. Simone's heart began to pound.

"Are you hungry or thirsty? Anything you need, you let us know," the pretty one said. "You will not be harmed, I assure you." She smiled.

Simone swallowed. "Why am I here? Who are you people?" Her voice cracked as she looked at the woman with the pretty eyes up and down, surveying her fashion. She concluded that not only was she pretty, but she also had style.

"Collateral." Simone watched the pretty girl reach for her Gucci purse and remove a cell phone. "Call your mom. Tell her some friends of her friend want their money back. Drop it off at Franklin and Fulton, on the steps of the train station. Tell her if the cops are called, she knows what to expect. Just remember Breeze."

The pretty-eyed girl's voice was filled with threats, even though she was smiling. Simone did what she was told. Her hands shook as she pressed the buttons on the cell phone. Tashy picked up on the first ring.

"Tashy?"

"Simone? Where the hell are you? Your grandfather is looking for you. The lady, Lillian, called here—"

Lillian hadn't informed Tashy about Wayne's murder; she'd just asked if she knew where Simone was, 'cause she wasn't home when Scooter got home. Simone cut her off and spoke in a low, cracked voice.

"Listen! Some friends of your friend want their money. They said to drop it off—"

"Simone, what are you—"

"Tashy, this is serious. I've been kidnapped. They said for your friend to drop the money that's theirs at the train station." She looked at the pretty woman and mouthed, "Where?"

"The steps of the Franklin and Fulton train station," the pretty woman answered into the phone for Simone, with the smile still plastered on her face. Afterward, she gave the phone back to Simone.

"Tashy, they said if the cops get involved, you know what to expect. Remember Breeze."

The pretty-eyed woman snatched the phone from her and ended the call. Tears began to fall down Simone's face.

"You're talking about Ruby, aren't you?"

"You're a smart girl. Hopefully, your mother and Ruby are just as smart." The pretty-eyed girl walked back to her BMW with her female friend, leaving Simone with the two goons.

"Please don't kill me or my mom! I hate Ruby!" Simone yelled. The pretty-eyed woman was halfway in the car when she looked back at Simone and smiled. "Then we have a lot in common. Hopefully, no one else will end up like your boyfriend."

She got in the Beemer and pulled out of the hangar.

When the call ended, Tashy quickly placed a call to Ruby.

"Yo," Ruby grunted after answering the phone on the second ring.

"Ruby, they snatched Simone!"

"What? What the hell are you talking about?"

"That bitch kidnapped my daughter. She said to drop the money you owe her at Franklin and Fulton train station." Tashy's voice was filled with rage. "Ruby, I don't give a fuck who or what happened between y'all, but the bitch involved me and mines. Make it right, Ruby, 'cuz if something happens to my daughter, I'm gonna blame you." Tashy ended the call.

Chapter Forty-three

In the measure that she glorified herself and
lived luxuriously, in the same measure give
her torment and sorrow.
—Revelations 18:7

Temperatures in New York were just above freezing the morning Ruby and Mecca walked the empty bike path of Brooklyn's largest park. Ruby hung on every word Mecca said while at the same time thinking how the Italian sun had given her a golden hue. Mecca looked good and healthy. Her once thin face, from lying in a coma for months, was now full, and Ruby could tell that she had put back on a healthy weight. Mecca filled her blue denim jeans by Citizens of Humanity nicely. Ruby noticed how her hair, which was without extensions or a weave, had grown a few inches past her shoulders. Both women walked with their hands in their coats. Mecca preferred for them to meet at a warm spot, but Ruby felt the park at the time was a suitable place to talk and be out of sight.

"So how'd you know that was Wise's sister?" Ruby asked.

"When I first saw her, I felt she looked familiar," Mecca reported, looking straight ahead as a group of pigeons flew off in fear of their approach. "Then, while I was in Italy, I had this dream. I saw her in my dream. It was a while back, but it made me remember."

"A dream?" Ruby asked skeptically. Mecca glared at her aunt, as if she was insulted.

"Yeah, a dream! The dream just helped me remember. Is that hard to believe?"

Ruby, sensing her frustration, changed her tone. "I'm not saying it like I don't believe you. I just wanna be sure."

"It doesn't take a rocket scientist to figure it out. You know she's behind what happened to Breeze and his family. You said it yourself. She just bounced without a trace."

"Yeah, I . . ." Ruby's response was interrupted by the ringing of her cell phone in her leather bomber jacket pocket. "Yo," Ruby answered, annoyed that her conversation with Mecca had been interrupted. Mecca watched Ruby's facial expression change from a calm one to one that was shocked at the news she received from her caller. "What are you talking about?"

Ruby listened attentively as Tashy revealed the news about Simone's kidnapping and issued a threat. A threat Ruby didn't appreciate. Before she got a chance to respond, Tashy ended the call.

"Who was that?" Mecca asked.

"They kidnapped my girlfriend's daughter. They want me to pay the ransom they said I owe." Ruby had a fearful look in her eyes. A look Mecca couldn't remember ever seeing on her aunt's face.

Mecca sighed. She knew just as well as Ruby that Daphne was responsible for the kidnapping. Only Mecca knew why it was said that the ransom was what Ruby owed. Still, Mecca held her tongue.

"What are you gonna do?"

Ruby stared off into the distance. Unsure of her plan, she answered just the same. "What can I do? I don't know what I owe or where Daphne is."

"I can help you find her. Me and her got pretty close. Give me a day or two. I'll let you know what I find out."

"I don't have a day or two. They want the money tonight," Ruby said.

Mecca paused to think. "Give me your phone," she said. "When they call back, I'll tell them that you're scraping it up. She'll talk to me. Meet me at your crib tonight."

"A'ight," Ruby answered.

Just before they exited the park and walked to their own vehicles, Ruby turned and spoke. "I just wanna know where she's at. I don't owe the bitch shit but a bullet in her skull."

Mecca watched her get inside her truck and entered her own rented car, welcoming the warmth. She removed Ruby's phone and smiled to herself. When she started the car up, she mumbled, "Much smarter than you think I am, Lou."

***

The Honorable Francis Nicoletti sat behind his mahogany desk in a snow-white shirt with red suspenders and a matching bow tie, reading a sworn affidavit given to him by Detective Levy and Agent Doyle, who sat in chairs, anxiously waiting for him to sign it.

Both Levy and Doyle couldn't read the judge's expression as he stared down at the file of papers they'd both spent long hours preparing. He nodded sometimes, raised an eyebrow, and grunted for what seemed like a lifetime to them. Levy fidgeted uncomfortably, while Doyle stared at the top of the bowed head of Judge Nicoletti.

Judge Nicoletti finally looked up at Doyle and Levy with his blue eyes behind rimmed glasses. His pale skin had deep lines, and the double chin jiggled when he spoke.

"The Davidson phone, I'll authorize the wiretap. There's probable cause, but Williams and Carter, I'm denying. Being friends with a target of an investigation is not probable cause, gentlemen. I need more. You got your wire for thirty days. Hopefully, that wire will give you PC on the other ladies. You gentlemen, have a nice day. This meeting is adjourned."

A bulimic, reddish-brown-haired female stenographer packed up her equipment and left the office. Judge Nicoletti removed his glasses and rubbed the bridge of his nose. When the stenographer was gone, the judge smiled at Doyle.

"You owe me a lunch, Phil. I'm starving." The judge gave a sly grin, then continued, "You never know. The right restaurant may get you more wires."

Doyle and Levy stood up, prepared to leave. It was Doyle who spoke first, with a grin. "Never knew you could be bribed."

Nicoletti put on a black blazer, then patted Doyle on his back as they walked toward the office door. "For a plate of lasagna or veal Parmesan, I would have authorized wiretaps to be placed on the Oval Office."

"I knew that dame was bad news. You sure know how to pick 'em." Scooter and Tashy sat in the office of Scooter's bar and grill on the Queens–Long Island border. Tashy raised a disappointing eyebrow at her father's comment. She knew he was exhausted and stressed.

"Don't start," Tashy said vaguely, sitting on a leather sectional, rocking back and forth nervously. Every time her phone rang, she would get jumpy and answer it quickly. A knock at the door interrupted their conversation.

"Come in," Scooter ordered.

The man who entered was someone Scooter was expecting. He stood up to shake the man's hand, which always reminded him of frog's legs. The guy's thin frame and college professor look were a deceptive contradiction to what he was really about.

"Glad you could come at such an early hour, Sonny, but this is one of those 'desperate times calling for desperate measures' situations," Scooter said, gesturing for Sonny to take a seat in front of the mahogany desk.

"I kind of figured it was something that was extremely important for you to call at such a time," Sonny said softly.

Behind the humble, intelligent demeanor, Sonny was one of the most, if not *the* most, dangerous men Scooter had ever met. He was handsome, in a Babyface sort of way, and his brown eyes were direct. He had even features and curly hair that was graying at the temples. His athletically slim body made him look ten years younger than his fifty-three years. Besides him being a stone-cold killer, what made him more dangerous was that he was an ex-marine honorably discharged after serving his country for twenty years. Ten in Special Forces and another ten in the NYPD, which he'd retired from. He was a trained killer who knew powerful people and could get information on any person he wanted. That helped when he was looking for someone, because even if you were hiding in an igloo on the frozen tundra, Sonny would find you.

"You want a drink, Sonny?" Scooter walked over to his personally carved black marble bar and poured himself a glass of Grand Marnier. Sonny waived it off.

"No thanks. Liquor was never a choice breakfast for me." Scooter half smiled at his humor.

"I called you here because some people have kidnapped my granddaughter," Scooter said without hesitation. "This is my daughter, Tashy." As Scooter gestured to Tashy, Sonny nodded.

"I assume it's your daughter Scooter is talking about," Sonny said with a serious expression as he looked at her.

Scooter had used Sonny for many different "services" in the last decade, after he was introduced to him at a campaign fund-raising event for a friend who was running for the state senate. The introduction was short and to the point when one of Scooter's associate mumbled in his ear, "I want you to meet Sonny Brown. Anything you need taken care of, he can do it. And I mean anything or anybody, you dig?" Afterward, anytime Scooter needed Sonny's "assistance" in dealing with a problem that was considered "expendable" or a "potential threat," Sonny handled it efficiently.

"Do we know who is responsible?"

"Her name is Daphne Carter. She's from Brooklyn. She's affiliated with the Shower," Tashy answered.

"You mean the Shower Posse?" Sonny's eyebrows rose in surprise.

Tashy nodded.

"How did you all get into a run-in with the likes of the Shower Posse?" Sonny inquired.

Sonny remembered that when he worked as an NYPD detective while on leave from the service a case involving the Shower Posse came in. In the eighties, Jamaican posses reeked murderous havoc on many U.S. cities, especially New York, Miami, and places like D.C. Sonny recalled the brutality and savagery of the Shower Posse's murders. They loved to dismember their victims.

"Long story," Tashy said abruptly.

Sonny looked at his Patek Philippe watch. "Long morning. I got time. Need to know what I'm getting into and where to start."

After Tashy gave Sonny the rundown, he simply stated, "We need to talk to your friend Ruby."

Scooter reached in his desk and pulled out a stuffed envelope and handed it to Sonny, who stood up, straightening his Ralph Lauren Purple Label suit. He grabbed the envelope and placed it in his inside pocket.

"Always a pleasure," Sonny commented before exiting the office.

"You sure he can get Simone back?" Tashy fretted.

"He's the best, Tashy. No one can hide from Sonny Brown. That man is probably the only person in this world who could find Osama bin Laden."

"Why doesn't he?" she asked.

"'Cause nobody is really looking for him."

The FBI technicians finished installing the wiretap and electronic listening devices in Ruby's brownstone right before she pulled up in front of her home. Agents sitting in a van with a telephone company logo watched Ruby from the corner of the block. She looked nervous as she exited her Jeep cautiously, looking up and down the block as the sun began to rise. The chilly morning left dew on cars and patches of grass that surrounded small trees enclosed behind small black wrought-iron gates. The temperature got a little warmer as the sun began to rise, promising, at the very least, a sunny day.

When she entered the brownstone, she went directly to the first-floor kitchen to fix a much-needed cup of coffee. When she turned the lights on, she was momentarily startled by the person sitting at the kitchen table.

"What are you doing here, and how the fuck did you get in?" Ruby asked with force.

"I really need to talk to you."

"Listen, Mona, enough is enough," Ruby sighed.

Chapter Forty-four

The suspicion of an ulterior motive is anti-seductive.
Never let anything break the illusion.
                    —Robert Greene, *The Art of Seduction*

Junior McLeod exited the terminal at Miami International Airport and put a pair of shades on over his piercing gray eyes. An aqua blue Nautica deck shirt, white cotton Nautica short pants, and white track sneakers gave him the typical Miami everyday look. He wore his long dreadlocks neatly packed in a red, yellow, and green knitted cap.

Whenever Junior visited the States, Miami was the place he enjoyed time in, as it was with many Jamaicans who came to the United States. After hailing a taxi and telling the driver that the Setai Hotel was his destination, Junior stared out at the familiar landscape of the city. It'd been a few years since he'd been back in the United States, as he'd been uninterested in traveling ever since the September 11 attacks, and there probably wasn't a place on the globe he hadn't visited, anyway.

However, this visit was urgent. Urgent enough that the person he was there to see had booked him a room at what was now considered one of Miami's best hotels on Collins Avenue. The Setai Hotel was an oceanfront spot in the center of South Beach, among tropical gardens and pools. The place was top-of-the-line luxury, and Junior's suite put the *l* in *luxury*. Setting down his Tumi luggage, Junior took in the view of the crystal blue ocean from the deck of his room. The ocean smell reminded him of Jamaica. Getting comfortable, he removed his cell phone from its case on his waist and dialed a number. The person picked up on the second ring.

"By the looks of this room, I guess this meeting is more serious than I figured." The accent wasn't lost on the person on the line. A voice and accent the person hadn't heard in years. The feeling was mutual when Junior listened to his response.

"I don't think it could get more serious, old pal. I'll be there in five minutes. I know you don't eat meat, except fish. They got this restaurant on Washington Ave. It's a seafood place. How 'bout we grab a bite?"

"Pleasure, then, brethren."

The line went dead, and Junior went to his carry-on bag and removed a sealed cigar box. Removing the seal, he took out a tightly rolled leaf of Jamaican weed and went to the deck, where he lit it and inhaled deeply. When the potent smoke filled his chest, he held it momentarily, then exhaled a thick white cloud of smoke. Junior felt relaxed.

Thirty minutes later Junior sat in Joe's Stone Crab Restaurant, eating a healthy plate of baked fish, steamed vegetable brown rice, and freshly blended mango and banana juice. Before the dishes were served, he was able to get reacquainted with his host.

"You look like you haven't aged a bit."

"Whatever it is you want, flattery will work in your favor. Too bad I can't say the same for you, old friend. You need to change your diet and habits." Junior smiled.

Agent Doyle shrugged his stooped shoulders at Junior's comment. The relationship between the two men went back years, to when Junior led a vicious attack of the Shower Posse on the streets of New York and Doyle investigated them. Unable to catch Junior himself in a RICO indictment because of Junior's son, who ran the day-to-day dirty work, the FBI decided to indict Donovan and other members of the posse, including Daphne. It was an indictment that led to the raid that resulted in Donovan's murder, Daphne's conviction, and a bloody war on the streets.

Agent Doyle had set up a meeting with the then forty-year-old Junior at a Brooklyn hotel, knowing the murderous reputation he had. Junior commanded a posse that did not hesitate to murder a federal agent, and afterward, Junior respected Doyle even more.

Doyle personally sent a reef of roses to the funeral of Donovan and his condolences to Junior and his wife. He expressed the same condolences at the Brooklyn meeting, where Doyle made the only unethical decision of his long career. It was a decision in which, he felt, the ends justified the means.

At the time, too many bodies were popping up around New York and his caseload was growing because of the posse. So for Junior's promise to stop the war going on in the streets, Doyle gave Junior the names of the informants among Junior's crew. Among those informants were a few people who were responsible for the indictment and convictions.

"A diet? The only thing I need to cut back on is police work. It aged me beyond my years," Doyle said before ordering a huge plate of fried jumbo shrimp, baked salmon with a butter dip, and buttered noodles, which he washed down with white wine.

Junior studied the aging cop and laughed to himself at his style. His white, short-sleeved polo shirt fit loosely around his upper body but was stretched by his protruding gut. The navy blue Dockers were wrinkled, and he wore no socks with a pair of not-so-shiny hard-bottom shoes. The seventies-style Vegas shades made him look even more comedic. After their meals, Doyle got right down to the point of calling Junior.

"Junior, it's like the talk we had twenty years ago in Brooklyn . . . ," Doyle began as he stared directly into Junior's gray eyes. Immediately, he remembered that time when he told his partner that he felt like he was going to pass out after staring into Junior's eyes.

He relayed to Junior everything that had been going on in the investigation of Ruby and the murders. Junior listened intently. When Daphne's name was brought up, Junior's eyes squinted and he folded his arms across his chest.

"Over the wire we placed in Davidson's home, we received information about the kidnapping of Tashy Williams's daughter. Tashy Williams is the daughter of a guy named Scooter Williams." Doyle paused, waiting to see if the name registered. When it didn't, he continued. "This Scooter is a powerful guy with connections high up in city government and the underworld."

The two men paused as a waiter walked over and asked if they needed anything else.

"Let me get another glass of wine," Doyle said, "and the check."

When the waiter left, Doyle looked around at the other tables. They were mostly filled with young, tanned couples having giggling conversations, oblivious to the New York federal agent and the old, dangerous Jamaican gangster who was responsible for at least 5 percent of the homicides in New York in those years.

"So what can I do for you?" Junior asked.

"Talk to Daphne. Tell her to let the girl go. There will be a war bloodier than any of your past ones combined." Again, he paused as the waiter brought his drink and the check.

"And what about the murders already done? Will Daphne have to go to jail for them?"

Doyle sighed. Once again, the ends were justified by the means. "What does she want? I know you know what this war is about, Junior. She still confides in you. This is off the record."

Junior knew he could trust Doyle's word. It was not like Doyle would go incriminate himself and risk ending his career behind the walls he'd put so many people behind, and Junior had enough dirt to do just that!

"Davidson is responsible for the murder of Daphne's older brother years back. She wants revenge," Junior murmured.

Doyle looked into his eyes and, with a serious expression, said, "I'll give her Davidson, she leaves the country, and the murders go unsolved."

"What about what's on them wires?"

Junior did not know that Doyle had lied about receiving the information from the wiretaps. He'd actually got it from an informant on the street who was a member of Daphne's crew. He had to keep some cards in his hand covered.

"There's nothing on them to implicate Daphne in the murders. If she leaves the country, the kidnapping goes unsolved and there is a statute of limitations on that charge."

"I'll call her," Junior replied.

Doyle sipped on his wine. "Can you guarantee the release of the girl?"

Junior chuckled. "Have the years and bad diet clouded your memory, too?"

Doyle smiled. The world could do without a Ruby Davidson, he thought, rationalizing everything.

Outside the restaurant, before both men went their separate ways, they shook hands.

"I have to go," Doyle stated. "I have a flight scheduled to New York leaving in an hour. So what will you do while you're in the States?"

Junior smiled mischievously. "I still got moves, mon. I'm going to a reggae club to dance with the young people."

"Time for me to take off this Miami attire and get back to the icebox up north. It was nice seeing you again, Junior, and once again, thank you." Doyle chuckled.

"It's nothing, mon. Soon me call you for a favor. I just hope I don't have to book a hotel in Jamaica to ask." Junior nodded.

Too many things were going through Daphne's mind for her to concentrate on a casual sex partner doing what most women would say was a good job at eating pussy. The dark-skinned Taye Diggs look-alike moaned between Daphne's legs while she lay on her back with her legs resting on his shoulders. She had situated herself in the Bronx condo, on a king-size bed in a room that was plush and comfortable. From time to time, he would look up at her between his moans and hard breathing and notice her staring into space. Her mind was in some other place. It bothered him that she wasn't into it while he was doing her a service, and he wondered how she would act when the roles were reversed.

"Stop. That's enough," Daphne suddenly snapped.

"What's wrong? Did I do something wrong?" he asked. Daphne got off the bed and walked to the armchair, which held her clothes.

"No, it's not—" Interrupted by the vibrating cell phone, she removed it from her jeans pocket and looked at the screen. "Hello," she answered softly.

"Daphne?" the voice hummed.

Daphne instantly recognized the voice as Junior's and looked back at her naked partner and placed her hand by her mouth for him to remain silent.

"You're in Miami? Why?" she inquired.

Junior never came to the United States without informing her so that she could have something arranged for him. Most of the time he would stay at her guesthouse and she would arrange for a car to pick him up and take him wherever he wanted to go. This was unusual.

"I had some urgent business to take care of," he replied.

"Are you coming to New York?"

"Are you on a private line?" he asked.

"Yes."

"Go public and call me at this number," Junior ordered.

Daphne didn't hesitate in leaving the condo and giving her lover a rain check. She had enjoyed the guy's company and he had a mean tongue, so she would definitely be back, but when Junior called and said something, Daphne would stop everything to get it done. Even a bomb-bursting orgasm.

On the way to a public phone, she made a call on her phone, asking if Ruby had made the drop yet. She had already made it clear to Tashy how much she wanted. A quarter of a million in clean, hard cash. When she found out the drop hadn't been made, she was furious.

"They think it's a game? Show them it isn't," she said into the phone, then hung up.

As she parked her car in front of a bar where a group of young guys stood, Daphne studied them before exiting. She realized they had to be hustling in the freezing cold. From the way they were bundled up, they had been out there for hours, and once they saw her, they tried to get her attention. A beautiful black woman jumping out of a luxury car didn't intimidate these young cats.

Ignoring them, she went into the bar and used the pay phone on the wall in the back. Music and smoke filled the bar, which was good. It would mask her and her conversation with Junior from prying ears. Daphne made the call. It was answered on the first ring, and Daphne never had a chance to speak.

"Let the girl go."

"I don't understand what . . ." Daphne's heart skipped a beat.

Junior cut her off. "Daphne, you know what I'm talking about. Forget the money and let the girl go. You can still get what you seek. She is at her home now. Get it over with now. When it's done, there is a flight booked to yard. LaGuardia, tomorrow morning, nine o'clock. Be on it."

"Junior, why are—"

"No need to get into it. Get it done." Junior ended the call.

Daphne hung up the phone, confused and infuriated. Who had told Junior of the kidnapping? Even more confusing was why he wanted the girl let go. Who had talked to him about that? Daphne thought about who she was related to and realized Tashy's father was powerful, but that meant nothing to her or Junior. The Shower Posse feared no one. Except the FBI.

Was Junior in bed with . . . Immediately she chased the thought from her mind. Junior would never. She would get to the bottom of it in Jamaica.

Simone knew it was now or never. She faked as if she was asleep on the cot while her two dreadlocked watchers were also asleep on their own cots. One of them was supposed to stay up while the other slept in five-hour shifts, but these two smoked weed all day and night, and after eating Jamaican takeout, they'd fallen asleep.

The first night they did it, Simone fell asleep at the same time they did, after catching a contact high from the weed. Plus, the full stomach of brown rice and beans, plantains and roti, didn't help her cause, either.

This time, she stayed up. As one of them snored, she knew she could tiptoe without waking them. They had made a fatal mistake by leaving her untied, thinking that fear overcame her will to escape. They were wrong.

She steeled herself, repeating that she was the daughter of Tashy Williams and the granddaughter of Scooter. They had learned to take fear head-on. Slowly, Simone rose off the cot, and her face scrunched as she got a whiff of her own body odors after two days without a shower. Though it was light outside, she was unsure as to what time it was and couldn't see the sky through the dusty windows, which needed to be cleaned. There was a door at the far end of the hangar that she knew was open. It was one of those doors with a lock on the outside, but once inside, you could just turn the knob

Still, she could hear her own heart as it drummed within her chest. Opening the door slowly, she stepped out into the cold. A welcoming cold. She took in her scenery and realized that the warehouse was on a long block of other warehouses. At the corner, she saw the Manhattan Bridge and knew she was in Brooklyn. Even though she didn't know exactly where, she was happy to be in the city.

Did her captors assume that she knew nothing of the city since she lived in Long Island? Well, they were wrong, and she was glad that the city was her playground and she knew how to get around it. So she ran. Back in the warehouse, a cell phone rang and awakened one of the men.

"Blood clot!" he barked as he shook his companion. "Fresh, get up! The Yankee gal, where she?"

He looked at his phone's screen to see if he recognized the number, and when he didn't, he calmed down and answered.

"Paul?" Daphne asked.

"What go on, Daphne?" he greeted, as if everything was normal.

"Let the girl go."

Paul thought he heard wrong. "Come again?"

Daphne sighed and growled, "Paul, let the damned girl go. Don't ask questions. Just do it, now!"

Paul couldn't have been more relieved. The kidnapping didn't matter, anyway. He didn't want to think about what would have happened if she hadn't said that. They didn't fear Daphne, but they did fear her connection with Junior McLeod. None of them wanted to be on his bad side; it was an express trip to the grave.

Paul looked at his partner, shrugging his shoulders.

"Who dat? Daphne?"

"Yeah, mon."

"We got to find that Yankee before she return," Fresh said.

Paul shook his head. "Nah, mon. Everything cool. Daphne say let the youth go."

"Just listen, Ruby!"

"Listen to you tell me how you broke into my crib? Listen, Mona, you don't know me that well. I got a lot of things on my plate right now, so don't make me have to beat your ass in here for real," Ruby said in a leveled tone. To accent her point, Ruby pointed her index finger and showed her the rage in her eyes. Tears welled up in Mona's eyes.

"Ruby, someone kidnapped Simone. That's why I'm here!"

"Don't you think I know that?" Ruby snapped. "You sneaking into my house don't help bring her back."

Mona wiped a tear that flowed down her face. "I know, I know, but I think Simone's mother and grandfather are sending someone after you. They're blaming you."

"What? Where did you hear that?" Ruby asked.

"I called Simone's mother, and she told me what happened. She must have been in the middle of a discussion with her father and another man. She forgot to press the end button on her phone, and I heard the conversation. I was worried about you," Mona said in a worried tone.

Ruby was tired of Mona's obsession, but with her revelation, Ruby put that aside for now. Mona might have saved her life with the info. Did Tashy actually think she was behind the kidnapping of Simone? Tashy must think Ruby was petty. Why would she ask for a quarter million when she knew Scooter was worth millions? And she knew Scooter would pay the ransom and would use the whole issue as an excuse for why Simone should stay in Long Island with him. Which would be ironic, since she was kidnapped from Long Island.

"How long have you been in my house?"

"Long enough to hide in the closet and watch some men break in here and put in wires. I think the feds are listening to us," Mona whispered.

The agents in the van outside went still when they heard Mona's statement. They looked at each other as one picked up a walkie-talkie and announced, "We've been made."

Agent Doyle's voice came through the walkie-talkie, responding to the agent in the van. "Shut it down and get out of here."

The agents left. They did not know Doyle was parked five cars behind them on the opposite side of the street, watching Ruby's home. He was there to make sure Daphne got her revenge with nothing else getting in the way. It would kill two birds with one stone, he figured.

With the murders of Breeze and his family on Ruby, he could say that she was killed in revenge. The murders of the family would be solved while Ruby's killers were on the run. That was Doyle's plan. Unethical, but society wouldn't lose a prominent, productive member, and he wouldn't have to spend his last year on a wild-goose chase and dealing with mountains of paperwork.

"You sure it was the feds?" Ruby whispered, grabbing Mona by the hand and leading her toward the door.

"It definitely was. I heard things they were saying. They were happy that the wires were in place, and they tested them by speaking to whoever is somewhere listening," Mona explained.

"We gotta go, then," Ruby mumbled.

"Where are we going?" Mona asked as Ruby pulled her toward the exit.

"Somewhere other than here. I have to think."

Drinking a cup of coffee from Dunkin' Donuts, Doyle waited. He knew Daphne would be pulling up any minute, and the agents hadn't made him aware that Ruby's life was in jeopardy, after hearing what Mona had told her about a conversation she had with Tashy.

They were angry that they had got made and forgot to mention it to Doyle. If he had known, he would have warned Daphne that Ruby knew.

He watched as Daphne, in a green Camry, parked the car across the street from Ruby's house, on the empty block. It was perfect timing. Then his peripheral vision caught some movement, and as he turned, he recognized a familiar face walking up the block. The man was also looking at the brownstone, as if he were searching out an address. Sonny Brown was here to kill.

Chapter Forty-five

But in the end, she is bitter as wormwood,
sharp as a two-edged sword.

—Proverbs 5:4

Furious that she couldn't put her plan of revenge in play by making Ruby rich, then taking it all away, along with her closest friends, Daphne looked down at her phone as it received a text message from Ruby. The text infuriated her even more as she sat across from her brownstone. It simply said, "Come and get me."

Ruby was taunting her.

She knew she should have killed Simone. Killing her would have definitely made Tashy and her family ready to kill Ruby for their loss. Daphne could have then killed Ruby without anyone suspecting her of the murder. But now Simone had to be let go on Junior's orders.

It was now or never. All the years of planning her revenge and how she would do it went out the window. Daphne had begun to plot and scheme about Ruby as soon as she found out who Ruby was. When she came to the federal prison in Ohio, and they met, the last thing she thought was that she would meet this gangster from Brooklyn that she'd heard so much about, the woman rumored to have killed her brother, Wise.

Daphne had first heard the rumor while she was in middle school, while listening in on a conversation in the girls' bathroom. One girl told another, "That girl Mecca, the light-skin one from Langston Hughes? My cousin said her aunt killed two guys last month. She threw one out the window and shot the guy Wise on the staircase. Her auntie ain't no joke."

The other girl replied, "I don't like that bitch Mecca. She think she all that!"

Just as Daphne walked out of the bathroom stall, the girls stopped talking. They didn't even look at her in the face; they just walked out. She could hear them mumble as they left, "That's Wise's sister."

Daphne knew who Mecca was. She had heard a lot of girls in her school talk about the pretty girl from Langston Hughes whose mother and father got killed while she watched from under the bed. The girl whose aunt was notorious in Brownsville.

Getting to know Ruby while in prison, Daphne realized that if she weren't responsible for her brother's murder, she would have really liked her. She admired her strength, even though underneath the hard exterior there was a woman yearning for true love, a woman who wanted to be paid attention to, and not just because she had a nice body or money. She was someone who wanted to be appreciated for who she really was.

Daphne had sensed that. She saw herself in Ruby, but Ruby was the cause of her pain. She had taken the person who meant the most to her. Daphne remembered how lonely she felt after her brother was killed, how Christmas changed, how abuse from her steppops went unchecked because her strong, fearless brother was gone. And this woman who was now in the same prison as her was the reason for all of her misery.

So she'd plotted.

She didn't understand why Junior wanted her to change her plan. When she was released from prison, she'd told him all about her plan, and he'd told her, "I understand your pain, but why go through all that instead of just getting right to the point?"

Daphne looked him directly in the eyes and replied with steel in her voice, "I want her to feel how I felt. I want her to be happy for a moment, then miserable even longer. I want the people around her to feel pain and blame her. Then I want her to die slowly."

Junior simply nodded. "It is not good to hold that much pain for so long. It could end up destroying you. Before you leave Jamaica, I want you to go see Doc Benjamin."

After she visited Doc Benjamin, her feelings didn't change. Doc Benjamin told Junior, out of earshot of Daphne, "The hatred for her enemies is too deep, brethren. She is driven by it. To try and stop her would be like being her enemy, too."

Junior shook his head and thanked him. He said no more on the topic.

Mecca smiled as she sat in her rented car, low in the passenger seat, watching the drama about to unfold on her aunt's block. It was Mecca who had text messaged Daphne the "Come and get me," using Ruby's phone. Unlike Daphne's, Mecca's plan for revenge was playing out perfectly. She'd even pulled one over on Lou.

Momentarily.

She recalled the dream she'd had last night, where they talked in the airport. Lou was the baggage handler who helped her carry her bags to the ticket counter. He was angry, and she wasn't in the mood for a long speech, so she blocked him out by thinking of being with Miguel. His touch, his smell, his voice covered everything Lou said, until she heard him say, "When you fly on a plane, you gamble with your own life. No fault in that, but gambling with other people's lives is an act of evil. . . ."

Her dream then switched to her seeing her aunt's demise the way she'd planned it. It reminded her to book a flight leaving that afternoon for Italy. She had spoken to Miguel that morning, and he'd informed her that his team won the European championship. She was sorry that she couldn't be there with him to celebrate, and he agreed.

"I know how we can celebrate, though," Miguel stated.

"How?" she asked, filled with a childish excitement.

"When you get back, let's get married."

"I'm coming back today," Mecca said, astonished.

"Good. I'll have everything set up."

"What about my dress and all?" Mecca asked. She wanted her wedding to be picture-perfect and not rushed. Still, it was Miguel, and she knew she was going to do it regardless.

"I know your size. I measure you every night," he replied with a seductive humor.

"You're fresh."

"Don't worry, baby. I'll get the perfect dress by Vera Wang. You'll see."

It was all set, and Mecca couldn't wait to get back to Italy and be in the arms of Miguel. He was her world. She just wanted to witness her former world go away, the same way it had come to her. Violently. So she watched, and something began to happen that wasn't part of what she'd planned.

Agent Doyle got out of his car, with his gun at his side, and approached Sonny Brown.

"Sonny!" he cried out.

Sonny Brown turned suddenly to the voice coming from the street. He smiled at the familiar-faced agent, the same agent who had tried for years to bring him down for murders that Brown was rumored to have committed. Not only had he tried to bring Sonny down, he had tried to link him to Scooter Williams but never could. Doyle told himself that this was one time he could link Sonny to Scooter, but he wasn't here for that, and he didn't want Sonny to mess everything up.

"Agent Doyle," Sonny said, looking at the gun in his hand, "what brings you to Brooklyn?"

"I was about to ask you the same thing," Doyle said, approaching Sonny to pat him down. From the corner of his eye, Doyle saw Daphne walking down the sidewalk, looking at Ruby's home.

Daphne glanced at Doyle and Sonny Brown curiously. She didn't know the two men, but the white man and the black man looked out of place. In fact, to Daphne, the white one looked like a cop.

Then the sound of a door being unlocked came from Ruby's brownstone. A second later, Ruby and an unidentified woman came out. Ruby immediately saw Daphne and reached inside of her coat, drawing a gun, as Daphne did the same.

Doyle looked up at Ruby, and the second he took his eye off of Sonny Brown, he heard a loud boom and he felt a blow to his chest that knocked the wind out of him, leaving a burning sensation. He couldn't breathe. He felt hard, cold ground beneath him and blacked out to the sound of gunfire erupting all around.

Ruby immediately aimed her .40 caliber at Daphne and fired repeatedly. It roared on the quiet block, causing people within their homes to frantically dial 911. Ducking behind a car, Daphne aimed her silenced .45 at Ruby. It sputtered softly, shattering windows and splintering doors all around Ruby. Both women were too busy shooting at each other to notice Sonny Brown shoot Agent Doyle, who lay dead on the sidewalk as a pool of blood began to form under him.

Mecca watched in amazement and confusion. Who was the black man, and why did he just shoot that white guy? And why was he now aiming his gun at Ruby and shooting?

Ruby pushed the woman that was at her back into the vestibule of the brownstone as she screamed. She then turned back to Daphne and unloaded her .40 caliber at Daphne, who hid behind a parked car. Then her body jerked from Sonny's 9 mm Beretta bullet tearing into her shoulder, and she looked at him, shocked. She turned her aim toward him, and before she could get a round off, Sonny sent a slug into her chest.

Mecca watched as a spurt of blood ejected out of Ruby's open coat.

Daphne saw Ruby drop. She was confused because she knew it wasn't her bullet that took Ruby down. She got up from behind the car and watched the black man walking away from the scene in a hurry. She quickly walked up the steps to the wounded Ruby and kicked the gun out of her hand.

"Hey, Ruby, don't look too good, bitch!" she grumbled, bending down over her.

People were now looking out windows at the scene. Mona sat in the vestibule, in the corner, with her legs to her chest, crying. Daphne heard her sobs and aimed her gun at her and put three bullets into her face. Somewhere in an apartment, someone screamed.

Ruby couldn't move. The bullet had gone through her chest and out her back, shattering her spine.

"Fuck you, bitch," Ruby mumbled between labored breaths. "Your brother died a scared bitch."

Before Mecca had revealed who Daphne was, Ruby had had suspicions at one time. It was customary for inmates in prison to show other convicts they were acquainted with photos of family, friends, and themselves on the streets. Once Ruby got to know Daphne, she showed her many pictures in her photo albums, most of which had been sent by Mecca, of her and Shamel.

Daphne never showed her one.

When Ruby inquired about it, Daphne told her, "I don't want to be reminded about what I am missing."

It was a reaction that Daphne had when Ruby was showing her pictures that gave Ruby her first suspicions. She had a photo of her and Wise that they took together in the famous club in the Bronx known as the Fever. The couple had posed, holding each other from behind, with Wise's arms wrapped around her waist and holding her hands against her stomach. Both of them had matching gray sheepskin coats, while Wise wore a hat, and Ruby had her hair out in a Jherri curl. As soon as Ruby turned to the picture, Daphne looked away, as if she hated seeing it. She played it off, as if something else had caught her attention, and walked off of the bleachers in the prison yard.

"I'll be back, Ruby. This chick Karen been owing me for months."

Ruby saw Karen across the yard, and her suspicions of Daphne became doubtful, because it was a fact that Karen owed Daphne money. Eventually, she made Ruby forget about it, and when she told Ruby she would put her on when she got out, that got her attention.

The next time Ruby became suspicious of Daphne's relationship to Wise, things had already began to happen. The robberies of the spots, then her sudden disappearance, brought those old thoughts back to the forefront of her mind. She wanted to act on those suspicions, but she never realized that she was being rocked to sleep, as she did with Mo Blood.

Now, lying paralyzed on the steps of her brownstone, the same one Daphne put down a payment for, she looked into the face of a woman hell-bent on avenging her brother's murder, which took place twenty years ago. Ruby had to respect the way she'd sought her vengeance. It was the most cunning, well-planned, patient plotting and acting she'd ever witnessed a person do. She had to admit, Daphne was a dangerous enemy.

Daphne chuckled and watched the mist form from both of their breaths in the cold weather. She watched Ruby's eyes blink as she struggled to hold on to her life force, which was slowly leaving her body. Tears rolled down her face as her life flashed before her.

"That's what I always admired about you, Ruby. You're a fighter. Even lying here, dying, you just have to get the last word in. You're the toughest bitch I ever met," Daphne said as sirens roared in the background.

"Get . . . it . . . over . . . with . . . mu'fucka," Ruby panted.

"For the record, if my brother died a scared bitch, no one will ever know that but you and God," Daphne announced as she pointed her gun at Ruby's head. "Now go tell God and my brother how scared you were."

She squeezed the trigger.

Wrapping her Burberry scarf around her mouth and nose, and fixing her Dolce & Gabbana shades, she quickly walked to her car and sped off to the airport, leaving the city of her childhood, a city she loved more than any place on earth, for good.

Mecca drove up and watched Daphne pull off and parked in the same space. She jumped out of the car and ran toward her aunt, screaming.

When the first police responded to the call of shots fired, they saw Mecca bending over the still corpse of Ruby, crying and hugging the body. The officers noticed Agent Doyle a few yards away, lying in the gutter but not moving. The blank look in his eyes indicated he was gone. People who lived in the neighborhood began to emerge on the street, still in shock at what had taken place in their peaceful, cozy, middle-class neighborhood.

When some of them were questioned, the police received a bunch of jumbled stories of what took place. Unfortunately for the investigators, no one got a good look at Daphne's face, which was covered by a scarf, or at Sonny Brown, because most of their attention was directed at Ruby, the neighbor they all recognized.

One knockoff version of Spike Lee told the police, "I don't know her personally, but I know she wasn't your average middle-class woman. I saw her in *Don Diva* magazine. She's a tough chick." Afterward, he pushed his oversize glasses up the bridge of his nose, played one of his favorite hip-hop songs on his iPod, and rode off on his mountain bike.

Within minutes, the Brooklyn block was flooded with ambulances, cops, and law enforcement officials from various agencies. When the news went out that a federal agent had been killed, everyone except for the director of the FBI showed up. The only thing Mecca shared with the investigators who questioned her as they sat in the back of an unmarked Crown Victoria was, "She's all I have. I have no family besides her, and now she's gone. I don't know who did this."

And the tears flowed. Happy tears. As chaos tore through Ruby's neighborhood, Tashy and Scooter found peace when Simone's voice came over Tashy's cell phone.

"'Ma, come get me please. I got away from those people. I'm at the mall on Fulton Street in Brooklyn!"

Tashy and Scooter arrived in his Phantom as quickly as they could, almost getting a speeding ticket on their drive to Brooklyn. When they pulled up in front of Albee Square Mall, a teary-eyed Simone ran out to the car and jumped in.

"Take me home."

Scooter dropped them off in Harlem.

When Daphne reached Jamaica and inquired about Junior's decision for her to kill Ruby immediately, he told her everything he and Agent Doyle had discussed. He told her about the deal they'd struck years ago and how it related to her. "If it wasn't for that agent, you would still be in prison, Daphne. His influence is what got you that sentence. You were supposed to get fifty years."

Nodding, she looked out at the street from the chauffeured 600 Benz and wondered. "So who was the guy who showed up and killed the agent?"

"I'm not sure, but I'm willing to bet that girl's family sent him there to get your old friend. He and Agent Doyle must have known each other. Maybe he was sent there to kill anyone who was around, and Doyle wanted to save you," Junior answered. "Did he see you?"

"Yes, he did."

"Then I guess we'll never know." Junior shrugged.

"Will there be anything else?"

"No, thank you so much." Mecca grabbed the cup of water and aspirin from the Jennifer Aniston–looking stewardess on an Alitalia flight bound for Italy. She sat alone in her first-class seat, listening to the CD player on her lap.

Realizing she had no useful information to give the authorities about her aunt, Mona, or Agent Doyle's murders, they'd let her go. Mecca told them she had just returned from Italy with her boyfriend and had seen nothing. Before leaving, she told them if she found out anything else, she would call them immediately. She told them she wanted to know who her aunt's killer was.

She realized she no longer cared how Lou felt about her deceiving him. He wasn't there in real life, experiencing the emotions that she experienced from the betrayal. How much did he really care, anyway? Why was he so fixated on trying to put her life in order, but not on putting the people around her in check? Why didn't he try to convince Ruby not to set up her father to get robbed? Why didn't he tell her aunt not to have sex with Shamel? Why didn't he stop Tah Gunz from shooting her, or Karmen from sleeping with her man and him cheating himself?

She didn't want to see or hear from Lou anymore. She didn't need him. She'd got what she'd come for, and if she had to pay in the hereafter, so be it. She'd been through it all and might as well enjoy heaven on earth with Miguel.

"So, your hands are washed of me?" Mecca was startled by the voice of Lou, who now appeared in the empty seat next to her. She knew she wasn't dreaming.

"How did you—"

"That's the least of your problems, my love. The question is, why? Why would you deceive me? Deceiving me means

you've gained control of yourself. Use that control more pos-itively and you'll get further in life." He paused and looked around. "But you didn't use that control properly, and life has a way of getting its own revenge. This you will see soon."

Mecca didn't like Lou's tone. As she thought, the plane began to shake violently. She immediately gripped the seat tighter, and her heart thumped loudly in her chest. She felt the sharp descent, and the pilot's voice came over the intercom.

"Passengers, this is your captain speaking. We are experi-encing some difficulties. Please remain calm, and follow the instructions given by the flight attendants."

Mecca looked at Lou, who sat next to her with a self-serv-ing smirk. The stewardess who had served her earlier rushed to the seat across the aisle and fastened the seat belt with a look of panic across her face.

"The plane is going down too fast," she said and looked over at Mecca. Mecca looked at Lou.

"Lou, I'm sorry. Please stop it. I'm a changed person, I swear."

"I would fasten my seat belt if I were you," Lou responded.

"Lou, don't do this. I'm getting married. I plan to live a positive life with my husband. I'm going to raise a family, and I'm not going to raise my children how I was raised. I swear!"

The pilot's voice came over the speakers again. "Ladies and gentlemen, please fasten your seat belt and duck your head in your lap."

"This is it, Mecca. The end of it," Lou said as their bodies jerked from the plane's rapid descent.

Tears rolled down her face. She took one more look at Lou before she ducked her head.

Lou looked her in the eyes and said, "It's done."

The impact of the plane awakened Mecca. Instead of being on a crashing plane, she was looking up from her bed into the eyes of her favorite doctor as a white woman in a long white coat opened up the blinds in the all-white room, letting in the sunlight.

"'Today is a beautiful day, Mecca. It is also your day, remember?" The handsome black doctor held her hand.

Mecca nodded. "What time is it?" she asked while wiping the cold out of her eyes with the back of her hand.

"It's seven thirty. Your hearing is at nine o'clock. You should get ready now."

The doctor left the lady in the white uniform in the room. Mecca looked at her, and she smiled through puffy red cheeks.

"Good luck, honey. I hate to see you go, but you deserve to leave this place."

She waited until the lady left, and got off her bed and looked at herself in the room's full-length mirror. She smiled at her own reflection.

"Yeah, today is my day," she mumbled. "I'm going home."

Chapter Forty-six

Lest you ponder her path of life—her ways are
unstable; you don't know them.

—Proverbs 5:6

Family court, Brooklyn

The small courtroom fell silent when the tall, broad-shouldered, bespectacled judge Norman Pastel entered from a door situated behind the bench.

"All rise!" the bailiff announced.

Once everyone stood, the judge responded, "You may be seated."

Mecca looked down at the judge. He reminded her of Marlon Brando in *The Godfather*. As she sat down, she turned, looking at the spectators' section, smiling at her aunt and friends of her aunt that she didn't know but saw every time a court hearing took place.

The judge's voice was a deep, rich tone. "I understand this is a hearing on a report and recommendation from the staff at the psychiatric facility in Bronx County."

A slim woman of six feet stepped up to the podium situated in the middle of the courtroom, between what would normally be the tables for the defense and prosecution of a criminal defendant. This wasn't the case of a criminal; the hearing was to determine Mecca's madness.

"Michael T. Moore, Your Honor. I'm here on behalf of Miss Sykes." The pale-skinned guy pointed to Mecca, who was sitting next to a black woman and a man dressed impeccably, while Mecca wore a plain white dress shirt, blue slacks, and black leather loafers with two-inch heels. Her hair was pulled back into a ponytail.

"Are you her attorney, Mr. Moore?" the judge asked.

"Yes, Your Honor."

The judge folded his hands and placed his elbows on the bench desk. "Proceed."

"Your Honor, this is a twenty-year-old case that I will bring you up to speed on, being that you're new to the case. A case that's been heard over and over for many years by the now retired Honorable Stanley Doyle." he paused to look down at papers he had on the podium. "In 1988 . . ."

Brooklyn, 1988

Fourteen-year-old Mecca watched as her aunt surreptitiously placed a snub-nosed .38-caliber revolver handgun inside an empty sneaker box and placed it in on her closet shelf. Her aunt Ruby didn't notice her niece, who she'd taken in when she was eight years old, after her parents were murdered in their Brownsville apartment in 1982.

Mecca and her aunt lived in a Coney Island apartment in the same building as Ruby's friend and lover Monique Johnson and Mecca's half sister, Dawn. Monique and Mecca's father had an affair while Mecca's father and mother were together. It was no secret in Brownsville that Dawn was Bobby Sykes's daughter, because the news had spread like wildfire. Mecca's mother was infuriated at the news but didn't bring it up to Bobby, because she was in love and it was a fling when they broke up.

When Mecca's mother saw Monique's baby, she had no doubt it was Bobby's. She hated Monique, but she didn't take it out on the baby. She was mature enough to invite Monique over so that their babies would know each other.

When Monique moved to Coney Island, it was Ruby who made sure that the girls grew up together as sisters. At first, the girls got along wonderfully, but after the murder of Mecca's mother and father, Mecca's attitude toward Dawn and Monique changed. They got into fights often because Mecca initiated them.

Despite their problems, Monique still loved Mecca as if she was one of her own. Mecca clung to Monique to make Dawn jealous. It was revenge for Mecca, because Dawn had tried to steal Bobby Blast's attention when they were younger.

Then, one day, while Mecca and Dawn fought over a Barbie doll that they both claimed was theirs, Dawn told her, "My daddy bought me that. He loved me more!"

That was when Mecca started to plot her demise.

It was years later, when the girls were fourteen and had started to blossom, that Mecca carried out her plan. One day, when Ruby was out and Monique slept in her bedroom, Mecca retrieved Ruby's gun from the sneaker box, grabbed a pillow, and walked up to a sleeping Monique and shot her twice in the head. She walked out of the apartment and down the hall to the apartment Monique and Dawn lived in and knocked. Dawn answered.

"Mecca, what's up, girl?" she asked, looking at Mecca, who had a strange look on her face, with her hands behind her back.

"Nothing."

Mecca walked into the apartment when Dawn turned to walk to the bathroom. She was in the middle of curling her hair with a hot iron when two shots rang out through the complex. Dawn's body slumped to the floor.

Mecca stared down at her, smiling. "Hey, Dawn, don't look too good, bitch. See if Daddy loves you now."

The shots were heard by the neighbors in the building, and they opened their doors, looking into the hallway as Mecca walked by as if she didn't see them. The gun was still in her hand at her side.

She climbed into the elevator and rode it down to the first floor and sat on the steps in front of the building. She was arrested and taken to the police station. When Ruby arrived, Mecca told her interrogators, "Those bitches got what they deserved."

After a psychiatric evaluation by defense and prosecution experts, it was determined that Mecca was unfit to stand trial. She suffered from various mental illnesses. One doctor testified, "When she was a very young child, she suffered head trauma when she fell in her neighborhood playground. This concussion went untreated, resulting in brain damage."

Another psych testified, "Her head trauma, coupled with the emotional trauma of watching her parents being murdered at such a young age, only worsened her already unstable mental condition."

On the recommendation of both defense and prosecution experts, and subsequently stipulated by both attorneys, Mecca was committed to a psychiatric facility for the criminally insane. Every year she would have a hearing on her condition.

It was later decided that she would never be tried for the murders, but she could be released from the facility only on the recommendation of the staff of the facility. Those hearings would be held every year.

"Your Honor, I call my first witness, Dr. Paul McLeod, Jr.," Mr. Moore announced.

The courtroom was hushed as a well-dressed man who appeared to be in his fifties walked to the witness stand. He wore his dreadlocks in a ponytail. Mecca recognized the gray-eyed man as he stated his name for the record and told the court his occupation and dealings with her.

"I'm a clinical psychologist who has worked with Mecca Sykes for the last five years," he said with a Jamaican accent.

"And you have with you your report and recommendation. Is that correct, Mr. McLeod?"

"Yes, I do."

"Can you tell the court your recommendation?" Mr. Moore asked from the podium.

"Yes. It is my professional opinion that Miss Sykes's treatment is complete and she is ready to reenter society as a fully functioning, mentally fit adult."

"And you base your opinion on what?" the judge asked, looking over his glasses.

"Your Honor, in the last five years Mecca has shown so much maturity that she even helps the staff counsel other patients when those patients suffer psychotic episodes. The patients practically trust her more than they do us, and under our watchful eyes, we even have her give them the medication when they don't want to take it from staff."

The judge nodded his head, and Mr. McLeod was excused.

"I would like to call Dr. Benjamin Mason, Your Honor," Mr. Moore announced.

A thin, wiry man in his midforties walked to the witness stand with a slightly stooped posture. His complexion was olive toned and dull, and he had brown, bold eyes. He was clean shaved and had short graying hair on his head.

Dr. Mason was born and raised in Senegambia, West Africa, and moved to the United States in the 1970s, after earning a degree in psychology at the University of Cairo, Egypt.

As he sat on the stand, Mecca didn't bother to look at him and instead looked at the lawyer paid by Ruby to represent her. Dr. Mason had opposed her release at her last hearing five years ago, where he'd simply stated, "It is my opinion that Miss Sykes's behavior and mental condition deem her unfit to function normally in society." Now she wondered what he would have to say.

After explaining his credentials to the judge and informing the court that he had had the occasion to work with Mecca for the last seven years, he expounded on their relationship by stating, "A lot of my time with her was short. She isn't on my caseload. Dr. Parker has worked with her for the twenty years she has been at the facility."

"Surely enough time for you to render a report and recommendation, correct?" Moore asked.

"Indeed."

"And your recommendation is?"

"Contrary to the one five years ago, I must say," Dr. Mason remarked with a smile, "today a different Miss Sykes sits before you. Not the manipulative, impulsive young girl I saw seven years ago. With Dr. Parker to credit, assisted by the staff who testified prior to me and others, what you see today is a mature, mentally developed woman ready for a productive livelihood among society."

Mecca couldn't believe her ears. She turned to stare at a man she'd come to hate. A man other patients at the facility called "Doc Devilman." Her eyes watered, and she felt strange inside.

When he walked off the stand, he passed by her and smiled. "It's your time, Mecca. Make the best of it. Good luck." With that, he left the courtroom.

"Your Honor, I call Daphne Carter."

Moore's voice was followed by the double doors of the courtroom opening, and a heartbreaking, lovely, statuesque, golden-brown-skinned woman with beautiful, pale hazel dreamy eyes strutted in. Her knee-length black Versace dress showed her dancer's legs. Her perfectly done hair surrounded her oval face, with a ripe mouth under her small, pudgy nose, which she applied makeup to smartly. Every man in the room stared in awe, while the women glared as her Chanel No. 5 perfume filled the room. The sight of the woman brought a smile to Mecca's face. Daphne Carter took the stand and crossed her legs after stating her name for the court. She went on to explain her job at the facility and how it related to the treatment of Mecca.

"I am a mental health counselor. I've been working at the Bronx County facility for ten years. I have counseled Mecca every two weeks in her anger management groups and have had one-on-one talks with her on many occasions."

"I understand your staff deals with a small amount of patients. How does that affect the patients?" Moore asked while sipping on a glass of water that had been placed on the podium.

"With a small amount of patients, it affords us more time to deal with the patients' needs individually. Mecca is on Dr. Parker's caseload, and Dr. Parker keeps me informed of her progress before she comes to groups or sessions with other doctors. This is so we know what type of individual we are dealing with."

Her voice was smooth and gentle on the ears and had captivated every man in the court.

"Miss Carter . . ."

"That's Mrs. Carter," Daphne corrected him.

Mecca smiled, as if she was in on a secret that no one knew about. Daphne was married to her childhood sweetheart, Donovan. He was an American-born Jamaican who she kept a picture of on her desk. He was very handsome, and once in a while he came to the facility to pick Daphne up. They lived in Brooklyn together, and she told Mecca that Donovan was a master chef who ran two Jamaican restaurants in Brooklyn.

"Tell us about Mecca's progress, Mrs. Carter."

Daphne smiled, looking at Mecca. She was a twenty-three-year-old woman when Daphne began working at the facility. Well, she appeared to be a woman, but when Daphne became involved with her, she realized this was still a little girl in emotional pain, trapped in a woman's body. She'd walked in on Mecca unaware when she was having a conversation with herself in the voice of a small child. Then her voice changed to her regular one.

She would listen to Mecca speak to herself as if she really was speaking with another person. The conversations were mainly about seeing no reason to change her life. Mecca seemed to blame her behavior on the death of her parents. Most memorably, Daphne heard her say, "How am I supposed to feel after my mother and father were killed in front of me? Am I supposed to just forget that? How did you expect my life to turn out? This life is all I know!"

Daphne's heart went out to her. Besides Dr. Parker, Daphne was the only other staff member that had established closeness with her beyond the call of duty. She treated Mecca like a daughter. As her condition improved, Daphne shared a lot of personal things with her. She told her about how her brother was murdered and how much it hurt her. The abuse she'd witnessed her stepfather administer to her mother. Things Daphne told Mecca made her sad but gave her strength.

"We can't let these things control us, Mecca," she'd told her. "We have to pick up the pieces and put it back together and make our lost loved ones happy by doing good in life."

She'd watched Mecca grow over the years. There were setbacks when she became angry and had psychotic episodes where she had to be sedated, but those incidents gradually became a thing of the past.

"She has made the best progress I've seen in any patient since working at the facility," Daphne testified. "She is very ready, sir."

"Thank you, Mrs. Carter."

As she walked off the stand, she stopped at Mecca's table and reached over to hug her. Several tears had fallen from Mecca's eyes, and Daphne wiped them away.

"I love you, Mecca."

"I love you, too, Daphne."

She left the courtroom, wiping her own tears away with a handkerchief.

"I call the last and final witness, Your Honor. Please bring in Dr. Louis Parker," Moore announced.

In walked a man standing six feet, with a glowing dark brown skin tone, penetrating black eyes, a mole at the corner of the left eye, a close-cropped, sharply lined graying beard, cut-glass cheekbones that made him incandescently handsome, and a perfectly rounded, short Afro with graying temples.

His presence was commanding. He walked with an air of authority. He was in charge. He looked expensive in his tan suit by Ralph Lauren Purple Label, white Dior Homme dress shirt, and silk tie. He'd complemented his suit with a pair of brown suede Hermès bit loafers and a rose gold Breguet watch. His scent of Attitude Armani overshadowed the scent left by Daphne. This man looked serious.

"Please state your name for the record," the judge commanded.

"Louis Parker."

Moore went into action. Dr. Parker was his most important witness. Even though the other staff members' testimony was compelling, Mecca's release from the facility depended on Dr. Parker's opinion and recommendation.

"Can you tell us your occupation and duty at the facility, Dr. Parker?"

As serious as he looked, to those who knew him, he was a kindhearted, devoted Christian man who genuinely cared for the patients under his control. He treated everyone fairly, and he made his patients feel as if they were in a family setting more than in a psychiatric institution.

"I am a clinical psychologist, a professor of behavioral sciences at Columbia University, and author of two books on psychiatry. I am the managing director of the Bronx County psychiatric facility."

Mecca stared at the man who for the last twenty years had been like her father, brother, mother, friend, and sometimes foe and watcher. She had a love/hate relationship with the man, who was caring, but at the same time stern in administering discipline when she got out of hand. This was the only person alive that knew everything about her. He had her life down to a science. He knew when she was in a bad mood, a good one, or just sad. He knew her thoughts, her weakness, everything.

She was brought to him a broken-down, lonely, angry, frightened fourteen-year-old who wanted to prove to the world that she was tough. He saw right through it all. From the beginning they argued daily. She screamed that he knew nothing about her.

"Those files don't mean shit, motherfucker!" she would yell.

He would remain calm and wait it out. Their arguments turned to long conversations about her growing up without parents after watching them being murdered. Conversations that were tearful for her, and for the first time in his career, someone's story brought him to tears. Mecca became Dr. Parker's personal task.

"Dr. Parker, tell us about Mecca Sykes and what it was like working with her for twenty years," Moore said, taking a seat next to Mecca. Dr. Parker smiled, showing a set of perfectly white teeth.

In 1998 officials from the Brooklyn family court and juvenile facility literally had to strap down a young teenager to a hospital gurney and wheel her into the Bronx facility. Dr. Louis Parker and his staff were awaiting the new admission. They were forewarned by her attorney that she was not a happy camper.

The staff wasn't shocked by her behavior; they'd seen it all before. Nobody wanted to be admitted to a "crazy house" involuntarily, especially a teenager. Mecca was immediately sedated and put on suicide watch for her first week. Once she was calm, Dr. Parker paid her his first of many visits in a dimly lit padded room that brightened after he walked in. After introducing himself, Mecca simply stared at him.

"Double homicide? Wow, you're a real mean young lady."
He leaned against the padded wall.

"And what?" she growled. Mecca sat on a chair that had
been bolted down and was connected to a plastic desk on the
wall. She rolled her eyes.

He held up his hands. "I'm not your enemy, dear. I'm here
to help."

"I don't need your help," she snapped.

"Obviously you do. I mean, the average fourteen-year-old
girl, as pretty as you are, usually doesn't kill two people and
something isn't wrong."

"Maybe they deserved it," she mumbled, rolling her eyes
and neck simultaneously.

"I doubt that," he stated. "But let's talk about that for a
minute."

Mecca studied the gold nameplate on his white coat.
"Listen, Dr. Parker . . ."

"Call me Lou. That's what everyone calls me."

Within a two-year period, Dr. Parker was able to break
through Mecca's tough exterior, which he called a "defensive
front." At her first five-year hearing, Dr. Parker felt they were
making progress, but still opposed her release. He had determined that she was not ready and was still showing antisocial
behavior.

Then, at the last hearing, he again opposed her release but
explained in depth about her condition and treatment.

"Under hypnosis, Mecca has imagined an envious version of
herself living a life of crime where she is the heir of a drug-deal-
ing empire headed by her aunt, who I know personally as a
hardworking woman in the Department of Corrections. More
strangely humorous about this life as a big-time drug dealer
who controls her Brownsville neighborhood is that her other
characters are me, my staff, and her fellow residents at the
facility. She envisions some of them as her close friends who
became her enemies. Enemies she is seeking revenge on."

"Who does she envision you as in this imaginary tale?" the
judge asked Dr. Parker.

"A cross between the Devil and God."

"Dr. Parker," Moore continued, "at Mecca's fifteen-year hearing, you informed the court of this imaginary tale of a life of crime, which she shared with you under hypnosis. How did you go about dealing with that?"

"With the help of staff like Dr. Carter, Mason, and McLeod, the progress begins by digging beneath the emotional scars and anger to bring out the good that all humans have sub-consciously within them and that they suppress with the emotional baggage. We knew from the start that her problem started in childhood, with the murder of her parents.

"I presented her with different scenarios in problem-solving sessions called Thinking for a Change and Anger Management. For example, one scenario that I presented her with was, what if she found out her aunt was responsible for her parents' murders?"

People in the spectators' section all looked at Ruby, who was embarrassed by the comment.

"We wanted to know how she would deal with it," Dr. Parker continued.

"Initially, she wanted to seek revenge on her aunt, and when other scenarios were introduced, such as characters in her imaginary tale betraying her, she wanted revenge on all of them. Within the last five years, she eventually began to see the foolishness in her tale. A psychologist from centuries ago, named Sándor Ferenczi, termed when another person becomes part of a person's ego, internalizing that other person's charac-ter introjections. Mecca's character in her imagination was her father. He was a drug dealer in her Brownsville neighborhood.

"Another way I dealt with her was by replaying her child-hood to her. I had pictures of her as a child, along with family and friends, up to her teenage years, prior to being admitted to the facility. Under hypnosis, we traveled back to those days.

"I found out that she wanted answers as to why things happened that made her sad. The untreated head trauma only added to her condition. Fortunately for her, she was a young lady when the trauma occurred, and her brain had not fully developed. The trauma only caused her development to slow down, so at fourteen she actually had the mind of a nine-year-old, one who felt anger and felt unloved by everyone. Along with growing up in Brownsville, her mental state fueled the feelings of rejection and depression."

Moore stood up and walked to the podium. "So today, twenty years later, what is your recommendation, Dr. Parker?"

He sighed and looked at Mecca as his eyes filled with tears. Sniffles could be heard throughout the courtroom. His testimony was emotional for many, even the judge.

"Mecca is ready to go home."

"Surprise!"

Mecca's friends at the facility cheered as she returned from court accompanied by Dr. Parker and Ruby. The recreation room was decorated with balloons and glittering banners that read FAREWELL, MECCA!

Mecca smiled as she took in the faces of all the people she'd grown to love over the years. Her friends and fellow patients who had put up with her mean attitude and treatment of them.

"I should have never stolen her nail polish," Tamika told herself.

"Listen, everyone!" Dr. Parker announced. "Mecca's aunt is here to take her home. We have a podium set up so everyone can say their last words and good-byes. Miguel, make it short, and don't be up there giving a sermon."

Miguel was a young Puerto Rican patient who happened to be Mecca's best friend. Mecca sat next to Ruby and Dr. Parker in a metal folding chair as her friends walked up to the podium one by one and said their good-byes.

Karmen, her sometime friend who had been at the facility since 1990 for killing her boyfriend, who had smacked her in the face for yelling at him, got up to speak. She had cut his body into pieces and had fed them to her pit bulls. She'd kept his head in the freezer. It wasn't unusual to see the two of them competing for the interest of the boys within the facility. As she spoke, she rubbed one of her braids that fell over her shoulder.

"I know we were at each other's necks, Mecca, but all in all I admire you. You're a real chick. I'll miss you."

Karmen walked away. Next came a brown-skinned girl two years younger than Mecca, named Tamika. For years, they'd hated each other, after she found out that Tamika had stolen nail polish from her makeup kit. When Mecca found out from Karmen, who wanted her to do something so Mecca could get into trouble, Mecca got a razor and slashed Tamika while they played in the rec room. Tamika needed thirty stitches to close the wound. Afterward, she was placed in a rubber room for a week, and when staff found out Taheem had given her the weapon, he was transferred to another facility.

"I never said I was sorry for stealing your nail polish. I'm sorry, Mecca." Tamika walked toward her with her arms out, and Mecca stood to hug her. "You deserve this more than any of us," she told her. Tamika was there for killing her baby by dumping her newborn in an incinerator.

Next, a tall, handsome, athletically built man three years older than Mecca rose to speak. He was admitted to the facility a year after her for chopping his younger cousin's head off in an East New York building.

He told the cops, "That motherfucker stole my bag of weed."

Shamel was Mecca's first crush. He was placed in the rubber room for a week when he beat up Taheem for giving Mecca the razor to cut Tamika. He knew Taheem did it so Mecca could get into trouble.

Mecca had told Dr. Parker that Taheem hated her, which was why he'd given her the razor. She explained he hated her because she wouldn't be his girlfriend. Dr. Parker understood why in her imaginary tale of crime, Taheem shot her, placing her in a coma for three months.

In his cool tone, Shamel spoke. "I'm gonna miss you, Mecca. You know how we do. Stay up. I love you."

Shamel walked over to hug her.

"Oh, boy!" Karmen said as Miguel began walking to the podium. Everyone laughed.

Miguel was the most talkative guy in the facility. All he talked about was how he was a street-ball legend from Bushwick, Brooklyn. He bragged and showed pictures of him at Rucker tournaments. He had articles about him being one of the best high school players in the country. He would talk for hours. It was Mecca who loved to listen, though. Miguel was her second crush once she found out that Shamel was messing with Karmen.

Miguel was admitted to the facility in 1997, after he stabbed and killed his father and then shoved a broomstick up his dead father's ass. Miguel's father had molested him since he was seven years old. Basketball was his escape from his horrible home life. His mother died of a drug overdose a year after his father first molested him. He immediately fell in love with Mecca when he got to the facility. He didn't care that at first she paid him no attention when he sent her cards he'd drawn of beautiful landscapes. He was an extremely good artist. He wrote her notes of how he wanted to travel the world with her, go to places like Paris and Italy. He said he would become a basketball star and spend the money on making her happy.

Eventually, Mecca began speaking to him. She found him to be cute. It didn't matter that he was talkative. Mecca put his stories into her imaginary tale. Every day she sat with him, listening to him talk about growing up in Bushwick and being the neighborhood star. He never talked about his personal life.

"I hate to see you go, Mecca, but I'm happy that you get to go. I don't know what I'm gonna do now. I look forward to our talks. Can I call you?"

"Oh God, don't do it," Karmen joked.

"Shut up, Karmen," Miguel said. "Anyway, I love you, Mecca. You're my best friend, and you will always be that. I never had—"

"Okay, Miguel," Dr. Parker interjected. He knew Miguel was about to go into one of his speeches.

"A'ight, Dr. L. Bye, Mecca. I love you." Miguel went over to a crying Mecca, and they hugged tightly.

Dr. Parker walked Mecca and Ruby out to the parking lot. Before they exited the facility, the old, stooped-shouldered, bald-headed janitor they called Stone came over to them.

"Hey, Mecca. You leaving finally?" His voice cracked.

"Yes, Stone, I am." Mecca walked over to hug him. For twenty years she had watched him clean up blood, vomit, feces, and other human body fluids from off the floor of rooms and the halls. He was a nice old man who treated the children like his grandkids. He snuck in candy to give them. Mecca was one of his favorites. He reached in his old uniform and pulled out a picture.

"She would have loved to see this day."

Mecca grabbed the picture, and a tear dropped from her eye. The picture was of an old black female patient all the people called Nanna.

Nanna had spent thirty years at the facility, after killing her two sons, who she believed were possessed by the devil. She told the judge, "My sons, Kaheem and Brian, were sent here by Satan to tempt me. The Bible say, 'Don't tempt the Lord thy God.'"

In 2002 Nanna died of a heart attack. She was seventy-seven years old.

"Good-bye, Stone." Mecca hugged the old janitor.

Outside, Dr. Parker hugged Mecca. He prayed Mecca's behavior, which had made him recommend that she be allowed to reenter society, wasn't an act. He had seen plenty of patients act as if they no longer suffered from mental illnesses. They "introjected," as psychologist Sandor Ferenczi called it, other people's character. They acted normal when they really weren't. He felt strongly that Mecca wasn't acting. If she was, she was one of the best actors he'd ever seen. Hollywood would definitely be her calling.

"Remember, if you feel you need someone to talk to, or you're feeling stressed or depressed, I'm a phone call away," Dr. Parker said as he wiped Mecca's tears with his hand. Mecca hugged him tightly.

"I'm gonna call even if I'm not depressed," Mecca responded.

Ruby shook his hand. "Thank you for everything."

"It was my pleasure. Mecca made me realize this job was worth taking."

With that said, Mecca and Ruby got in Ruby's '07 silver Range Rover. Mecca waved at Doctor Parker as they drove off, and he returned the gesture.

They drove in silence for a while, and Ruby looked over at her now thirty-four-year-old niece. She looked like the spitting image of her mother, Big Mecca.